The King's Furies

STEPHANIE CHURCHILL

July, 2019

ISBN-13: 9781079341119

For Chloe

Agrian Royal Family

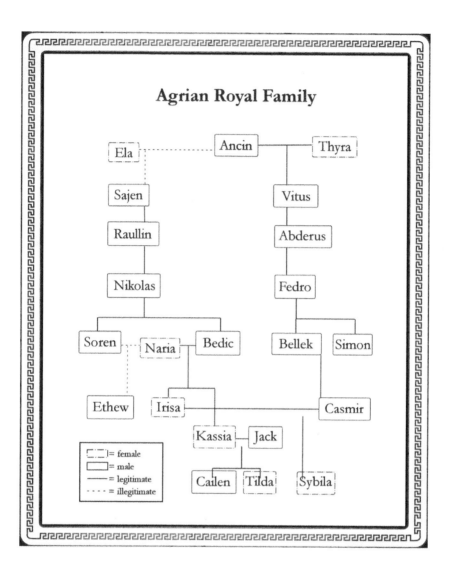

Characters

Addis	Wife of Wolf (Wigstan) of Bauladu; Daughter of Negus Bazin
Ancin	King of Agrius; Father of Sajen and Vitus
Anton Mathiasen	Man of Torrine
Aksel	Lord Cilgaron, Honor of Cilgaron
Alexio	King of Pania; Elder brother of Naria, Irisa and Kassia's mother
Andreu	Chamberlain, Bellesea Palace
Annor	Scriptstóri of the Bibliotheca
Bazin Assefe Amare	Negus (King) of Aksum
Bedic Sajen	Former prince of Agrius; Irisa and Kassia's father
Bellek Vitus	Former king of Agrius; Casmir's father
Cai	Friend of Irisa and Kassia from Corium; Squire of Isary
Cailen	Son of Jack and Kassia
Casmir Vitus	King of Agrius
Conrad	Grand Scriptstóri Bibliotheca, Prille
Ethew	Half-brother of Irisa; Lord Torrine
Evet	Casmir's mother; Wife of Bellek Vitus
Geres	Man of Glenna
Helene	Lord Cilgaron's daughter
Ildor Veris	Cousin of Casmir; former Chancellor of Agrius
Ingólfer	Magistrate of Lyseby
Irisa Sajen	Queen of Agrius
Isary Branimir	Prince of Elbra
Iteya	Sister of Addis; Former heir of Negus Bazin
Jachamin Guimer	Mercenary
Jack	Husband of Kassia
Kassia Sajen	Sister of Irisa
Kiros Assefe	Man of House Assefe, a prince of Aksum
Luca	Captain of the Palace Guard and Constable of the Palace, Bellesea Palace

Melku	Son of Negus Bazin and prince of Aksum
Orioc	Former scriptstóri of the Bibliotheca; short-lived Grand Master
Rigard	Palace Steward, Bellesea Palace
Roderic	Master of Stable, Bellesea Palace
Roswen	Lord Cilgaron's mistress
Simon Peares	Chancellor of Agrius; Uncle of Casmir
Soren Vitus	Elder brother of Bedic Sajen; Irisa's uncle and father of Ethew
Sybila Vitus	Princess of Agrius; Daughter of Casmir and Irisa
Teklu	Son of Negus Bazin, a prince of Aksum
Travian	Master Sergeant of the King's Guard, Bellesea Palace
Tugredd	Guildsman of the former Lyseby Slavers Guild
Wimarc of Dalery	Noblemen from the Honor of Dalery
Wolf (Wigstan) Argifu	Lord Bauladu, Honor of Bauladu

Bellesea Palace
Prille
Agrius

NO ONE HAD TO DIE. His master had promised him this. Especially not the child. By the gods, but he wanted no harm to come to the child.

It was a morning like every other when his master had presented his request. Annor had only just arrived after navigating the long, narrow steps down to the dark room where his master lived. He'd set the bucket of steaming water on the floor for his master's morning ablutions, except this time, rather than wash himself in silence, his master had spoken, had explained to him the details of a plan and Annor's role in it.

"While it might feel distasteful at first, everything will be made right in the end, for your actions will serve as the linchpin to the unfolding of greater things."

Annor wanted to be a part of greater things. It was one reason he worked so hard at his craft each and every day. In truth, it took very little persuasion for him to agree to the scheme. He just wanted to be sure no one had to die.

A gust of wind whipped down out of the gray northern sky, jerking Annor back to the present. The biting air sank deep into his bones, reminding him of deepest winter only just passed even while it teased him with hints of the coming spring. Annor glanced overhead to a thickly woven vine, still barren, snaking its tendrils through an arbor. On the brightest summer afternoon, the vine would be full, providing ample shade to obscure his presence. Today its barrenness did nothing but filter a pale, watery light into the narrow alcove in which he huddled. On this blustery, overcast afternoon, however, it mattered little, for there was no sun. He suppressed a shiver and pulled his cloak more tightly to himself.

From his secluded vantage, Annor watched a pair of nurses sit with heads together, gossiping, no doubt, over the latest goings-on amongst the rank and file of the palace servants, while a young girl, only just turned two years old, played with a doll on the far side of the square, out of reach and outside the attention of her minders. She wore a heavy woolen cloak, its hood pulled up against the wind. A bright spill of hair escaped one side, flowing down over her left shoulder like a bounty of king's gold. She appeared the very image of her mother.

Voices echoed from the adjacent arcade, announcing the arrival of a group of men. Annor pressed his back against the weather-worn stone of the wall behind him, wishing he could become one with the granite. He watched as the young girl looked to see who entered into her favorite play area; then, rising onto sturdy legs, she abandoned her doll to charge toward the man striding purposefully in her direction. He swung his arms low, scooping up the girl and swinging her onto his broad shoulders.

Startled out of their private conference, the nurses jumped to their feet then bobbed in obeisance, all the while keeping their chins low. The man seemed not to notice. He only had eyes for the young girl.

"A message has just arrived for you," announced a page, breaking into the domestic scene as he scurried toward the group.

"Whatever it is can't be so important just now. I've come to see my daughter."

"But," the page persisted, "the man said the matter is

urgent."

"Perhaps," he replied, narrowing his eyes in scrutiny of the page's bullish perseverance, "but at the moment, I tend to someone more important."

The page backed off a step, and the man turned and strode away with the girl securely ensconced on her perch. The page hastened to follow while the nurses bustled to gather their things.

Patting the side of his robe and finding the key concealed there, Annor finally relaxed. Once the nurses scurried off, he slipped over to the place the girl had just been, and, picking up the discarded doll, crept away, satisfied that everything was as it should be. His master would be pleased.

※ *1* ※

Bellesea Palace
Prille
Agrius

"WHAT BRINGS THE DISTINGUISHED captain of the Palace Guard into his king's private apartments?" I asked Luca as I breezed into the large sitting room. I arched an imperialistic brow at him, though he was not misled by the gesture, knowing well the depth of my approval of him. Sybila, who sat perched atop my shoulders, waved a hand at him, her little arm rotating just past my ear as the sleeve of her cloak flapped against my cheek. I brushed it away. "Whatever it is, it had better be something vital to the security of my kingdom, for I intend to give my daughter a giggle fit before sending her off to her nurses so I can ravish my wife in the seclusion of our chamber, with or without an audience."

I swung a giggling Sybila down off my shoulders then flashed Irisa a shameless look. Her lips twitched, and a light flush rose to her cheeks. I strode purposefully toward her, grabbing her around the waist to kiss her.

Not happy to be left out, Sybila pushed her way in between us, begging to be scooped up once more. Always easily swayed by my daughter, I obliged her. Once she had my full attention, Sybila pressed one small palm against each of my stubbly cheeks, rubbing my face between them.

"Papa, play like Lizzie!"

Lizzie was a dog, a sleek fawn-colored levrier gifted to me on the New Year a year ago. While the hound served as my prized hunting companion, most of the time Lizzie followed Sybila like a shadow.

I tilted my head at Sybila. "*Play* at being Lizzie?" I snapped my teeth at her hand, just like Lizzie after a bone. "I *am* Lizzie!" Sybila squealed, and I paced the room, snapping at her hand and growling, sending her into continual fits of laughter.

While a king was not expected to be a particularly good parent, I had broken tradition, deciding to be a true father to my children. A father like mine was not. Early on after Sybila's birth, some at court felt the need to comment on the frivolous nature of my childish games. If I happened to overhear the muttering, the offending courtier would receive a dark look for his trouble, silencing the censure. It only happened a few times before the entire court learned to quiet its murmuring on the matter.

"My lord..." Luca's address interrupted my play. I turned my head to acknowledge him. "I was just updating the queen about the problems with Tugredd, the former Lyseby slavers guild member."

"Luca, you neglect to mention your true reason for being here," Irisa interrupted with a mischievous smile. Turning to me, she added, "His wife has good news."

Luca ducked his head in modesty, but his eyes beamed

his delight.

"What about his wife? Is Chloe well?" I asked, though I had a pretty good idea I knew what.

"I would say so. She is with child, Your Grace," Luca replied.

I clapped the captain on the shoulder and offered him my sincere congratulations.

"She looks forward to setting up our home in preparation for the babe's arrival. She would be honored if the queen would lend her wisdom."

Irisa agreed readily. I knew she would be pleased to help Chloe, for the two women had a history together. Chloe was a one-time slave, freed by Irisa, who then became a maid in Irisa's household. When she'd married Luca, she had left Irisa's service to find a new life of her own with her husband.

I offered Luca my own wealth of good advice from one father to another, and then after a time, Luca brought the conversation back around to the other matter he had come to discuss: the Lyseby slavers guild member.

"I thought I had persuaded Tugredd to my way of thinking?" I tried to sound casual but knew I failed to completely hide the irritation in my voice. At that moment, I also noticed the page who had followed me from outside and still hovered in the doorway. "Leave that message over on the table," I instructed him, waving a hand in the direction of the indicated furniture.

The page nodded timidly, doing as he was told, then dashed out of the room with such haste that he nearly tripped over a stool. Luca watched him go, amusement plain at the corners of his mouth. "It seemed so, yes, my king," he answered, "but after you spoke to him, he had a chance meeting with Geres of Glenna, and their conversation rekindled his ire. He is planning to make for home at first light tomorrow. Who can say what new trouble he will stir?"

My mood darkened, but I suppressed the scowl that threatened to twist my countenance. The presence of Sybila always mellowed my reactions, for I did not want her to see my anger. I had vowed not to lose my temper in front of her. I spun a squirming and giggling Sybila around to face me, pecked a kiss onto her cheek, and then set her down. Pacing to the window on the far side of the chamber, I clasped my hands behind my back, and stared out the window, my gaze only partially taking in the magnificent view as I considered the state of matters with Lyseby. It felt as though it was all I did these past weeks.

It had been two years since the edict to eradicate the slave trade in Agrius, and for the most part, the kingdom had accepted its fate. Not all honors in Agrius had dealt directly in the trade, and those regions transitioned relatively easily. But for some, like the port city of Lyseby in Cilgaron, slavery had long been a vital part of the economy. For those places, the edict had been more damaging and the resistance to it stronger.

It was difficult to blame them. A man does not easily give up what has been profitable to his purse, especially when done only because of the principles of those who have power over him.

Irisa hadn't been patient over the Council's decision to enact the slavery edict slowly, even though I'd explained the wisdom in it many times over.

"Irisa, the well-being of the common people rests on the shoulders of their lords. If the noble purses are empty, who do you think will suffer first?" She tried to argue this point, but I drew her into an embrace, brushing away a loose strand of hair from her cheek with a finger. "You understand them, Irisa, the common people. You were raised as one of them, and this is why they love you. Your compassion for them is why I love you. I know of few other noble ladies who would care as much as you. But we cannot suddenly remove the foundations upon which these barons stand without expecting worse consequences. Trust me in this, Irisa, for I have seen it happen in other lands. Take away a farmer's field, and what is he to live on?"

"But they are not farmers, Casmir. They enslave other humans! It is deplorable!"

"This is true, but so many more would suffer if their lords were brought to such a swift ruin. We must replace their original foundation with a temporary one if anyone is to stand. And besides, if the lords were to openly rebel, we would have civil war on our hands. The cost would be too great. I fear it would crush Agrius. For the sake of all of us, we cannot let that happen."

Irisa did understand, as I knew she would, even if she did not like it. She had worked alongside the King's Council these past two years to ensure the process did not take too long, offering numerous suggestions that could only spring from her unique perspective.

As the largest trading port for slaves in all of Agrius, we focused much of our attention on Lyseby, working closely with Ingólfer, the leading magistrate of the city and long-time supporter of the Vitus family. Ingólfer had done his job well, persuading the local guilds into a smooth transition. The peace had not lasted long, however.

For the last several months, a steady stream of reports regarding a simmering mood of rebellion arrived in Prille. News of the recent meeting between Tugredd of Lyseby and Geres of Glenna was just one example of what seemed to be taking place more and more openly in Lyseby, and now in Prille.

I turned away from the window. "So Tugredd is still here in Prille? He has not left the palace?" Luca nodded. "Tell him I wish to see him. Now. Send him to the audience room off the Council chambers. Then get a message to Ingólfer telling him to report on the situation there. It's too long that Lyseby has been a thorn under my saddle."

"At your word, Your Grace," Luca said, his mouth thinning into a bloodless line as he bowed his way out.

I turned back to the window again to think, vaguely aware that my daughter had found new mischief, for something crashed to the floor and Irisa exclaimed over it.

"It is nap time for you, my little imp," Irisa said, her patience flagging. Calling out for a nurse, she instructed, "Take her to the nursery, and make sure she has a bit of bread before her nap this time so she does not wake early today."

After a moment, encircling arms snaked around my waist, and I felt Irisa rest her cheek against my back. I looked down to see her fingers entwined together at my belt and placed my hands over top hers.

"I'm tired of the whining, Irisa, the wrangling, and the positioning... it's no wonder my father did not covet the role of ruling. It can be ever-tiring."

Irisa said nothing, though I knew her thoughts fled instantly to Ildor Veris, my father's cousin and the former Chancellor of Prille who was killed trying to take the throne two years ago after he had taken Irisa hostage. Veris had been the puppeteer behind the scheme to remove Irisa's grandfather from the throne of Agrius, and put my father in his place, thinking him to be more pliable than Irisa's father would have been. And he had been correct. Once Bellek was crowned, Veris wielded the real power of the realm, and for twenty years had been successful in pulling the strings, like a puppeteer in the market.

After my father's death three years ago, Veris intended to continue his surrogate rule through me, except that he hadn't anticipated Irisa's strength, or her ability to persuade me to see the man's scheming even when I didn't want to believe it. Rather than be the biddable wife Veris had anticipated, Irisa proved herself worthy to the task of queenship. Initially indulgent, Veris' irritation turned to outrage which turned to attempted regicide. He'd ordered our murders, hoping to place Irisa's half-brother, Ethew, on the throne. We had survived, and Veris had paid for his treason with his life.

Irisa unclasped her hands from around me, sliding them up my back to my shoulders to knead the knots of tension she found there. I relaxed my chin to my chest as she worked deft fingers along the corded muscles. After a moment, I turned gently in her arms to face her, keeping her arms around my neck.

"Should I just give the crown to Luca, do you think? Abandon all these peacocks to their dithering and scheming?"

She tilted her head to the side, pretending to consider my proposal. "Perhaps we could take up a life of piracy, join Swain Golden Tooth?"

I grinned and tightened my hold. "That is one possibility." I leaned in to kiss her right temple, moving my hands down to settle on her hips. "Though can we wait until tomorrow to abdicate? My afternoon has of a sudden become deliciously interesting."

"Casmir, it's the middle of the day. Can you bear the scandal of it?" Her voice was light and teasing.

"Mmmmm..."

"Casmir?"

She tried to pull away as she said my name, but I pretended not to hear her. She nudged me again. "What did the page bring?" I continued my ministrations, easing her backward across the room as my fingers fumbled to find any fasteners on her clothing. She brought her hands up to my chest and whispered, "my love" in a way that recalled me to my broader surroundings. I raised my head at her persistent interruption. "What did the page bring?" she asked again. "The message, over there on the table?" She tilted her head toward the place the parchment rested.

"Nothing that will help me further my pursuits at the moment, I can assure you." I leaned into her once more.

"And as much as I hate to remind you, you must meet Tugredd," she scolded.

"Tugredd can stew," I grumbled, though I knew she had the right of it. "Curse Luca's efficiency," I said and snatched up the parchment.

Breaking the seal, I scanned the contents, my face hardening as the significance of the contents washed over me. When I finished, I stood silent.

"Casmir, what is it? What's wrong?"

"Your brother Ethew is gone."

❧ 2 ❧

Bellesea Palace
Prille
Agrius

"WHAT DO YOU MEAN, he's gone?" Irisa's voice held an edge of hysteria.

"He is not at his manor in Torrine, and no one knows where he has gone." My lips curled downward, revealing the suspicion I felt. "I would have thought that after two years of unconditional favor, after our pardon and granting him a title, he'd have settled into his role on that island, firming up his loyalties to the Crown."

Ethew was Irisa's half-brother, born to her mother and her father's older brother Soren before Irisa's parents had wed. The circumstances of Ethew's birth remained shrouded by mists of both mystery and tragedy. Because he had grown up from infancy with their uncle Alexio, Irisa's mother's oldest brother and the king of Pania, Irisa hadn't even known she had a brother until Ildor Veris tried to put Ethew on the throne of Agrius to become the puppet-king I refused to be.

After Veris' death, Irisa and I thought it wisest to keep Ethew close at hand where he could be watched. If he proved faithful, we gained an ally. To accomplish this, we split the Honor of Haern between Irisa's sister Kassia and her husband Jack, and Ethew. In the time since, Ethew had not given us any reason to be wary of him.

"I prefer to have Ethew near at hand, and neighbors close to keep an eye on him, rather than allow him to disappear back to your Uncle Alexio and that morass of Pania's vague political affinities," I'd assured the Council when they'd disagreed.

Eventually, the members agreed, but it hadn't prevented individuals from grumbling about Ethew on a regular basis. Between the two of us, Irisa and I had done our best to placate them, pleading Ethew's case over and over again. Even so, it hadn't taken long for the subject of Ethew to turn bitter on our tongues, and we had grown ever-weary of discussing him even between us.

"Who sent the letter?" Irisa asked. I dropped the message onto the table and made a vague motion toward it with my hand. She rushed to the table and took up the parchment, consuming the message as would a beggar starved for bread.

The message was from Jack, who had gone to Ethew's manor in Torrine. When he'd arrived, Ethew was nowhere to be found, and no one seemed to know where he had gone. Jack determined that the situation seemed dire enough to send word.

"That two-faced son of *Rakallin*," I spat. Picking up a wine flagon, I swung my arm back to dash it to the floor, thinking better of it before doing so. "As if we didn't have other things to worry about. We should send someone to

Torrine to find out what sort of devilry is afoot."

"Casmir, we don't know that it is anything subversive." Irisa's plea sounded weak, as if she didn't believe it herself.

I let her comment pass. Instead, I strode to the door, swinging it open with the force of a bear on a rampage. "Andreu! Get a scriptstóri in here then prepare a courier immediately!" Without waiting for a confirmation, I slammed the door shut then turned and stalked back into the room, my mood blacker than it had been in months.

"Perhaps his departure was on such urgent business he didn't have time to instruct his household?" Irisa bestowed hopeful eyes upon me, but I returned her look with a doubtful one. She pressed on: "Surely his absence can be explained?"

"For his sake, I hope so. My mood will not be so forgiving a second time."

The chamber door opened a crack, and Luca pushed his head through. "Your Grace, Tugredd awaits you as you requested."

"He shall have to wait a bit longer. Another matter requires my attention at the moment."

"Yes, my lord." He turned to leave, clearly resigned to not knowing the cause of my agitation.

"Hold a moment, Luca."

"Your Grace?"

"I'm sending you to Torrine."

"Of course, my lord," Luca replied again, failing to hide his confusion.

Just then a scriptstóri entered, and I paced back and forth across the room, hands behind my back, dictating the message I wished Luca to deliver. Luca listened, and his eyes widened as the full implications of the situation broke over him.

Once I finished with the scriptstóri, I met Luca's gaze,

my head tilted in question. "You understand the situation in Torrine now?"

Luca nodded heavily. "Yes, my lord."

"Good. Once he's finished," I said, indicating the scriptstóri as he finalized the details of the message before sanding and sealing it, "I want you to leave as soon as you can take sail."

Luca nodded then turned to leave.

"Oh, and captain?"

Luca turned back. "Yes, my king?"

"Bring Jack when you return. I want to hear of his experience there personally."

Watching Luca depart, Irisa ventured, "Wouldn't it have been better to send another..."

"With more experience? Irisa, he is captain of the guards and constable of the palace. He doesn't hold his position because of his family title. He earned it two years ago when he helped me regain my throne. I trust his instincts. His skills were honed in the lowest orders of garrisoned men. He knows when someone is prevaricating, and he'll be able to see who is telling the truth and who isn't. He'll get answers, one way or the other, trust me."

"Asking me to trust you makes me all the more suspicious, my husband," Irisa quipped with a smile. I grinned at her. Spotting the nearby flagon I'd almost thrown not long ago, I took it up, thankful I'd thought better of smashing it to the ground. I drank from it directly rather than pour a measure into a cup, eyeing Irisa over the top as I did so. "Casmir," she scolded, "if Sybila sees you do such a thing she will do it too and not see the reason against it!"

"I'm not sure I see the reason against it?" I winked at her, and she softened, my gentle teasing having the desired effect. "Now, come, my love. Let's go see Tugredd and talk some sense into him. Lyseby is enough trouble without Glenna stirring the pot. I swear, Irisa, it's worse than herding cats trying to keep these pretentious peacocks in tow." I took another swig from the flagon then reached out for her hand, smiling provocatively. "And then, my Adonia, we can pick up where we left off, when news of your brother so rudely interrupted us."

❋ *3* ❋

Lyseby
Honor of Cilgaron
Agrius
Helene

A FLOCK OF BLACKBIRDS took to flight, scattering like a quiver of arrows loosed into the air simultaneously. Their angry calls pierced the relative peace of the market in rapid staccato, an indictment at the loss of their feast. Helene stepped lightly around the pile of refuse which had been the focus of the horde, continuing on her way without a look at the source of the reprimands.

The day had started off brightly, the sun full and unhindered from the bank of clouds which had hidden it away these last many weeks. Helene drew in a full breath of air, still crisp from the recent winter.

Her father's ship, the *Tristram*, had docked three days ago, and she knew he had spent the time since his return meeting with leading members of the city's merchant guilds as well as tending to any other business a nobleman of his position as baron of the Honor of Cilgaron must oversee. Helene and Roswen, her father's woman, had come to Lyseby to greet him and escort him home to Croilton Castle, the center of his rule in the Honor of Cilgaron. While she would not go so far as to say she had tried very hard to escape Roswen, it was true that she'd made a weak attempt at it, surprising herself by her success. She'd had no malicious intent, had simply wanted to have a look at her father's newest caravel docked in the harbor, but she knew Roswen would think it unseemly so knew better than to ask the older woman to take her.

She would not be able to evade Roswen for long, and certainly her maid Eleanor and the guardsman who trailed her would not let her stay away forever. But at the moment, the draper shop she now passed would serve as an excellent diversion.

"My lady of Cilgaron, how good it is to see you! I do not believe I have seen you since the last fair day up at Angorlum during harvest?"

"I kept close to home this winter, yes."

"It is good you have come, for only just this morning I took delivery of a lovely bolt of toley wool, bright as can be!"

The man turned and disappeared momentarily before returning with an armful of red fabric. Helene's eyes widened at the sight, for only once before had she seen such a shade of red, more vivid than any summer berry.

"I believe your maid would agree with me that it brings out the luster of your dark locks." He glanced briefly over her shoulder to Eleanor for confirmation.

The man's comment seemed somehow indelicate, but when he turned his attention away once more to find another item to show her, Helene decided that he had meant it sincerely. She was not a good judge of social proprieties, for usually it was Roswen or her father to decide and then, most often, to bristle. For the merchant's sake, she was glad that her father had not been on hand to hear him, for she knew his words would have upset him.

After lengthy consideration, she made her purchases, including the toley-colored cloth, thanked the man, and left the draper's shop. Stepping out once more into the street, she glanced quickly around for Roswen but saw no sign of the older woman. Before she thought better of it, she turned quickly and made her way through the midday crowds down Market Street toward the busy docks.

She was just passing an enormous new warehouse nearly completed when a voice called out at her over the noise of the men hauling supplies up the gigantic system of scaffolding erected along the building's side.

"My lady, what a delight and surprise to see you here! It is most fortuitous indeed that you are here, for you save me a trip to Croilton. If I might be so bold to say, that is."

The man was tall and narrow of frame, dressed stylishly even if not ostentatiously. He was not noble-born, most likely of the merchant class. Even so, he was near enough to her age, and his face handsome enough, that a thrill raced through her.

She smiled brightly and inclined her head. "How may I help you?"

While her reaction would not be considered flirtatious by most, to her the interaction smacked of rebellious independence. She was not used to speaking to strange men alone.

"I was asked to deliver this message to your father from a courier just arrived from Sarsala. I believe he would wish to see it immediately, but it was not going to be convenient for me to deliver it for a few days yet."

"You needn't be bothered to travel, for he is here in Lyseby. He only returned from a journey a few days past."

"Your news is better than any I could have hoped to hear!"

And then, as if possessed by an impish spirit, she smiled slowly, adding, "I could escort you to him even now if it pleases you?" To anyone else, her invitation would have been construed as a simple courtesy. But to Helene, whose father was bearishly protective of her, beyond what would be expected of a baron of the realm, it felt a coup. She was not used to thinking for herself.

The man beamed his delight before glancing quickly at the guard who hovered uncertainly behind her. "You have my most humble gratitude, my lady." He offered a slight bow at the waist. "I would be both delighted and honored."

Empowered by her newfound independence, she added, "You may call me Helene."

"My lady, Helene," he added with his own slow smile. "My name is Anton Mathiasen, and I have only recently arrived in Lyseby from the south." He offered his arm, and she rested her hand lightly upon it as they turned together back toward the city and away from the harbor.

"How long have you been at sea?"

"My home port is Torrine. I have only been aboard ship two weeks, but your warm welcome has now made me feel as if I have been away far longer."

She wanted to meet his look, but she dared not. Other women, more practiced in the subtle arts of such interplay, would know how to respond to his subtle flirtation. All Helene could do was steal a glance from the corner of her eyes and blush.

Anton noticed and smiled more broadly. "My task has suddenly gone from burdensome to delectable."

❀ *4* ❀

Bellesea Palace
Prille
Agrius

FRENZIED SNOWFLAKES FELL LIKE crystalline faeries, dancing, teasing and whirling, falling then spinning up and away as I took the reins from Roderic, the master of stable.

"Your brigandine is secure, Your Grace?" the master asked.

"Of course."

I frowned as I turned my head away, but Roderic's keen eye missed nothing. He patted my velvet tabard to feel for the shoulder straps beneath to be sure, despite my assurance. "Good. See that you leave it on."

I swung up into the saddle then glared down at him for his gruff manner. "I could have you replaced for your insolence, you know."

"Indeed you could, Your Grace. How careless of me." Roderic's mouth maintained its scowl, but a mischievous light lit his eyes as he smacked my horse on the rump, causing it to move off. "My entire existence serves only to do your bidding."

I tossed my head back with a hearty laugh and waved in reply as I moved toward the outer courtyard beyond the stable.

Roderic had been master of stable since my youth. In fact, he had taught me to ride. And while the older man respected me, he saw past any mystique my blood implied to the immature whelp of a boy I had once been. He was also a far better horseman than me, and he never let me forget it.

"Does my protective cage have to be so heavy?" I'd asked the armorer the day I received word that the Council demanded I wear the protective layer whenever I rode beyond the palace precincts. The leather tunic was fully lined with oblong steel plates riveted to the fabric, and over time the weight seemed to increase substantially.

"It is to serve as your protection," the man had replied. "We cannot risk losing you again."

I had glowered by way of reply, but now as I rode out into the courtyard to meet the group for the afternoon hunt, I murmured my silent thanks. I would not risk losing my life like the day Ildor Veris had nearly taken it from me. And besides, it provided an added layer of warmth in brisk weather.

Once I saw that the falconer had the birds at the ready, I patted my strong-bodied bay and gave the signal to move out.

We moved along the broad King's Road north out of Prille. Freshly laid with flagstone the previous year, it was an easy ride despite the biting wind which blew down from the north, sweeping across the fallow fields. While eager for the hunt, most of the men clung tightly to their cloaks until we reached the sheltering bluffs providing a barrier on the north side of the road.

I chatted amicably with those around me, pretending to be excited for the upcoming release of my new gyrfalcon. The truth was that I did not enjoy falconry all that much, never mind the status of the pastime. The use of gyrfalcons was in the province of kings, and it was my duty to entertain with the use of them. Lesser nobles were not to own them, and for the members of today's hunting party, the opportunity to fly the magnificent bird was one not to be missed.

I much preferred to chase the hart, for in the pursuit of it there was a certain recklessness in the speed, the full abandon to the run which allowed my courser freedom, and the skill required with bow and arrow to bring down the magnificent animal once it tired. The bay I rode now, Ascelot, had been my preferred hunting mount for many years, but Ascelot was no longer a young horse. Perhaps, in the fullness of spring, it would be time to find a new one.

The call to stop rang out as the first of our party entered the middle of the wide plateau overlooking the River Caton carving the island southward toward the Tohm Sound. Here on the windswept flatland overlooking the river, the snows still settled stubbornly within the dips and hollows of the land in and amongst the tall grasses, providing a playground for wintering hare and grouse.

The hunting party dismounted, gathering in a large group to watch the falconer prepare the birds. Once my bird perched securely on my wrist, I ordered the hounds released. Soon they had done their work, and a hare scared from the safety of its hiding place. I waited a breath, then pulled off the bird's hood, slipped her jesses, and whistled her off. Within a heartbeat, she had reached her pitch, then stooped in pursuit of her prey. The party let fly a raucous cheer as the falconer rushed to the bird to hood her once more before taking the hare, cutting off a portion, and offering it to the bird as its prize.

I received the praises of my companions then offered the bird to the next eager participant. With my role in beginning the hunt over, I edged my way to the back of the group, happy to let others enjoy the sport for which I had little enthusiasm.

"My king, a word, if I may?"

A younger man moved into position at my side, watching as another eager participant released a falcon.

"Wimarc of Dalery, if I recall correctly?"

"Yes, Your Grace."

I knew the man's father, the elder Lord Dalery, who had done his best to contain the slave uprising in his honor on the southern tip of Agrius. It was my visit to Dalery to put down the uprising that persuaded me that Irisa had been right about slavery. It needed to end, and it was then I'd agreed to consider the edict abolishing it.

"You have my attention, for at present the birds are all taken." I smiled indulgently and waited for the man to get to his point.

"Thank you, Your Grace. While I recognize that I have only recently arrived in Prille, I could not help but take notice of the whispering of certain men of Lyseby and Glenna, Tugredd and Geres in particular."

"Your eyes do not deceive you," I replied cautiously, eyeing Wimarc before shifting my attention to Geres who stood near the forefront of the hunting party, the silver gyrfalcon on his wrist. "And your ears are keen."

"Tugredd of Cilgaron is a member of the Lyseby slavers guild."

"A former guild."

"Indeed. A former guild." Wimarc waited a moment as

if digesting the notion. "He seems to have been stirred by Geres' meddling these last many days. I am curious: I hadn't been previously aware that the citizens of Glenna pushed so hard against the slavery edict?"

I turned toward Wimarc full-on, scrutinizing the man with a shrewd look. "Lyseby needed little provocation to rekindle the flame of outrage. You have personal dealings with these men?"

Wimarc appeared amused by the notion. "Hardly, my lord. I only observe and take note of what I see."

"It can be a dangerous thing to observe men who wish not to be seen, my lord of Dalery."

Wimarc bobbed his head in acknowledgment. "Indeed, it could be."

I turned my attention back to the man from Glenna, Geres, who cheered with the other men at another successful catch. "Then perhaps your observations could be put to use. Would you care to visit the King's Council to share what you have just told me with the wider group?"

"If you ask it, my king, I will of course attend. But pardon me for asking -- does the Council not already know these things?"

"It is true, yes. Yet you still saw fit to confide in me all the same." I offered a wry smile to Wimarc who ducked his head, embarrassed at being caught out in his less-than-subtle attempt to slip into the king's confidence. I let the man stew in his discomfort for a moment before slapping him on the back. "You serve me well, good sir."

"Thank you," he replied with a bow before moving away to rejoin the other men.

I watched him for a while, taking note of the way he interacted with the group, the way he laughed and joked, his easy affability. All the while, Geres of Glenna remained blissfully unaware that he had just been discussed. Wimarc's father had long ago lost interest in the politics of Agrius. His son, however, was seemingly eager to engage and wished to make a name for himself. His assessment of the situation in Lyseby had certainly been on target for one so new to court. Perhaps he was an asset worth cultivating.

It was later, back in the palace after returning from the hunt, that I intercepted Geres. The men stood congregated in the hall to take refreshment and warm themselves after a long afternoon in the cold. I approached the group huddling near the generous hearth and its burning fire, coming alongside the man of Glenna as he warmed his hands.

"You will excuse us, good sirs," I eyed each of the other men around the fire, "if I have a word with my lord of Glenna?"

The men nodded themselves away, leaving me alone with Geres.

"You have some influence at court, it seems."

Geres appeared surprised by my straightforward approach, uncertain where the conversation would go. "You praise me too highly, Your Grace," he replied, doing his best to appear humble and ignorant of my meaning even while failing miserably.

"I expect much from those who attend me at court. When one enjoys the benefits of nearness to the throne, return service is required as payment."

This comment made Geres' right eye twitch. I waved a passing servant over, and taking two goblets, offered one to Geres. I took a light sip while my companion drank greedily, uneasy under the scrutiny of his sovereign.

"I am your faithful servant, my king," he replied finally.

"Are you?" Geres had just placed the rim of his goblet to his lips to drink again, but this comment shocked him into sputtering the liquid back into the cup. "I am curious to hear your understanding of the royal prerogative, of the workings of the Fiortha Court and its subsequent impact on the governance of the realm."

"Your Grace?" he faltered, trying with all his might to sidestep where he knew his king led. "I am a simple man, uneducated in the philosophies of the world."

"Come, Geres, you know of which I speak. Kingship. It is a form of contract of sorts, where I as your king act in consonance with the stipulations of such a contract. You, in turn, as a subject of my kingdom, offer me service. I provide the leadership and legitimacy, you the loyalty. It is how it has been done in Agrius for generations. I am the platform upon which the law, and therefore the government, by common counsel of my barons, exists." I gestured with my hand as if the concept was straightforward enough to be child's play.

"You speak in a tongue foreign to me, of political ideologies and abstract tenets. Again, I am an uneducated man in the ways of scholars. Do you speak of absolutism?" This time his jaw clenched.

"If you think *'by common counsel of my barons'* means absolutism..." I shrugged. "I refer to kingship, that ancient establishment upon which Agrius has been built."

"Yet your commands have the force of law, and all are bound to obey."

"And those commands come from within the community of the realm, as I have said." As I spoke, a log in the fire broke in two, with one half dropping into the embers below, releasing a hiss and sending a flurry of glowing ash up into the flue above. "Again I ask you, what is your understanding of the royal prerogative in the governance of the realm?"

"My king, I do not wish to argue with you."

"And yet you do so by your actions."

Geres' face burned bright red, though he had the wisdom to refrain from pressing his case even harder. "What would you have me do then?" His tone bordered on waspish.

"Abide by the law, Geres. You tread a dangerous line when you whisper in the shadows."

"Do I break the king's peace when I converse with others regarding disagreements with our king?"

"Geres, I simply suggest that it is unwise when your whispered words incite others to illegal activities."

"And now I am to be held responsible for the actions of others?"

"Not held responsible, no. You simply bring yourself under heightened scrutiny. I only advise wisdom before your actions cross over into the illegal."

"Thank you for your advice, my king," he said as he tossed the dregs of his cup back. "I will keep it in mind."

"See that you do."

I turned back to the fire, signaling that our conversation was over.

And with that, Geres turned and walked away.

The empty space he had occupied was quickly filled by other courtiers eager to catch my ear. As it often did, their drivel passed right over me even though I smiled and nodded. My mind, however, was elsewhere. Even as I listened, my eyes followed Geres as he bounced from person to person, finally stopping near a man I did not recognize.

I finished the last of my drink, and, placing a hand on the shoulder of the man bending my ear, offered, "My apologies, but there is something I must tend to." The man sputtered at the abrupt dismissal, but before he could form a useful reply, I strode away, depositing my empty goblet on a table as I went.

In truth, there was no urgent matter in need of tending. I was tired and simply wanted to see my wife and daughter, to retire to a peaceful evening free of the jostle for position. Other men tried to catch my attention as I went, but I kept going. *The scheming sons of Rækallin can go to Myrkra*, I thought. "On the Luskka Ferry," I muttered, not realizing I'd said it aloud until the door valet glanced curiously at me as I passed.

❊ *5* ❊

Bellesea Palace
Prille
Agrius

"THAT WILL BE ALL for this morning, I think." I pushed my chair back and stood, signaling the other men at the table to do the same. I rolled my shoulders, easing the stiffness from them after a long session of sitting. "The clerks will finalize all we have discussed this morning and add it to the rolls for the full Council."

The eradication of slavery in Agrius had presented a barrage of new issues to be worked out within the Council -- matters which touched on nearly every aspect of life, though resting most heavily on the issues of revenue and its generation for the coffers of the Treasury. Agrius had long been indebted to the financiers of the Min Tirrell in Odrana, a disastrous result of the darker proclivities of Agrius' former king, Nikolas; appetites which reached beyond the means of the Treasury.

Despite my right to bitter memories of the man, my

cousin Veris had done much to improve the condition of the Treasury during my father's reign. My father had little patience for such matters, so he had divested the power to Veris. It was only my removal of slavery as an income source that had injured the Treasury's new found health.

Thoughts of my cousin Ildor made me instinctively reach over to massage my left shoulder, finding, in particular, the muscle which had been rent and torn by his blade when he'd tried to kill me. The wound had healed, but it still gave me trouble, remaining stiff and achy when I didn't regularly stretch or move it. It was an irritation I did my best to hide from everyone, even my wife, for it served to remind me of my own weaknesses.

Before I could be tempted to pick up another dispatch for perusal and action, Irisa swept into the room, immediately stamping out my desire to work. As she made her way toward me, a twinge of thrill spidered through me. Dressed in a gown made of -- I honestly knew not what, nor did I truly care; I noticed only the way it clung to her curves as she moved. Her blue eyes fixed on mine as she crossed the room, and I sucked in a breath, releasing it slowly. I allowed a mischievous smile to curve the corner of my lips, hoping beyond hope that I would never grow tired of the sight of her.

When she reached me, she came immediately into my arms and pressed herself against me, peering up provocatively. "Have your minders left you all alone?"

She traced the line of my chin with a single finger, and I drew her in more closely, breathing in the scent of her hair which always smelled of lavender. I leaned in close and whispered near her temple, "I can think of worse things. Some matters are best tended to without my councilors around."

A light flush rose across her neck and face. Even after

so few years of marriage, my flirtations still caused her to blush the way she had done when we first met. This, of course, made me flirt all the more, causing her to blush more deeply and making her even more desirable.

"You seem happy today, my love, despite the work." She kissed me lightly then pulled slightly away to study me.

"I should be prepared to answer with a deeply philosophical evaluation of my own contentment, but I know you would see right through me." I pulled her close again. Irisa laughed, the sound of it warm and bubbling like a gentle brook. "We tended to mundane matters, my Adonia."

"And those are...?" she asked, glancing at the scattering of papers on the table behind me. "Have you had time to review the merchants' requests regarding changes to the annual fair? I think they are quite reasonable and will result in a sizeable profit, even if the ideas are somewhat unusual."

"Nothing so dramatic. Taxes, plain and simple."

"Are you getting any closer to resolving the most hotly contested portions?" She raised a brow, clearly interested in the work taking place. "For you know my opinion on the matter: that lightening the tax burden on areas hard hit by the slavery edict might be the safer approach."

It was this side of my wife that endlessly fascinated me. Certainly, I called her Adonia for her resemblance to the goddess of the same name, and I hoped to always delight in her beauty, but her greatest attraction had always been her intellect and compassion. And it was this aspect of Irisa that also continually confounded the Council, for they were not used to a woman, be she queen or otherwise, taking such interest in the minute details of the governance of Agrius. Indeed my mother and sisters had never been, and whenever she visited the Council meetings as she often chose to do, many of the councilors ended up visibly dazed, bewildered or distracted by her contributions, much to Irisa's amusement. In fact, I had come to the conclusion that their befuddlement only caused her to participate even more.

"We will have the good workings of a plan to put forward to the full council this afternoon, yes. It's likely the lords of Berig will pick apart each and every section, but there's no surprise in that." I shrugged.

"So, you are free until the midday meal then?" Her face lit up, the sunlight from the far window setting her hair aglow.

A spark fired through me. "No, I'm afraid not." I took in the sight of her lips, trailing my eyes along the gentle curve of her cheek toward her ear where a wisp of curl had escaped its pins. "The next hour has very suddenly, and very completely, become spoken for."

A hint of disappointment flickered on her face until I brandished a wolfish look, and she caught the direction of my thoughts.

"You are a very fiend!"

"I do not deny it," I admitted somberly.

She placed her hand on my cheek. "My love, I hate to disappoint you."

"Then don't," I murmured, snatching her hand away then turning it to plant a kiss in her palm.

"Casmir, there is a very important matter just beyond, in the upper courtyard, that needs your personal attention."

"And it cannot wait?" my ardor cooled only minimally at her resistance. Even as she spoke, I continued to consider ways in which to press my case with her.

"Your daughter has a gift for you."

"Does she? Since she is the only other female I know who can turn my head..."

"As it should be," she whispered, peering up at me for a moment before offering a small smile.

I snatched her hand once more and kissed her knuckles, then tucked her hand into the crook of my arm. "We most certainly should not keep the little enchantress waiting."

We made our way together in search of Sybila, finding her in the courtyard waiting alongside her nurses, bouncing with excitement and beaming a look of pure delight. My attention shifted, and behind her I noticed a magnificent black horse standing in the center of a large group of admirers. With great reluctance, I broke my gaze from the horse and back to my daughter, crouching down next to her.

"Sybila, your mother tells me you have something for me?"

She moved toward me and wrapped her arms around my neck. "Horse for Papa!"

I swept her up and stood, shifting my attention back to the magnificent animal in the center of the courtyard. "My little goose has given me a horse?"

And what a horse! Standing tall and proud, the animal's glossy coat gleamed in the midday sun. His luxurious black mane had been braided and tacked out with tiny silver bells. An unusually short, narrow caparison quilted and embroidered with the colors of House Vitus lay under his saddle, matched with rein covers that also displayed silver stitching. Prancing impatiently, the horse looked in want of a good run. Roderic whispered near the horse's face, keeping one hand on his lead while stroking his nose with the other.

Not wanting her father to forget her, Sybila placed her hands on my cheeks, turning my head and attention away from the horse to look directly into her face. "For Papa," she emphasized again, her look turned serious.

I gave her a heft then glanced at Irisa who stood a little way apart at the edge of the cobbled yard. "And what am I to call him?" I asked Sybila. When my daughter did not answer, I looked to Roderic for help.

"He was called Sevaritza by the trader, was bred in Ukaina, and the firstborn his foaling season. But of course, it is up to you to decide. Name him what you will."

I circled the courser, running my hand along the sleek flank and shoulder. "Sevaritza," I stated. "What does the name mean?"

"I am told it is a Ukainan word for wyvern, Your Grace."

I considered the information. "Sevaritza it will remain then. Will that suit you, my goose?" I asked Sybila.

She nodded sagely, and I turned to Irisa. "You did this?"

"You are not the only sovereign in Agrius who can negotiate, my love." Laughing, she crossed the distance between us and added, "Ascelot has served you well but deserves his retirement. He was a fitting beast for a prince, but a king... A king needs a horse from Ukaina."

I shook my head slowly in awe at my usually frugal wife then turned back to take in the sight of Sevaritza. Without realizing Irisa had taken Sybila from my arms, I moved closer to the animal, taking the reins from Roderic. Sevaritza twitched his nose as I ran a hand along his neck before moving around to put my foot to stirrup.

Once seated, Sevaritza settled immediately under me, and I turned him in a few tight turns before walking him around the courtyard. Sevaritza responded to my slightest touch, his movements fluid and graceful. After a time, I steered him back toward my waiting family and dismounted.

"The horses of Ukaina have more than earned their

reputation, it seems," I declared as I tossed the reins to Roderic. I planted a kiss on Irisa's cheek before turning to escort her inside.

❀ ❀

It was late when I finally made my way back to my apartments after greeting a late-arriving foreign deputation. As I entered, I found Irisa sitting propped up in bed, reading. I eyed my valet and Irisa's maid with a look that left no misunderstanding regarding my intentions this night, and without a word, they straightened from their tasks and left.

Irisa moved aside the coverlets and stood just as I reached her. I pulled her into a fierce embrace, kissing her hard on the mouth. When we pulled apart, she smiled up at me. "What was that for?"

"Thank you for my gift, my love, for Sevaritza. He is worthy of the most noble of men."

"If this is how you thank me, I shall be sure to give you more gifts."

"Oh, I'm far from finished offering my thanks," I murmured, pressing her back onto the bed as I fumbled to lift my shirt over my head. It was as I did so that a bolt of fire bit through my shoulder. I gasped.

"Casmir, what's wrong?" Irisa furrowed her brows and sat up in alarm, pushing me away to examine my shoulder and the jagged white scar across it. "How long has this been happening? Ever since the wounding? Does it hamper your sword training?" She prodded at the scar, pressing her fingertips against it.

"No," I replied shortly, pulling her down toward me and burying my face in her hair as I kissed her ear. "I am entirely capable."

"Casmir, I'm serious!"

"So am I," I mumbled, putting an end to further conversation.

Later as we lay together cocooned in the warmth of each other's arms, Irisa traced the smaller scar on my cheek. I twirled a strand of her hair around my finger.

"My Adonia, if I don't tell you often enough, I love you more than life itself."

Irisa kissed my cheek softly before nuzzling into me. "And I, you," she replied, though I could tell her words were losing force as she drifted toward sleep.

"Adonia?"

A barely audible "mmmmm..." was the only reply. Her gentle breathing signaled that sleep had finally claimed her.

I kissed the top of her head, luxuriating in the absolute intimacy I felt with her. Not one to dwell on such things normally, the moment filled me with an overwhelming warmth of affection. Then out loud, as if to Irisa, I whispered, "Once we find Ethew and get the matters with Lyseby settled, I can't imagine life being more perfect."

❋ *6* ❋

Bellesea Palace
Prille
Agrius

A HEAVY WEIGHT OF night's darkness still blanketed the room when I awoke. The air carried a frosty tinge, for it was yet too early for servants to kindle the fire to heat the chamber. I didn't want to be awake so early. The day's ride was not my idea, but I had agreed to it.

I rolled toward Irisa and gazed at her sleeping form, listened to her slow, rhythmic breathing, watched her shoulder gently move with the cadence. Brushing away her plaited night braid, I leaned forward and kissed the warm flesh of her neck. She did not stir at my touch, but it hadn't been my intention to wake her.

Resistance tugged at my consciousness as a powerful desire to stay cocooned in bed threatened to override my promise to go riding with Wimarc, the young lord of Dalery. The man insisted that I allow Sevaritza to stretch his legs after too many long days of stabling, though I suspected he simply hoped I would offer to let him ride Sevaritza.

"I'll make it worth your while," the young lord had promised with a glimmer in his eye. I argued that there was too much work to do, but the more I'd argued, the more Wimarc pressed me. Finally, I'd agreed, though the compromise came at the expense of sleep. I didn't mind, for in this way I could accomplish both tasks, work and sport. My day still might follow its normal course of productivity.

I kissed Irisa once more then slipped out of bed, dressed quickly, and crept from the silent room. I set my feet on a path toward the stables, but before getting far, I diverted to the nursery. With a light hand, I pushed the door open a crack, sending in a filtering of feeble light from the corridor. It highlighted Sybila as she slept peacefully with one arm slung carelessly over the side of her bed. I smiled then stepped back into the corridor, easing the door shut as I went.

Power surged beneath me as Sevaritza's muscles pulled and stretched, flinging man and beast across the landscape, hungry hooves churning up the miles beyond Prille. There was no feeling quite like it, the exhilaration of racing at top speed as if flying. Was this what my gyrfalcon felt like as she stooped from the sky above to the earth below in pursuit of her prey?

After a time, I pulled rein and eased Sevaritza from his run, slowing to a stop.

"By the gods, what a magnificent beast!" I exclaimed to the air around me. It was the longest, fastest distance I'd ridden him in the time I'd had him, and he let me know it too. Showing his displeasure at the disruption of his run, the animal struck a hoof into the hard soil, snorting and tossing his head in agitation. Despite the clouds of steamy breath puffing from Sevaritza's nostrils from the cold early morning air, his coat glistened with the sweat of a good run. I leaned down to pat his neck then eased back against the cantle to catch my breath. Sevaritza settled, shifting his weight from one side to the other with a satisfactory creaking of the leather tack.

I stretched my aching shoulder and drew in a breath of crisp air. The sun had dawned under the heavy shadow of winter memories, biting the trees and tender grasses with a late frost. A brisk wind blew down from the bluff overhead at a nearly vertical angle, whipping my cloak wildly about me.

Wimarc's horse had not been as swift as Sevaritza, so finally, he reined in next to me. His cheeks blazed red with cold, his lips purple. The man looked utterly miserable. I had learned only as we'd prepared to ride out how much he detested the cold. Wimarc caught my amusement at his discomfort and tried not to scowl. I laughed outright.

"Don't blame me, for this was your idea, remember?"

"Perhaps, though had it been up to me, I would have chosen a more civilized hour. Like after a full meal, for instance." Wimarc blew hot air on his hands.

"Ah, but riding out at such an early hour brings along other benefits. No one else is as daft as us, so you don't have to compete for my attention." I waved my hand around at the silent and empty clearing surrounding us. "Though to be honest, I'd have preferred that you compete for my ear if it had meant a cushioned seat near a roaring fire as opposed to this."

We had not ridden out completely alone, for no king has such a luxury. Though this far from the palace, I'd ordered my accompanying guard to wait just over the previous rise. The solitude brought with it an unexpected pleasure, and one as peculiar to me as would be the sight of a mythical creature bearing the body of a man and the head and tail of a bull.

I laughed once more as I reached behind my cantle for the extra cloak I had rolled up there and tossed it to him.

"Now, are you going to tell me what this is about, or do I have to build you a fire first?" I knew he'd called me out here for more than just a ride.

It took him a moment to decide to admit it. "While I agree with you about the fire, cushions, and flagon, you'll be thanking me for bringing you out here once you hear what I have to say." Wimarc twisted in his saddle to look over his shoulder then turned back to study the line of trees ahead of us. "The trees have fewer eyes and ears than the palace walls."

I compressed my lips. As the son of one of the largest landholders in all of Agrius, Wimarc would inherit a vast wealth upon the death of his father, along with the huge responsibility of managing it. He had come to serve at court only six months ago because as his eldest son, his father wanted him to learn the ways of court. I had not thought to question my trust in this ambitious young man, and now as the wind cut through the gaps in the trees in the vulnerability of the open meadow, exposed and unprotected, I wondered if I should have been more wary.

The question had no more than formed in my mind when a movement at the edge of the trees captured my attention. A single rider came out from the dark wood, moving slowly toward us. The figure's face remained hidden under a deep hood, concealing his identity. I made a quick mental tally of the location of my weapons, though I noticed that Wimarc appeared unconcerned. His hands rested casually clasped together before him. Clearly, the two men had an assignation; this meeting had been planned.

The newcomer came to a stop just an arrow shot from

us.

"You had an easy ride of it, I trust?" Wimarc called across to him.

The man ignored Wimarc's question initially, and instead studied me with cool detachment. When the moment drew overly long, he answered. "As well as can be expected, considering the hour." He walked his horse closer, nose to nose with Wimarc's mount and near enough to Sevaritza so that he tossed his head. I resisted the urge to ease him back a step.

"Your Grace, may I present Jachamin Guimer?"

I tilted my head in acknowledgment. "And to what do I owe the pleasure of making your acquaintance? My friend here has told me nothing, and in this, I am afraid you have the advantage, for I presume you know why you are here?"

"Of course," the newcomer replied, giving nothing away regarding his feelings on the meeting.

"Guimer," I said, as if tasting the name on my tongue. "The name is familiar, yet I cannot place why I would know it."

"Your Grace," Wimarc broke in, "you met him a few years ago when last you visited Dalery."

My eyes widened at the news. "You are the assassin who finally brought down the slave rebellion's leader."

"You make it sound like a bad thing, my king," Jachamin broke in, a slow smile hinting at the corners of his lips. "But I prefer *mercenary* if it's all the same to you."

"Your tactics were... heavy-handed," I observed.

His eyes flashed at that, and the freedom I'd reveled in only moments before dissipated, melting away as easily as a sugared wafer on Sybila's tongue. I moved my gloved hands over my face, partially to brush away the loose strands of hair which had fallen over my left eye, but also to give myself time to think.

"Casmir," Wimarc broke in, annoyingly comfortable enough to use my familiar name, "Lyseby is a problem. In fact, you have many problems that defy conventional solutions."

I shot him a hard look. "And you think that hiring an assassin... *mercenary*," I corrected myself with a dismissive wave of my hand, "will fix these problems? We have only begun to try *conventional solutions*. I am not about to condone as common practice the murder of those who would oppose my rule!" I gave each of the men a cold, hard stare.

"Casmir, I only brought you here to hear him out."

"Yes, because you know the palace walls have ears. You said as much. This was to make the ride and early hour worth my while?"

"Casmir, I..."

"You have mistaken me for another king -- my father, or his hound Veris. I am *not* him, nor will I ever be," I growled. "You have wasted my time."

And with that, I made a savage jerk on the reins, wheeling Sevaritza around to leave the two men staring after me.

Sevaritza's hooves pounded furiously into the hard earth as if he was just as eager to get away from the men as his rider. With each thundering beat, my anger pulsed. Wimarc had presumed too much.

Or had he? Perhaps my anger bubbled from somewhere deeper, a seed of truth. I wanted an assassin to take care of the problem. I truly did, and the notion had tempted me far more than I'd let on.

But I was not that man -- the man Veris had wanted me to be, the man my father was, nor was I the man who sat the throne before both of them. I was stronger than that.

No, it wasn't true. I slammed the door on those thoughts and continued back to meet my guard.

As I topped the rise and began the descent toward the waiting men, I spotted a new rider just arrived. He'd clearly brought news of some importance, for his horse stood lathered and panting despite the brisk morning air. Spurring Sevaritza on, I raced headlong toward them.

"What news?" I called ahead as all heads swiveled toward me.

"Casmir, it's Sybila," the man half shouted, half panted.

"What about her?"

"She's gone. Taken..."

Without waiting to hear more, I dug my heels deeper into Sevaritza's flanks, spurring him without mercy. Once home, I bypassed the flock of grooms waiting to take Sevaritza, riding directly to the upper court and the domestic area of the palace. Upon reaching my chambers, I finally threw myself from the saddle, finding that a servant waited to throw open the door for me.

The room bustled with clerks scurrying, messengers coming and going, and my steward directing them all. I fought through the chaos to find Irisa standing on the far side of the room, leaning against a table with one hand. She had been crying, for her cheeks glistened with wetness, and her face was mottled with red, her eyes puffy. I reached her in several strides, and when I took her into my arms, she swayed heavily against me. Her knees buckled under her, and I lowered her gently to the floor to cradle her there.

"My Adonia," I began, my throat tightening on the words.

"Sybila... gone..." she whispered.

A blind fury threatened to rise up inside, but I pushed

it down and asked through gritted teeth, "How did this happen? Who was watching her?"

"The nurses..." She gasped a sob then took a strangled breath. "They took her to the courtyard outside the quadrangle as they do every morning. She played, happily content." She sniffed, and I wiped her face with my sleeve. "They were talking, and when next they looked up, a man carried her away..."

The fury rose up again, and my next words came thickly off my tongue. "A man... what man? A guard, someone else?" Irisa did not reply as shudders shook her frame. "My love," I prompted.

"They only saw the back of him, the swish of his cloak as he rounded a corner. And Sybila's scream..." She broke off again, her sobs coming furiously. She buried her face in my shoulder.

I lifted her chin to meet my eyes, and the pain I found there broke something inside me. "In all the vastness of the palace, no one else saw anything?"

She shook her head. "They were in the domestic quarter, Casmir. They are never under full watch there. Never!"

"Irisa, I swear to you I will find her. I won't leave a single stone standing in Prille if that's what it takes."

Irisa seemed not to be listening, so I rose and gently lifted her into my arms, carrying her to our bedchamber where I placed her on our bed. She fell back limply onto the pillows. I watched her for a moment, grinding my teeth and biting back fear, anger, and confusion.

When my cousin Ildor had held Irisa captive with a knife to her throat, I swore I would never let anyone else dear to me face such danger again. I should not have been out racing Sevaritza or wasting my time with Wimarc but should have been here protecting my family. I had failed, and for that, my daughter was gone.

I signaled a maid over to me. "Send for Luca's wife, Chloe. My wife needs her support just now."

The maid nodded and hurried off.

I would find the man who had done this, and I would kill him. One way or the other, I would have my vengeance. Taking a deep breath, I leaned over and hovered near Irisa's ear. "I promise you, my Adonia, I will find who did this. We will get Sybila back."

After brushing a light kiss onto her forehead, I turned and swept from the room like a storm of fury breaking from the clouds.

❊ *7* ❊

Bellesea Palace
Prille
Agrius

"TRAVIAN!"

My bellow resounded off the gleaming surfaces of the
corridor, but the only reward for my effort was the sound of
my boots pounding the floor and my cloak flapping behind
me. I charged on, my pace matching my mood, impassioned
and furious.

With Luca away in Torrine investigating Ethew's
disappearance, Master Sergeant Travian filled the role of
constable of the palace in his place. I bristled at the man's
elusiveness in this moment, and the fact that the sergeant was
simply off tending to the search for Sybila did little to ease my
irritation that he wasn't immediately at hand.

"Travian!" I called again, rounding the corner and
nearly colliding with a young man carrying a basin of water.
The basin spun from his hands, smashing to the floor with an

enormous crash and sending water everywhere. The cacophony behind me only just penetrated my awareness before I was too far away to care.

I was about to call out again when Simon Peares, my uncle and Chancellor of Agrius, appeared in the corridor just ahead.

"Simon, where is Travian?"

Simon stepped in beside me as I maintained my brisk pace. "Travian is busy arranging a circuit of riders to scour the surrounding countryside beyond Prille."

Despite being my father's younger brother, Simon had spent little time at court during my youth. The two brothers had been estranged all of my life, though I'd never really understood the reason for it. However, knowing the disposition of my father, it was understandable. Simon had been kind to me the few times I had met him, and after the death of Ildor Veris, I asked him to come to Prille to serve the Crown as Chancellor.

A hulk of a man, Simon stood almost a head taller than me, who was already taller than average. His broad chest and extravagant white beard had inspired Sybila to call him 'Bear' when they were together.

"The gates have been shut, yes?" I asked. "No one is to go in or out until I order otherwise?"

"Indeed, and Travian has already ordered the palace searched and has sent out men to turn over every stone in the city itself."

The man was efficient even if he remained elusive. "Tell him to search it again, and to keep searching it."

We pushed through a collection of petitioners awaiting the day's audience in a small antechamber off the corridor and entered the great hall. A clerk approached me, his arm full of parchments. He selected one to hand over. I took it and gave it a hasty read. After a moment of conferring, I moved on. More clerks pressed forward, and I gave them begrudging attention.

Another clerk pressed yet another scroll into my hand, but without a look, I thrust it immediately at Simon. "Enough!" I growled, turning away and shoving through the crowd. Anyone who still had not received what they needed from me sidled away.

"Sigeric!" I raised a hand and snapped my fingers.

A short man with a constant squint bustled over, doing his best to keep the pace I set. "My king, how may I be of service?"

"You have prepared warrants to go out to the surrounding cities?"

"Of course, Your Grace," he replied. "Travian has already ordered it."

I shot him a dark look, my impatience overcoming my better sense, and was about to ask something else when Simon cut me off.

"Your Grace, may I have a word? In private?"

I gave the officer a final instruction before allowing Simon to lead me to the far side of the hall. I leaned against a column and crossed my arms, daring the older man to tell me something I didn't want to hear. "This had better be urgent. My daughter needs me, and I've been stuck in this hall far too long. Likely the rogue who has taken her is halfway to Mercoria by now."

"Indeed your daughter needs you, but you do her no good by racing about, snapping at those who serve you. You are king, not a toddler. You have a guard and officers to do your bidding." Simon stopped speaking and searched my eyes. "You are not the only one injured here. Sybila is dear to me too, to everyone who has ever met her. We share your heartbreak, your anger, your desire to find the man who did this and bring him to justice."

I ground my teeth but kept my mouth shut, allowing Simon to continue.

"Stop pacing around like a caged beast, lashing out like a tyrant in the pursuit of your justice." At this, I opened my mouth to argue, but Simon held up a hand and continued. "You have to trust that those around you are doing their jobs, that everything is being done, and has been done, to find her. Casmir, you are a man of action. No one is in doubt of that. But let us work. There is no wisdom in biting the hands of those who serve you."

Simon took my shoulder and prodded me toward the door. "It is early hours yet. Get out of the hall, out of the clerks' rooms; find an outlet, something soothing. Visit Sevaritza. Groom him. Do something, anything, just…"

"Stay out of the way," I finished for him.

"Yes." A compassionate smile curved Simon's mouth, and he pat me gently on the shoulder. "I will send Travian to you later to report once he has had a chance to do his job. Let the man work."

While the morning had started off brisk, the day had turned warm in the time since my return to the palace. After wandering aimlessly for some time, I entered the cool interior of the upper stables, shrugging off my cloak and letting it drop to the floor just inside the door. I made my way down the wide central aisle, absentmindedly stroking the noses of the horses that pushed their heads out as I passed. Wide-eyed grooms stopped their tasks to look at me as I went, most of them slipping silently away in fear of their king's mood. I ignored them.

Finally, I came to Sevaritza's stall. The tall black had been well tended in the hours since my unforgiving ride back and stood munching on a meal of grain. I reached out a hand to caress his neck. A headache threatened to take hold, so I slowed my breathing and closed my eyes to smell the scents of fresh straw, fodder, and horse flesh. I allowed the muffled sounds of the courtyard outside to wash over me like the gentle murmur of a waterfall.

Every instinct told me I should be out actively searching for my daughter, but Simon had the right of it. I needed to let others tend their duties, duties for which they had been trained. And I would allow it; for now at least.

After some moments, the sound of soft footfall broke into my reverie. Someone entered the stable. I turned to identify the intruder.

Wimarc.

A bolt of anger shot through me, flaring instantly as would a spark to naphtha and quick lime. Was it only coincidence that the very morning Sybila was taken he had insisted we go for a ride far from the palace?

The young lord had not noticed his king, for I stood in deep shadow. I stepped out.

Wimarc turned startled eyes to me. "Your Grace, my apologies, but I did not know you were here! Had I known, I would have come another time." A look of confusion crossed his face when I took several slow steps toward him but remained otherwise silent. "I am sorry to hear about Sybila. I cannot imagine how difficult it must be for you. She was your heir."

Without giving him a chance to say more, I closed on him, grabbing the collar of his tunic in a bunched up fist. I pushed him back hard against a post.

"She is my *daughter*," I growled, my words coming from somewhere out of the darkness of my misery, "and at this moment, I am no king, just a man whose daughter has gone missing."

I tightened my hold on his tunic and twisted. His eyes widened in fear, his youth showing in the whites of them.

"Was it your job to get me away from the palace so I would not be here to protect her?" I felt a fleck of spittle land on my chin. Wimarc swallowed, shook his head then opened his mouth as if to speak, but I shouted, "Don't even think about lying to me!"

"No! I knew nothing of what happened, I swear to you on my inheritance, may it rot in my father's coffers if I do not tell the truth!"

I was about to respond when a shadow fell over us, and a hand pressed my shoulder. I gave a violent shrug, swinging around on the newcomer who jumped back, holding up his hands.

"Whoa, stay your hand! Casmir, it's me, Wolf."

A dim light of clarity broke through the mist of fury fogging my vision, and I hissed a breath between my teeth before bringing up a hand to rub my eyes. I kept my other hand twisted in Wimarc's tunic.

"You are returned from Odrana," I stated finally.

"Just now, yes. And none too soon, it seems." Wolf eyed Wimarc briefly before returning his attention to me. "How has this man displeased his king so that it requires summary judgment and immediate execution?"

Wolf offered a mischievous smile, and I could not help but return my own, even if it lacked force.

Wimarc sensed the shift in the mood and jumped in. "Your Grace, I swear again that I knew nothing of the plan to take your daughter. I only wanted you to meet Jachamin.

There was nothing sinister in my mind."

"So you have said," I returned, and this time my voice betrayed my fatigue. My grip on the young man's tunic loosened and fell away.

Wolf nodded to the door with his head, and Wimarc took the opportunity to make his swift exit. When he'd gone, Wolf led me to a nearby crate and forced me to sit.

"I am sorry about Sybila," he said simply.

I said nothing but nodded as I slumped forward, thrusting my head into my hands, working my fingers back over my hair. Wolf sat next to me.

"You are still wearing your riding gloves," he observed mildly.

I lifted my head and looked at my hands, examining the gloves with their exquisite stitching. How was it I still wore them and had not bothered to take them off in all the time since returning to the palace? It was a mundane thought, a useless concern. Yet somehow the simplicity of the query seemed easier to ask than questions about Sybila.

Wolf lifted the cloak I had shrugged off at the entrance and handed it over. I took it without a word.

"We have known each other since we were boys," he commented off-handedly.

"I have no better friend, Wolf, and you know it."

"So you know I'm here for you always. And you know I'll always tell you the truth, whether you want to hear it or not."

He said nothing more for a moment, allowing his companionship to serve as a salve. Then, after a long while, he added, "When I heard what Addis had done -- to me, to you, to the kingdom -- I felt a strange mixture of fury and helplessness. We did not get along all the time, and we rarely saw matters the same way, but I thought we were friends. Her betrayal crushed me more than I thought possible."

The stable remained quiet around us. Aside from the shuffling of horses' feet, nothing else stirred. No one dared intrude on their king's grief. As Wolf spoke, I stared at the riding boots I still wore, boots that gleamed even after my long ride, for I had never once dismounted.

Wolf continued, "I stewed back home in Bauladu, even after matters were sorted with the Council and I'd retained my lands and title. Financial matters had deteriorated enough that I had no other choice than to seek the services of the financiers of Min Tirrell. I carried my anger through all the miles to Odrana and during my stay there. I thought that feeding it, keeping it sharp, would hone my senses, would make me a better weapon to get back at Addis. But I found the only person my anger injured was me."

"You have been reading too much of what the priests peddle," I grumbled.

Wolf shrugged. "It was my own experience, no more than that."

I stood, wringing my cloak in my hands before heaving it to the floor once more. "She is a child, Wolf! An innocent child!" I threw up my hands and paced angrily away before turning and stalking back. "If the craven coward who took her has a grievance against me, he should be man enough to tell me to my face. As it is, I will find him, and I will kill him."

"Assuming it is a man." We both looked at each other, remembering Addis' betrayal. "You have to find a way to contain your fury or it will consume you. Casmir the father wants revenge, and that is only normal. But you are more than that, whether you want it to be so or not, and you cannot let it control your life. You are more than just any man; you are king."

"And the *raggeit* who took my daughter would do well

to remember it too."

✻ *8* ✻

Bellesea Palace
Prille
Agrius

"I THOUGHT I MIGHT find you down here."

I stepped into the golden light of late afternoon, entering the small square beyond the water gate. Irisa sat on a small bench along a low, stone wall, her eyes closed. The rings of fatigue etched so deeply around her eyes matched my own. Chloe sat next to her, a silent companion.

I nodded to Chloe who acknowledged my approach, but Irisa did not move as I neared.

"This is where you found out, the day Ildor Veris tried to kill you," she said at last.

She needn't clarify what she meant, for I recalled all too well the moment to which she referred.

After leaving us for dead along the coast of Pania, Veris' ship returned to Prille to announce that the Agrian king and queen had died in a storm. Veris had planned to place Irisa's half-brother, Ethew on the throne in our place. But we had survived, had returned to Prille with the pirate, Swain Golden Tooth, under the cover of darkness and through this very water gate. I confronted Veris in the same council meeting which would have officially selected Ethew to be the next king. When Veris escaped, he'd come upon Irisa eavesdropping and had taken her prisoner. This was the place I'd found them, with Veris holding a knife to her throat. Veris knew she carried my child, and he had used the information against me to force my hand.

And it had almost worked except that Irisa's maid, Chloe, wasn't going to let that happen. She killed him before he killed me. It seemed somehow fitting that Chloe was here with Irisa now in the very place it had all happened.

I sat next to Irisa and took in the sight of her pale, smooth skin which was now also drawn, tight to her cheekbones. Her lashes quivered, but her eyes remained dry as she held them shut. She held a blanket in her lap, folded neatly and tucked under her hands. Sybila's blanket.

"I am going riding with Travian," I said, finally finding words.

She said nothing, but I knew she had heard me. Her short exhalation of breath told me she was not pleased.

I picked up her hand and pressed it to my lips, holding it there for a long moment. It felt cold in my grasp, fragile and limp as if she had been ill.

"Simon thinks it a good idea, says my pacing has been driving him near to mad."

She turned to peer at me through blue eyes now alive and penetrating, even in her pain. "Do what you need to do," she whispered, her words floating on the air like a thistle seed.

I left her to tend her own grief and made my way to

the stables where Sevaritza stood saddled and waiting for me.

Travian already sat his horse, waiting for me in the lower ward just inside the main gate. He nodded as he saw my approach then raised a hand to the small group of palace guards who would accompany us. We rode out together in pairs, the rhythm of hooves on cobbles echoing off the walls and buildings as we threaded our way through the crowded streets. Once people recognized me among the guard, a hush of silence fell over those we passed. Sybila was loved by them, and it felt a balm to my spirit to know of their support even if it did nothing to change the circumstances.

"I hope to have word yet this evening from the leader of the Nos Nari," Travian said as we began our circuit north then along the ridge west of the King's Gate. The land climbed steadily here, and as we crested the summit, the view below us showed the city of Prille spread over the rocky cliffs along the Tohm Sound, its ancient streets descending toward the water like a twisted and sinuous serpent.

We paused to take in the sight, and I eyed my companion, the tall and enigmatic Travian. He was older than me by many years and was only recently come to the King's Guard after Luca appointed him his second in command. Because of his history with the underground Nos Nari, he had seemed to me at first to be cold, calculating, and empty of feeling. Luca offered me assurance that this wasn't the case, but my initial assessment had been difficult to shake.

"They have put in a triple effort to learn news of your daughter, my king," Travian continued. His eyes flashed a dangerous look, and I nodded.

I didn't want to know what Travian had promised the group of blackguards, but whether I liked it or not, the request had been a necessary evil. Operating out of the deepest scummy filth that was the underworld of Prille society, the Nos Nari had turned from a once Crown-sanctioned group under the control of the former Agrian king Nikolas, into a rogue network of shadowy figures who operated outside the law. There was not much to be done about them, but we had managed to maintain a healthy truce. And now, it seemed, I needed them.

We kicked our mounts and rode on, and I considered what Travian had said, what he'd implied would happen on Sybila's behalf. In my pondering, I caught the glinting of the sun off the spear tips of the guardsmen who rode just ahead of us. Deadly but effective.

I would bring down the full force of the Crown and everything at my disposal to find Sybila. And family or not, if I found any connection between Ethew's disappearance and her loss, he would pay for it with his life.

By the time I returned from my ride with Travian, I found a light meal set in the family apartments where we had chosen to take our meals as of late. I brushed through the small assemblage, passing into my bedchamber. I smelled of sweat and horseflesh but decided not to wash. I peeled off my tunic and tossed it at a valet who offered me a fresh one.

"This will have to do," I muttered as I swept back out into our private hall. I eyed the food but chose a cup of wine instead then edged to the fringes of the room to drink it in relative solitude.

I had downed most it and had just begun to feel the relaxing aftereffects of the liquid's soothing embrace when a familiar voice spoke up.

"I beg your forgiveness, Your Grace."

I turned to find a downcast Wimarc, his lips drawn,

and his eyes avoiding my own. He appeared a pathetic puppy.

"For what? You said you were not a part of what happened."

Wimarc tilted his head slightly to the side as if weighing my response. "And I spoke truth. My apology is that I was an unwitting part of what happened, even so."

I inhaled a deep breath then crossed my arms across my chest, letting my cup rest on my forearm. I directed my focus across the room, taking in the group of somber diners. Spying a passing servant, I waved him over to refill my cup then sipped it slowly, watching Wimarc over the rim.

"You only did what you thought best," I offered finally.

Relief washed over his face as he clung to my words as would a drowning man to a lifeline. "Thank you, my king."

"Call me Casmir." I let a slow smile spread my lips. "At least here, in privacy. At court," I added, flicking my hand in the general direction of the other parts of the palace, "I am still your king, and you will address me as such."

Wimarc matched my smile and straightened his shoulders. "Of course," he returned, but then his face grew somber once more. "If I may..." He paused for a moment, as if searching for the bravery to continue. "I also wanted to clarify about the mercenary I introduced you to, Jachamin Guimer."

"I thought I made myself quite clear on the matter."

"Yes, you did. But I am not confident you understand all that the man can do for you." I must have looked about to argue, so Wimarc quickly pressed on: "I have a proposal, one that might give you something by which to judge any future involvement."

I lifted an eyebrow and sipped my drink.

"Send him to find your brother-in-law."

"I have men looking into it," I snapped, beginning to grow weary once more.

"And if they discover nothing? Let Guimer show you that he can do the work without stepping on proprieties."

I set my attention on a point somewhere beyond Wimarc as he spoke, letting his words and the implications behind them wash over me like the surf on the beach. How was what this young lord offered any different from my own use of the Nos Nari?

I sipped at my drink a while longer as I considered. Wimarc waited patiently beside me, content that he had made a firm case. I spied Irisa sitting with some ladies on the far side of the room and sensed my escape. Tossing back the last of the contents of my cup, I pushed the empty vessel into Wimarc's hands and walked away, doubtlessly leaving him standing there in confusion.

Irisa stood to greet me, and I gave her a light kiss on the cheek just as Travian entered.

"I have just heard from the Nos Nari," he began quietly, but as the din of the room hushed, he eyed Irisa then looked to me.

"Come with me," I said, taking Irisa's arm and leading Travian into the privacy of our bedchamber.

Once the door closed behind us, I turned to face the master sergeant, taking a deep breath. Irisa dropped into a nearby seat, straightening her back. She folded her hands neatly in her lap.

I nodded to Travian, indicating he continue his report.

The man's lips hardened into a thin line. "The leader of the group has only just come to me."

"What's his name?"

Travian's gaze turned aside, clearly uncomfortable with the question. "His anonymity is his shield. He is not known to most, and if his name is known..."

"His name!"

"He goes by the name Oda."

"And what did Oda have to say?" I forced lightness in my voice, but Travian could not miss the threatening undertones.

"Despite doing their best work, the Nos Nari have discovered little of use."

"But even a 'little' is something."

"Yes, though how significant..." Travian inhaled a slow breath. "A ship was chartered for the purposes of taking *certain cargo* on a long journey." He eyed me, his words heavy with a meaning that I did not miss. "Certain cargo could mean..."

"Sybila. And?"

"But the certainty was not significant enough to deem worthy of report, Your Grace, until I asked. They know no more. She may still be here, but if the ship is for her, someone means to take her off the island."

"Keep after it." I hardened my jaw.

Travian nodded then left.

I moved to the hearth, slumping into a seat in front of the fire.

Irisa slipped up behind me, putting her hands on my shoulders and moving to run light fingertips across my cheek. "Come to bed, my love," she whispered.

I placed my hand over hers and squeezed. "Not yet."

She leaned over and kissed me gently then retreated to call her maids to assist her in her nighttime ablutions, leaving me alone with my thoughts.

I watched the dancing flames. Ethew gone, my daughter taken. Ethew's disappearance had been a prick to my pride, it was true, but it had been little more than that. But

Sybila... The very force of it was a dagger to my heart.

I sat unmoving, staring at the dying flames turned to ember long into the night until the fingers of dawn began to threaten a watery light. Finally, I went to find my bed.

❊ *9* ❊

Bellesea Palace
Prille
Agrius

2 years ago

"DO ALL BABIES FIGHT *sleep?*" I asked as I paced the room, still entranced by the sight of my newborn daughter tucked safely into the crook of my left arm. She had only just slipped into sleep, and the room echoed with the absence of her cries.

Irisa lay in bed, exhausted but unwilling to sleep as she had been instructed to do by the midwife, and watched me through half-lidded eyes. All was quiet in the corridors beyond, for it was late into the night. Everyone else had long since found their beds. Aside from the irregular hiss of the candle's flame, the only other sound to break the silence was the occasional gurgle of Sybila's rosebud lips as she worked her mouth in slumber.

"All babies do fight sleep, perhaps," Irisa whispered, "but I wonder if it is the willful ones who do it most often?"

"Indeed?" I arched a brow at her then eased down onto the bed, carefully shifting so I could recline back against the pillows. "Perhaps she takes after her mother then?" I smiled wickedly at her before turning *back to stare at my new daughter.*

The babe was barely a day old, and in that time, I had hardly relinquished the care of her to anyone else except for her to be fed and changed. I'd instructed that every petitioner seeking an audience be turned away. As such, the women accused me of over-indulging her.

'A king has higher duties to tend. Let us care for her,' they said.

But that mattered little to me. She is my daughter. I am a king, but I am a father first.

I snuggled Sybila more tightly to my bare chest, enjoying the warmth of her even though the night air carried the close heaviness of recent rains. Irisa edged closer to me, taking in the sight of the scar running down my shoulder, the remnant of the wound I'd received from my cousin Ildor when he'd tried to kill me. It was barely six months ago, but the memory was as fresh in both our minds as if it had just happened yesterday.

"Does the wound still pain you?" she asked.

"My Adonia, you worry too much. You need only concern yourself with your own healing."

"The midwife assures me that I should feel much better in a month or two. While painful, birth is a natural thing. But your wound worries me. It looks as if," she began, but I leaned carefully down and kissed her head.

"Irisa, I'm fine." And then, looking once more at Sybila, I added, "Thank you for the gift of her."

"You are welcome," she murmured quietly. "But as I recall, you had something to do with it too."

My mouth twitched.

Just when I would have leaned down to kiss her again, Sybila awakened from the jostling. Her face puckered, and her red-tinged cheeks puffed with anger. Soon a howl of rage boiled up from out of her tiny body, piercing the silence. I swung my legs over the side of the bed and began once more to gently bounce her as I circled the room.

While she would not admit it to me, I knew Irisa had been

surprised by the immense and immediate attachment I'd had for Sybila. But it seemed she had forgotten that my sister Kathel was much younger than me. I remembered her as a babe, and in the years she'd lived in the palace, I'd always doted on her, perhaps in compensation for what was lacking in the paternal love of our parents.

Sybila quieted as I told her a story, the deep tones of my voice calming her. I made my way back to bed, easing once more against the pillows as I neared the end:

"At last, the great wolf Ulfer showed itself, and with one great swipe of a paw, it flung the last of the Furies to the dust. 'You have defeated the Furies I sent against you, but this last vengeance is mine!' cried Loxias as he lifted the two-headed ax. 'The deed was mine to do in the first place, and finally, I do it with my own hands!' And with one broad stroke, he separated the great wolf's head from the rest of his body."

My tone softened as I spoke, my words a mere whisper. Sybila's eyelashes quivered in the soft light like feathers on the wisp of a breeze. Her face relaxed and her breathing slowed for the sleep which claimed her at last.

"Why do you tell her such tales, my love?" Irisa whispered. "Surely there are stories better suited to her tender age than these tales of wolves and battle?"

I quirked a smile. "No daughter of mine will grow to be a mewling kitten. I expect her to have steel in her spine, like her mother."

"You want her to learn to avenge the wolf's devouring of her father, like King Loxias?" She matched my smile with one of her own.

"I have no plans to be eaten by a wolf any time soon, but surely she will meet her own adversary in time?"

"And send her Furies to seek vengeance only to use the sword of Loxias?" Irisa laughed gently then turned serious. "No, I would say she shall be more like her father."

"Whom have I avenged, my Adonia?"

"None, my love, for that is not your way."

I slid gently from the bed and walked carefully across the room toward the cradle to place my sleeping daughter in it for the night.

When I returned, I wrapped my arms around Irisa to pull her close. She brought her hand up to my chest and traced my scar once more.

"Vengeance is a double-edged sword, my love," she whispered, feeling her weighty eyes begin to close. "Easily meted out, but often leaving a scar in the process."

"Is my wife a bard now?" I asked. "Or perhaps a prophetess that she can see the future?"

"I simply relay a lesson learned from your cousin, that vengeance often comes at a cost."

"Both wise and beautiful." I kissed the top of her head. "Sleep now and I will keep the wolves at bay."

❊ *10* ❊

Bellesea Palace
Prille
Agrius

HOW MANY NIGHTS HAD I spent like this?

Was it this chair or another in which I sat each night as all of Prille slept beyond the walls of the palace? The darkness felt a comfortable blanket to me, the anonymity I found in it a balm to the treachery of my grieving heart.

Strength.

It was what I needed to show to those around me. I needed it for me. It was a shield. If my shield remained in place, I could not feel my pain.

A shudder washed over me, and I clamped down my jaw, grinding my teeth together to keep them from chattering. I knew my flesh was cold, but it was no colder than my heart. I had to keep it cold. If it was cold, I could not feel it.

Cold on the inside, on my flesh. Strength on the outside, as a shield, to keep others away.

Maintaining the balance day after day exhausted me.

With each coming and going of the sun, maintaining the delicate dance took more effort, and my nights turned longer, sitting and staring at the dying flames until I found little comfort in it.

I hadn't heard Irisa approach, but she soon knelt before me, taking my hands in her own. Her hands felt warm, full of life, a contrast to my own which felt like ice. She peered up into my face, but I would not meet her look and instead gazed beyond her.

"My love..." she prompted, but I continued in silence, as a statue of stone. I caught sight of the gleam of tears in her eyes from the feeble light of the night candle as she whispered, "Casmir, what am I to do for you?"

The rawness of pain in her words cut me like a sword thrust to the heart, but the pain of it only matched the open and bleeding wound already there.

Sybila had been missing for a week, and despite regular, full-scale searches, there had been no sign or even the tiniest scrap of information beyond what news the Nos Nari had provided to Travian days ago. If she had been taken out of Prille, it had been on the breath of a specter.

In the last weeks, I had done my best to be attentive to Irisa, considering the circumstances, but my thoughts were far from her even as I did so. With each day that passed, I felt the fog of pain increase, forcing me to pull away from others. I knew Irisa needed more from me. The quiet moments of the evening just before sleep were perhaps the hardest on her because they were the few private moments between us most days.

"Come back to bed, my love." Irisa ran her hand up my arm. "Your skin is covered in goose flesh, and you will catch your death sitting here. You do not need to sleep, but you need to come back to bed."

This roused me. "How can I?" My voice sounded brittle and cracking to my own ears. "How can I go to my rest when she is out there somewhere, alone and scared..." I cut myself off with a shudder as sorrow spilled from my eyes. "While I sit here helpless."

Irisa rose, curling herself onto my lap. She wrapped her arms around my neck as I leaned my forehead against her shoulder. She smoothed my hair with gentle hands as the moments passed interminably, my nearly silent sobs shaking my shoulders. Finally, the wave of anguish passed, and I raised my face to look at her.

Irisa searched my face with new intensity. "A piece of my heart was torn out the day she went missing," she whispered. "I fear that if she is never found, the wound will never heal but will continue to bleed out for the rest of my life. I die a little every day as it is. I cannot bear to lose you too."

A single tear rolled down her cheek as she unburdened herself. I saw it, but rather than respond, I looked away. What words were left to say, after all?

With a defeated sigh, Irisa stood and offered me her hand. "Come," she whispered. I took it, and she guided me back to bed.

The fuel of my pain had finally exhausted itself, and I fell almost immediately into a fitful sleep.

When my eyes opened on a new day, I forced my limbs to move, to ease myself upright. My body felt leaden, weighed down as if with rings of iron. Irisa slept still, but I had no wish to wake her. While I should have stayed abed, for I hadn't managed to find even a handful of hours' sleep, I could not remain still any longer. Activity kept the furies at bay.

I stood and made my way to the next room with one ponderous step after the other. My head hurt, and I felt the haze in my thoughts that comes from a lack of rest. Andreu was already about his work even so early and had laid out my day's attire. The fabrics displayed commonplace colors, held little by way of adornment. I shook my head.

"The crimson, Andreu. The new one Irisa had made from the fabrics of that foreign mercer. And the jeweled collar."

His eyes rounded wide in mild surprise, but he checked the emotion quickly then spun to retrieve the garment as I'd asked.

Once dressed, I looked at myself in the mirror. Black smudges ringed my eyes, the only visible evidence of the phantoms visiting me in the night. Not usually one to succumb to the lure of extravagant attire for everyday matters, this morning I stood every inch the king. Perhaps it was time I did so more often. The crimson tunic provided a luxurious backdrop for the bright emerald and garnet jewelry spangling my wide collar. It would do well to distract attention away from my fatigue.

I waved off food to break my fast and slipped out of my apartments, deciding I would make my way to the administrative chambers to immerse myself in work. The duty guard outside my door straightened when he saw me, but I nodded his way in greeting and proceeded down the corridor, thinking vaguely about the day's tasks while fighting the melancholy which haunted my waking moments.

My steps slowed as I inhaled the breeze wafting through several open windows just above a small garden below, catching a hint of the scent of early blooming vervain and mint. With little conscious decision, My feet had turned of their own accord, and soon I found myself following a more circuitous route through back corridors and service alleys. Perhaps I meant to search out the garden, or maybe I wanted only to enjoy the peace of such early morning, free to think my own thoughts.

Finally, I emerged into the same garden I'd noticed moments earlier and chose to follow a path that wound off to the left. Little grew in the fertile beds as it was too early in the year, but soon I came to a small patch of green, the source of the fragrance that had led me here. I stooped to pick a sprig of mint then retreated to the wall behind me where I sat on the ground, oblivious of the cold, hard earth beneath me.

I rolled the plant between my fingers, breaking up the fibers of the leaves to release the oils which contained the powerful scent. The pungent odor revived my senses, and the haze I'd experienced upon waking dissipated. With it came overwhelming pain, my ever-present shadow.

My fingers worked to tear the leaves into tiny pieces, dropping them to the ground beneath my feet where I sat. I leaned my head back against the wall, closing my eyes.

As I did so, I overheard footsteps and opened my eyes to peer at the sight of a maid carrying a pail. She had stopped before me, frozen in place upon seeing me. It was not a place frequented by nobility, was only a working garden to supplement the kitchen supplies. Likely at such an early hour, she hadn't expected to find anyone here, never mind her sovereign.

It was rare that I felt lonely, for I had Irisa beside me, close advisers to add wisdom, courtiers about continually, and little free time. But something about the sight of this lowly maid who stared at me as if I would pounce on her elicited a forlorn and desolate feeling from deep inside. It defined the gulf I experienced between me and others.

It added to the pain of loss that gnawed at me, eating away at any hope of peace in my spirit.

I was just about to speak, to find some way to reassure her concerning me when she finally came to herself and skittered away, dropping her pail to clatter to the hardened path.

The whole encounter left me feeling somehow emptier than when I'd arrived.

I was not just any man. I was a king.

Sometimes kings must do hard things.

The offer Wimarc presented me on that windswept plain north of Prille rose again to the forefront of my conscious mind, solidifying my determination to act.

"I spoke with the Constable of Torrine who was away tending to village matters at the time his lord left. He has no idea where Ethew went, and no one has heard from him since."

Luca stood before me, having just returned from his journey to Torrine on Haern to determine the state of matters there. Irisa had brought him to me in this chamber where I sat in conference with my uncle Simon, Wimarc, and a handful of other men in my closest confidence when he found me.

I stood as I listened to Luca's report, repaying his news with a cold, hard stare. I then shifted my attention away long enough to notice how quietly Irisa stood at the back. Turning my head, I glanced from face to face, taking in the expressions of each of the rest of the men in the circle around me.

Luca cleared his throat. "Ethew had only just left before Jack arrived," he continued. "The lesser servants knew little more, and despite the pressing I gave them, they could add nothing beyond the fact that their lord left in great haste.

He appeared packed for a journey, though a brief one."

"Is there any evidence to connect his going with the disappearance of Sybila?" Simon asked from his seat at a long table. Luca shook his head.

"What of my brother-in-law, Jack? Has he returned with you?"

"No, he had already returned home. I sent him word to attend you at court."

I slumped back against the table then brought my hands up to my face, rubbing my palms into my eyes before tousling my hair with my fingers. I knew my fatigue showed as obviously as I felt it.

"Your Grace, it's possible that Ethew's disappearance and Sybila's kidnapping could be related. We should consider..." Simon began.

"Uncle, not now," I interrupted. "I am in no mood for speculation but fortification. What I need is for the palace garrison to increase its muster."

"We have done so, many times," Simon pointed out gently.

I flicked him an irritated look. "And you will do it again."

Luca nodded, doing his best but failing to hide his frustration, and left to act on my orders.

It was later that night, in the evening hours before retiring to bed, that I received the final piece of bad news.

I sat at a table, playing merels with Wimarc when the man assigned the task of telling me the news was admitted to my chamber. He approached me slowly, his face pale with anxiety. He dropped to a knee, waiting for permission to report.

I gave it and listened to him with outward calm, while inside, fiery ice burned in my veins.

Taibel Rebane -- the man who had imprisoned then tortured and nearly killed Irisa's father, and the man who had conspired with my cousin Veris to take the throne; the man who had been imprisoned these last two years rather than be put to death -- had escaped.

When the distressed news bearer finished relaying all the details, I dismissed him. The room had fallen silent all around me during the unfolding of the story, and now everyone remained quiet, watching to see what I would do, how I would respond.

I waved my hand, indicating that the harpist continue to play. He hesitated a moment, his fingers hovering over the strings until I nodded at him again. He then began to play, haltingly at first, and then with more confidence.

Irisa met my gaze, but I looked away from her and back to Wimarc. Lowering my voice, I murmured, "Set up a meeting with your mercenary."

❋ *II* ❋

Prille

Agrius

Annor

HE HATED THIS PLACE, the pervading dark, the damp cold that penetrated the stone foundations so far below ground. How he dreamed of lighting a fire for heat like the ones that burned so brightly in the chambers of the king and queen. But that was a privilege reserved for very few, and this was not the place.

His master had allowed only a single oil lamp to burn because even the tiniest pinpoint of light pierced darkness like the shrill call of a trumpet in a crisp, autumn glade. Though they had secured the door, fastening it tightly from the inside and disguising it from the outside, his master still feared discovery. The work they did, his master explained, would only be understood as treasonous, and all their preparation and work to this point would be for naught. So for the loyalty he owed his master, and for the cause his master believed in,

Annor carried on his work despite the discomfort it brought.

Annor set a tray beside his master who waved him to serve it to their guest first. He would never admit to his master how much their guest scared him, but it was true. When Annor had arrived outside the man's cell door deep beneath the palace in the place the Palace Guard kept their closest prisoners, he pulled the key from its hideaway. He had stared uncertainly at the object in his hand for only a moment before inserting it into the greased lock and turning. The door opened silently, revealing a pair of gray eyes that glistened in the darkness like two pools of mercury in firelight.

The stranger had stood there motionless, his eyes boring into Annor with a malevolence that suggested he meant to kill Annor before fleeing. Annor knew that the man had no reason for animus against him, for Annor was his savior. But in the dark of the prison corridor, amidst the sounds of human suffering and anguish, Annor could only imagine his own death. Finally, a sinuous smile twisted the man's lips, and he'd followed Annor out of the prison.

Now as Annor handed their guest a cup, he studied the escaped prisoner, and his fearsome guise seemed less frightening. While his fine, charcoal colored hair matted against his head, he still managed to wear it in an elegant style. His hollow cheeks displayed the privations of prison, but a fire lit his eyes even so.

"No one knows of this room, you are certain?" he asked the master. Annor was struck by the deep, resonate timbre of his voice, velvety smooth like a ripple of rich fabric.

"No, and it was only by chance that I discovered it."

"Very good. My passage has been arranged?"

"Yes, you may leave as soon as everything else has been sorted."

"Good, good." The guest sipped from his cup as he

considered the man across from him.

Satisfied that the men had everything they needed, Annor made his way to the corner of the room and the pallet on the floor. Kneeling down, he picked up the doll that had fallen into the rushes there. He placed it next to the girl as she slept, brushing back the cascades of tumbled hair the color of a bright wheaten field on a summer's day.

"There is one slight change of plans," Annor heard the newcomer say.

"Oh?" His master broke a piece of bread from the loaf and did his best to chew it with a casual air, as if anything their guest required would be no burden.

"The girl is going with me."

Annor froze. This had not been part of the original plan. His master had promised him that no harm would come to the girl, that once their guest, this Taibel Rebane, had been freed from prison, Sybila could return to her mother and father. She had only been taken as a distraction, to allow them to free Rebane in the chaos of the palace. Annor's heart froze at the thought that the young girl would be taken away from her parents. This was not what he had agreed to. But he was committed now. His actions would be considered treasonous, his master had told him. There was no backing out.

"You will be well compensated for your trouble," Rebane assured.

His master tilted his head. "Of course. Thank you, my lord. You are most generous. Your ship will be ready to sail soon, as soon as I receive word."

❋ 12 ❋

Bellesea Palace
Prille
Agrius

15 years ago

IT WAS THE SMELL that arrested my senses first, before either sight or sound. A man, or so I guessed him to be from his man-shaped form, stumbled along in the middle of a row of other prisoners making their way along the quayside toward a transport cog. A filthy, ratted cloth hung loosely over an emaciated frame which now showed only the haunted vestiges of a formerly youthful vigor.

I followed two paces behind my father as we walked together amidst the King's Guard. The sight of the prisoners startled me, for never before in my nine years of life had I ever seen anything like it. Yes, I was aware that Agrius had prisoners -- as did every kingdom -- but I had never actually seen prisoners, and nothing had prepared me to see the contamination and defilement encrusting them. Dejection and inhumanity radiated disgustingly from their bodies.

I wanted to ask my father about these men, but I knew better.

Better to ask Grand Master Lito at my next lesson. The Grand Master would answer truthfully and without retaliation for an honest question.

A guardsman called the group of prisoners to a halt in deference to the passing of my father and me. Most of the prisoners kept their heads down, drooping chin on chest, but one man in the middle of the row, the one I had noticed first, kept his head held high. And rather than staring at his feet, he focused his bold attention on his king. My father noticed as well, and anger suffused his face with red.

"Our prisons have not changed, have they?" he asked to no one in particular.

"Your Grace?" the lead guard asked as he took one uncertain step toward us.

"Our prisons are still dark hell-holes, infused with misery and hopelessness, are they not?"

"Most certainly, my king."

"Then why does this brazen skingi have the pluck to stare down his sovereign in such a way?"

The guard glanced over his shoulder at the prisoner my father had indicated, his face darkening with embarrassment and disgrace. I sensed my father shudder with rage underneath his huffing chest. That he would do something unpredictable, I knew. It was his way. He had been in his cups already, even at this early hour, and it only followed that any reaction of his would go well beyond reason.

I tensed as I waited for events to unfold, but I did my best to keep from shrinking away. I straightened my back and held my head erect. I was not a baby. I knew full well how to hide my emotions from others just as my mother had taught me all my life. "You will be safer if you do this," she'd always told me. If my father would embarrass himself in this encounter, it would not touch me. I would stay above it.

Fortunately for me, I needn't have worried. Cousin Ildor appeared, and I breathed a deep sigh. My cousin would make matters right, I knew. Cousin Ildor always knew what to do.

"My king, what is amiss here?"

"*This skingi has defiled the illustriousness of the Crown with his ill-considered attention.*"

"*My apologies, my king.*" *Veris moved closer to my father, lowering his voice so that only we could hear. "You should not concern yourself so publicly over such a thing. I will see to the man, make sure he is punished for his presumption." Veris put his hand on my father's shoulder and patted it reassuringly, glancing briefly down at me as he did so.*

I heard my father inhale a large breath then release it slowly. "Very well. As you say. I trust you to take care of it."

And with that, my father moved off, waving a hand at me to follow him. I stepped into place behind him, but we had gone no more than three steps when my father stopped and turned.

"*Cousin, I've had a thought. This would be an excellent opportunity for my son to learn something." He raised his hand to scratch the side of his nose. "Take him with you. I want Casmir to see what happens when someone insults the king."*

A fleeting cloud crossed the features of my cousin, but it passed as quickly as it had come. "Of course, Your Grace, as you wish. My prince, if you would please come with me."

"*Make it the last lesson the skingi will ever know.*"

I felt my eyes grow wide in direct disregard of my usual outer discipline. I quickly schooled my face back into passive indifference. I knew better than to voice my doubt, for even if I'd asked, no one would give me the satisfaction I sought. And no one would countermand my father. Certainly not Cousin Ildor, for he was a faithful servant of the Crown, of Agrius itself. No, my cousin would act on the pronouncement without thought, for it was the king's justice. He would do his duty.

I expected that he would take the prisoner aside, somewhere out of sight to mete out the requested sentence discreetly. Punishment as my father had required, but punishment on principle alone. Justice must be served, but it need not be so public. So it was with great shock when, rather than go to a private place, the guard directed the prisoner to the far side of the public quay in full view of the dockworkers and sailors. Two men took each of the prisoner's arms and pulled them behind his back. The lead guard handed my cousin a long, triangular dagger called a rondel.

My cousin eyed me only briefly, and then as if another man took over his body, a new light lit his eyes, hinting at something maniacal. I physically sank back, my mouth suddenly dry. This was a side to my cousin I had never seen, and it frightened me.

He said nothing as he walked toward the man, the point of his borrowed rondel dagger held out. He circled the tip in front of the man for a moment, gauging his reaction, then pressed it against his chest just above his heart. The man twisted in the grip of the men who held him, but their grasp remained strong. Ildor pressed harder. The prisoner screamed, and I bit my tongue, tasting blood.

A cruel smile twisted Cousin Ildor's lips as he pushed the dagger deeper and deeper, pressing with both hands to pierce between ribs. My breaths turned quick, shallow. I wanted to vomit so turned away as I fought against every instinct in my body to run and hide from the horror before me. I did not flee, but neither did I watch.

My mother's words came to me: "Hide your thoughts from them, my son, and it will go better for you. If they don't know what you are thinking, you have the upper hand."

But I had never expected this from my dear cousin. I could not reconcile what I witnessed with what I knew of the man who had been like a father to me my whole life.

Screams pierced the peace of the morning, and I covered my ears, squatting down to make myself into a ball. After a time, I sensed the ordeal had ended so chanced a peek to find the prisoner slumped to the ground. My cousin straightened and turned back to me, a pleasant smile brightening his face.

"And now, my prince, to our midday meal," he said, as if he'd just done nothing more than comb his hair. "Come along." He swept his cloak over his left shoulder and strode away.

My father had ordered the deed, I told myself. Cousin Ildor could only obey. My gaze switched to the dead man lying in a pool of his own blood, to the retreating figure of my cousin, then over to the line of prisoners hovering on the far side of the courtyard. None dared to look at me. Finally, the two guards who had held the prisoner grabbed the dead man's arms and dragged him out of sight, leaving behind a trail of blood.

Kings had to do hard things sometimes, I reasoned all the while pushing the horrific experience far, far into the deepest recesses of my soul. Someday I too, when I was king, would have to do hard things.

A tear threatened to streak its way down my cheek, but I wiped a hasty hand over my eyes then set my face and followed after my cousin even though I was certain I wouldn't be able to eat a thing.

Kings had to do hard things or find others to do them for him.

❀ *13* ❀

Bellesea Palace
Prille
Agrius

"THREE IN A ROW again!" Faulkner, a courtier who attended me and Irisa in the privacy of our chambers this evening, leaned across the table, taking a token from the board and placing it with his collection.

I heard the words and replied without conscious thought, but the interaction itself flit over my consciousness like a light breeze. A memory from my youth occupied my mind, and my fingers had simply been moving tokens from space to space without awareness.

I had no first-hand knowledge of my father's throne-taking, for, at the time, I still occupied my mother's womb. I'd heard the stories of the violence throughout Prille as the soldiers descended over the city, though most who told the stories didn't know I overheard their whispers. I thought it all gossip and untrue. As I grew, however, I came to know my father's baser inclinations, his brutish ways. Brutish with those he deemed beneath him, at least; but to me, his son and heir, Bellek had merely acted indifferently. His vices were far more interesting than a young boy.

I would not be the man my father was. Or the man Ildor Veris had been. I'd sworn it on my daughter's life.

Sybila.

She was gone.

Another wave of fury rolled over me, leaving brittle scars of its going in the hollows of my soul.

Kings must do hard things or find others to do such things for him.

So be it.

"My king, you are in danger of losing this third game to me, and your purse along with it." Faulkner slapped his palm on the table as an exclamation to his point.

The sound startled me out of my pools of blackness, and my eyes snapped open, bringing my mind back to the present. The game of merels spread on the table before me, and I eyed my nearly empty purse sitting alongside it. It was still in the early hours of the evening. Other men played games around us, and Irisa sat ensconced on the other side of the room with her ladies. A musician played out a quiet tune for the enjoyment of anyone who cared to listen, but I found no pleasure in any of it.

After a time, Faulkner rapped the table with his knuckles, declaring, "I win again!"

I slid the entirety of what was left of my coin over to him without thinking. Games of chance were not best played when one's thoughts hovered in dark places. Faulkner stood and offered his thanks for a good game then made his way to find another table.

I sat alone for a moment, my mind tumbling over the

bleakness that had swept into my thoughts of late. Helplessness was not a state of mind with which I cared to be so intimately familiar. But there it was.

A change in the ambiance of the room came when the door opened and Rigard, the palace steward, entered and made his way toward me.

"Your Grace," he said, offering a brief bow, "Your uncle has asked me to inform you that Magistrate Ingólfer's messenger has arrived from Lyseby. Do you wish to see him now, or should I settle him first and have him attend you tomorrow?"

Pushing myself away from the table, I responded, "Tell him I will hear his initial report tonight. Send him to the audience hall outside the Council chambers, and have Simon meet me there as well."

"As you wish," Rigard replied, bowing his way out.

"You were gone before I knew you'd left. I would have gone with you, had you told me."

Irisa hadn't spoken in accusation, only surprise, and I knew it. Even so, her words left me feeling guilty, for I had intentionally gone without her.

"Simon went with me. I did not want to take you away from your ease."

I let my gaze drift around the room, wanting to avoid looking at her in case she could read my thoughts. Tables lay empty of board games, and the stools occupied earlier now sat vacant. All had long ago gone to bed, and in all honesty, I had hoped that she had as well.

A valet stirred from a chair and moved in to help me prepare for bed, but I waved him off, making my way to a table for a small loaf of bread.

"What did Ingólfer's messenger have to say?" she asked, watching me curiously as the valet shuffled aside.

I tore a chunk from the loaf and popped it into my mouth, chewing slowly as I ordered my thoughts. Speaking out of the side of my mouth, I muttered, "He was elusive."

"Elusive because he knows something or because he is afraid he knows nothing?"

I took another bite and chewed again as Irisa stood from the cushioned chair she'd occupied near the hearth, her curves showing through the thin fabric. I turned and paced away lest my thoughts of her distract me from what I meant to do next.

"Ingólfer was long loyal to my father, despite the political tensions of the region. He was active to support reconciliation after the edict on slavery when the trade guilds balked. Remember how welcomed we felt when we traveled through Lyseby?" Irisa nodded. "I am convinced that was purely the result of the force of Ingólfer's will upon the citizenry. He is magistrate for a reason. But if he had as much control in the region as he has wielded in the past, why the problems?" I shook my head. "I want to trust him, but I am uncertain because of his inability to tell me more about what happens in the shadows. Either he does not want to tell me, or he doesn't know about it and is afraid to admit it. It's nothing his messenger said, more what he didn't say."

"Do you have reason to question his loyalty now?"

"I've given that some thought, and no, I don't think there is a reason to question his loyalty. His evasion didn't seem deceptive. Full of self-preservation? Maybe. But not openly deceptive."

"Did you ask if he thought there might be any connection between the trouble in Lyseby and the disappearance of Rebane from prison?"

"The messenger had not yet heard that news." I compressed my lips. "But once I explained the situation, he thinks it unlikely."

"I wonder if he would even know if there was," Irisa queried mostly to herself.

"Ingólfer is perceptive enough to know that his city will be under heightened scrutiny when he hears of Rebane first hand if he doesn't already know. The question is, will he admit what he knows? He is loyal to the Crown, but like every man in his position, he is also shrewd and gifted at self-preservation."

Irisa nodded and turned, but before she did so I caught the hint of hurt in her eyes.

"Rebane will be found, Irisa," I offered more gruffly than I'd intended.

"He imprisoned my father, had him tortured."

"I know." The fact that he had been Ildor Veris' lackey bothered me more, but I kept that thought to myself.

"I thought that holding him in prison was the right thing to do," she continued, "was more just than having him put to death. He would have killed my father, was only prevented because the Serdar saved him in time. I thought that if we'd killed him, we'd have become just like him."

It was a topic we had discussed at length, many times over. What more was there to say? I'd wanted him executed for treason, but Irisa had pleaded clemency. I knew she blamed herself, but I had no words of comfort for her. Justice was never so simple.

Irisa crossed the room to stand behind me and slipped her arms around my waist. "If he is connected to Sybila..." she broke off, swallowing back whatever it was she was about to say. "My love, come to bed," she said instead.

When she moved to unfasten my coat, I stayed her hand. I swallowed, shoving away my desire, knowing that if I let her continue, I'd not make it to my next meeting. Turning around and taking a step backward, I replied, "No, Adonia, not tonight."

Her look of pleasant longing melted away. "Casmir, is something amiss?" Her face held a question, but it also hinted at suspicion.

Irisa Sajen, daughter of Bedic Sajen, heir of a deposed ruling house, was a crowned sovereign with as much right to power as me. So far in our marriage, we'd found agreement on most matters of state. I shifted my eyes away from her face momentarily then steadied once more. While Irisa the queen may have given my plans a fair hearing, Irisa my wife would not. She would be upset. And for that reason, what I was about to do I did on my own. I forced shut the door to my emotions.

"I must go," I said, more sharply than I'd intended.

"Go? Casmir, what is the matter? Has something happened I should know about?"

A knife of guilt stuck its sharpened blade into my gut, but I forced the feeling away. In its wake came a hardened feeling akin to anger disguised as defensiveness. My mouth thinned into a brittle line.

"Nothing you need concern yourself with," I muttered.

A flash of challenge lit her eyes. "Nothing I need concern myself with, or nothing you wish to tell me?" She moved around to face me.

I scowled and brushed past her. "I have to meet someone," I snapped, surprised that I'd admitted even that much.

"At this hour? Casmir..." she warned, but I ignored her and strode for the door.

I was protecting her, I reasoned. She would understand that later, even if not now. It would be worth it, I persuaded myself as I closed the door with a final thud.

The corridor outside lay dark and silent. Disappointment with my own behavior toward Irisa muddled about with the anger and defiance only just roused. I entered a small chamber far from my apartments. Full darkness cloaked the room save for a pool of moonlight reflecting through a tiny window into the center of the room.

A disembodied voice spoke out of the darkness: "We thought you might have changed your mind, that you wouldn't come."

"I said I would come," I snarled, "and here I am."

"My fee is 250 crowns and not a bezant less."

I moved further into the room, into the watery silver light. I began to make out the outline of a man leaning up against the far wall. His fee had already been agreed to. I saw no reason to respond.

The man read my lack of response as hesitation.

"Hiring a shadow to do what others cannot or will not do is not unusual for a king, *Your Grace*. You will be glad of it, once I've returned."

I clenched my jaw. "My decision does not waver, nor do I need your reassurance," I growled.

I saw movement out of the corner of my eye, but I was not surprised by it. I knew Wimarc would be here too.

"Jachamin only meant..." the young lord began, stopping when he read the sneer on my face.

"I know what he meant. Here is your fee." I held out a sack of coins, and Jachamin stepped forward to take it. Just as his hand moved to close around the bag, I snatched it back from his grasp. "Bring him back alive. If you can do this one thing as I've asked, we will see how else you may be of use to me." I hurled the pouch at the mercenary's chest.

Jachamin Guimer caught it, and with an aggravating hint of amusement on his face, he pocketed the money and turned to leave. "One more thing, my king," he added as if something had just occurred to him. "I do what the job requires. If anyone gets in my way, friend or foe," he began, but I cut him off.

"You heard my stipulations. Just be about your business, mercenary," I snapped.

Another smile spread the man's lips, and he exited.

I was left feeling as if I'd just done a deal with *Rækallin* himself.

I slipped back to my bedchamber and found it dark and cold, and Irisa abed, though I knew full well she did not sleep. Her breathing came too quickly, was too shallow for deep slumber. In the dim light, I considered her form, the rounded curves beneath the sheets, the drape of her hair across her pillow. Once I'd undressed, I slipped beneath the coverlets. As I did, the sheet covering her shoulder slipped down to reveal warm flesh beneath it. While any other time I would have moved into her, I knew I would find no welcome this night. Instead, I turned to face the cold, outer wall and closed my eyes, feigning a sleep I knew would be long in coming.

✻ *14* ✻

Foredeck of the Lazlis
Tohm Sound
Agrius

Kassia

"I WILL *NOT* WEAR that!" Kassia stomped her foot, acting very much like her two-year-old son Cailen, she knew. But she didn't care. "I don't care that the Queen of Agrius *is* my sister, I will not look the part of a pretentious peacock just to visit her. She knows me well enough in that regard, and I have no need to try to impress those around her as if I was some mewling lady of the court!"

From his position by the window, foot propped on a stool as a servant laced his tall boots, her husband Jack barked a laugh, quickly coughing to cover it up. Kassia whipped her head around to glare at him, her eyes daggers of blazing heat.

The servant finished with Jack's boots, and he strode toward her, taking her shoulders between his hands and giving her a look he often used on Cailen when he tried to reason with the toddler. "Kassia, mark my words, no one would ever dare call you mewling. Or demure for that matter." He flaunted his most winsome smile at her, and she scowled in return. "It is late spring and green things have begun to grow, but on the waters crossing the channel, the winds will be fierce. Don't dress to impress. Dress to stay warm. At least wear the cloak? You can wear your homeliest homespun underneath with none the wiser."

That same dark lock of hair which so often fell down to cover one of his eyes distracted her, and she forced herself to clench her hands so she would not be tempted to brush it off his forehead. "I will wear the velvets, but only because they are warmer," she humphed.

Now as she stood aboard the ship crossing the Tohm Sound from their home on the island of Haern, the very winds Jack had warned her about whipped her once neatly coiled strands of hair free of their pins. They lashed at her neck and face, blowing about like striking serpents. While she would never have admitted it, she wished she had opted for the cloak too, as Jack had suggested.

She thumbed aside her tousled locks to spy her husband standing near the deck railing holding Cailen and pointing out various landmarks of the fast approaching city of Prille. The boy's dark hair stood on end, ruffled from the day aboard ship. The spring weather had held steady for many days, but today a storm brewed farther out at sea, and the winds heralded news of it. She tucked the corners of the blanket more tightly around her infant daughter Tilda, snuggling the child closer to her breast as she slept peacefully despite the weather and rough seas.

She turned her attention to the outline of Prille, the buildings coming into better focus as they rose and fell in a haphazard line up the incline from the port below to the heights of the city overhead. Where was the palace, she wondered? It was her first glimpse of the city of her father's birth, the city of Jack's birth too, for, in the past two years since Irisa and Casmir had come to their small village in Pania as castaways, Kassia had never gone to visit them as king and queen of Agrius.

"Mama!" Cailen called to her. She traversed the deck and allowed her son to point out a large ship anchored in the deep water of the Sound. His finger quivered with excitement, for they had nothing of its like near their small manor. She made an approving murmur and kissed his cheek before eyeing Jack then returning back to the place she had left nearer the center of the ship's deck.

She had been prepared for uneasy feelings at first sight of her father's city. She remembered all too well the dread that wore down her heart those years ago upon arrival in Brekkell, home of her intended husband, Isary of Elbra whom her father arranged for her to wed in exchange for his support to retake the throne of Agrius. She had never had much love for the aristocracy, but since learning the identity of her family, she'd made an uneasy peace with it. The feelings invading her heart now were quite different from what she'd expected, however. Her heart raced with excitement. Perhaps she was simply eager to see her sister.

A crowd of finely dressed individuals awaited their landing. Kassia scanned the line of faces, immediately picking out Irisa and Casmir standing at the forefront of the group. They were yet too distant to make out Irisa's expression, but Kassia imagined that her sister smiled at her.

As the ship grew closer, she studied Irisa, tall and regal, wearing a voluminous gown of pale blue and gold, her sleeves trailing long to the ground. A wool cloak draped her graceful shoulders, held at her neck with an enormous round sapphire. Irisa held her arm up, shielding her eyes with her hand while the wind whipped tendrils of her hair about her face. Casmir stood next to her dressed in velvets and fur with precious jewels adorning his collar, every inch the king of Agrius. His bearing now was quite different from the man he'd appeared the day he showed up at her home in Pania. She would never have guessed that either of them was the same person as before. They were not, of course. She knew better.

When their ship nestled into its berth, Kassia steeled herself for what would come next before handing off Tilda to a nurse. Once her feet touched solid ground, Irisa rushed toward her. Kassia took in the scent of lavender and basil as she returned the embrace.

"My sister, how I have missed you!" Irisa leaned in to kiss Kassia's cheek.

"And I you," Kassia returned.

The sisters maintained their embrace as floods of memories came rushing back, of her escape from Corium, of her time with the swamp people in Porpio á Fen then at the Serdar's in Islay Bay, her near-marriage to Isary of Elbra, of her father's past and her own future. There was much to face here in Prille, but for just this moment, none of it mattered. She squeezed her sister then released her and pulled back.

Now as she viewed Irisa's regal bearing, bright and beautiful despite the grief Kassia knew lurked under the surface, she wished she hadn't waited so long to visit. No matter her own demons, she must do this for Irisa.

"Thank you for coming," Irisa murmured softly.

"Of course," she whispered back.

Casmir turned away from Jack to greet her. He placed his hands on her shoulders and, embracing her as Irisa had done, kissed her cheek. "You are most welcome to Prille." He pulled away and studied her face, and a brief hint of grief washed over his expression. It was quickly gone, however, replaced with a bland smile. He swept his arm behind him, saying, "Come. We have palanquins waiting to take us to the palace. After you settle, we will dine. After that," he said, turning to Jack, "I will beat you at hazard!"

Had she not already met him and taken his true measure, Kassia would likely have been intimidated by Casmir, for the man before her appeared unreachable. He was Casmir, King of Agrius, and the most powerful man she was likely to meet in her lifetime. Recalling him now as she'd last seen him, at his weakest, dirty and injured, the formality of his manner struck her as brittle, perhaps contrived, as if he'd tried too hard to achieve it. Perhaps this was his court mask Irisa had often spoken of.

Shaking off her meditation, Kassia straightened her spine and surveyed the immediate area around them, noticing for the first time the large contingent of soldiers flanking them. Irisa had often spoken of her relative freedom to move about Prille, so the size of the guard surprised her. She must remember to ask her sister about it later, but perhaps it had something to do with Sybila. She took her place beside Irisa as Jack fell into step beside Casmir. The pair of women followed the men as they made their way toward the palanquins.

"Cailen and Tilda, they are beautiful," Irisa murmured.

Kassia's eyebrows shot up. "Thank you, I wasn't aware you had seen them."

"Only a peek from afar. Your nurses had them in hand as you disembarked."

Now that they sat close together in the confines of the palanquin, her first impression of Irisa faded. Gone was the serene queen whose duties rested lightly on her shoulders. Instead, Kassia observed her pale skin, her drawn and sorrowful eyes. Taken together, it told a different tale than the one Irisa likely wanted to show to the world. The stress of the last many weeks had clearly taken its toll. How could she respond to a woman who had just praised her children when her pain regarding her own missing child was likely unbearable?

Irisa read her mind. "Kassia, you needn't walk on eggshells around me. Sybila is missing, but your children are not. They are alive and well and safe. You do not need to feel guilty for your own happiness."

So Irisa had not changed that much. She still thought of others before herself, always wanting to put others at ease. But Kassia knew it had to have taken something out of her to extend such a grace. The furtive look she directed at Casmir told a more complex story.

"Casmir is not holding up well," Kassia ventured.

"No, he is not," Irisa replied, her mouth hardening into a firm line.

Irisa provided no more explanation, so Kassia picked up her sister's hand and curled it into her lap before turning away to watch as the city passed her by.

Soon the palanquins reached the palace and stopped inside a private courtyard. Grooms helped the women climb down from the conveyance, and Irisa led Kassia inside a small antechamber, then down through a long corridor, and finally out into a covered arcade alongside a quadrangle. At the end of the second arcade, she paused outside a large oak door as a servant opened it, allowing the women to enter.

"These were my rooms when I first arrived in Prille. You and Jack may use them for as long as you are here. Geralt will see to your needs. You need only ask him."

Irisa smiled vacantly, and Kassia wondered if she saw memories of her early days at the palace. She sobered when

Jack entered behind them.

"Thank you, sister," Kassia said. "We will be more than comfortable."

"I will let you settle until the meal. We will dine privately tonight to allow you to adjust to your surroundings. For now, refresh yourselves, and we will speak more later."

When she had gone, Kassia turned back to the empty room to find it echo with the magnificence that was Prille's palace. Her father's home. A place she'd never wanted any part of since learning of his true identity as a prince of Agrius, a would-be king.

Jack seemed to sense her thoughts. "Kassia..." he began as he moved to embrace her.

"Don't worry about me," she interrupted. "You should take the opportunity to take in the memories of your old home."

"But we didn't live in the palace, Kassia, just in the lower yard with the tradesmen," Jack teased gently. "And besides, my memories are my father's more than mine. I was a mere babe in arms in those days, so all I know of this place comes from his stories."

Jack's father Rem had been a metalsmith at the palace during the reign of Nikolas Sajen, Kassia's grandfather, and he had struck up an unlikely friendship with Kassia's father, Bedic. After Bellek's arrival, Rem had fled with much of the palace household, his young son Jack in tow.

"I am more concerned about you," he added, kissing the top of her head.

Kassia peered up into Jack's face as he brushed hair from her forehead. "Perhaps I can gain some sense of my father, as your father knew him, while we are here. You know how things were between the two of us when he died, but I would still love to know what turned him from the man I remember as a child into the man he became in Brekkell," she whispered.

She pulled from his embrace and turned to face the room, wrinkling her nose. "But for now, let's see what we can do to make this place a little less pretentious." Jack stifled a laugh at her pragmatism as she paced across the room, taking in the gleaming marble and shining surfaces of the rich wood tables and chairs. "Though we only need to wait a bit. Once Cailen arrives with his nurses, he'll set matters aright!" She picked up a delicate glass vase and turned to Jack. "Want to guess how long this has a chance of surviving?"

The door opened, and the nurses entered with Cailen and Tilda in hand. "Mama!" Cailen squealed as he came rushing toward her.

"We shall see," Jack laughed.

❀ *15* ❀

Bellesea Palace
Prille
Agrius

Kassia

"THAT MAN THERE," IRISA said, pointing a discreet finger at a barrel-chested man with a white beard, "is the Lord Treasurer, our Chancellor, Casmir's uncle Simon." She laughed quietly. "I will do what I can to keep you away from Simon's clerk, the man at the far end of that table," Irisa continued. "More than likely, he will try to introduce himself later, but we'll keep him at arm's length."

"Why?"

"Trust me, you don't want to know," she laughed. "And those men over there are minor lords of Sarnas and Valnia."

Irisa rattled off name after name with ease. The patina of sadness shading her face yesterday afternoon had faded. A new glow had appeared, the aura of a queen, a woman comfortable in her role.

Kassia, on the other hand, felt awkward and out of place. As Irisa continued to explain the ways of court, she'd stopped listening, occupied herself by picking at her food. Most of it meant nothing to her. These people meant nothing to her. She was too exhausted to pretend to care. It couldn't be soon enough that the dinner ended and she could escape.

"Kassia, I've lost you."

"Yes, sorry."

"No, you're not."

"No, I'm not. I'd rather poke out my eyes with an embroidery needle."

Irisa tipped her chin up and laughed a laugh that bubbled up in a way that reminded Kassia of their childhood. "Come on," she said, pushing her chair back. "Let's make our escape."

"But I'll miss the jugglers," Kassia offered.

Irisa caught her sarcasm and shook her head before leading the way through crowds.

"Hide our escape," she whispered conspiratorially to the door valet as they dashed through the door and out into the chamber beyond. Finally, they reached the upper courtyard across from which stood the Bibliotheca, the bastion of ancient learning for generation upon generation.

"I would often go to the Bibliotheca when I was new to Prille. That hulking pile of stones became my respite from the world when nothing about my life made sense. I will show you my favorite hideaways inside later, but I do not wish to disturb the scriptstórii, for they are likely preparing to retire for the night. For now we can stand atop the steps where no one will bother us."

Kassia nodded and followed Irisa as she stepped out

from under the shelter of the arcade. Irisa glanced about to make sure the way was clear and that no one observed them too closely before flitting around the edge of the courtyard toward the Bibliotheca. Swift footfalls took them up the deeply worn steps to stand just outside the main entrance to the institution. A low drone, like the sound of a distant hive, settled over the courtyard below them. Clerks and servants came and went, completing their remaining duties before retiring for the night.

Kassia closed her eyes and breathed in the serenity.

"My new world overwhelmed me," Irisa murmured, "and I needed to escape to clear my head and make sense of my thoughts and confusing feelings. I found a sort of solitude here, in the Bibliotheca. The day before my wedding to Casmir, I missed you more than anything, Kassia. I wished you were here."

"Were you afraid to marry him?"

"No, I was eager to do so." Irisa offered a self-aware smile as a light flush painted her cheeks. "But I was nervous too. And before you say anything sister, it's not what you're thinking. It was simply that so much in my life had been overturned. The idea of becoming a queen -- me, a girl who had only ever known poverty... that is what gave me pause."

Irisa glanced overhead, toward the quickly deepening hues of the sky as twilight ushered away the brightness of day. Kassia felt herself relax as she followed Irisa's gaze to take in the clouds, smiling when she found a familiar shape from within them.

"There is a sparrow, sister." Kassia pointed out the abstract shape on the far horizon where a streak of yellow and orange color offset her cloud sparrow as if it escaped a fiery furnace.

Irisa grinned. "And there is a chariot!"

They continued playing the childhood game, with it coming a feeling close to serenity.

"Thank you, Irisa."

Irisa turned inquiring eyes toward her. "For what?"

"For helping to put me at ease when you have far bigger worries than me."

"Kassia, do not compare our struggles, for your cares are just as real to you as mine to me. It's not a competition."

"That's my sister. Always looking out for everyone else before herself."

Irisa's blue eyes met Kassia's green ones, hints of sadness returning once more. "It is my duty as queen," she deferred.

Kassia sighed. "Duty? You are too humble, Irisa. Queenship has nothing to do with it. You did things like that even back in Corium when the idea of ruling sovereignty would have been madness. It is just who you are, and you can no more hide it than a leopard can hide its spots. Your current station has not changed you. It's why you pushed so hard to eradicate slavery once you became queen. You saw the people in the streets as real because you were once one of them."

"Casmir would have done it in time," Irisa protested, though her eyes suggested that she did not truly believe it.

"Perhaps, but we'll never know for certain, will we?"

"No, we won't."

Kassia heard the catch in Irisa's voice, saw the sadness in her sister's eyes, and her heart broke. "Irisa, tell me about Casmir. I watched the two of you together tonight. He understandably misses Sybila, but there is something more."

"Yes." Irisa examined her hands as she gripped the balustrade, seemingly reluctant to say more.

"There is something in his eyes. A hint of danger perhaps. He is not the Casmir I met in Pania," Kassia ventured. "It is almost as if he has become... feral."

Irisa rocked back almost imperceptibly on her heels at Kassia's harsh word choice, but she quickly recovered. "First Ethew missing, then Sybila. When Rebane escaped, I thought Casmir would break. But he didn't break, Kassia. Something solidified in him, something deep down and unreachable in a place I cannot follow." She shook her head to make sense of her own words. "I fear that you might be right: *feral* might best describe what he has become."

Irisa's eyes turned pleading, and Kassia wasn't sure what to say. She chewed on her lower lip as she considered how to help.

"More than that, he struggles with his confidence," Irisa continued. "He would never admit to it, of course. What man ever would? But I know it. I can see it even though he tries desperately to hide it. At night when I find him sitting alone in a chair before the cold hearth, there is a look about him that says he is haunted with a fear that the darkness will overtake him, that he will become like his father, or even worse, like Ildor Veris."

"How could he think that? He is not the same man. Not even close."

Irisa shook her head. "No, he's not. You know it, and I know it. But does he?"

"So the search has been futile for all of them?"

"Yes. And it eats at him like a cancer, Kassia. He feels powerless to do anything about it. No king, no man for that matter, can easily accept such a thing."

Kassia nodded. "Yes," she said weakly. "I know how he feels."

"Of course you do, sister. And that is one of the many reasons I am glad that you and your children are here."

Irisa offered a weak smile before Kassia noticed an

entirely new emotion flit across her face as glistening eyes released a tear.

"There is more, isn't there?" Kassia asked, and Irisa nodded. When she remained silent, Kassia picked up her hand. "Tell me."

"Sybila is two."

Irisa said it as if that alone should tell Kassia all she needed to know. Kassia tilted her head in confusion. "Yes, she had a birthday not long ago."

"Do you not think it strange that she does not have a sibling?"

"Irisa, it is not so unusual that..."

"No! Kassia, there is something wrong. There has to be. I have failed, and I wonder if Casmir doesn't hold me responsible. We don't talk about it, but I know he must wonder." Kassia opened her mouth to speak, to contradict the illogical reasoning of it all, but Irisa held her off. "Don't deny it, Kassia. He is king, and a king must have an heir. With Sybila gone, the throne is vulnerable. I feel so guilty for even thinking such things, as if wanting another baby is disloyalty to my missing child! And thinking of my own children simply as heirs..."

"My sweet, you are under more stress than anyone can possibly understand. There are two sometimes irreconcilable sides to who you are, who you have to be. And besides, you are young. There is plenty of time. Casmir the king may be concerned, but in the end, it won't matter. Sybila will be found. Casmir will not stop until she is, I know for certain. In the meantime," she continued, flashing a wicked smile, "you just have to work harder at conceiving another babe, no matter how unsavory the deed may be. I know it must be a chore, for one must only look at the man to know it."

"I'm not sure what you mean."

"Mmmm hmmm..." Kassia replied, her eyes narrowing at Irisa who flushed. "My poor, poor sister."

"He has never been tested in this way before. Is steel forged in the spine of everyone put to the fire? I think not. Some men break."

"Then we will hope that he draws strength from those surrounding him, supporting him."

"If he will allow it."

"He loves you, sister."

"Yes. But even in that love, there is a gulf between us. In some ways, it has always been there and always will be. He was born here, to this, while I, we, were born to the dust and the dirt of a back alley. There is love between us, yes, but sometimes our pasts can be a foreign language that no amount of well-meaning can decipher. It is in the time of testing, as in this hour, that the strain is felt the most."

"Every marriage experiences strain, sister."

"Yes, but not every marriage also carries the weight of a crown. *Two* crowns. Our marriage is not just for us, Kassia. It is for the kingdom, first and foremost. And the kingdom will always, without fail, come first."

"Irisa, you are strong enough for this task. You share a hurt with him, it's true. You both grieve for your daughter. But a mother's heart was made to bear the pain and rending for a lifetime, for that is what it means to give birth to a life which you must ultimately free back into the wider world. But men... often their pains are born of a pricked pride which, in its unbending, bleeds away the very strength it was meant to contain."

"Little Katava, the philosopher!" Irisa laughed and with a conspiratorial smile added, "Are you trying to suggest to me that men are simply brittle?"

"You never heard it from me."

Irisa looked about to say more, but just then the sound of clattering of hooves and the jingle of tack interrupted them. Her face drained of all color, and she all but flew down the stairs toward the riders entering the square.

Kassia stuffed down her surprise. "Irisa, who is it?"

"Those are the colors of Torrine," Irisa threw over her shoulder.

"Is it Ethew?" Picking up her skirts, Kassia hurried to follow on her sister's heels. When they reached the mounted men, Irisa froze as the lead rider dismounted, followed by another man whose hands had been tied together.

The stranger pressed the bound man forward.

"Ethew," Irisa breathed, taking in the sight of her half-brother.

"My queen, I bring you a gift," the stranger said before Ethew could speak.

Irisa snapped shrewd eyes on him. "And you are?"

"Jachamin Guimer, Yar Hátin," he offered with a broad smile and a gallant bow.

A strange light flickered across Irisa's eyes as she took in the sight of Jachamin, but soon it was gone. She turned to Ethew.

"Greetings, sister," Ethew offered. "I bring you news of Sybila."

Bellesea Palace
Prille
Agrius

14 years ago

"*IT'S ABOUT TIME!*"
 The outburst came with the sound of a hand slapping the table. I blinked as I crossed the flagged floor of the King's Council chambers, my eyes flicking from left to right to find that most of the councilors watched me. I knew they wondered how their young prince would react, but I kept my features passive as ever. I breathed in a slow breath through my nose and kept walking. Upon reaching the side of my father, I stopped, stood patiently waiting for my father to speak.
 "*Wasting time with those idle, namby-headed clerks in that hulking waste of stone?*" *My father raised a shaky cup to his lips and took a deep drink from it, but it was hastily done, and liquid spilled*

from the corners of his mouth onto his chest. He wiped at it with a sleeve as he turned baleful eyes back on me. "Nothing to say?"

"I was at my lessons, Father."

"Eh?"

"My lessons. I was studying the Ballad of Trardreer, and Grand Master Lito has asked me to memorize..."

"Bah!" he interrupted. And then as if flicking at a buzzing bee, he swiped at the air with his hand, his fingertips just missing my cheek.

I took a step back.

I knew that if I looked around the room full of gathered advisers, I would see looks of resignation, some of shock, and others of embarrassment. I needn't look, however. My father's routine of insult and offense was as regular and predictable as the hands of the water clock in the great hall of the Bibliotheca.

"Sit! Find you a place over there, out of the way. You are here to watch and learn, but I don't want to see you while you do it."

I made my way around the table in the center of the Council chambers, and only now did the councilors whisper among themselves. Several cast me sidelong glances, and others uttered phrases of mocking determination about the value of the present sovereign of Agrius. I knew they spoke truth, but the insults conflicted me just the same.

Finding a seat along the back wall, in a corner of the room which put me out of the direct line of sight of my father, I sat and listened, even if I had little interest. If this was what it meant to rule a kingdom, I wanted no part of it.

I felt certain I hadn't dozed off, but my attention had flagged enough so that when the meeting ended, the sounds of shuffling feet startled me. I looked up to find the men departing and a shadow loom over me.

"My Prince," said the voice, both familiar and welcome.

Cousin Ildor.

He offered me his hand, and I took it. Once we had left the chamber, he finally spoke.

"Casmir, you do not do yourself a disservice by locking your heart away from your father. He is a man who is incapable of appreciating the good gifts he has been given."

"And that is why we are lucky to have you, cousin."

My cousin smiled down at me. "I will always keep you safe. Never fear."

"But my mother can..."

"Your mother can't be bothered just now, son. You know that." He pulled me along, and finally, we found ourselves in the courtyard of the upper ward. *"You have me, and I will watch over you. You needn't concern yourself with either your father or mother, for they can do nothing for you."*

He stopped then turned and knelt down to eye level with me. "You will be king someday, Casmir, and until then you must learn the craft of kingship. I will be your guide, for your father cannot. And if the task should prove too much for you, you only need rely on me."

He peered over his shoulder as if to confirm that we were alone. "Agrius cannot abide another king like him. Until then, I will continue to lead as I have done. As you continue to grow, I will teach you all you need to know." Ildor smiled, taking my hands between his own. "And even when you are king, I will be there for you just as I have been for your father."

I lunged forward into his open arms. Even if I felt isolated from everyone else in my life, even from the playmates of rank who had been chosen for me to be my companions of quality, I felt safe with Cousin Ildor, he had never given me reason not to. It was as if the very gods had sent him to Prille, just to watch over me.

❊ 17 ❊

Bellesea Palace
Prille
Agrius

"KASSIA HAS FINALLY SETTLED on household officers after all this time. Prodding her only slowed her down because she refused to let go the reins of control for much of it. *'If I have to be the lady of the manor, we'll do things my way,'* she says. With the fire flashing in her eyes, most are happy to let her lest the wrath of the gods fall on them!"

Jack laughed, and I laughed with him. He had matched the cadence and tones of his wife perfectly. His dimpled smile and the warmth of light dancing in his eyes when he spoke of Kassia told me all I needed to know of his love for her, the happiness of their match. She'd never wanted the land or title I'd granted them, but she'd agreed to it for her love of her husband. Jack was a lucky man, and he knew it.

I watched my unlikely brother-in-law from over the rim of my goblet as he continued to tell story after story of his time in Haern since arriving there from their former home in the obscure village off the coast of Pania. Jack had taken to his tasks as lord of the manor, it seemed, and had thrived as I knew he would. His days of helping his father support a small community of exiles had prepared him nicely for this.

I stretched out a hand for the flagon across the table, but a servant saw my movement and hurried to reach it first. I waved the man back and took it on my own, pouring a full measure and taking a deep drink. The cool liquid slid down my throat, and I closed my eyes in appreciation. My father would have approved of it, for he'd had a taste for fine things.

My father.

I felt the familiarity of a black cloud descend at the thought of him. My father sought comfort in his cups and in the touch of his many mistresses.

I am not my father.

I took another sip. Warmth washed through my limbs, suffusing my toes with tingles. Indeed, I was not my father. My fingers clenched the goblet. My father had sought solace in his cups, and it had killed him.

"What a wonderful feast, thank you," Jack said, drawing my attention back to the present.

"You are most welcome. Your coming has been just the distraction we needed. Let's hope it is a harbinger of better things to come." Surprised by my own candor, I raised my cup toward my brother-in-law who returned the gesture, and together we drank.

The warmth of Jack's companionship, his ability to see through the masks of court and its pretensions and get straight to the heart of matters had enabled this husband of my wife's sister to fall immediately into my confidence. I had come to know him as a wise, perceptive man, yet in all the opportunities to inquire about the details of the troubles in

Prille, Jack asked not a thing.

Kassia had described Jack as introspective and thoughtful, with a discerning sense of understanding the world. Perhaps it had been all the adversity in his life as an exile. Whatever it was, I was thankful for him. Thankful for the companionship without the questions, or even the judgment to go with the questions. He would have made a very good king, had our roles been reversed.

Perhaps even a better one than I was.

I took another sip.

"Our wives, they seem to have left us," Jack observed. "I admit I was paying too much attention to the entertainment."

"The troupe was very good wasn't it?" I smiled. "Our wives slipped away very discreetly some time ago."

Jack nodded. "They have much to discuss."

"Undoubtedly. It is good for Irisa to have her sister here. Thank you for coming."

Guests rose from their seats, beginning to mill about in groups for conversations as servants moved in to clear the food from tables, removing benches and boards along the length of the hall as they worked. I stood, and Jack followed my example.

"While I have enjoyed our pleasant conversation, there are some men here I think you should meet because they won't leave me alone about it until they do. You are the husband of the queen's sister after all, and a man newly come to power and position with a connection to the throne and an ability to catch the king's ear. That makes you an irresistible curiosity to most." I smiled wryly at him.

"As you wish, *Your Grace*."

Jack flashed a cheeky grin. Never one to stand on ceremony, it seemed to amuse him more than anything to address me as *Your Grace* with a mocking glint in his eye.

I nudged his shoulder, and we moved away from the table, goblets in hand just as a commotion erupted near the hall's entrance. A group of men pushed through the quickly quieting crowd, a bound man at the forefront.

Ethew.

I threw back the rest of my drink then backhanded the cup to Jack. A renewed surge of anger rose up, ending my newfound contentment. I clenched then unclenched my fists, forcing my breathing to steady.

The group reached the upper end of the hall, and Wimarc moved around to the front. He dropped to a knee before me.

"Your Grace, I bring you your brother-in-law."

I studied Ethew for a moment, and then taking a step back, I eased down into the chair a servant had brought for me. I tapped my signet ring impatiently on the chair's arm for a few moments before finally waving Ethew forward. Once he came near, he shifted from foot to foot, his gaze switching between me and Irisa who had made her way up to sit next to me.

"Remove his bonds," I ordered, and Luca moved forward to slit through the ropes.

"My lord of Dalery?" I asked, looking to Wimarc. "Explain."

"My king, this man was apprehended by..." he paused, glancing briefly at Jachamin, "...one of your ships off the coast of Haern. Luca was given custody to bring him to Prille to answer to you."

"Luca, remove Lord Torrine from here to meet with me in private."

✿ ✿

Irisa took Ethew by the arm and walked him to the side table to offer him something to drink.

"Brother, we have been worried about you."

"Have you?" He rubbed at his wrists where his bonds had been. "There was no need, sister, truly. I am fine. Have been fine."

I watched the pair through hooded eyes as I leaned against the lintel supporting the fireplace mantel. I'd retrieved a new goblet on my way out of the hall and sipped from it now, keeping my focus on Ethew all the while.

Irisa smiled kindly. "But Ethew, we did not know."

"No, Ethew," I added sharply, "we did not." I straightened and walked toward the pair.

Irisa shot me a look, and Ethew's previously placid mien clouded over as he watched me make my way forward.

"If I had known that I would eventually end up apprehended because of my actions, I can assure you I would have sent word immediately."

"So perhaps you will tell us what those actions were, why you left no word with your man at Torrine, and why I had to send someone to inquire after you then another man to hunt you."

Irisa turned her piercing blue eyes toward me, and I cringed at my slip. I hadn't intended to tell her about Jachamin and wondered if this was how a mouse felt when cornered by a cat. I ignored her, keeping my countenance closed off as I continued to stare down her brother. "You are here now. Enlighten us."

I took a seat but did not invite Ethew to do the same. Instead, clasping his hands calmly before him, Ethew looked to the floor as if gathering his thoughts. "A man arrived in Torrine some weeks ago seeking a night's shelter. My retainers were happy to offer hospitality as is tradition, and the man ate and drank at my hearth. As he enjoyed my wine, his lips loosened. He would not say who he was or how he knew, but he let slip of a plot in Prille, uttering the name Sybila."

Irisa let loose a quick gasping inhale but recovered quickly. I remained stony-faced while Ethew continued, "Once he realized what he'd said, he became tight-lipped and was gone before first light. No one saw him go, so we knew not how to follow him."

Irisa placed a hand on my shoulder. The gesture pleaded for prudence in its subtlety, but such a recommendation did me an injustice. Inscrutability was the first lesson I'd learned as a child.

"A man shows up at your hearth, speaking of a plot involving my daughter, and it does not occur to you to send word to me immediately?"

"Rumors blow on the wind with regularity, Your Grace. I cannot give credence to them all. In retrospect, my decision was perhaps unwise, even naive."

"Unwise?" I sneered at the older man, stood, then walked to meet him face to face. "*Unwise*, you say? To say the least."

My hand closed into a fist which I held tightly at my side, and I ground my back teeth. My temper burned so hotly I feared losing it. I paced away from Ethew to gather my thoughts and felt the searing gaze of Irisa upon my back.

"I thought you would be better served if I took immediate action to find the man, for I deemed that finding the truth behind the whisperings to be of more value than the whisperings themselves. I reasoned that if I could find him and interrogate him, I would have something to bring to you. He had spoken of taking sail for the eastern coast, and I knew I had to act quickly. Someone somewhere had to have seen some evidence of his going, and I wasted no time in trying to catch him before he became unreachable."

His assessment made sense even if I was in no mood to show it. "And what did your investigation reveal?"

Ethew's face darkened as if as a result of some memory, as he uttered his reply: "We never found him, but we encountered others who overheard his loose lips after he left my hall."

"And did they know who might be behind a plot involving my daughter?" I stepped toward Ethew again, and he flinched.

"The man had a tendency to boast of his connection, yes."

"Ethew, tell us," Irisa pressed, her voice quivering.

"Aksum seems to be at the center of the spider's web. Send to Aksum, for there you may find answers."

❁ *18* ❁

Bellesea Palace
Prille
Agrius

"I WANT TO GO."

I arched a brow in surprise at the audacity of Wolf's impassioned demand.

He'd arrived at the palace this evening, coming back immediately when news of Rebane's escape reached him in Bauladu, despite having just returned home from his long trip to Odrana. The man was my oldest friend, and therefore there was never any pretense between us. It was the passion with which Wolf had uttered his desire to journey again that surprised me.

I wanted to go to Aksum with the delegation too, by the gods. Of course I wanted to go. It had taken every remaining ounce of control I'd had left not to board the *Sjórinn Mær* immediately after Ethew's news and go to Aksum. I wanted to kill the man -- or woman, I mused as I thought of

Wolf's wife Addis -- who had taken my daughter. But I could not. The Council would not let me. And my bitterness over the denial felt like bile rising in my throat.

"*A diplomatic mission to assess the situation*," they'd decided.

Diplomacy over outright accusation.

I'd argued that I should personally lead the delegation. As king, I felt it my right. But they had denied me. They said I was needed in Prille. Despite their words, I understood what they really meant: they didn't trust me to keep my composure when my daughter was concerned. They did not trust me to be diplomatic. In the same way, they did not trust Wolf because Addis had fled to Aksum, the place of her birth and the place her father ruled as king. Was Addis behind the disappearance of Sybila? The connection seemed obvious. Why had she done it? For spite, or something more sinister?

Wolf had come to me after the somber evening meal only hours after the Council had made their decision. We'd escaped the suffocating hall and now sat together hours after the household had gone to bed. Every part of the palace beyond the doors to this room lay silent, for the midnight bell had just struck. The hearth's fire created diabolical shadows licking the wall with menace, an eloquent mirror of moods of the two men who sat hunched forward before it, elbows on knees.

"We are quite a pair, are we not?" I asked lightly despite my own bitterness.

A light of amusement broke on Wolf's face, and he leaned back, sighing. Couching his cup on his lap, he reached behind his head to pillow it against the wall. A stark laugh broke from his lips, and he took a deep draught. "Indeed, we are. With both our feet held to the fire, it's a wonder neither of us has broken."

"Who says we haven't?" I returned, more sourly than I'd intended.

Wolf's look curdled again, and he stood, pacing to the far side of the room.

"Casmir, I have a right to confront her, to apprehend her and bring her back."

"Wolf, they won't let you go."

"So tell them I'm going!"

"It's not up to me."

"For all the fury of *Myrkra*," Wolf yelled, "of course it's up to you! You're the king!" He threw up his hands and spun away. "What good is being king if not to override the Council?" Wolf lifted his arm as if to dash his cup against the wall, held himself in check. "And now that I think of it, what good is it being the friend of the king?" He reconsidered his previous hesitation and threw the cup anyway. It shattered, sending red wine splattering in all directions and rivulets running down the wall. Ruby pools captured the firelight, sparkling like droplets of blood.

Wolf paced back to his seat, and, bending over his knees once again, uttered a groan, rubbing his hands over the top of his balding pate.

I knew my friend's outburst had everything to do with Addis and not me, so I stayed quiet. The Council's decision not to allow Wolf to go could be debated, but their decision regarding my own involvement had been wise, even if I loathed the fact and would never admit it to another soul. Yet in my self-admission, my anger boiled too hot to accept it with grace.

"I will see what I can do," I gave in at last. "But do not expect much. The Council is quite firm in its decision. My uncle Simon will go in my stead, as Chancellor. I trust him to do what needs to be done if they will not allow me. But I will see if they cannot be persuaded to send you along too."

An overwhelming sense of fatigue washed over me, and I yawned. "It is late enough now that I ought to be away to my bed." I stood and stretched. "Irisa is likely asleep, and I cannot stay awake much longer."

Wolf nodded. "Is she still furious with you about your mercenary?"

"Yes."

Irisa had confronted me after our interview with Ethew. I'd admitted to hiring the man without consulting her, and she had responded to my confession with a look of wounding that still haunted my memories.

"Why didn't you trust me enough to consult me?" she'd asked, her eyes displaying such hurt I'd had to turn away.

"Would you have agreed?"

"No," she'd responded, her voice hard and edged with a tint of bitterness. "He's my brother. He would have returned on his own once he found his answers. There was no need to hunt him like an animal!"

"You say that with such certainty now that you know where he's been! How easily you take his side!"

"There are no sides! Casmir, be fair!"

I'd said nothing in response, but had turned and left the room with her standing there watching me stalk away.

The haughty contempt of an enraged nobleman I could handle in stride, but the way in which I'd disappointed Irisa had left a pit in my heart deeper than I'd expected. The question of trust still hung between us. I'd easily avoided her today, busying myself with a full day of Council meetings, reasoning that the decision regarding who would travel to Aksum a more important matter than righting things with Irisa. And this evening I had stayed away intentionally, excusing myself to spend time with Wolf, hoping she would be asleep before I came to bed.

Wolf shook his head in consolation. "I am certainly not one to give marriage advice, but you need to fix this."

"I know, but I have such little practice."

"With humility?" Wolf taunted good-naturedly, but his arrow struck home just the same. A twinge of resentment tickled at the back of my mind. "Casmir, you have something most people in the world will never know or understand - a marriage made up of two people who love each other. Stop being a king long enough to be a husband. You were wrong in this. Apologize and have done with it."

"Says the man with a successful marriage of his own. If only it was as simple to fix as you say. My life crumbles around me and now my oldest friend criticizes me?"

"Poor Casmir. You are a helpless victim now."

My nostrils flared, and I shot him a scathing look then turned and left.

I brooded on my way back, annoyance prickling my already unsettled mood. When I reached my bedchamber, I found the room dark as I'd hoped. A night candle burned on the table, and I could see my wife's sleeping form as I removed my clothes and slipped gently into bed so as not to disturb her.

Her whisper cut the silence. "You have nothing to fear. I have no intention of discussing my disappointment with you tonight. I'm too tired."

Nothing in my life had prepared me for this. I'd certainly had no lessons from either of my parents in how to conduct a successful marriage, loveless or otherwise. I thought again of my father's domineering ways, his treatment of my mother, his disregarded wife. She'd born him four children, and once she'd done her duty, he'd had no more use for her.

He'd looked the other way when Ildor Veris all but locked her away, allowing her to appear at court, but giving her no other freedoms and very little status.

My mother had not the strength or support to fight back. How could she? In secret I would visit her, doing so when I knew Cousin Ildor was elsewhere occupied. I'd never been close to her, too divided in my duty to my father and the kingdom as I was. And to this day I still carried regret. After Irisa and I had wed, Evet left for her dower lands, taking my youngest sister, Kathel with her. I could have argued more strongly that my mother stay, but in truth, I didn't want her to. She was a reminder of too much of my past, a past I wanted to put behind me in favor of a new future for Agrius.

Irisa didn't deserve the same treatment. I wanted to make things right with her. I just didn't know how.

"Irisa," I replied, rolling toward her, but she stiffened and pulled away. I pressed my case with tenderness, and eventually, she gave in to me, though the encounter left me wholly unsatisfied. As I rolled away to find sleep, my thoughts remained on Irisa and the effort required to mend a strained relationship. No wonder I had become so skilled in the use of my court mask. It was easier.

❀ *19* ❀

Bellesea Palace
Prille
Agrius

Kassia

"SIMON, THE LORD CHANCELLOR, will go," Irisa explained to Kassia as they walked along. She ticked off the names on her fingers. "And Luca of course. Ethew asked to go since it was his discovery, but Casmir would not abide it, and the Council conceded, refusing him. It took little by way of argument. No one trusts him, and while I would love to give him a chance, I have to admit I think it's unwise to send him. Casmir has sent him back to Torrine with the instruction that he keep watching and listening for news. Mostly he just wants him out of the way."

Bright sunlight filtered down from between the bows of overhanging branches in the garden behind the palace. The spring day had dawned warm for a change, and the sisters abandoned their woolen cloaks in favor of lighter linen. While green buds poked from the early bloomers, it would be some weeks before the brilliance of the full garden would spring to life once more.

Kassia took her sister's arm now as they walked, falling companionably into silence. Memories of her time in Caelnor Palace in Brekkell had long since faded, the wound healed over. Since her marriage to Jack, her dreams had been mercifully free of the pain of the scars her past had given her. But now that she was here in Prille, thrust once more into the intrigue and maneuvering of court, she fought a renewed battle for mastery over the painful memories the present situation conjured.

Most of the time she succeeded in the struggle. It was later that afternoon, however, that the ghosts reappeared as uninvited guests.

After spending the afternoon with Irisa visiting the Bibliotheca and viewing the latest updates on the work to restore the damaged records pertaining to their grandfather's rule of Agrius, Kassia escaped the bustle for some time alone with her son, Cailen. As the sun made its last grasp for dominance in the western sky, she sat with him along the side of the great hall as Cailen played with a set of intricately carved wooden figures, a gift from Casmir. The boy played contentedly as she watched the flurry of activity. Servants scurried about, preparing for the evening meal.

She enjoyed the solitude even in the midst of the bustle, as it allowed her time to ponder recent events and those not so recent. Sitting in Prille's great palace, in the very hall that had witnessed generation upon generation of events in her family's past, she pondered what her life would have been like had Figor never come to find her that fateful day back in Corium.

An image of Figor popped into her mind's eye, of his expensive silks, the garish colors, and the giant sun medallion around his neck.

"Kassia, you look to have seen the phantom of my father's lost youth. Is anything amiss?"

Jack swooped around a great column, bending his bulk down to the ground next to their son. He picked up a figure and joined in on the boy's play.

"Rem would not be pleased with your jest," she teased, feigning a guise of superiority. "His youth was only lost because he was forced to raise such a troublesome boy on his own."

Jack flashed her a villainous smile, dimpling his cheeks in the way he did when he felt overly cocky and continued to play with Cailen, lining up the fallen figures while the boy proceeded to knock them over once more.

"I was just contemplating my life, and how lucky I am," Kassia continued, tilting her head haughtily.

"To have married such a handsome rogue, you mean?"

"Rogue indeed, for rogue you are! Aren't you in rare form today, sir?"

"Surely not so rare?" He scooted closer to her, slipping his hand up under her skirt, brushing a thumb across her ankle with a light touch.

"Jack! Someone might see!"

"So?" He stood up and turned to lean over her, putting his face right in front of hers. "Can a man not show his wife affection?"

Kassia cast a hurried look about her, noticing the servants toss sideways glances in their direction, some with sly smiles. "Not when it might create a scene!"

Jack arched a brow then kissed her. "How scandalous, to kiss my wife in public." He kissed her again.

She squirmed away from him just in time to see Cailen reaching out to grab the apron ties of a passing servant carrying a tray laden with dinnerware.

"Cai!" she shrieked.

As if he had eyes on the back of his head, Jack spun and snatched the chubby hand away.

"Perhaps we should move away and let matters tend themselves here without any added assistance."

Kassia nodded her agreement and stood. Jack swept Cailen up from the floor and seated him on his shoulders. They made their way outside, crossed the outer courtyard, and turned to head through the arch to descend into the lower ward.

Jack took her hand. "As long as we have some time before the meal, I would like to show you something. I have been waiting for the most opportune time, and now is as good a time as any."

The bustle of people going about their tasks was nearly as palpable here as it had been in the hall, but somehow Kassia felt their presence to be less intrusive. *These are my people*, Kassia told herself, comparing the wealth of the hall and its occupants to her former life, the dusty streets of Corium, the city of her birth. She drew in a large breath and felt a wash of relaxation settle over her.

She was just about to utter another playful jibe at Jack when she stopped in her tracks, catching her husband off guard. A group of exquisitely dressed men on horseback had pushed their way through the crowds, entering the lower ward through the main gate as an oxcart would push through a field of wheat. The lead man pulled up just in front of Kassia.

The man threw off his hood as he peered down with distaste at the person who had dared impede his progress. The look of disgust lasted only a heartbeat, for almost immediately a look of recognition replaced his scowl, and a serpentine smile turned up the edges of his mouth.

"Lady Kassia, it is both a delight and a complete surprise to see you again." His sharply cruel eyes and the sneering curl of his mouth suggested anything but.

The sight of him threatened to send a torrent of dark and debilitating fear pouring over her, and she stood paralyzed. Kassia felt her knees weaken, but before she could respond, Jack stepped in between her and the shoulder of the man's horse.

"It should not be, sir, for her brother-in-law is king, her sister queen, as you well know," he snapped, his own lips curling with derision.

The man's horse snorted, its hot breath steaming from its nostrils a mere hands-breadth from Jack's face. Jack did not flinch as its rider edged it nearer.

"Of course he is. My apologies," the man said, though again, his expression did not match his words.

"Papa, who angry man?"

Cailen held out a fist, using one finger to point at the man high on the horse.

"His name is Isary, my son. And he is a prince without a kingdom."

Isary of Elbra glared at the toddler for only a moment before returning his attention to Kassia.

"It is just as well you are here, for I have come with news you will find interesting. Come, and I will allow you to listen in while I speak with the king."

Isary heeled his mount, and the animal moved forward, pushing into Jack's shoulder as he and Cailen spun to move out of the way.

"Come on, Kassia. Let's go see what trouble the *skingi* has come to stir."

❋ *20* ❋

Bellesea Palace
Prille
Agrius

"I COME HUMBLY TO ask a favor."

Isary Branimir of Corak, Lord of Brekkell and Prince of Elbra fit his title nicely, richly dressed in a deep blue over-tunic worked through with gold embroidery at collar, sleeves, and edges of its length. It reached to mid-calf over a pair of polished black boots. A wide collar spangled with tiny gems hung just beneath the tunic, and strung at its lowest point hung a large pendant of worked silver and gold filigree bearing the seal of the House of Branimir.

I inspected Isary, tapping my fingers on my leg as I took in the man's grandiose bearing which, despite his bending of the knee before me, belied the idea that he had ever done anything *humbly*. While I did not believe his pretense of humility for a moment, whatever brought him here was worth hearing.

But I was under no obligation to make things easy for

the man.

"The Kingdom of Elbra has a long history of independence, and, if we are honest with one another, has kept itself aloof from its neighbors. Until recently, I might add." I allowed acid to drip through my words as I spoke. "Why should Agrius help you?"

"Forthright speech. I like that." Isary's lips thinned, and his eyes narrowed. All signs of the humble prince disappeared. "You will help me because I know where Taibel Rebane has gone and why."

He could not hide the light of triumph that danced so casually at the corners of his eyes. He found gratification in putting me into such a position.

"And once you heard of Rebane's plot, you came straight to Agrius to offer your support. How magnanimous of you," I replied dryly. I waved him to stand.

He rose but said nothing in reply. He didn't need to say anything. He knew his bait would have an effect. It showed in his wide stance, the casual way in which he clasped his hands in front of him.

The man was an enigma in so many ways; to know what to do with him, a puzzle. He had plotted with my wife's own father to make war against Agrius in an attempt to take the throne for himself, with Kassia as his bride and providing his legitimacy. While I could appreciate the subtleties of political intrigue, the scheming, the shifting lines of loyalties, and the ever-changing political affinities, I knew my wife would not, and most certainly neither would Kassia. I wished now that Kassia was not present for this audience.

"How did you hear of this news?" I asked him.

Isary quirked a smile, as if the idea that he would share his source was ludicrous. "Come now, Your Grace. You have spies. Surely you know how well news travels in the back alleys?" At this last comment, Isary threw a calculated look at Irisa. I knew he'd meant it as a slight to the upbringing of my queen, yet I would overlook it this time.

"What do you want in return?"

"I want a royal bride, of course."

"And you think that simply sharing the whispers of rumors about the whereabouts of the traitor Rebane is worth the price of a royal bride? Seems a high cost for such a tidbit. We can find news of Rebane from other sources."

I stood as if dismissing Isary, but before I could signal that the prince be escorted out of my presence, Isary interrupted.

"I applaud your restraint. I admit that I would not react so serenely to news of the whereabouts of a man who had insulted both my sovereignty and my person."

"So far I have heard no news, only suggestions of rumors."

"Would you be nearly so cavalier if I told you that Taibel Rebane has your daughter?"

"Why would you even consider working with that man?" Kassia fumed. "I cannot believe you would bargain with him!" She paced across the small room, her skirts fluttering around her as she ate up the distance with large strides, her arms flapping like an agitated swallow.

We had retired to privacy to discuss Isary's proposal. I knew that if the news had caught me by surprise, I was not alone. Because of Isary's past, the matter would require a delicate touch. This time, not with my Council but with my own family.

I cast an inquiring glance at Jack who repaid my look

with a helpless one of his own.

I took a deep breath and turned my attention to my wife. "Irisa, you have been quiet. What do you think?"

"I do not like that we would be indebted to him."

Kassia nodded, fuming with smoldering anger. The light of the fire in the hearth reflected off her auburn tresses, setting them ablaze with the same fury as her temper.

"But if it brings us news of Sybila," Irisa continued, "we have to give him what he asks."

"And become his allies? I cannot abide it!" Kassia stormed in reply. Jack stood near her elbow but did not dare touch her. "He offers us nothing we don't already know!"

"Kassia…" Irisa reached out a hand to her sister, but Kassia pulled away. "We have not previously had word that Rebane was involved in Sybila's disappearance."

"But we know Sybila is bound for Aksum. Ethew has already told us. We don't need Isary so have no reason to help him." Kassia shook her head. "No. Just no." She turned and fled in a rustle of silk, leaving a trailing scent of jasmine behind.

I returned my attention to Jack who stood staring at the flickering flames, his hands clasped before him. The conflict I read on his face could not be more clear. He was a man of integrity, and I knew he understood our need to do all we could for our missing daughter. On the other hand, his first duty was to his wife.

I would not press him. His own internal debate cost him, and I understood this.

"We should help him, of course," Jack murmured finally, his voice strained. He did not meet my look. "He may not be a man of integrity, but you are. Sometimes that is reason enough." After a long moment, he glanced up. I saw a world of both pain and purpose on his face. "But there is one condition: where he goes, I go. Ethew says Aksum is behind Sybila's disappearance. If this *skingi* confirms that Rebane took her to Sékra, and that is where he goes, so do I. He will not get away from me again." Jack jut his chin in the direction of the audience chamber then let his statement hang there for the weight of his need to sink in, so I would follow his intention. "I should see to my wife."

I sighed and gave in with a nod. Jack made his way out, closing the door softly behind him, leaving me and Irisa alone. I moved to the place by the fire my brother-in-law just deserted and braced an arm against the lintel. I peered into the flames in the same way Jack had done, as if answers could be found there.

"He wants revenge, Irisa."

"I know. Kassia will blame me that he is going." Irisa came to stand beside me and slipped her hand through my arm, sliding in close to me. I pulled her into my arms, and she tipped her face up. "But if our cooperation brings back our Sybila..."

"Jack will mollify her. Let him take care of it."

Irisa looked doubtful. "If Isary's news is different from Ethew's, who will we believe?" I had no answer, and my uncertainty must have shown. "And worse, what if he tells us that Rebane has taken Sybila to Sékra, confirming what Ethew has already said? He offers us nothing new, and we've agreed to help him."

"We will have given him our word, that's why. Irisa, I would pay anything to find Sybila. If we must work with that man, then so be it."

"And he asks for Kathel? Would you sacrifice her?"

While it was true that it would soon be time to consider the marriageable future of my youngest sister, the idea that Isary would claim her was preposterous.

"Let's see what he has to say first. We can negotiate later."

❀ ❀

"You have a particular bride in mind?" I asked casually, as if I didn't fear what he might ask.

"Of course."

I watched him closely for some time, as if I hadn't fully made up my mind. "We have discussed your proposal and have decided to grant your favor. But first, you must tell us all that you know. Once we hear your news, we will decide its value."

If it was possible for Isary to straighten any more than he already was, he did so now, as if declaring some sort of distorted victory in a contest that only he seemed to understand. I wanted to wipe the look of superiority off his face, but I swallowed back my feelings on the matter even if doing so tasted like the dung scraped off the bottom of the dovecote. Irisa held out a hand and placed it on my arm, sensing my mood.

"Rebane has taken ship for Sékra, in Aksum."

Irisa squeezed my arm slightly. I narrowed my eyes at him. "You tell us nothing we don't already suspect."

Isary shrugged. "Then consider the news confirmed. You have already agreed to help me, have you not?"

"Perhaps. What bride do you seek?"

"The Negus of Aksum has daughters. Only one of them is married... for now." He needn't explain that he meant Addis. "You must see that one of them becomes heir rather than any of the Negus' sons. Whichever daughter he chooses, that is the one I want for my bride."

I wanted to breathe a sigh of relief, and it took

everything in me to maintain my mask. It felt laughable that he thought I had any say in the matters of Aksum. What he asked would not cost me a thing.

"And you think I have sway with regard to who will succeed her father, never mind who she will wed?"

"Of course. Once you reveal that you know he shelters the traitorous Taibel Rebane in his court, yes. The Negus would not want to invite the wrath of the King of Agrius who has allied with Elbra. In his humiliation, he will do as you say, for his people hold honor in higher esteem than anything else."

"He sounds like a virtuous man," I said dryly. "What do you propose I do?"

"Likely you've already prepared plans to send a delegation to seek her out. I will go with them. When you implicate the negus in the scheme regarding your daughter, it will put you into a position to exact a certain amount of influence over him. Use that influence to persuade him to marry off his daughter to me." Isary shrugged. "Anything you do after that is entirely up to you."

"By the gods, but that went well." I couldn't hide the mocking edge to my words. A wave of exhaustion washed over me as I collapsed into a chair. "That man had us where he wanted us the minute he walked through our gates, and he knew it."

My chamberlain removed my boots. The evening had retained what heat the day had managed to produce. Now barefoot, I swept outside onto the balcony overlooking the sound beyond the cliffs. A purple cloak of twilight took hold of the eastern sky, and I reveled in the breeze coming off the water.

Thankfully Irisa had been no more interested than I in tarrying after the completion of the evening meal in honor of Isary's visit, so we had stayed as long as courtesy required before offering our best wishes and retiring early together.

I took in one last, full lungful of night air and ventured back inside, taking up a flagon from the table as I loosened the ties on my shirt. Pouring myself a cup and then one for Irisa, I crossed over to where she sat under the ministration of her ladies who combed out her long, golden tresses. I offered her the cup, but she made no move to accept it.

I eyed her quizzically. "What is it?"

She didn't answer immediately. Her face remained skillfully and unusually reticent, as if she hid an internal struggle. Finally, she dropped her gaze, staring at her hands which she held tightly in her lap. "I fear saying anything, for it seems we have finally found a fragile peace between us, and I do not wish to break it."

I raised the cup to my lips and drank from it all the while watching my wife over the rim. Indeed matters had been strained between us since Ethew's arrival, but her fury over the matter had subsided in these last two days. Though I suspected that she'd only become weary of arguing rather than that she'd changed her view to see things my way.

I wanted to be impatient with her, but I fought back the emotion and set the cup down, leaning against a table and crossing my arms.

"Even so, now that the notion has been suggested, I must hear what it is that bothers you."

She raised clear blue eyes up to my face, waving away the maid who brushed her hair. "The Council and their decision not to allow you to go to Aksum... are you upset with them?"

"Am I upset with them? Do you truly have to ask?"

"You want to force them to change their decision. You plan to impose your will on them."

She had said it as an accusation, and I immediately bristled. "As far as I am concerned, the matter is not settled. How can I be content to stay here when my daughter needs me?" I shrugged.

"We don't even know if she truly is in Aksum. If Isary speaks true. He has every reason to lie, simply to manipulate you and get you to agree to help him."

"You disbelieve your own brother who suggests that Aksum is behind it?"

She shook her head. "No, but that does not negate the fact that there is reason to be cautious with Isary. That is why we send the delegation: to assess the matter."

"But neither do we have no reason to think that he does not speak true, that she is not there." As had been my way of late, my anger peaked in an instant. I did not want to take it out on Irisa, but it was becoming more and more unavoidable. "How can you ask me to stay here, doing nothing?"

"Casmir, you do something when you send a delegation. It is Simon's role as Chancellor to act on your authority in your stead. How is that nothing?" She stood and walked toward me, her eyes pleading.

"Because I am her father, Irisa!"

"And I am her mother," she whispered, hurt evident in her trembling voice. "I think you forget that you are not the only one who bleeds inside." She turned and moved to put out the lamps on the far side of the room before retreating to bed.

I had not intended to wound her, but I had. A knife of guilt pierced me, and I wished desperately that I could take back the heated words. Yet despite this, something inside me remained resolutely hardened toward her even if I could make no sense of it. How could I make her understand if I could not understand it myself?

I should have gone to her, offered her something. But anything I offered would have been merely platitudes, meaningless words that would not be enough to feed her need.

Our gulf grew wider, and each of us seemed helpless to prevent it.

❋ *21* ❋

Bellesea Palace
Prille
Agrius

Kassia

SHE WASN'T MEANT TO be here. Not alone at least. Not inside the palace, and certainly not out there, along the shore of the Tohm Sound just beyond the newly fortified water gate. Yet here she was, and there she would be.

Checking one last time to see that the duty guards were looking the other way, Kassia slipped through the wicket door in the larger gate and crept along the dock, jumping down to the water's edge on the far side, out of view of anyone who might come through the gate.

She drew in a deep breath of air tinged with salt and smiled, for from here she could take in the vastness of the water, could hear the busy port and its sounds of commerce and trade, but no one could see her. She had found solitude at last, and the peace of it provided a welcomed balm to her trouble-weary soul.

In the days since Sybila's kidnapping, King Casmir had decreed that all members of his family have a personal guard at all times, even within the palace. But in all the years of her life, Kassia had never been one to do what was expected of her. As such, she wasn't terribly concerned with what her brother-in-law wanted. At least not when it came to her freedom.

Kassia had slept poorly last night. It had been many years since the phantoms of her past had come to visit, but they had come last night in her dreams, visions of the two men from her Mosrad Prison ordeal. While those memories had mostly become faded and distant in recent years, yesterday's arrival of Isary had awakened them with a fury. She couldn't talk to anyone about it, not even to Jack. While he would be compassionate and kind, he could never truly understand her trauma. How could any man?

A bright, warm spring sun beat down overhead, reflecting off the rocks scattered along the shore. There was no wind here, so close to the towering palace walls behind her, and a small trickle of sweat beaded its way down the small of her back. The warmth made her smile despite her fatigue. Pulling her feet free of her shoes, she wriggled her toes then dipped them into the cool water. It wasn't freedom, but it was near enough. Finding a boulder large enough to serve as a seat, she sat on it and made herself comfortable, allowing her mind to roam freely, taking stock of the life she now lived far from those dusty streets of her youth.

She didn't dislike her new life in Haern, though she'd expected to. Moving there had been a sacrifice on her part. Jack, of course, had been beside himself with joy the day the message came from Casmir and Irisa, offering him a position amongst the aristocracy of Agrius. With that position came land and responsibility. And while she was within her rights to ask him to refuse, Kassia could not allow her husband not to accept. It meant too much to him, being back in the land of his birth. Rem, Jack's father, had been elated for his son, but despite Jack's invitation for Rem to come with them, he'd declined. His new life in the small village on the shores of Pania, his new wife, and the quiet world they inhabited, was enough for him in his old age, he'd said. Let the past be, he'd pronounced.

Jack was sad to leave his father behind, but the allure of what awaited him was enough to temper his grief. "I'll visit," Rem had promised. And he had. Several times, in fact, once he had grandchildren to make it worth his while.

Kassia had been less keen to leave their small cottage in that secluded Panian meadow. It had been her dream, the reason she'd wanted to leave Corium before she knew her father was meant to be a king of a distant land. She was safe there. She was happy. But as she had come to find out the hard way, life didn't always follow the path of expectation.

"I'll make it up to you," Jack had promised one night as they prepared the final packing necessary to move their household across the sea. "I know how you despise court life. We will keep our household small, nothing beyond what is required for the proper running of the place. And you can run it on your terms, as you please."

"But you will have a status to maintain, must not appear to be the poor beggar who was given a position out of kindness."

"But I was a poor beggar who was given a position out of kindness," Jack pointed out, a grin broad on his face. "My brother-in-law is a king, and I am a simple smith, remember?"

"I do seem to recall hearing something about that,

yes."

"You will be safe there. And you will never be alone. Never again. I swear it."

It had only been a short year and a half now that they had lived in their gifted manor on the island of Haern, but it had become home, and Jack held true to his promise. She had been happy. Her past had distanced itself, and she thought she was finally free of her phantoms.

Until Isary of Elbra slithered into the Agrian court, finding a way into the confidence of her sister and her sister's husband. Kassia scowled at the thought.

When she'd first met Isary as his intended bride, she had not been overwhelmed by his appearance, for he would not likely ever become the subject of a bard's tale of lovers. He was not particularly handsome. His eyes were too close together and his nose too pointed. His attraction had come from his charisma alone, and she'd found herself immediately smitten.

His allure didn't last long. In snippets of overheard conversation with his lover, she'd learned the truth about him: once her father's bid for the throne of Agrius had been successful, Kassia would be the heir to the throne. And when the time came for Kassia to wear the crown, Isary would rid himself of her, claiming the throne as his own. But his plans had failed, for very soon after news reached Brekkell's shores of the impending marriage between the eldest Sajen daughter and the heir of the Agrian throne, Isary changed. He grew cold toward her, cruel and mocking. All support for her father's rebellion faded, and Isary lost interest in her as a bride. What use was she to him now? Fearing for their lives, Kassia and her father fled Brekkell under the cover of darkness, eventually finding Jack, and making their way to live in safety in Pania.

With Isary in Prille, Kassia wasn't sure she could feel safe. The fact that he wanted to accompany the delegation to Aksum to find yet another new bride tempered her fear somewhat, but now Jack wanted to go along. She knew Isary to be a spiteful man, and she feared for her husband's life. She and Jack had fought over it last night. He had tried to convince her that he needed to go with Isary, but she didn't agree. His reasons to go sounded weak in her ears, yet he insisted upon it with an urgency that defied logic.

She knew Jack had a past that he tried to keep hidden from her. More had happened to him in his youth than he had ever let on about. But she was not blind. She understood more than he knew. And it was his past that drove him to follow Isary.

Which was why she needed him here. Safe. Why did he ignore her need so much? She tried to push away the melancholy that had settled over her spirit, but she grew weary of resisting, allowing it now to wash over her.

She dropped the tumbled rocks she'd been mindlessly gathering, and glanced at the blue waters of the Tohm Sound. Sea birds circled and called overhead, swooping lower and lower in an investigation of the intruder to their beach. She raised a hand to shield her eyes from the glare of the sun, and as she did so, a familiar voice called out for her.

"Kassia?"

She needn't even turn and look to know who it was.

"How did you know I was here? No one saw me come, I know for certain."

Cai came and sat down next to her on the rocks, folding his legs in front of him and wrapping his arms around his knees to rest his chin on one of them. "Except someone did see you come down here. I did."

"Of course you did," she returned, turning finally to

look at him.

Cai the orphan, the son of a temple prostitute who had adventured with her on her journey from Corium to Brekkell, Cai the orphan who had been taken into the service of Isary of Elbra and had done so, regardless of the man Isary was, because what else was a poor orphan boy to do?

"How are you? You have grown, look to be well taken care of."

And he had grown. While she had remembered him as a boy, he had put on height and weight, likely from the work and the training he had been put through as a squire in training. Even though she had not necessarily known he had traveled here with Isary, it did not surprise her that he'd come. He would have been a part of Isary's retinue, sent along to serve the knights of Isary's household. No, it didn't surprise her that Cai was in Prille, but it did surprise her that he had found her when she was certain no one knew she was here. Except that this was Cai, and nothing about Cai should have surprised her.

"I have. They feed me well so long as I do my work," he said plainly, as if having food wasn't something one took for granted. "And they train me, teach me all kinds of things so I can be a knight someday," he beamed.

"And are you a good student, Cai?"

"Of course!" he returned, his impish grin belying the truth of his words. "But now I want to come to Haern, to serve with you and Jack," he said, turning suddenly serious.

"Is Isary abusing you?" Kassia asked quickly.

"No, I rarely see him, and his men are good to me. I just miss you."

"Will he let you free of your oath to him, do you think?"

"I don't know. I hope so."

She patted his arm. "I don't see him releasing you out of the goodness of his heart."

"No, you're probably right."

The pair fell into silence, the only sounds coming from the lapping of water, the call of the birds overhead, and the distant shouts of men training in the lower courtyard. She was certain Isary had to be among them, how else explain how Cai had seen her sneak past on her way to the water gate? She imagined him flaunting his skill with a sword, even though he had never had reason to use it in the field of battle. He just wanted to make sure others knew he could if necessary. She shuddered at the thought of him holding a blade, recalling the fear she'd felt as he pushed her back violently against the wall of the abandoned manor in the Elbran countryside.

Tendrils of the dark memory preyed on the peace she'd only just reclaimed.

"How did we get here, Cai?" Kassia whispered. "How did two orphans end up so far from the life we used to know?"

After a time of consideration, Cai spoke, his voice lowered to reflect the seriousness with which he'd thought through her question. "I don't know, Kassia. But I do know that we are here now, and we have to make the best of it. Besides," he added with a wicked grin, "it's not so bad, you a princess and all. Your sister is a queen, your brother-in-law a king. Not many street orphans rise so high in the ranks, do they?"

"No, I suppose you are right. You always were, you imp," she teased, tousling his hair as she used to do back in Corium. Narrowing her eyes, she added, "Watch Jack, Cai. Keep him safe. I'm relying on you."

"I will, Kassia, I promise. And I will find a way to rid myself of my oath to the House of Branimir."

"No matter what?"

"No matter what."

"We should get back. I want to see if there is any chance Isary accidentally slipped and fell on his sword." Cai looked startled by the idea then spread a grim smile. Before he could offer his own retort, she added, "A girl can dream, can't she?"

❊ 22 ❊

Bellesea Palace
Prille
Agrius

Kassia

"So the Sajen daughters have come to bid me safe journey?"

"If by safe journey you mean I hope your ship sinks over the nest of a sea monster, then yes," Kassia quipped under her breath.

Irisa grabbed her arm, shoving her slightly aside with her hip, then smiled brightly at Isary who had heard Kassia but seemed more amused than offended. "Please excuse my sister. She slept poorly last night, and didn't mean it."

"Yes, I did," Kassia mumbled.

Irisa stepped in next to Isary, taking him by the arm to escort him to his waiting ship. But before Irisa could steer him away from her, Isary's eyes turned hard even as he kept a smile firmly fixed on his face. She knew the look all too well, had seen it too many times to count.

"You should be grateful to me, my lady."

"And why is that?"

"Your husband," Isary murmured, looking pointedly over her shoulder to the place Jack stood somewhere behind her, "was given a very generous grant by my hand. All he had to do was accept it with the good graces of a man who should have known his place."

"Oh? That's not how I see it."

"And how do you see it, if I may ask?"

"My understanding is that you sent your men with instructions to murder him on the way to your so-called grant, but he turned the tide and got to them first."

She could tell that Irisa had not heard the story before, but she did her best to hide her surprise. For Isary's part, his face darkened as his eyes narrowed at her. "Your husband is an interesting man. I very much look forward to getting to know him better, this son of a smith turned courtier." He smiled again, the cold, calculating smile she had come to know all too well, and her insides froze. "Yes, I think he and I will find much to talk about."

"My lord," Irisa broke in, "we should find your ship so you can board. I am certain you have much to do to settle."

"Of course, forgive me." He picked up Kassia's hand. "My lady," he said, kissing it before she had a chance to snatch it away.

Kassia watched them go, her countenance blazing, wishing that with each step he took the dock would open up to dump the pompous prince of Elbra into the murky waters beneath.

It was for this reason she sensed rather than saw Jack come up behind her. "If looks could kill, I'd warrant that cock-sure, fen-sucked cur would have died a thousand times over."

"A million times over," Kassia corrected.

"What did he say to you this time?"

"That he is going to murder you in your sleep in retribution for his failure to steal the throne of Agrius."

Jack turned an amused eye on her. "Did he really?"

".Something like that."

"Kassia, I'll be fine."

"I know, I've instructed Cai to make sure you are."

Jack took her by the arm and spun her away from the water's edge, turning her to walk back toward the city.

"I've survived much worse than threats from that puffed up cockerel, and I'm sure I'll survive him too."

"Jack, for the love of all you hold dear, why must you go? Rebane is not your problem."

"You have no interest in finding the man who tortured and nearly killed your father? The man who has likely taken the princess of Agrius, your own sister's child, your niece?"

Kassia felt panic rise in her chest and her eyes cast about fervently for some response. "Yes, I do, but..."

Her pleading was fruitless, she knew. Jack would go along on a fool's errand and leave her. She would be left alone. Her heart thudded mightily in her chest, and she fought to breathe. Her fear was ridiculous, she knew, but it still felt as real as the bulge of her husband's forearm under his fine tunic.

"Kassia, come with me, I would show you something," Jack said finally.

"But the departure..."

"There is much yet to load, and many things that must be tended to first. There is time. Come," he invited again.

She nodded and leaned into him as he held her firmly by the arm, a mercy Kassia could only breath thanks for, for her legs felt too wobbly to support her own weight. By the gods, but she didn't want to be so weak-minded!

They progressed up through the streets, back toward the palace, and entered into the lower ward through a tradesman's gate. Taking a sharp left, Jack led her along the road past workmen's buildings, past barns and workshops, all serving the needs of the palace.

Finally, Jack stopped outside the door to a smithy, and as he placed his hand to the door to open it, he turned to her.

"This was my father's before he fled Prille. We lived in the room just above."

Kassia entered behind Jack, and they greeted the men working inside. Jack had obviously already been by, for the men asked no explanation of who they were. They simply went back to their work, leaving Jack and Kassia to their conversation.

Kassia glanced around the room, taking in the counters and tables, the neatly maintained rows of tools and pieces of work. Jack next led her into another room, empty of workers.

"This was where my father spent most of his time, working with gold and silver."

Kassia took in the sight of a table holding the tools of the smith's trade: hammers, snips, files, and blocks, all laid out in neat order.

Jack leaned back against the table and studied her for a moment before opening his arms to her. She went to him, and he enveloped her in a secure hug.

"Your father would come to visit my father in this room. They formed a fast friendship here."

"How did it come to be?"

"I think your father liked to escape the palace. I don't imagine his father was a very pleasant man. He seemed to find peace here away from his father's eye."

"How was it your father was so loyal to House Sajen, knowing what my grandfather was like?"

Jack considered her question for some time before answering. "I don't think it was so much Nikolas that he was loyal to, but your father. Because they were friends, he knew the kind of king Bedic would be. I do not know for certain, but I imagine Bedic often explained his hopes and dreams for Agrius after he became king in his father's place. My father was furious with the coming of Bellek, because the overthrow meant your father would not have his chance to undo the tyranny of your grandfather.

"When we had to flee Prille, he was alone. My mother was dead, and none of his family survived. It was just him and his tiny son. There was no one else, and he had to make it for my sake." Jack spoke the words quietly, as if remembering the events that had taken place so very many years ago. "My father said that he experienced a fear beyond words. But he had to survive, had to keep going, for my sake, if for no other reason."

Kassia pulled closer to Jack's chest, burying her face into him.

"This is why I will not let the likes of Prince Isary of Elbra best me, Kassia. I will return safe, for I will not leave you alone, nor will I leave my children without their father. No force drives me more powerfully than that."

"I am still afraid," she whispered. "I know Isary. He is cruel and vile. He will try to do you harm because he feels wronged by you. And just because he can."

"Kassia," he whispered, thrusting a finger under her chin to raise it to meet his look. "Do you trust me?"

"You asked me that once, long ago. I didn't know how to answer you then. But now I have given you two children, and many things have changed. Of course, I trust you."

"Then trust me enough to know that I will do whatever it takes...anything....to come back to you. I promise you, I will return." He kissed her lightly, and she relaxed somewhat.

"Jack, I have a gift for you, something I want you to take along." She thrust a wrapped parcel into his hand.

He opened it, revealing a wooden panel with a painted portrait of his wife upon it.

"What is this for?"

"I meant it to be a simple token, but now it carries more weight." When he seemed confused, she explained: "Now it serves to remind you of your promise to return to me. It binds you to that promise."

"Thank you," he said simply.

"And Jack? If you break your promise," she said, flicking her head to the side, "I swear I will kill you myself."

He tucked the portrait into his tunic, and the motion drew her eye to the dagger at his hip. It was not his usual arming dagger, but a more elaborate one with a curious design etched upon it.

Jack caught her notice of it, and before she had a chance to comment on it, he slipped his hand over it to cover it, taking her by the arm to guide her back to the quay.

An hour later, Kassia stood beside her sister at the water's edge. Both women stood quiet and resolute, each of them caught up in the worries of her own mind as the ships bound for Aksum pushed off. Kassia watched the ever-shrinking figure of her husband, catching the last glimpse of him waving before his ship turned into the wind, blocking her view of him.

Taking a deep breath, she turned, intending to take Irisa's arm so they could return to the palace. Instead, she found that Irisa still stood rigid, staring blankly after the ships and paying no mind to anything else happening around her. To Kassia's eyes, she seemed uninterested in either the ships or in returning to the palace.

Kassia guessed that Irisa and Casmir had argued that morning even if Irisa had not admitted as much. Tensions were high between them, she knew, and it was for this reason Kassia had been able to forgive her sister so easily for her support of Isary's plan. Wouldn't she have done the same if it was her Cailen or Tilda to have been kidnapped? This thought helped her resolve the conflicting emotions she felt over the issue at least, and it proved how strong she had become in the last couple of years.

She placed a light hand on Irisa's arm. "Come, sister. Let's walk a while. There is no need to hurry back."

After a moment, Irisa's look sparked with recognition, and she nodded. Kassia waved away the palandiers who had stood at the ready to take them back to the palace. Instead, a discreet contingent of foot soldiers stepped into place behind them, following at a considerate yet watchful distance as they made their way back into Prille, following the winding and steep main road up the hill.

Irisa did not seem interested in talking, and Kassia felt relief for it. It allowed her own thoughts to wander, settling unsurprisingly on her husband and his going. Jack was gone, and now there was nothing more she could do for him. He would have to deal with Isary in his own way. She knew his skill with the blade, and she would have to rest in that knowledge.

Trust me, he'd said. And she would.

Bellesea Palace
Prille
Agrius

FROM THE WINDOW OF my chamber, I observed the ships weigh anchor. Three Agrian ships, the *Arvök*, the *Arnborg*, and the *Dögun*, as well as the ships from Elbra. Each appeared as a bright jewel, sails whipping smartly in the sun as they navigated the placid waters of the Tohm Sound, heading ultimately for the land of Aksum. They carried my uncle Simon, the Lord Chancellor of Agrius as my own personal representative, Luca to guard him, Isary, and my brother-in-law Jack along with a contingent of men-at-arms.

I felt nothing as I watched them, as if the sight of the ships was nothing more than the progression of common merchant vessels loaded with wares to sell in distant lands. Irisa had gone to see them off, but before she had gone, she'd pleaded with me to come too. I refused, and we'd argued.

"What purpose would my presence serve?" I'd asked.

"Simon is going in my stead, Luca to watch over him, and Isary to meddle. There is not enough room for me."

"But you are king," Irisa snapped back, clearly losing her patience with me. "And they are going to find our daughter, Casmir! They go on our errand!"

"As should be *my* duty!" I snapped back. "But I must remain here, *helpless* while they do!" I swiped at the surface of a table, brushing a scattering of parchments and sending them fluttering to the floor.

"Your duty is to Agrius, Casmir," Irisa replied gently, turning sad eyes to the scattering of parchments on the floor. "Simon loves Sybila too. He will do everything he can to get her back."

"While I am here. *Here!* Do you understand, Irisa? I am stuck *here* while my daughter is out *there!*" I flung my arms in the general direction of the Sound. "While other men negotiate for her as if she is something to be bargained for. It is my duty! It should be me!" I knew I sounded petulant, but my frustration ate away at my bones.

"She is my daughter too, or have you forgotten yet again?" Irisa replied calmly. When I said nothing, kept my back turned, she moved to the door. "I will send them off, demonstrating our mutual approval and well wishes. You can remain here and brood, if that is what you wish." At that, she left, closing the door quietly as she went.

Yes, brooding. I knew I was brooding. But I'd never felt so powerless as a king, as a father, as a man. Now as I rubbed at my wounded shoulder, stiff from disuse, I turned away from the view. I would change, would visit the practice yard for a chance to unleash my rage upon any opponent foolish enough to face me in such a black mood.

"You are *Rækallin* in the flesh, I swear by the gods, Casmir. Or you are possessed by his minions at the very least." Wolf tossed me a flask, and I caught it with one hand, quaffing a good measure then wiping my mouth with the back of my hand. "If you and I were not friends as we are, I would have supposed you were doing all you could to kill me before dumping my body into the Sound. But we are, and I know you were not. I can only imagine this has something to do with Rebane?"

I eyed Wolf then took another swig of the flask to avoid answering Wolf's question. Yes, I had seen Rebane's face in the fight. I'd wished it had been Rebane, and I had reacted accordingly. I had shown the traitor mercy, and that mercy had been repaid with more treason and treachery, not just against the Crown, but against me personally. Oh, yes, I had seen Rebane's face in the fight, and I had dreamed of thousands of ways to kill him. As king, I was oath-bound to uphold justice. But I was a father first, seeking a father's justice. It was good I had to stay home in Prille. If I met up with Rebane in Aksum, likely I'd kill him on the spot.

I tossed the flask back to Wolf who took my silence with a shrug and the offer of a hand to help me up.

"Ah, Your Grace, I have been sent to tell you that the grand scriptstóri seeks an audience with you." Wimarc waited at the door to the armory as Wolf and I left our practice arms with the armorer. "And our mutual friend would like a word."

"Tell Grand Master Conrad I will see him after I've cleaned up and changed. The other business I will tend to later."

"As you wish," Wimarc returned, offering a perfunctory bow with a conspiratorial smile before leaving Wolf and me to our business.

"Casmir, do you think it wise to continue to meet with the man, after Irisa..."

I swung on him. "Are you telling me what to do again?"

"No. Yes. I just think you need to consider Irisa..."

I held up a hand, interrupting him before he could say more I did not want to hear. "As you told me sagely the other day, I am king. I will do what I think best."

"Of course, Your Grace," Wolf replied stiffly, his eyes hard.

"I must change," I said grumpily.

"I wonder if you haven't already."

I eyed him severely and Wolf turned away, shaking his head in disgust. I stood alone in the yard. After a moment, I swung around and made my way back to my apartments. A valet helped me strip off my sodden clothes before leaving to fetch hot water for washing.

A few moments later, Irisa entered.

She stood motionless, betraying none of her thoughts and taking in the grubby clothes piled in the corner while I stood alone in the center of the room wearing nothing more than braies. Before I could think of what to say or do, my valet returned with hot water. Irisa dismissed him and took it upon herself to take up the sponge and soap.

Twirling an imperious finger, she said, "Turn."

I obeyed, facing the window as my throat tightened on any words I might say. She began sponging off my back and neck, heedless of her costly garments and the water inevitably dripping onto them.

"So they are safely away?" I asked, searching desperately for something neutral to say after our argument that morning.

"Of course," she replied quietly.

She continued to work in silence, and when she finished my back, I turned back around to face her. She would not meet my eyes as she continued to sponge off my torso then my arms, finally finishing up with my hands, taking them into her own, one at a time.

"You were injured," she observed, carefully dabbing around a gash on the back of my hand.

"It's nothing. I was in the practice yard and must have taken a hit without realizing it."

She nodded. "I should bandage it."

After she'd retrieved a small bandage and tied it securely around my hand, she turned to find a clean shirt for me, but I stopped her, grabbing her hands. I pulled her close. Still, she would not meet my eyes with her own.

"Thank you," I stated simply. She looked up. "Your gown is wet," I added, a smile tugging at the corner of my mouth.

"It's nothing."

She tried to pull away, but I held her fast.

"Irisa," I began, uncertain what else to say. *When had it become so hard to speak to my own wife?* After a moment, when she seemed to want to draw away again, I added, "I'm sorry."

I wasn't sorry, but I needed her to be near me. At least for a moment longer. My words seemed to be the balm she needed, for finally she willingly leaned into me, resting her head on my bare chest. I held her there, and after a moment I felt her shudder, feeling wetness against my skin where she had buried her face.

"What has become of us, Casmir?" she asked, her brokenness and pain cracking her words and pouring from her eyes.

My heart ached, but I felt incapable of doing anything about it. Nothing either of us had tried helped, and I feared making matters worse. We were both exhausted from trying.

I didn't want to try.

"I must go see my steward," I said at last.

She sniffed and lifted her chin to peer up at me. I met her despondent look and took in the redness of her eyes, the tears streaming down her face, her raw, bleeding need. I leaned over and kissed her forehead.

She responded with yielding softness, and memories of all we'd shared in the last few years came flooding back, overwhelming me. I knew I should do more. So much more. But what could make her feel better, take away her pain and offer her reassurance? I had nothing of my own to heal her. How was a drowning man to save another when he couldn't save himself?

Having nothing else to offer, I retreated back once more into my best defense: silence. The court mask I had relied upon since childhood. Rather than provide a morsel of food to the starved, I backed away, retrieved clean clothes, and dressed quickly, leaving her to stand alone, drowning in her own private grief.

❋ *29* ❋

Bellesea Palace
Prille
Agrius

11 years ago

"YOU LOOK WELL, MY son," *my mother whispered in my ear.*

It was an unusual thing for me to converse with my mother. Cousin Ildor discouraged me from speaking to her, though I'd never understood why, and he would not answer my questions about it. In the end, I trusted my cousin implicitly, even if the instruction made little sense. She was my mother after all. And I missed her. But my cousin had his reasons, I was sure.

I didn't know how to reply so rather than speak, I nodded slightly. I had grown much since I'd seen her last, was nearly of a height with her. I was only in my thirteenth year and would grow much taller. Everyone said so.

She placed a warm hand on the back of my neck, though even in the movement, we both kept our attention focused toward the front of the hall, to the place where my father and members of the Council stood around a table.

The ceremony of betrothal between my older sister and her future espoused, a nobleman from a far-off land, could not have been any more boring. Interacting with my mother seemed a much more preferable diversion.

"I hope we find a match worthy of you, my son, for you deserve nothing less than a blissful marriage, never mind that it be wishful thinking."

I nodded again, for I was in no position to agree or disagree. Marriage would be contracted for me, regardless of my wishes. I had every expectation that the state of it would be similar to that of my parents'. Likely my mother thought the same, for she gave my neck a delicate squeeze.

I wanted her to say more, anything more. I did not want to be like my father.

Not in marriage.

Not in anything.

She'd just stirred hope in me, but just as the seed of it rooted in my heart, my mother's hand tensed. She stiffened and dropped her hand, stepping back from me.

I searched the ring of faces surrounding my sister and her betrothed and spotted Cousin Ildor standing in his usual place just beside my father. He stared directly at my mother, and his dark look suggested that he'd just sucked on a bitter fruit. His eyes blazed at her until he noticed me watching him. He softened his look.

Soon enough the crowd dispersed, the ceremony over.

"Your future will bring you here one day, boy, eh?"

I turned to identify the speaker, finding a man towering over me. I searched my memory to recall the man's face and place it in its proper holding. Aksel, Lord Cilgaron.

The Honor of Cilgaron sat to the north of Prille around the midpoint of Agrius, and east along the coast. Cilgaron was one of the wealthiest in all of Agrius, for Lyseby in Cilgaron was the busiest slaving port in the kingdom. Lord Cilgaron had amassed great wealth since the coming of my father to Prille, and he held considerable power at court.

"I have a mind to talk to your father about his plans for your future. A union of Vitus with my own house would not be a bad move for him, I think." Cilgaron leaned down as if to whisper a confidence to me. "My house is of Sajen blood, you remember. Your father could be wise to unite our families, considering our history. There are those who might plot rebellion otherwise, to bring back a Sajen rule." He puckered his lips, seemingly impressed with his own wisdom. "I know your cousin over there has the ear of your father. I think you would find my daughter, Helene, a pleasing mate."

Cilgaron laughed then slapped me on the shoulder once more before he moved off. What he had suggested made me uncomfortable, and I glanced quickly around to see if anyone had observed our conversation. Noticing that no one paid me any mind, I flew out of the hall, making my way to the one place I always found peace for a troubled soul: the stables. Visiting my horse was an uncomplicated thing, a leveling act, for regardless of station, men the world over had horses.

I found the stable unusually quiet for this time of day. Roderic, the master of stable, was nowhere to be found, though a few young boys went about their work. As it usually was, the air felt cool, the atmosphere peaceful. The smell of fresh fodder always calmed me, and I stopped to close my eyes, inhaling the sweet scent of alfalfa.

A noise broke through my reverie and I opened my eyes to locate its source. My eyes settled far down the long row of stalls on a girl no more than a year or so younger than me. She stood silently watching me next to an unfamiliar horse. When she saw that I had noticed her, she pulled back against the wall behind her.

"Who are you?" I asked in my surprise, more harshly than I'd intended.

The girl still said nothing, and I walked slowly toward her. She was plainly dressed, and, while clean and tidy, it announced her as a person of modest means. Perhaps a merchant's daughter?

"I am sorry if I frightened you. What is your name?"

The girl lowered her eyes, and her lashes fluttered like the delicate wings of a butterfly. I waited patiently for her answer, and finally, she risked looking up. "Elin, Your Grace." Her voice matched her fragile gaze.

Clearly, she knew who I was. Why would she not? Everyone knew me.

I was my father's heir, destined to follow in his steps.

"And is this your horse? She is lovely."

Lovely? Who called a horse lovely? I stared at the floor, uncharacteristically tongue-tied. I'd sounded ridiculous. The girl was lovely. The horse was... "a fine animal, I meant." I stepped in more closely, noticing the warmth of her coloring and the rosy hue which tinted her cheeks.

"She is lovely, Your Grace, but no, she is not mine!" she exclaimed. Her eyes opened into round orbs, blue like the summer sea. "I was simply waiting for my father. He will be finished with his business soon, and then we will leave. I only wanted to see the animals. I am sorry if I am not meant to be here. I should leave." She threw a hasty look over my shoulder.

For some reason, I didn't want her to go.

"Elin, you need not worry. You have done nothing wrong in being here. What business brings your father to the palace?"

She took my measure, as if uncertain that I really did not mind her presence. "He is a stationer. The scriptstórii often purchase materials from him, and he has come to meet with the grand master. I sometimes slip away to see the horses when we come. He does not know I am here."

I loved hearing her speak and opened my mouth to ask her another question, but she glanced past me again as if she wanted nothing more than to leave. Did she fear me? I only wanted to hear her voice again.

"If your father makes books, does that mean you enjoy reading

them?"

She looked at me warily again, as if pondering whether or not I mocked her. "I am often able to read the books commissioned before his clients come to retrieve them. That is, if I am lucky enough to sneak into my father's workshop after the household has gone to sleep." She smiled mischievously, and I caught my breath at her beauty.

My heart pounded out a loud rhythm in my chest, but I willed it to slow. "Do you know this one?

> *The fair Adonis, turned to a flower*
> *A work of rare device and wondrous wit."*

She gazed at me with open admiration, and it only encouraged me to continue, for how I desired her admiration!

> *"First did it show the bitter baleful stir;*
> *which her assayed with many a fervent fit;*
> *when first her tender heart was with his*
> *beauty smite..."*

"Your Grace," interrupted a deep, booming voice.
I spun around. "Roderic, I was only just..."
"Here to order your horse saddled and readied for your use?" Roderic measured the girl disapprovingly before giving me a meaningful stare.

I swallowed. "Yes, of course. What else?"

Roderic's mouth twitched with humor, and I moved aside to let him go about his work. When I turned back again, I found that Elin had gone.

That night I dreamed of a young girl with eyes the color of the summer sea.

I knew I could not have her, or anyone like her. My future lay with duty. I would wed the woman matched for me, and that was all there was to it. I would learn to guard my heart against her. The sooner I learned it the better.

Bellesea Palace
Prille
Agrius

"I HAVE CONSIDERED YOUR warning, Your Grace, and I have brought news."

Geres of Glenna, the man whom I had recently admonished for his connections to the troublemaker Tugredd of Lyseby, knelt on one knee before the dais, carefully attired in a richly decorated tunic of embroidered vines encircling forest animals. Spring had begun to weave toward summer, but despite the warmer weather, Geres wore a light cloak draped about his shoulders, held in place with a gigantic enameled brooch boasting a blue sapphire.

"I hope that my news will make amends for my previously ill-considered behavior."

I straightened in my chair, though the motion had been slight enough that likely no one but Irisa, who sat beside me, noticed. A tiny muscle at the corner of my jaw worked, the only thing betraying my anxiety over whatever news this man of Glenna had brought us. If it was possible for progress to be made on the Lyseby question, perhaps this was the time. Perhaps the news would serve to distract me from my bitterness over having been left behind.

Wimarc of Dalery took in the interaction standing off to the side of the central aisle, just below the dais. I glanced his way and our eyes met. Irisa caught the exchange, and though I could not see her, I sensed her displeasure. She disliked the young lord, and though I had never told her of it, she felt certain that he had arranged the introduction between me and the mercenary, Jachamin Guimer. She most certainly did not like Guimer, indignant over the influence she felt he had over me.

Since his retrieval of Ethew, Jachamin had become a fixture at court, for with his effective service, I saw no reason to dismiss him. And with Luca away in Aksum, it seemed fitting to bring him into my service.

I saw her take in sight of him now standing just behind Geres, wearing the royal insignia at his shoulder, marking him as a king's man.

I returned my focus to the man kneeling before me. "You are most wise for your reconsideration, my lord of Glenna."

I waved him to standing, and he ascended the steps to kneel once more before me. This time, in my impatience, rather than invite him to stand again and find his ease, I let him remain there.

"What has caused you to abandon your scheming in shadowed corners?"

Geres wisely let the unfair remark pass, appearing to remain a contrite and dutiful vassal. "My king, I only spoke with Tugredd out of frustration. I merely vented my feelings with him. The change to my fortunes has been significant, and as you can imagine it has been more than difficult." I eyed his exquisite attire with bemusement, and Geres had the sense to look embarrassed before continuing. "If he took my comments as affirmation for whatever he had already planned to do, then that responsibility is on him.

"After your warning that I be more cautious, I instructed my man to ask some discreet questions, to see if I could get at what is behind the trouble there. I want to prove faithful to my sovereigns, Your Graces."

"And?"

"Someone else is behind what stirs up the guildsman and the city. Tugredd is only a player, not the instigator."

"And you know who is?"

Geres shook his head. "My man's source was very skittish, and he seemed too fearful to say more. That alone says something. I would hate to suppose without evidence, but I am certain you can divine the answer."

"Thank you, Geres. We will see to it that you receive accommodation and refreshment."

The palace steward stepped up to lead Geres away, and I stood, looking first to Wimarc and then to Guimer. It was only as an afterthought that I turned back to take Irisa's hand.

We retreated to the Council chamber, along with those Council members who had been present in the hall.

I leaned against a table and folded my arms across my chest. "Thoughts?"

"I recommend we send men to Lyseby to root out the truth. Have them collude with Ingólfer to get to the bottom of this."

"Except you forget that Ingólfer already has a significant network of informants. If he doesn't already know the truth of what's going on, sending outsiders will hardly produce anything new."

"I think you should leave matters to stew there. What can an uprising in Lyseby really do? Surely Lord Cilgaron would put down any open rebellion as is his oath-duty to the Crown?"

"You don't know Cilgaron if you think that," someone else replied. "He cares more for Croilton than city matters."

I listened without comment. I had my own suspicions about Lord Cilgaron and his ambitions, and Geres had hinted as much.

All the while the men talked, I caught occasional glimpses of Irisa who stood stiffly to the side. I knew she had little patience for what we discussed. The councilors presented nothing which hadn't been suggested before. Everything mentioned was a tired argument, discussed and rediscussed in previous meetings. Inaction had plagued us since the slavery edict, fueled by hopes that the trouble would die down. It hadn't.

Soon she spoke over the noise of the heated debate. "Hasten to finish the tax reform, show them partiality, and present them with something of true significance for their purses, even if it is a hit to the Treasury."

I watched the noise die away. The men gave her their attention, even if their interest seemed fragile.

The work on tax reform had made a tedious progression, for no lord of the realm was eager to impact his own profit by giving another a break. If the Lyseby tax burden was reduced, the Treasury had to be filled by other means.

"And when you have something to offer," she continued, "I will take it personally and present it." The men stared at her now. She continued with more confidence. "Surely Aksel, Lord Cilgaron would be pleased by such an offer, and as a result would do all he could to aid our cause."

She paused to make eye contact with each man. "A softer touch is needed. Send me. I will go."

The silence of the room felt palpable, and for a moment no one said a thing. And then, as if propelled by the weight of the idea, heads began to nod, slowly, one at a time. It seemed as if Irisa had struck a chord.

After a moment for this thought to sink in, someone spoke up from the back of the room. "Cilgaron has a slippery past at best. Would it work, do you think? He could be behind it all for all we know."

Other heads nodded, but no one spoke out against the idea.

I cleared my throat.

"My lords, if I may?" Wimarc broke into the trance-like agreement of the other councilors, and all eyes snapped to him. I smiled to myself. "I have kept my own counsel during this discussion. I am not an official member of the Council, and my time here in Prille has been short relative to your more seasoned and mature experiences. If you recall, my family was called upon to assist in putting down the slave rebellion that started in Dalery early in our king's reign." He looked to me in silent query, and I nodded my encouragement. "I may not have experience with the finer points of policy making, but I do know the mind of a rebel. This issue is so deeply rooted that I am not confident in the success of... well, in your words, Yar Hátin, a *softer touch*. I recommend that our king travel to Lyseby himself, put down the disquiet in a similar manner to what was done in Dalery."

It was the opening needed to bring back the louder protests, and before Irisa could try to calm the assembly, returning them to her way of thinking, the tide had turned away again.

After the waves of debates ebbed and flowed for a

time, I finally raised my hands to quiet the group.

"My good sirs, I think I have heard enough. You have shared your thoughts and concerns, and I will ponder all you've said. We will come to a decision tonight, for I think action must be taken immediately."

The meeting moved on to other things, and when it did, I saw Irisa slip away.

The confrontation didn't come until later that night when we finally had time to ourselves.

Irisa's maids were just finishing brushing and plaiting her hair into one long braid down her back as I breezed into our bedchamber, exhilarated after a game of merels with Wimarc. Certain for the first time in weeks that matters had turned into a fair wind, the sight of her attire, a light, loose-fitting shift falling askew off one shoulder, stirred my desire for her. I swayed toward her, eyeing her maid with a look that communicated I wanted to be alone with my wife. The maid scurried away.

Irisa stood when I reached her, and I leaned in to kiss her neck, moving my hands down her back to her hips. But rather than respond to me as I'd hoped, she pulled back. Confused by her refusal of me, I reached for her again.

"You are going to Lyseby," she stated simply. I dropped my hands, the fire of my desire doused instantly. "You couldn't go to Aksum, but you are going to Lyseby."

I set my jaw, crossing my arms over my chest. I stared at her with narrowed eyes, impatience oozing from every pore. "Yes, I am." Defiance rose up in me, clawing at my chest with sharpened talons.

"You told the Council that we would come to a decision. *We*, meaning you and me. Together. But I was not involved. You decided. You alone." Her words hung in the air. "You will start a war."

"If war comes, it is not because I started it. This conflict has been brewing for longer than I have worn the weight of the crown."

"But if it starts on your watch, no one will know the difference." She glared at me. "Or care."

"Irisa, I can't send you."

"You could not go to Aksum, and now you will not allow me to go to Lyseby."

I scowled, not knowing what to say in response. Likely it would be petulant. I strode away from her.

"If only Simon was here," she whispered as if to herself, but I overheard her.

"But Simon is not here," I growled. "He is on his way to Aksum. Unfortunately, you are left with only me to guide the people of Agrius!"

"Casmir, you do me a disservice! I am not questioning your abilities!" She threw up her hands. "I only meant..."

"I know what you meant," I said and turned back to the door, flinging it open. "I think I will find others more eager for my company this night."

I stormed out, leaving the door to our chamber standing open as I went.

Irisa bit the inside of her cheek as she moved to close the door. Once the latch clicked, she pressed her forehead against it and closed her eyes, letting loose a long sigh. After a time she turned around, leaning against the door, taking in the large chamber, the broad doors leading out the balcony overlooking the sound. In the last few years since her marriage to Casmir, this chamber had witnessed the highlights of her life; her biggest source of joy, of love and life and cheer. Now it all lay quiet, dark, and lifeless.

She reached up to rub her temples with her fingers. Tears would not be summoned, despite her desire for them. She shuddered a deep breath into the hollow place just under her ribs. Her daughter missing, her husband distant from her, her kingdom on the brink of civil war. Utter loneliness of the likes she hadn't felt since the first night Figor had left her with Miarka in Corium washed through her grief-stricken, joy-shriveled soul.

She chewed her lip in indecision. Should she go in search of Casmir, try to make him see reason? Who could say where he would sleep? She tried not to think on it. The alternative was for her to go to bed alone. She remembered the look on his face, the set of his jaw, the defiance and angry pride which had driven him of late. No, he would not soften, would not have his mind changed. She was tired of arguing, tired of trying. What use was it?

She looked then to the far side of the dark room, took in the sight of the cold, empty bed, and walked toward it.

If Casmir would not share it with her this night, it was all she had.

Once under the coverlets, she curled into herself, turning her head toward Casmir's pillow. Inhaling the scent of him, she wanted nothing more than to go back to the simpler days and nights when troubles could be soothed away by nothing more than his touch and the intimacy of their marriage bed. It was long into the night when she finally fell asleep, the scratching mice in the corner her only companions until morning.

Bellesea Palace
Prille
Agrius

Irisa

"IRISA, TAKE CARE OF yourself." Wolf directed a wary glance at Casmir who stood on the far side of the hall tending to details for his departure to Lyseby.

It had been two days of frenzied preparations since Casmir had decided he would personally lead a contingent of soldiers to the port town himself. And in those two days, Casmir kept a careful and cool distance from her. Her feelings of loneliness had not abated; if anything, they had increased.

"Won't you stay? Please?"

Wolf was more Casmir's friend than hers, but somehow his going at this moment in time felt like a betrayal.

Wolf's face fell. "No, I should go. There is so much to be done in Bauladu."

"He still has not asked you to come with him?"

Wolf tried to hide his hurt, but Irisa could see through his valiant attempt. "He said there is nothing here I need concern myself with, and that any news from Aksum would be a long time coming."

"So he sent you away?"

"Not in so many words. But yes. And as a good king's man, I obey."

Casmir had done a thorough job of distancing himself from those around him, finding slights where none had been intended and lashing out at those who only sought his good. It was only now that Irisa discovered that Wolf had also fallen victim. It seemed as if the foundations of Casmir's very world had cracked around him, and while everyone who loved him wanted only to offer help, he seemed determined to widen the cracks that would swallow him whole.

"I wish you were going with him," she admitted.

Wolf grimaced. "He has others to tend him now."

"That's what I'm afraid of." She laid her hand on his arm. "He knows you will be his conscience, and he doesn't want that. Not when he surrounds himself with those who will tell him what he wants to hear."

"Irisa, promise me you will stay strong. He needs you."

"He doesn't seem to think so." She could no longer hide her anger.

Wolf bent over, putting his face just under hers, forcing her to look him in the eye.

"He doesn't seem to think he needs anyone right now. But here's the thing: he has taken a blow. Several blows. His pride wasn't just pricked, Irisa, it was slashed in two, thrown to the ground, and stomped on. It wasn't just his personal pride either. It was his kingly pride, and that's almost worse. It's his identity, Irisa, his whole world. Right now he is trying to make sense of it."

"You defend him?"

"His heart was shattered." Irisa made to protest, but Wolf lifted a finger to quell her rebuttal. "As was yours, Irisa. I do not deny it. But women find comfort more easily than men, for women find consolation among other women. They confide in one another the matters of the heart. Men, not so much, and kings..." Wolf shook his head. "He is isolated, has always been, even in his youth. His father had little use for him, his mother was kept from him, and Ildor Veris... the man manipulated him, Irisa. Intentionally, even in his youth. Can you imagine betrayal like that from a man who was closer to you than your own father? Few have been able to travel his road with him. Now he has you, but it is still not natural for him. He has learned to guard his heart well. I know this hasn't been easy for you, and Casmir seems to have forgotten that you are a mother whose heart has been broken too. He has turned selfish and unthinking. But he will come around. I know him. He must deal with his furies, but he will conquer them."

"And if he doesn't?"

"He will."

"Even with louder voices whispering honeyed words in his ear?"

Both of them turned to see Casmir end his conversation with a groom before waving Wimarc over to him.

"I do not like that man, Wolf."

Wolf compressed his lips into a thin line. "He is young."

"But even if he was old, I do not think he would be wise. Foolishness and wisdom do not necessarily favor one age over the other."

"No, not always."

"And if this Wimarc seems set on starting a war? And if Casmir listens to him, thinking it a way to prove himself?"

"It isn't who he is, Irisa."

"You and I both know that, but he seems to have forgotten it. I wish you could do something."

"I will see what I can do."

She grasped his arm more tightly, squeezing it. "Wolf, I don't deserve you."

"Most women don't."

She tilted her head back and laughed then flourished a bright smile, her darkness momentarily lifted.

Wolf smacked his hand over his heart, pretending to stagger backward. "That's a smile that could kill a man, right there. Promise me you'll flaunt it more often?"

Irisa dropped her chin, unnerved by this brazen compliment even while grateful for it.

"Thank you, Wolf," she whispered quietly. "I should let you tend to your preparations. Rest assured I will send word to you immediately upon hearing news from Aksum."

"Thank you, dear lady." He leaned toward her and kissed her tenderly on the cheek. "You have given me some things to ponder." His attention trailed to the place Casmir now stood talking to Wimarc. He took a breath as if to say more but frowned instead before moving off.

Irisa stood alone for some time as activity swirled around her. She felt like a bird flying against the wind in a storm at sea.

She and Casmir had argued bitterly that morning, perhaps the most bitter argument of their marriage, and in her mind's eye, she recalled the scene.

Casmir's chamberlain, Andreu, fit a tabard over the top of his brigandine jacket while Irisa tried once more to appeal to his better senses, to persuade him that his arrival in Lyseby in such a manner, with a ship full of soldiers, could only stir trouble.

"What will happen in Prille while you are gone? What are we to do without you?"

He'd tilted his face toward her, raising an eyebrow. "Do you realize how much you disparage your own crown when you argue your last point as you do?" He waved Andreu away, and the man bowed his way carefully to the outer fringes of the room. "You are a crowned sovereign as well as I," he said dismissively. "You will be here to rule even if I am not."

He faced her fully now, his attention fixed on her, his look imperious. His mood drummed up within her the tattered remnants of an old insecurity. She fought against it, pushing it back down.

"Casmir, you know as well as I do that as a woman, my crown is somehow reduced in size."

"Then it is up to you to change that fact," he snapped. "Irisa, you sit on the Council and have every right to be there. Use the power your crown gives you."

"The same right and power you yourself dismiss?" She offered him an imperious look of her own. "Twice now you have disregarded my counsel and have courted the advice of men who don't have your best interests at heart."

"And you know this to be true? I would be curious to know how."

"I have eyes to see, Casmir!"

He pressed his lips together. "And who might these individuals be?"

Ice solidified his tone, making his question hard, biting.

"That lord of Dalery is merely a glib youth, but he has your ear even so. But more than him, the man I fear is

Guimer. You know little about him, where he has come from, what his affinities are, yet you rush headlong into his confidence."

"And what influence do you think Jachamin has over me, exactly?"

She walked a dangerous path, and she knew it. She didn't care. "I suspect that he pushed you into going to Lyseby," she stated honestly.

"He pushed me? For what reason?"

A dangerous glint lit his eyes, but she pressed on in spite of it. "I don't know," she admitted, "but by making you go to Lyseby..."

She got no further. Ferocity lit up his face.

"He did not *make* me do anything. By the gods, Irisa!" He balled his fists so tightly they turned white. "Do you think me so weak-minded that I can be led by my nose, persuaded to do things I have not chosen to do? I am king, and the decision was *mine alone.*"

"Yours alone? And I have no say, no influence?" She jammed her fists into her hips, furious with him. "Your mother had no influence, Casmir, don't you see? And Veris stood behind your father, pulling his strings. You have become just like your father, like Veris too, and you will not see it!"

Casmir's eyes widened into orbs, the ice behind them melting with fire.

"You go too far," he hissed.

But she hadn't. She'd merely spoken truth. He just didn't want to hear it. He had disbelieved her when she'd warned him of Ildor Veris' schemes, and now he did the same thing with the new voices at court. Would he never learn?

"You know what my father did, what Veris did to me, how I hate them each for it. Veris tried to take away everything I hold dear..." He paused and took a shaky breath. "To accuse me of being like either of them is an insult, and from you, of all people, Irisa." He shook his head then spun on his heel and left.

She had not seen him look at her that way since before their marriage, the day he'd accused her of conspiring with her own father to be ambushed on their journey to Bauladu. She learned that his anger that day had been fueled by his fear of losing her, but in that moment, the heat of it had shaken her to the core. Was he any different now? She was not sure.

A page approached her, returning her to the present moment. "The king wishes you to join him."

Irisa steeled herself for what she knew was coming then crossed the hall to meet him, conflict raging within her, confusing her feelings on their coming separation. Everything she thought she knew had shifted under her feet.

"It is time to depart," he stated, holding out his arm for her to take.

For a moment she searched his eyes, looking for any sign of remorse, regret over the bitter words which had passed between them, but she found nothing. Only his court mask.

Lifting her chin, she smiled pleasantly at him for the benefit of those around them. There was no warmth in her look and none in his.

When they reached the palanquin which would take Casmir to his ship, the *Sjórinn Mær*, he turned to her. Speaking in a voice pitched loudly enough for all to hear, he instructed her, "My queen, rule wisely in my absence." Then he bowed over her hand and kissed it.

She returned his parting in kind, and he moved away, climbing into the palanquin. When he raised his hand, indicating he was ready to move off, Irisa stood fixed to her spot and watched him pass through the courtyard and out of the gates. He did not look back. The gleam on the gold of his crown was the last she saw as he disappeared into the crowded streets.

She hadn't noticed Kassia standing near, but now as the crowds thinned, her sister came alongside her. Irisa offered her a hollow smile, but Kassia did not return it, took her arm instead. "Come, sister," she instructed. "Let's get you to your chamber."

Irisa followed along, oblivious to everything around her. When finally they reached her apartments, Kassia dismissed the servants. As soon as the door closed behind them, Irisa drifted toward her bed. Grabbing the corner post, she leaned her forehead against it, feeling a surge of raw emotion.

Kassia came alongside her and pulled her into an embrace as the tears brimmed over.

"Let it out, dear one," she whispered. "You have been so strong, but it's alright to cry."

They sat down on the bed together, and Irisa leaned over and, tucking her feet under her, pillowed her head on Kassia's lap.

"It's like a dagger to my heart, Kassia, and I cannot bear it. I feel like I have broken, the parts of me scattered to the winds. First my daughter, and now Casmir."

"I don't know what passed between you two this morning, but it doesn't matter. I am here."

"I feel that I've lost him," she sobbed.

"I fear he has lost himself, dear sister."

Kassia rocked her gently as a mother would her grief-stricken child, stroking her hair.

"Was a person meant to take this much strain without cracking? I cannot do it anymore."

"Just be a mother and wife this day. Tend to your

bleeding wounds. There will be time enough later to be the queen Agrius needs."

Deck of the Árvök
Eastmor Ocean

Jack

I KNOW ISARY. HE is cruel and vile. He will try to do you harm just because he can.

Kassia's words echoed in Jack's mind, tumbling around and around, repeating over and over until they had become part of the background tapestry to his days aboard ship.

He is cruel and vile.

As was the makeup of many men Jack had met in his time.

He will try to do you harm just because he can.

A smile tugged at the corners of his mouth. Let the pocked bag of worms try. He welcomed it.

In truth, Kassia's warning had done little to impact him. At least not in the way she'd intended. Kassia wanted him to be wary of Isary because she worried for him. It was her right. Isary had damaged her, and that damage had left scars. But in scarring Kassia, Isary had invited Jack's enmity even if the flames of that hatred had burned low in the last few years. No, Isary's arrival and Kassia's warning did not worry him. It had merely stirred up something long buried.

He pulled back from the railing and the spray of salt water, absent-mindedly fingering the sheathed dagger at his belt.

"A good day to hunt a traitor, eh?"

Simon Peares, Baron of Hambelin, and Chancellor of Agrius stood behind Jack with hands on hips, a bright look on his face as if reveling in the sea air whipping through his hair. The Árvök dipped and crested, breaking through the waters and causing the deck to roll. The older man did not appear to be thrown off balance but rather kept his footing as if having lived a thousand days on a sea-going vessel.

"Indeed, it is always a good day to hunt a traitor," Jack replied, allowing his gaze to stray to the *Aurica*, the ship that carried the Elbran prince.

Simon caught the look, and Jack quickly checked himself, turning once more to the railing to take in the sight of the sea below.

The story of what Isary had done to Kassia was not a secret, but Jack had determined to keep his thoughts on the matter private. He now feared his lapse revealed more to the Chancellor than he'd intended, and he hoped the man would let the subject lie.

To Jack's relief, Simon said nothing. Together they watched as a pair of dolphins emerged suddenly from the water a stone's throw off the port side. Like silver streaks of firelight, the animals leapt and played, swimming and dancing in and out of the water.

"I don't imagine they had dolphins in the foothills of

the Sidera Mountains?"

"Not many, no," Jack answered with a wry grin, imagining such creatures playing in the shallow waters of the streams that flowed out of the foothills.

"I thought not." Simon paused, as if his thoughts drifted on to other things, but after a while, he continued: "I lived near the sea when I was a child, when my father served as castellan at Blackdown. There were many creatures of the sea, of course, but my favorites were the dolphins. I didn't have many childhood companions, so in their way, they became my friends. I even swam with them from time to time, though my father became furious when he learned of it." He laughed at the memory. "Such beautiful creatures. Intelligent.

"They came to the little cove just below the fortification in the winter of each year for protection from the stormy seas. One particular year brought a new type of creature to our little bay. Initially, I thought their interest in the dolphins a curious thing. But my child's understanding did not grasp what was to happen. Rather than find safety in the protected cove that year, my dolphin friends met their deaths, for the herd of *hákarls* were not interested in play but in feasting. The cove became the dolphins' prison, and they were destroyed. As a boy, I was devastated, of course, to witness such carnage. I wanted revenge on the *hákarls*, but my father warned me:

A predator is what it is, Simon. He is being true to his nature. But you are a man. In seeking revenge, a man becomes that which he hates.

"I didn't figure his advice worth much at the time. I didn't see any way I could become a hákarl, for I was a boy and they fish!"

Simon laughed at the memory, and Jack offered a

good-natured laugh of his own as his gaze drifted back toward the *Aurica*.

Simon followed Jack's look. "I've never met a more conceited, disdainful, pretentious brute in all my days. We can be thankful that his elder brother will sit the Elbran throne after his father, and not him."

"Truer words have never been spoken," Jack agreed, scowling.

"My lord, I do not mean to pry into a man's private world, and far be it from me to cause you offense, but I know the man's transgression against you. And while you may not want it, you have my sympathy."

"I thank you, sir," Jack replied even if he didn't mean it. He wished the Chancellor would speak of something else.

"I don't love the idea of supporting the shameless jackanape either, but our king has ordered that we set aside our personal feelings. We go to Aksum in search of Sybila, a little girl who, like any other little girl, cares nothing of politics or the machinations of adults in the trappings of power. She needs her father and mother, and they need her. In the case of most children, it would not matter who her parents are. But for Sybila, it matters more than anything. That fact that her father and mother are king and queen of Agrius will complicate everything we are about to do. This is why we must proceed slowly, with extreme caution and care."

"Of course, my lord, I want nothing more than to find our Sybila."

Jack had spoken lightly in an attempt to keep his voice steady. Even so, Simon narrowed his eyes, and Jack resisted the urge to fidget.

The scrutiny lasted only a moment. Soon a twinkle appeared in the older man's eyes. "Very good, my lad." He clapped Jack on the shoulder. "That, of course, was my official admonishment. The Chancellor has a duty to attend. However," he held up a single finger, "Simon Peares is also a husband and a father. It's hard to say what dangers await us in Aksum, what dangers await that prince." Simon tossed his head in the direction of the *Aurica*. "In my duties, I must, of course, ensure that any dangers the prince of Elbra encounters during our time do not impede our attempts to save Sybila."

Jack cleared his throat. "How do you plan to go about our task? We can hardly barge in demanding her back."

A thoughtful look crossed the Chancellor's features, and he rubbed at the white hair on his chin for a moment. "I will seek an audience, of course. We are entering the Negus' domain under purely diplomatic auspices, first and foremost. That is all we must appear to be, and that is all we will publicly admit to. If indeed, the Negus has conspired to take the girl, there is no doubt he will be suspicious of our motives. However, if he knows nothing of it, we may be able to elicit his help. If his daughter Addis is to blame, rather than the Negus, we will still have to tread lightly, for we do not know his feelings toward her after her conspiring in Agrius. Our first task will be to find someone willing to confide in us."

"So a simple thing, really," Jack observed dryly.

Simon caught the edge of mockery and curled a smile. "Indeed. Which is why there may not be time for much of anything else."

"You might be surprised at how many tasks I can manage simultaneously."

Jack looked again at the *Aurica*. The vague shape of the ocean-going caravel loomed just ahead of them, its sails lost in the glare of the sun as its last rays chose that very moment to dip below the dark blue waters of the Eastmor Ocean. Twilight fell over the world.

"I am off to my bed now, and I suggest you do the same," Simon advised, "for the captain assures me that tomorrow we will have our first glimpse of this land of Aksum. And then the mighty Sékra, the city of the Negus, will soon follow."

Jack nodded then turned back to the railing as Simon left him to his thoughts.

Later, as he lay on his bunk below deck, Jack thought of Kassia, of her whispered words upon his departure: *I know Isary. He is cruel and vile. He will try to do you harm just because he can.*

And he drifted into a dreamless slumber.

Sékra

Aksum

Jack

DUST AND GRIT, WITH *a taste of the ages.*

Jack licked his lips, surveying the rise and fall of Sékra's outline as the Árvök maneuvered along the busy waterfront of Aksum's principal city. It was nothing he had imagined it would be.

"What a colorless place, this Sékra," Luca observed coming alongside him.

"Truly," Jack agreed. The dust on his tongue seemed to make up the essence of the landscape, of the distant hills, the buildings, and even the water through which the Árvök plied. Then he flashed a bright smile. "Ah, but there are trees!"

Jack pointed at the line of the green leaves poking over the walled enclosures and rooftops of the city. Luca laughed and the pair watched the city slide by as the Árvök made its way into a berth alongside the *Aurica*. It was only after they'd stepped off the ship and onto dry land that Jack began to realize his mistake in assuming Aksum to be drab and colorless. There was so much more color and life to the city than he'd seen at first.

One only needed to look more closely than the broad sweeping judgment made aboard a ship's deck. For it appeared that in order to counter the dull, blanched architecture, the people arrayed themselves in bright colors which spanned the full breadth of vibrancy found in nature. The citizenry draped themselves in hues of amber, blue, yellows the color of straw and pansies, with reds like a berry or an apple; tunics of purple and green, silver and gold... many striped and woven with wild patterns to delight the eye.

And the people underneath the vivid attire could not be more entrancing to Jack's eyes. While he had never met Addis, stories of her beauty abounded. Darkly tanned skin with a tall, slender frame, her graceful movements and refined manners entranced everyone she met. The people of Sékra came in all shapes and sizes, but there was a casual elegance about their bearing, to the very least of them, that hinted at a common nobility shared across their culture. They were a proud people and a people who carried themselves with the dignity due that inherent nobility.

Jack pushed his way through groups of dockworkers making quick work of unloading the ships and filed past the hockers of wares and trinkets. The *Aurica* also unloaded, and Jack watched Isary and his retinue push through the crowds to join Simon who had already begun to talk with a delegation from the Negus'. Jack caught sight of Cai among the Elbrans and gave a brief nod.

By the time Jack reached them, Isary had already moved off, his face registering irritation, though Jack could only imagine the nature of the offending slight. Isary glanced over his shoulder, noticed Jack, and the prince's back stiffened, his eyes hardening into steel. He leaned in toward the man next to him, whispered something, and the pair laughed together. Isary smirked and strode away.

Disgusted, Jack turned to find Simon approaching him.

"We will be taken to the palace, but we will only be allowed a very limited personal guard within the palace. Luca, of course, and a handful of his choice. The rest will be lodged in the city, though I've been told they will be near at hand outside the palace walls." Simon delivered his news evenly, but Jack could tell the Chancellor was not pleased with the development. "It is the polite thing to do, I am told. It suggests our trust in the ability of the Negus to keep us safe."

Simon said this last part with compressed lips, and Jack turned his eyes southward toward the Betem Jebili, the Negus' palace, which dominated the far horizon. The ancient fortress of the Negus sat atop an enormous rock formation some distance from the coast. It stood as a watchman high on a natural rise, easily seen from all points within the city as a reminder that the Negus lived among them and yet remained apart.

"Do you think it a cause for concern?" he asked Simon at last.

"What else are we to do? If there is duplicity in the Negus, it is not likely to come in the form of a full-scale military front. No, I do not fear anything that would necessitate a full contingent of our own soldiers. Assassination in a palace, however, is not unknown." Simon's expression turned somber. "I am confident that each of us is a man trained in the art of self-preservation, and as such, I trust each one to keep a watchful eye on each of the others."

"I'll keep an eye on your back, that is for certain, but I

would not want that one keeping an eye on my back," Jack muttered, looking darkly in the direction of Isary.

Simon said nothing, simply clapped Jack on the shoulder then turned and waved the men forward to follow the delegation. Jack hefted his pack and found his place in the retinue, all the while working to make sure Isary stayed ahead of him. Kassia's warning may not have influenced him directly, but he was still a man of pragmatism. He rolled his shoulders, imagining how easy it would be for a man like Isary to slip a thin blade between his ribs, and moved on.

Jack tossed his pack onto the floor and looked around the room, taking in the strange surroundings. It felt a world apart from his manor on Haern, and especially distant from the leafy bower he'd known as home for years as an exile outside Heywood in Mercoria. Exotic woods inlaid with shiny tiles and polished stones, leather furniture, and silver-fitted decor made up the visual aspects of the room, while a thin filament burned incense in the corner, filling the room with a scent Jack could not name.

So far everything about his entry into the world of Aksum felt like an attack on his senses, overwhelming with newness. He sat on the bed and brushed his hands across his eyes, rubbing the fatigue away.

After leaving the harbor earlier that day and threading through more districts of Sékra, then through several bustling markets and progressing past a wealthy district full of magnificent homes, the travelers reached the Betem Jebili, the home of the Negus of Aksum. Upon their approach, the fortress rose a colossus above them, larger than he'd first suspected from Sékra's harbor.

To reach the fortress from the city, the party crossed a raised causeway over a deep gully. Wide enough to boast ten armed and mounted men riding abreast, the approach ended at a massive gateway on the other side, its doors created from huge timbers bound with iron bands. Everything about the fortress put Jack in mind of the mist-shrouded and hulking Mosrad Prison, or the Dark Fortress as the locals called it back in Corium, and he suppressed a shudder at the memory of Kassia's captivity there. To get his focus off such memories, he'd examined the gully below, finding the result less than reassuring. Jagged rocks made up the bottom of the gully, an unfortunate welcome for anyone who might tumble off the causeway.

A gust of wind had picked up just then, blasting a current of dry heat in his face, swirling eddies of dirt like the grasping fingers of the desert around them. He cleared the grit from his eyes and entered the fortress with the rest of his companions through the looming gate.

Standing several stories tall and nearly as deep as a city wall, the entrance into the Negus' stronghold would not have been an easy one for a marauding army to breach. Standing guard along the path through its great barbican stood six burly men positioned on each side. Dressed in brightly polished armor, halberds at the ready, none made eye contact, though Jack was under no illusion that they did not watch closely as each visitor passed by.

Once through the gate, a no man's land stretched before them, leading to a second curtain wall atop another rise, a second barbican situated upon its height. Jack's eyes trailed up the second set of walls, and it occurred to him that his first view of the palace in Prille had been one of awe, just as it was now. Though while Prille's palace showcased strength and wealth, it somehow also managed to communicate a domestic side, that while a fortress, it was also a home. The Negus' palace showed no such softness. If Sybila was here, he prayed to all the gods that they would find her soon.

Once through the second gate, the upper circle of the fortress presented a new side, a more luxurious and even more alien one. Buildings boasted colorfully tiled entries, with silken awnings sheltering doorways and propping up tent-like structures beside. External staircases led to upper floors and rooftop pavilions. Fountains decorated courtyards, and lush greenery made the air smell somehow cleaner, like a taste of spring on the mountain air.

"The Negus and his family live in the inner court," their guide said, sweeping a graceful arm behind him to indicate yet another wall, this one not nearly as tall as the first two they had passed through. "Your lodgings will be here in the upper ketema."

He clapped his hands and another man jumped forward. "Le'ul Isary, I will lead you to your lodgings while this man will show you of Agrius to yours."

And with that, their group split. Jack peered after Isary as he paced himself alongside his guide. His group processed down the wide street for a while before turning a corner past a large building that looked to be a chapel of some sort before disappearing from view. When Jack came back to the present, he realized his own entourage had moved on so ran to catch up.

After navigating a warren of streets, the Agrians arrived at their residence, a palace within a palace, for their accommodation had its own wall and gate. Once inside the gate, they entered a virtual paradise decorated with brilliantly colored ceramic tiles, a large central fountain spilling cold water over an elaborately carved marble statue. Arbors lined the walls, sheltering green vining plants and bright flowers. Exotic scents permeated the air, a welcome change from the dusty streets outside the walls of the betem.

After they had a chance to settle in and rest, a man arrived, tall, slender, and stately, dressed in a long, silk robe of crimson. His hands bore elaborate tattoos which disappeared up his wrists and under his sleeves. His head bore a flat-topped, round hat encircled with thin, gold chains.

"My name is Melku Amare Negus, and I offer you greetings in the name of His Imperial Majesty, the Negusa Nagast, Bazin Assefe Amare, though to honor your foreign tongue, you may refer to him as Negus Bazin."

Simon offered the man a slight bow in deference. "Our thanks to you, Le'ul Melku."

Melku raised a brow. "You know of the stylings used in Aksum, I see." He allowed only a slight smile to curl his lips, though his eyes shone with obvious delight and approval.

"I know that you are a prince of the esteemed Amare line, yes, son of Negus Bazin."

At this, Melku smiled more widely. "I have been sent to serve you during your stay here in the Betem Jebili, as the Negus' personal representative. If you find anything lacking, you need only ask. You have been given this complex, this *ye'inigida kifili*, for your personal use during your stay, and you may roam freely. Though I do recommend that you keep mostly to the place provided for you. While you may visit other parts of the betem, I suggest an escort. The guards outside your door will serve in this way."

Melku went on to explain other aspects of life in the betem, and the function of various buildings. Jack heard little of what was said, distracted as he was by the man's warning that they not wander unaccompanied. Melku had not required it, so they were not being held here against their will. But the warning did seem to have an odd ring to it, and he wondered how the instruction fit with the foreboding he'd felt upon arrival.

"I would invite your *balam* to join me," Melku said, indicating Luca, "and I will introduce you to your equivalent here in Betem Jebili, the Balam Baras." Luca nodded his agreement, and Melku continued, "A meal will be laid for you here this night rather than at court so you may recover from your long journey. We invite you to partake of it with joy as we look forward to honoring your arrival with a full feast in coming days."

He extended his arm, inviting Luca to come with him, bowed to the group then turned to leave.

"One moment, if I may, Le'ul Melku?" Simon cut in.

Melku turned back.

"What of the Negus Bazin? When may we meet with him?"

Something passed behind Melku's eyes, though the specific emotion of it was unreadable to Jack. "Negus Bazin will be most pleased to meet with you in his time."

And with that, he offered a careful smile, and left, with Luca in tow.

❀ 29 ❀

Betem Jebili
Sékra
Aksum

Jack

IT WAS THE BARKING dog that woke him. Or was it? Jack's eyes snapped open and he grasped for the dagger he kept near his head.

His heart raced, and it was only with great effort he fought against the fog of sleep to think through where he was. The Betem Jebili, he realized, the home of the Negus of Aksum.

The room lay under the gentle enchantment of night, his companions breathing rhythmically in sleep. None of them had been disturbed, so what had awakened him?

The dog barked again and continued to bark just beyond the wall of the *kifili*. He knew his pounding heart would keep him awake until it settled, and it would only settle once he looked into the cause of his alarm. Too many years of living in exile had taught him that apathy could kill.

He swung his legs over the side of his bed and placed his feet on the floor still warm from the previous day's heat. Rubbing the grit from his eyes, he blinked a few times and stood. Grabbing his shirt off the end of the bed where he'd tossed it the previous night, he slipped it over his head and made his way gingerly across the unfamiliar room to the window on the far side. He lifted the lattice that served as a window and poked his head out to listen. Nothing seemed out of place. Pushing the lattice open farther, he contorted his bulk through the space and dropped quietly to the ground on the other side. He crouched in the concealment of the bushes and paused, listening.

Guards stood posted at the door of his *kifili*, and they talked quietly with each other, their conversation casual. He peeked at them from hiding and found nothing amiss. Hearing nothing else out of the ordinary, he circuited to the back of the enclosure and crept away in the opposite direction. He was awake now. Why not have an unaccompanied look around the betem? Choosing a path at random, he set out.

An image of Sybila rose in his mind as he wandered. Imagining how his own son would feel, stolen away, far from his family and any familiar face... Anger boiled up inside him. He had only seen the girl once, but even from that one meeting, he could not escape the striking similarities she shared with her mother. She would not be too easily hidden here in Sékra, with her hair the color of the sun's glow on a white-hot summer's day. Was it likely he would come across the place Sybila was hidden? No. If she was with Addis, there was no way he would get close. But perhaps he might uncover other things in his night wanderings.

Just around another corner, there came the sound of

marching feet scrabbling on the loose gravel of the path. He had just enough time to pull back into a recess in the wall as four armed guards came into view. With no other destination in mind, he decided to follow them.

After following for some time, he felt his pursuit had probably been pointless. He was about to turn around to retrace his steps when they rounded another corner, revealing another quartet of guards on duty in front of a door, plain and unadorned, but heavily fortified even so.

The new guards stopped, and the four on post stood stiffly at attention.

"Hēli Kiros!" each called in turn. Other commands issued back and forth in barks, and though Jack understood none of it, one name stood out: Kiros.

No one had mentioned the name in his hearing before, but this Kiros had something in his possession that seemed valuable enough to guard. The circumstance screamed a mystery he wanted to uncover.

The duty guards completed their exchange, and the relieved men walked down the path in the opposite direction from Jack. Knowing there was no way to force his way past the guards, and with nothing more to do, he pulled back making a mental note to return later. He spun on his haunches.

Into someone crouching behind him.

In his surprise, he was unable to reach for his dagger quickly enough. A hand snaked out and grabbed his wrist.

"Jack, it's me, Cai."

Relief washed over him like the many waterfalls of Lynchport.

Cai tossed his head to the side, inviting Jack to follow him away and out of earshot of the men on duty.

"Cai, why are you out in the night?"

"I could ask you the same."

He had a point. "I couldn't sleep. Your turn."

"Me either."

Well, that cleared things up.

"Why were you watching that door?"

"I wasn't. I was following you."

"Why didn't you let me know you were following me?"

"Because then those guards you were following would have known you were following them."

"I can't argue with that."

Cai's cheeks dimpled mischievously, and Jack felt joy rise in his chest for the first time since arriving in Sékra. He clapped the boy on the shoulder.

"What are your thoughts on what's behind that door?"

Cai shrugged. "Dunno, but I'm going to find out."

"I don't doubt that. Just don't get caught." He nodded toward the path once more. "We should get back before anyone notices we're gone. In the meantime, keep an eye on that *skingi* of a prince for me. Get word to me regarding anything interesting. I don't know that Isary is involved in what happened to Sybila, but I want to know everything he knows. You might be the key to our finding her."

Cai nodded gravely. "That's what I planned to do all along." He smiled again. "If he doesn't know anything about Sybila, there must be something else to implicate him. I'm going home with you and Kassia."

Before Jack could reply, Cai dashed away, leaving Jack to find his own way back to his *kifili* and his bed. Finding sleep came more easily to him. He had an ally.

※ ※

A yellow-billed kite flew high overhead, its outline stark

against the washed-out blue of the hot Sékra sky, so close that Jack felt he could but reach out and touch it. High upon the ramparts of the Betem Jebili's outer curtain wall, he felt a part of the kite's world. Instinctively he reached out, realizing quickly enough their extreme height as a wave of dizziness threatened to unsteady him. Instead, he brought his hand up to shield his eyes from the onslaught of the sun's heat. The bird moved on, and Jack looked earthward once more, taking in the sight of Sékra's sprawl far below. Undulating waves of heat rose from the city, making it appear a breathing, sentient thing. He inhaled the hot air, like a blast from the furnace of a forge.

"This heat, it is not what you know back home?" observed his companion.

"In Agrius? Certainly not. Though in a way it is reminiscent of summers in Corium."

In the three days since arriving in Sékra, the heat had been unrelenting, and Jack found himself wondering how anyone coped.

"I did encourage you to avoid this midday heat, did I not?" Melku smiled compassionately as Jack wiped away a bead of sweat from his forehead. "This is why we have awnings overhead," Melku pointed, "to protect the men serving as guards so high with the eagles."

Melku had arrived at their *kifili* at sunrise that morning to invite Simon, Luca, and Jack on a tour of the betem, but none of the Agrians were eager to venture out at such an hour. Jack felt a keen lack of sleep from his night wanderings the night before. It didn't take much to encourage a head-shaking Melku to return at a more reasonable hour. He had, though he'd warned them about the heat.

Now as they stood high atop the outer wall of the betem, Jack understood the warning. A trickle of sweat ran down the middle of his back, and he longed to dip into one of the many fountains found throughout the betem. Simon and Luca had obviously given up on the view from so high up on the wall, for Jack caught sight of the back of them descending the steps.

Even so, Jack remained glued to his spot, his hands gripping the edge of the dun-colored bricks of the wall.

"Ask what you want to know but have not yet allowed yourself to put to words."

Jack's eyes snapped to meet Melku's, and in their brown depths, he found a sharp intellect inviting candor.

Jack inhaled a deep breath. "Tell me about Addis," he found himself asking before realizing he had even spoken. He immediately cringed. Perhaps everything they hoped to accomplish now lay destroyed as a result of his reckless question. His need had made him careless. He prepared for the worst.

Melku twitched a smile. "Yes, Addis is here. That is the question you truly wanted to ask, is it not?" In his amusement, Jack sensed the prince was happy the subject had surfaced at last. "She fled reprisals from your king and has taken refuge in the court of her mother."

Jack nodded. He wasn't sure how much more to ask, knew he was most certainly not ready to ask about Sybila. "And your father? What does he think about his daughter's activities in Agrius?"

"It is difficult to know the mind of the Negus," Melku replied cryptically.

The answer veiled something, for behind Melku's words hid the hint of another world of truths just beyond Jack's understanding. Feeling immediately at a loss for words, he struggled to know how to respond. The decision was made for him by the passage of a pair of t'ebaks along the wall behind them. Once they had moved out of earshot, Melku changed tack.

"Your friend, the prince of Elbra, he is a unique man."

"He is hardly a friend," Jack spat instinctively, though just as quickly, he moderated his tone, adding more tactfully, "Prince Isary came to Prille, asking our king if he could join us on our diplomatic mission to Aksum. Of course, our king could not refuse the honor."

"Of course," Melku replied slowly, and Jack wondered if the man sought to find a different meaning behind his words. A sly smile spread his lips. "We also have men in Sékra who do not carry what we in Aksum call *wami ts'shekimi.* The meaning lacks a simple translation. How to explain?" Melku gazed off into the distance, studying the waves of heat rise from the city. "*Burden of honor* -- perhaps that is one way to explain it?"

"I dare say every kingdom has such men," Jack returned. "It's when such men reside close to power that we need to fear them."

"You are not of the direct line of your King Casmir. Are you of another line of the *mesafint*, perhaps?"

"Mesafint?"

"It is what we call our noble peoples."

"Ah, well, no, I am not of the mesafint."

"Indeed?" Melku raised a surprised brow, and Jack did his best to stifle a laugh at the man's openly startled expression. "I just assumed, being a member of the king's delegation..."

"Not by birth anyway. My wife is the queen's sister."

"You are married to Le'elt Kassia?"

"Undeniably so, though how it came to be is a long story, and one which I will tell you some evening while we drink wine together." Jack placed a hand on Melku's shoulder and gave it a squeeze. "My own background is a little less illustrious, you can be sure."

"I have heard the story of your wife's father, of his connection to Elbra." Melku's look turned sympathetic. "But I never learned what became of the Le'elt Kassia. I am glad to know that she is safe. I would very much like to hear how it is that one not of the mesafint won the hand of a princess. And for her sake, I am glad he is a man of *wami ts'shekimi.*"

"You mentioned that Aksum has powerful men without *wami ts'shekimi*. Is there anyone I need be concerned with?"

It was Melku's turn to appear as if he had eaten sour grapes. "Tonight you will meet Kiros Assefe Negus at the festival of welcome."

Kiros. The man who posted a guard outside a fortified door.

"He is also of the mesafint?"

"Yes," Melku affirmed, flicking a glance at Jack before staring off into the distance once more. "He is of the House Assefe, a branch of the Negus' family."

"Separate from the Amare House?"

"Yes, though I will not weigh you down with the intricacies of how our royal houses are intertwined. You need know nothing more than that they are convoluted, and that we have many princes here in Sékra. And since we have no law requiring succession the way you do in Agrius, any of them are eligible to become the heir. The succession can become," he began but paused to think of the word, "messy," he concluded finally.

Another pair of t'ebaks turned onto the rampart just down from where Melku and Jack stood. Their brightly polished armor made them appear bulkier than they really were.

"Let us walk," Melku advised. "We have been standing here talking for too long."

The glint of the highly decorated short swords on the hips of the t'ebaks emphasized Melku's point. Besides, the sweat running down Jack's back had turned from a trickle to a rivulet. He nodded, and they turned as one, heading for the steps leading back down to the courtyard below.

Once they had reached a place of relative seclusion, Jack asked, "You mentioned that any of your princes are eligible to become Negus. Does that include your princesses?"

"You may know that the Negus' daughter Iteya was to follow her father before she died?" Jack nodded, and Melku grimaced at the memory. "She would have ruled well. Too well, I believe."

Melku meant that if Iteya would have been a good ruler, those who were her rivals would not have been pleased. Perhaps treachery had ended her life.

"And as a prince of Aksum, you are eligible to become Negus?"

Melku kept his chin dipped with humility but Jack did not miss the tension his expression revealed.

"Yes," he whispered.

❀ *30* ❀

Betem Jebili
Sékra
Aksum

Jack

IT WASN'T AS IF he'd tried to be late, but he was late. He had lingered after Simon and the rest of the retinue left for the feast, hoping to waylay Cai to learn of any news the boy might have discovered about Isary before the feast. He'd failed, and now that he was here, he hoped Simon would let the potential slight to their hosts pass without comment. After depositing his shoes and weapons as ordered by the door valet into a special niche designed for such things, he tugged at the bottom of his jacket, adjusting the lie of his belt, and crossed under the entrance arch and into the Negus' welcome feast.

Jack scanned the room for Simon, taking in the eight massive columns covered in tiles the colors of earth, fire, and water. They soared into the upper reaches of the lofty room, standing like sentinels at the sides of the opulent feasting hall.

Firelight caught the beveled edges of the tiles on the columns, causing them to shimmer as with a thousand suns. Luca stood watch near one further down the aisle, so he assumed Simon must be near there. He squinted, moving further into the room as he pushed through groups of people.

A massive carpet lay on the floor, and as he walked he curled his toes into the luxurious thickness of it, thankful for the strange custom of leaving one's shoes at the entrance. He imagined having a similar carpet in his own hall and smiled at what he imagined Kassia's reaction to such opulence would be. She would scrunch up her face and toss off an irascible comment, he was sure. The joy of teasing her would easily balance the significant loss of coin to acquire such a luxury. The corners of his mouth trembled with amusement even as a pang of yearning pierced him. He missed his family.

He spotted Melku standing near a group of other Aksumite courtiers and was just about to make his way toward the group when all eyes turned back to the entrance where a crier announced the arrival of the Elbran prince.

"His Most Revered Isary Branimir of Corak, Lord of Brekkell and Prince of Elbra."

The puffed up prince entered the hall, dressed in an elegant tunic of midnight blue and jade. A thin circlet of twisted gold and silver rested lightly on his head. These accessories did not surprise Jack. What did surprise him was the accessory draped upon his arm: Addis, wife to Wigstan of Bauladu, betrayer of kings and traitor of Agrius.

Guests moved immediately to welcome the Elbran and offer greetings, hoping, Jack assumed, to gain some sort of advantage with the visiting royal. Isary greeted each one with flamboyance he was known for.

Simon pressed up alongside Jack and, offering him a cup of something, he said, "That sniveling *putak* can stick his nose up the backsides of those posturing *bakhlid* all he wants, for what good it will do him."

Putak he most certainly was, but Isary wasn't sniveling. The man was as smooth as a fox. Jack quaffed his drink, not bothering to look to see what it was first. He didn't care. It would take the edge off no matter what it was.

Simon and Jack tracked the Elbran prince as he found a place at the table, near as possible to the top. Simon had long displayed the discipline necessary to appear more retrospect while Jack didn't bother. He watched the man with open disgust.

"The Aksumite mesafint don't seem to need much encouragement. You'd think he was here at the head of his own Elbran delegation rather than accompanying an Agrian one," Jack said bitterly.

"That doesn't necessarily mean that the Negus will see eye to eye with him. Keep that in mind."

Jack sniffed and turned away from the Elbran.

"Any success pressing your case for an audience with the Negus?"

"I spoke with a clerk this afternoon, and he was liberal with apologies, explaining that the Negus has been overwhelmed with work. He understands that we have come from a great distance, and he will get to us as soon as he can."

"And Melku has not provided any help?"

Simon was about to reply when another voice broke into their conversation.

"My lords, I offer my apologies for not making your acquaintance sooner than this. There is no excuse I could conceive which would absolve my dishonorable behavior."

A tall, elegant, yet undeniably muscular man towered over Jack. His oiled skin gleamed, and combined with his close-cropped hair and flowing Aksumite robes, he appeared strangely foreign to Jack. As he lifted his arm, the sleeve of his robe slipped away, revealing a telling tattoo. This man was yet another prince.

"My name is Kiros Assefe Negus."

Simon inclined his head and introduced himself and Jack. "Le'ul Kiros, there is no need to apologize. We have enjoyed the generous and gracious hospitality of your city, of your betem, and our needs have been met most satisfactorily."

Simon displayed flawless manners and smooth regard for the Aksumite prince. Had the Chancellor yet formed any suspicions about the man?

Kiros gleamed a bright smile then spread his arm to guide them along the length of the table to their seats. Another man dressed in elaborate robes, his tell-tale tattoo marking him a prince of Aksum, stood at the head of the table. Upon noticing the man, Kiros turned bodily away and back toward his guests.

"You are our guests this night, and we invite you to take your ease and continue to recover from your long journey. Be nourished and entertained, my friends. This night is for you. Enjoy the hospitality of the Negus."

Before he turned away, Kiros tilted his head and took in Melku out of the corner of his eye. "If you have more needs," he added, "you need only ask." He bobbed his chin to indicate Melku who received the duty with grace. Jack wondered at this interaction, wondered what Melku thought of his role as a mere steward.

"We thank you, Le'ul Kiros," Simon returned, "You are most gracious."

After Kiros left, Jack leaned in toward Simon, whispering for his ears only, "I would have liked to know who that other prince was, the one Kiros couldn't abide."

"Presumably another son of the Negus. You can tell by

the tattoos. Every child of the Negus is given one at a very young age, once the Negus has recognized the child as his own."

Jack noted the information. "How does any of this help us find Sybila?"

"It doesn't, but we must play the game."

"Do you think they know why we are really here?"

"If they have Sybila, of course they do." Simon shrugged.

Jack considered this. If Melku had truly befriended him as he'd led Jack to believe, why hadn't he let slip any information about either Sybila or Rebane? Simon had warned him that they may be surprised how matters would go, and indeed the warning had proven true. Everything they'd encountered so far was surprising. It was said that the Aksumites operated with a keen sense of *salay* as they called it, or intrigue. Perhaps it was all a game, despite the label of friendship affixed to their personal relationships.

The arrival of young boys bearing platters laden with meat, bread, and vegetables signaled the beginning of the meal. Servants plied each guest with mounds of the choicest portions, and Jack felt himself begin to forget the worries that had burdened him at the start of the evening.

Very soon, Le'ul Kiros stood. Spreading his arms wide to take in the assembly, he smiled broadly, saying, "It is with a most humble heart that I greet you, our guests from Agrius," he said, nodding toward Simon and Jack, "and Elbra," nodding toward Isary. "I must offer my apologies on behalf of His Imperial Majesty, the Negusa Nagast, Bazin Assefe Amare, that he could not be here tonight. It is most unfortunate, for it is not often that we receive such exalted visitors simultaneously. We offer our gratitude to your visit of friendship and return it with a salute representing our own."

Hardly friendship, Jack thought to himself. *You hide a traitorous skingi from our shores, a skingi who stole away a young girl, and you harbor him here.*

Jack gripped his goblet and scowled, beyond caring that he did not hide his emotions. As Kiros continued his speech, Jack eyed Isary who sat across the wide table from him. Addis saw the look and offered a sly smile of her own, watching back blatantly. She eased more closely into Isary's side, and the Elbran prince turned toward her in surprise. She leaned up to whisper in his ear, and a wolfish look spread across his face.

What a miserable pair those two make, Jack pondered as a cold finger of loathing slithered down his spine. The sooner their cause could be put forward with the Negus the better. Why Simon showed little outward impatience was beyond his understanding. He knew the Chancellor had worked daily to get an audience with the Negus but so far had been unsuccessful. There was much politicking at work, he knew, but he was sick of it. He ground his teeth.

Kiros sat down and dancers entered, spinning and whirling to undulating drums. He had no stomach for their sensual provocations, though Isary seemed to revel in them.

When finally the evening ended and guests began to rise from their places, Jack followed with relief. Taking a cup from a passing servant, he quaffed the contents then all but threw the empty cup into the hands of a different servant, keeping his dark look fixed on Isary the entire time.

Simon noticed his mood. "You look like a man who could use his bed." Simon turned Jack away from Isary and steered him toward the entrance where they found the niche containing their shoes and weapons.

Jack felt unsteady on his feet, so Simon retrieved Jack's things, handing him his shoes first. Jack reached out to take his sheathed dagger from the Chancellor, gripping the leather scabbard detailed with elaborate tooling along its length, but the Chancellor did not let go. Instead, the older man's hand remained fixed, his grip strong as steel. Simon locked eyes with Jack and twisted the weapon to reveal the unique design carved into the pommel's face.

Simon's look bore into Jack, but Jack did not flinch. He grit his teeth, remaining resolute in his refusal to account for what the Chancellor thought he understood.

"Does Kassia know about this?" Simon's eyes flicked to the etched design then back in challenge.

"No. And she never will."

"Does Casmir know? Is it why he sent you?"

"No."

After a moment's consideration, Simon released his grip. Jack flipped the dagger, tucking it into his belt as the Chancellor waved Luca over.

"Let's get back to the *kifili* before the evening turns into something it is not meant for," the older man instructed.

Luca nodded as they turned to go, but Jack did not move. "No, I want to take in some air before I do."

"Jack..." Simon warned, but Jack had already moved off, waved over his shoulder, and strode toward the door. The pair of men let him go.

No one was entitled to an explanation about Jack's past, and he didn't intend to give one.

Starlight glittered overhead, encrusting the night sky like one of Isary's gem-studded sword belts.

Jack breathed in a deep breath, allowing the fragrant night air to flow through him. How long he'd perched on the narrow ledge a stone's throw above a walkway overlooking the gateway to Isary's *kifili* he didn't know. His growing frustration with the stalemate they'd found themselves in and the way the Elbran prince flaunted his connection with the daughter of the Negus combined to put him in a dangerous place. He didn't want to take out his anger on his companions.

He pulled a leaf off the vine that grew near his left hand and chewed it in the way Melku had shown him. It tasted bitter but was good for his teeth, the prince had informed him. He leaned back against the wall behind him, closed his eyes, and crossed his arms as he chewed. The fog that had swirled in his brain during the feast had all but dissipated, and he felt a release in his shoulders.

Jack had left Simon and Luca purely out of irritation, it was true, and then he'd wandered aimlessly. He hadn't intended to come here despite what Simon might have suspected. Despite Melku's warning about traveling inside the betem alone, he wouldn't be in danger. He could take care of himself. Simon had seen the dagger, knew what it meant. And now he understood why Jack was in no danger.

He pulled another leaf and placed it on his tongue, allowing the moisture of it to soak in. He closed his eyes as the earthy bitterness at the plant's heart worked its soothing magic.

The betem lay quiet around him except for the chorus of night birds singing a nocturnal aria. Once again he breathed in the scent of the heady air, rich with exotic scents unique to Aksum. He stifled a yawn, deciding he was ready to make his way back to his *kifili*, when the soft sounds of footsteps padded along the walkway below. It was too dark to make out the identity of the person, but the veiling and robes indicated it was a woman.

The guards outside the *kifili* made no challenge when the visitor slipped in through the gate, disappearing into the Elbran prince's borrowed domain.

Jack touched his dagger, running a single finger along the wooden inlay of the pommel then turned and disappeared into the night.

❊ *31* ❊

Betem Jebili
Sékra
Aksum

Jack

"HELLO, CAI, IT IS good to see you." Jack gripped the boy's shoulder with his hand and ushered his young friend inside. "Does your *lord* know you are here?"

Cai shrugged. "Doesn't matter. He's not in the *kifili* anyway."

"Oh?"

"No, he's been very scarce recently. The rest of the men are bored and most have gone off to find their own amusement. He doesn't seem to have much use for us, and no one knows what is going on." He shrugged.

"You are in good company, Cai."

It had, in fact, been two days since their welcome feast, and aside from their short visits from Melku, a visit to Sékra's market, and their tours of other parts of the betem, they had done nothing of significance. Simon was away now trying once again to petition their cause. Jack's edginess was palpable, and he could sense the same in both Simon and Luca.

"Lord Peares hasn't had any luck seeing the Negus yet?" Cai asked.

"No. These Aksumites don't seem to be impressed by swift action. Melku won't say it outright, but their culture seems to stress hospitality and fanfare. It's as though they want to parade who they are and what they have before we can get down to the real matters. Though, to give them credit, we did come under a guise of friendship and nothing more. Another feast is scheduled for tonight, so maybe we'll get lucky and the Negus will attend." Jack grimaced.

At that Simon entered the room, his brow furrowed.

"What of Sybila?" Jack demanded of him, and Simon shook his head. He flung up his hands. "The longer we let this continue, the longer Sybila is away from her mother and father! We don't know what Rebane plans, and the longer we do nothing, the longer he has to accomplish whatever it is!"

"I understand, Jack. We all do. We are both parents, you and I, and I do not forget the little princess. But you must remember that we are their guests, and no amount of pressure will help our cause. Because we came under the pretense of friendship, with no other political agenda, they must receive us as such, no matter how galling it is."

Simon looked as disgusted as Jack felt. He paced across the room, clearly disinterested in discussing it more.

Jack trudged out into the courtyard with Cai right behind him. Another day brought its blistering heat, so he headed to the fountain and sat on the lip, inviting Cai to do the same. He dipped his hand into the cool water, splashing it onto his face.

"Where has he been, do you think? Your lord, I mean," he asked Cai at last.

"I am pretty sure he has spent his days and his nights with Le'elt Addis."

"You're pretty sure."

Cai nodded.

"And his nights," Jack repeated.

"Yes, they have become..." and the boy blushed a furious crimson shade.

"Lovers?" Jack finished for him.

Cai nodded once more.

"Care for a walk, Cai?"

Jack stood and headed toward the gate with Cai trailing along behind. When the door guard moved in behind them to follow, Jack waved him off. "No, I don't need a watch where I am going."

Isary was up to something, and that something threatened to undo all they had come for. Confronting the Negus with the accusation and proof of his subterfuge involving Taibel Rebane and his kidnapping of Sybila was to be the means by which the Negus would accept Isary as a suitor for his daughter. If Isary had already wooed Addis, there would be no need to coerce the Negus regarding Rebane. That strutting *skeit* would not ruin their chances of success.

"Where are we going?" Cai asked, running to catch up.

"To find Mclku. I am going to find out exactly what's going on, diplomacy or not."

Jack wasn't certain where he'd find the Aksumite prince, but he knew that if he clamored about enough, sooner or later Melku would find him.

The pair crossed a yard full of guards training in full regalia, and Jack nabbed the sleeve of a passing servant, asking him where he could find Melku. The youngster pointed to a tall, elegant building across the square. Jack nodded and strode off.

After passing through a series of rooms and inquiring several more times about where to find Melku, Jack pushed his way past the door guards he knew were there to protect the prince.

When he entered, he found Isary and Melku lounging on couches. Melku looked up, surprised to see Jack.

Isary did not seem surprised in the least, spread a wide sneer. "If it isn't Jack, the blacksmith who now plays at being a lord? Did you get lost trying to find the Negus' smithy?" He laughed heartily at his own joke.

Jack closed the distance between them. "You show up in Prille, fling around words of cooperation and plead for help, yet when you get here you carouse and," he paused momentarily to eye Melku, "bed the Negus' daughter, a woman who is already married to an Agrian noble, and a woman who schemed to have the sovereigns of Agrius murdered!"

At this accusation, Isary stood, and, gently setting down his plate of food, straightened to his full height, staring down his nose at Jack. He was half a head taller than Jack, but the man did not intimidate him. Jack could wield a hammer with enough force to bend steel. This cockerel had nothing on him.

"For all I know, you planned Sybila's kidnapping personally, setting up Addis to force the Negus' hand." Jack clenched his fists at his side, resisting the urge to launch himself at the pretentious prig of a man.

"I care nothing for the little Sajen brat. Is that what you wanted to hear, you soot-covered *anzvíti?*"

"Oh, never once did I ever think you cared a whit for

Sybila. She was only a means to an end, as would have been any child you've brought into the world." Jack bared his teeth as he spoke. "You would have married Kassia conceiving your very own Sajen *brat*. It would have furthered your greedy, insatiable desire for a throne of your own. Once you'd got what you wanted, you would have rid yourself of her."

"A child by that whore you call your wife?"

And then with the speed of a mountain cat, Jack covered the distance between them, knocking over the table in the middle of the room and sending dishes and flagons crashing to the floor. He pushed Isary back against the wall and smashed his fist into the man's face, breaking his nose with a nauseating crunch of splintering cartilage.

"I'll kill you, you Elbran bastard," Jack spit as a red mist of rage blinded his vision. His chest tightened with fury so that he could barely breathe. In the same heartbeat, he gripped Isary's throat and with the other reached down for the dagger at his belt, only to find he could not move it.

"Do not do this thing friend," Melku whispered, holding Jack's wrist with a strong grip. "You are a man of *wami ts'shekimi* -- of honor -- and I would not have you throw away your life for him. He is not worth it."

Jack shook his head, Melku's words coming to him as if through a long tunnel. Isary's face hovered in front of him, the man who abused Kassia, the man who had escaped his fate and justice. Isary watched him back, his eyes wide with a combination of fear and pure hatred even as his life's blood dribbled down his face.

Melku squeezed his wrist, and Jack's vision began to clear. He realized he had been holding his breath.

"He may be a man of no honor, Jack," Melku continued, "but he is a prince, and in Aksum, the punishment for killing a prince is immediate death. I would not have you sentenced in such a way, even for the likes of this one."

Melku seemed to sense Jack's decision, for he released his grip on Jack's wrist. Jack inhaled a deep, shuddering breath and took his hand away from the weapon. Even so, he did not let go of Isary with his other hand. He squeezed the prince's throat more tightly until the man's eyes bulged. Before he could pass out, Jack slammed Isary's head back against the wall with a final crack then released him.

Isary doubled over and began to cough violently, spitting up blood and phlegm.

Jack turned away, his anger drained and leaving him cold and empty, exhausted, as if he had just spent an entire day wielding a hammer in his father's smithy. Without looking back, he made his way to the door where Cai stood watching him with hooded eyes.

From behind him, he heard the scratchy, breathy voice of Isary.

"You're a dead man, blacksmith."

✻ *32* ✻

Betem Jebili
Sékra
Aksum

Jack

JACK THOUGHT OF HIS son Cailen and the infant Tilda as he pushed his food around his plate, leaving it mostly untouched. All around him swirled the activity of yet another feast, with musicians and dancers performing as they had done all the other nights. An image of Kassia sprang to mind. When he'd first met her, he'd been intrigued at her spit and fire. It was only later he learned of her vulnerabilities. He smiled at the way her temper would flare at the merest suggestion that she had any vulnerabilities.

"You have no appetite this night?" Melku asked as he leaned in toward Jack.

"I miss my family, Melku. That's all."

"That is understandable, my friend. One of the downsides, I would imagine, of traveling. Though I have never traveled outside the borders of Aksum, so I would not know."

He offered Melku a weak smile, though his heart wasn't in it. His mood leaned toward the desultory since his altercation with Isary earlier that day. He wasn't sorry for what he'd done. The preening prince deserved his suffering. But it was also just as well Isary and his contingent had not appeared for the meal, for Jack wasn't sure how to handle the public display of his work. Since Isary had stayed away, Jack was given one more night's reprieve.

A new worry entered his thoughts, and it niggled at the back of his mind. Isary could have chosen, for strategic reasons, to stay away. In another day or two, the discoloration and bruising of his broken nose would reach its pinnacle, and he might win some sort of additional favor with the Negus' court. It would be just like him to use the consequences of his own hubris in an attempt to gain sympathy.

Jack swallowed his wine, slamming the cup down a bit harder than he'd intended.

Melku offered him a sideways glance but said nothing. The Aksumite prince had offered little by way of conversation the entire evening, and now they continued in silence for what was left of it. Jack wondered what the man thought of Jack's display of anger toward Isary, but also about the accusations he'd let slip in the process.

"Come, my friend. Let us get away from this stuffy place," Melku said at last, pushing his chair away from the table.

"You couldn't have asked any sooner," Jack returned, pushing his own chair back.

The pair slipped away from the hall, and once outside Jack breathed in the hot, dry air. They turned to head out of the upper ketema and through the lower wards and toward the outer wall of the betem. Melku found the steps leading up to the upper reaches of the ramparts. Once there, Melku led them to a place well away from the t'ebaks on duty.

Jack read the gesture as a way for Melku to discuss something in private, something the pair could not discuss within earshot of the opportunists.

"I am sorry for your humiliation at the hands of the prince of Elbra," Melku offered finally.

Jack nodded, gripping the wall of the rampart with his fingers with such force he thought the brick might crumble. His right hand throbbed where it had struck Isary's nose, but the pain had been well worth it, he'd decided. An easy price to pay for Isary's treatment of Kassia.

"Your Chancellor, he was not pleased with you?"

Jack tipped his face toward the clear, night sky. A swath of stars spread across the heavens from one side to the other, and as he considered the vastness of them, how the sight of them made him and the problems of the world seem so small, he cursed his temper.

"Hardly," he muttered.

Upon returning to the *kifili* after the incident, Simon had been furious at the news. And while the force of his fury had not been pleasant to face, Jack felt a grudging acceptance of it even if he could not quite feel ashamed of his actions. Acceptance, because, as Simon had pointed out, the violence could anger the Negus, giving him reason to send them home in disgrace, and all without having ever learned news of Rebane or Sybila.

"Come with me," Simon instructed him, curling a finger toward Jack in the direction of another room where they could speak in private.

"Jack, I get it. I do." Simon swung away from him, pacing across the dark room. "But you put Sybila at risk when you act rashly. You let your temper get the best of you. If we lose a chance at Sybila because of it," he warned, letting his thought trail off.

"I will take care of it," Jack offered.

Simon swiveled back around, hands on hips. "You have kept your secret well." He nodded at the dagger in Jack's belt. "And I admit that knowing of your past gives me more comfort than I had at first, living in the Negus' control without our other armed men." Jack's hand went unthinkingly to his dagger pommel and the design etched there.

"You won't tell anyone?"

Simon sighed. "The fact that you were trained with the Morthingi? No."

"How is it you are familiar with them?"

"They are a secretive group, it is true. But in order for a troop of assassins to thrive in their trade, they must be reachable. People must know their trade. It's not so secretive as you might think as a group, even if no one knows the identity of the individual Morthingi themselves. Why do you carry their dagger if it concerns you so?"

"I don't, not usually. I only brought it this time, for," Jack began.

But Simon cut him off. "For this journey, because Isary would be with us."

Jack said nothing, admitting Simon's suspicions in his silence.

"Remember how I told you aboard the Árvök that I don't care what happens to that pig of a man once we secure Sybila's safety? I still mean it. You've jeopardized our purpose. As Chancellor of Agrius and the man who speaks for the king and with his authority, I order you to leave the man alone from this point on. Your mission of revenge will not be successful while in Aksum. Let's just be glad Melku stopped you. You'd have been put to death to be sure."

"And if I hadn't been, Kassia would do the work for them when I returned home."

He'd said the last part with a wry grin, lightening the mood. Simon barked a laugh, and the upbraiding was over.

Now, standing atop the ramparts overlooking Sékra below, he would admit none of these things to Melku. If Simon was the only other man alive besides his own father to know of his association with the Morthingi, it was one too many.

Melku took a deep breath, and Jack knew the man would ask the question he'd come so far out of the way to ask.

"Earlier today, you accused Addis of conspiring to have the Agrian king and queen killed. So the rumors are true?" Jack did not look at Melku, he simply nodded then closed his eyes, rubbing his temples between thumb and forefinger. "And you think she might have something to do with the disappearance of your young princess?"

"That is the news Isary brought the court at Prille, yes."

Melku shook his head, his head sinking with the apparent weight of sorrow.

"This news comes as some surprise to you? Do you think she is innocent?" Jack wasn't sure, but it seemed unlikely to him that Melku would think Addis innocent.

"Oh, she is very capable, that is for certain. If she believed there to be some benefit in murder, she would not be held back." Melku grew quiet for a moment, considering. "I will help you find your little princess. If Le'elt Addis is involved, I will find out."

"Thank you, Melku. You are a true friend."

"But until we figure things out, you must be careful. Le'ul Isary does not seem a forgiving kind of man." Melku grew quiet again, and after a moment, asked softly, "Your wife, you love her so much then?"

A bright moon hung overhead, spilling its silvery light over the ramparts and illuminating the small wooden plaque Jack now withdrew from inside his shirt.

"This is Kassia," he stated. "She had this painted before I came here, to remember her by."

Melku examined the portrait for a moment before handing it back. "She is beautiful. But even if she was not so lovely, she is a treasure to be protected. You do her justice in your protection of her."

Sighing, Jack slipped the portrait back inside his tunic.

"Isary could cause you trouble, you know that."

"Yes," Jack replied. "I think it likely."

"And if he does, there is not much anyone can do for you."

Jack nodded. "I should find my bed. I suspect tomorrow may be a long, difficult day." Even as he said it, he felt his fatigue wash over him.

"Indeed, my friend."

Once the two men parted company in the courtyard just inside the upper ketema, Jack turned to make his way back to his *kifili*. The shadows had a longer reach here, were deeper and more penetrating. The night had come on faster than he'd expected. His head hurt, and he wanted to sleep, craving the release it would bring his battered spirits.

A corner loomed ahead, and he paused, his senses pricking, though he'd heard nothing. Steadying his breath, he continued, keeping a sharp eye on the darkness around him.

A foot crunched on pebbles behind him and he whirled. A figure rushed at him, a flash of metal gleamed.

Before he had time to react, the figure collided with him, and he felt overwhelming pain.

Jack pulled away, and a blade clattered to the cobbles at his feet.

"I said you would die, *anzvíti.*"

Jack touched the place where his stomach burned, and his hands came away covered in blood. He looked up again to see the grinning leer of his murderer as the cobbles came rushing up to meet him.

❋ *33* ❋

Port of Lyseby
Honor of Cilgaron
Agrius

A CHILLY SPRAY OF salty water buffeted my face as I stood along the railing of the *Sjórinn Mær* which crested then dipped its way along the northern coast of Agrius, nearing the port of Lyseby in the Honor of Cilgaron. The fledgling summer sun had little power yet over the vast ocean whose icy fingers reached up from the pit of the deep to remind mere mortals of the fragility of life.

I wiped the spray from my forehead, staring pensively at the churning gray waters below, listening with passive interest to Jachamin Guimer explain our plans upon arrival.

"We will lodge first with the magistrate at Parthley Court. Lord Cilgaron is due to arrive in a few days' time to escort us to Croilton."

"That will give me time to speak with Ingólfer alone." I pursed my lips as I considered the arrangements. "How much notice was Cilgaron given?"

"I only sent word the day we left."

I nodded then leaned forward onto the railing. The trip to Lyseby and Croilton Castle had been decided upon suddenly, and there had been little time to plan it, but the decision to notify Lord Cilgaron as late as possible had been strategic. I did not want the man to have time to contrive any pretext concerning potentially treasonous plans which may already be in progress. If he'd hired a mercenary army to his cause of sedition, we would catch him in the act. But first, we needed to discover if the man was, in fact, the author of this sedition.

I inspected the ship just off our stern carrying the soldiers we'd brought from Prille. If there was trouble to be found in Lyseby, Guimer had prepared us well, I supposed. "Make sure the men don't cause a ruckus in town before we piece things together. Carousing soldiers in an already hostile city will only make matters worse."

"And the gods know I don't need matters to get any worse," I muttered to myself as he moved off, the words getting lost in the rush of wind whipping across the deck.

I glanced overhead, taking in the sight of my standard hung from the tall masts marking the ship as the king's.

That ought to send the rats scurrying.

I tugged at my tabard, smoothing the nap of the velvet and fur under my fingers before rolling my stiff left shoulder. The stout brigandine gambeson felt heavy, yet in the coming hours, it would offer me a sense of calm. The greeting awaiting the King of Agrius could only be guessed at, and I would not put much hope in the good wishes of the Lyseby citizenry. I knew how they felt about me.

When Irisa and I had moved to end slavery in Agrius two years ago, we had chosen what we'd believed to be a wiser path in enacting the edict. By staggering the requirements, it would give the affected merchants and traders time to adjust to a new way. Even with the adjustment, most in Lyseby had been hit hard, for the port here had served as the center of the slave trade. The city existed today because of it. Taking its eradication as a personal assault, much of the citizenry boiled in its anger. There was a reason I had not been back here in two years.

I directed my attention back to the churning gray waters below.

Just like men and their fickle affinities. Gray and churning, rising and falling, stinging like salt water...

When I was a boy, I didn't want to be king. That my father was king did not seem a good enough reason to require me to be one too. As I grew older and came to understand the fact that the world just worked this way, I'd resigned myself to it. My father cared little for the position he held, was more interested in the benefits of power aside from the responsibilities. If I had to do it, I would not be like my father. I would rule well.

"My king," interrupted the captain. "My apologies, but if I may?" I turned to find a sailor standing next to the captain. The wiry sailor hefted a rope, staring awkwardly at the decking below my feet as if he wished I was not there and was too afraid to ask me to move.

"Of course," I replied absently, only half-listening and only marginally less caring. "I do not mean to hold you up."

I moved aside, crossing my arms and closing my eyes, breathing deeply of the sea air. Bitter words had passed between me and Irisa at my departure, and while we seldom quarreled, something about our current disagreement seemed more injuring than any other. An aching pang of loss pitted my gut even while a fire of anger burned there.

You have become just like your father, and you will not see it!

Impossible! The only man I despised more than Ildor Veris was my father himself! How could she think I'd ever become like him? She had injured me at a time when I most needed her, when my life had already begun a descent into a darkness I couldn't control. Sybila gone, treason, and threats of civil war... Her words only added to my wounds. The force of the argument punched me in the gut once more, taking the breath from my body.

"Your Grace," a voice interrupted.

"What is it now?" I snapped. Opening my eyes, I found Andreu standing near, his face placid.

"My apologies, Your Grace, but it is time to prepare for arrival."

"Yes, Andreu, I'm sorry."

This ever-faithful retainer did not deserve my wrath. He was a lord in his own right, born of a noble house going back generations. When he gestured that I proceed below deck, I followed obediently.

"I was sorry to hear news of your daughter."

The sentiment was inevitable with the magistrate of Lyseby. The man served as the administrative leader of the city, independent of Lord Cilgaron's rule in the honor because he was appointed directly by the king. It was his business to keep the king's sensitivities in mind. But he was also a long-time family friend. Even so, the reminder of Sybila's loss stabbed my heart every time, no matter who brought it up.

I bobbed my chin in acknowledgment of his polite intent then sipped from the welcome cup before handing it over to my men in turn. "We are actively pursuing the *skingi* who took her," I offered.

"I am so glad to hear of it." Ingólfer turned and indicated the hall behind him. "You are welcome to Parthley Court and the hospitality of my table for as long as you have need of it, Your Grace."

I moved into step with the magistrate as we entered the hall.

"I admit my surprise when word came of your impending arrival. This is no mere progression through Agrius. Your journey has been prompted by something specific, else you would have come earlier." I offered only the ghost of a smile by way of response, and Ingólfer seemed to take the hint. "We will discuss your reasons later, no doubt, though I'm certain I can divine your reason without a seer."

"Indeed."

We sat in cushioned seats as my men bustled around the hall and servants presented trays of food.

"Your Grace, I offer my apologies for the state of my home. You cannot have helped but notice, and it brings me displeasure that you must be hosted in such condition."

As we'd entered Parthley Court through the gate and into the central courtyard, I had, in fact, noticed the workmen, scaffolding, and the condition of the outer ranges beyond the hall. It was impossible not to.

"The changes in the city's fortunes have caused me to alter the course of the renovations I began in the years before..." he paused, and after only a slight hesitation, continued, "...before the slavery edict."

"Which is why I was surprised by the state of the crowds that greeted me along the way." I narrowed my eyes at Ingólfer. "They were clean, happy, and smiling."

"Yes, Your Grace, your people love you."

I swatted away his comment as I would a buzzing insect. "You are not convincing, good sir. I saw the empty slave yards, the ruined districts and crumbling streets. There is little warmth here for Agrius' king. You purposefully brought out only the friendlies today."

Ingólfer looked abashed for only a moment before he recovered. "I thought I would let you adjust under friendly terms before ushering the harsh reality of the boiling pot that is Lyseby, Your Grace."

The fact that the man could have such control over the population communicated the enormous effort it had been. I let my guard down momentarily and offered a genuine smile. "I do appreciate it." I took another sip of the magistrate's excellent wine.

"And it is for this reason you have come," Ingólfer returned grimly.

"Ingólfer, I hold your oath of allegiance, but beyond that, you are a longtime family friend. You served my father as you have served me. I want to know who stirs the pot that boils, and I need to know why you have not yet found the man who holds the spoon." Ingólfer made to answer, but I silenced him with an upraised palm. "I would have Tugredd attend me tomorrow."

Ingólfer dipped his chin. "I am afraid he will not be cooperative."

I raised a brow. "It is not a request. I am done playing games."

❀ ❀

Despite a limited notice and the professed aggrieved state of his coffers, the magistrate of Lyseby provided an ample table that night. A carefully selected and sympathetic group of the city's leading members attended, and once the tasteful but reticent feast ended, Ingólfer and I retired to a secluded corner of the hall. On the far side, my men entertained themselves over games of chance.

"I have sent word to Tugredd, requesting his presence at midday tomorrow."

A servant handed me a goblet filled to the brim. I took it gratefully then lifted it in salute to my host. "To tomorrow then."

Away from the large court at Prille, Ingólfer's hall felt surprisingly intimate. I looked over to spy Wimarc and Jachamin huddled together over a flagon of their own on the opposite side of the hall. Wimarc barked an exuberant laugh while Jachamin slapped the table. "Again!" he howled, and the pair started a new game.

The warmth of camaraderie, the end of a long journey, a big meal, and wine all worked together to relax me more than I'd expected. I closed my eyes and sighed contentedly. Perhaps the journey would proceed more smoothly than I'd thought, considering the circumstances. And perhaps the time away from Irisa would also help settle the shattered peace of my world.

"I do not wish to intrude where I have no business," Ingólfer broke in carefully, and I pried open my eyes, "but I have long been friends with your family. How does the queen in these hard days?"

I clenched my teeth, the tranquility of these last moments shattered. I tried not to show any other sign that the man's question hovered perilously close to the overly intimate. A discussion of my wife was the last thing I wanted to have with anyone.

"She is coping as best she can," I offered flatly, hiding a scowl behind my cup.

"I am glad to hear it." The older man nodded as he drifted back into his own private thoughts.

I hoped that was the end of the matter.

Ingólfer rested his old bones back onto his padded couch, heavy jowls hanging over his collared tunic, his eyes half-closed as if sleeping. But I knew the sharp mind sheltering behind bushy brows and under the smoky-gray mop of hair on his head. I had long regarded Ingólfer as perceptive, a good judge of men and capable administrator.

"Your wife does you honor in her rule. She is a credit to your house."

"Indeed," I replied, wishing to discuss anything else but Irisa. I took another deep drink of the sweet wine, allowing the flavor of rich berries to linger on my tongue.

"My wife is gone these last five years, may the gods keep her," Ingólfer continued, oblivious to my souring mood.

I stared into my cup, swirling the contents like the Whirlpools of Frenau in the wilds of Dalery. "And free of harassment these last five years, I would imagine," I muttered under my breath.

Ingólfer's eyes snapped open, the intelligent, searching look I had come to know so well fixed on my face. The man saw the deepest parts of my conflicted soul, it would seem, and for some reason, it angered me. My fingers curled more tightly around the decorative pewter of my goblet.

"You may be the king," Ingólfer replied gravely, his eyes sharp lancets, "but you are young. Young enough to be my son." He paused to consider his next words, and I steeled myself for a rebuke. "Even so, I will withhold the advice I might give a man of lesser rank concerning the peace of a home, and his duty to keep it."

I took a deep breath, berating myself that I'd allowed my desultory mood combined with drink to loosen my lips. The state of my marriage was of no concern to anyone else, least of all the magistrate of a troublesome city, be he family friend or not. Even my oldest friend had meddled where he wasn't welcome. A muscle twitched under my eye, and I inhaled slowly. "It is late," I said, pushing myself up from my seat. "I am beyond tired and should get to my bed. I will need my wits about me on the new day."

"As you wish. My man will show you to your rooms, such as they are."

An elderly steward led me along a long corridor then up a tall, narrow flight of stairs. Rough-hewn stone lined the walls, doing nothing to promote a feeling of domesticity, and the impotent light from the man's lamp did little to dispel the deep darkness as we went.

Seems fitting.

I found the chamber given me, and though Andreu had already set a fire to burn in the narrow hearth set into a wall, there was little else to cheer it beyond a few brightly colored bed hangings.

Ingólfer did not hedge when he warned me of the dismal accommodation.

A sense of grim amusement washed over me as a valet helped me prepare for bed. After tending to a few other duties, I slipped into the cold bed, falling into an instant, fitful sleep.

❈ 34 ❈

Parthley Court
Lyseby
Honor of Cilgaron
Agrius

THE THIN LIGHT OF morning spilled into my chamber, and through my window, I could just make out the hazy smudge of the distant mountains beyond the foothills surrounding Lyseby. A brisk wind embattled the heights where Ingólfer's manor stood. The window rattled, and tiny drafts seeped in, stroking my skin like the searching, grasping fingers of a courtier.

I half turned away, and from the corner of my eye, I viewed Wimarc casually sprawled in a chair, his legs askew over the side. His hair hung about his face in disarray, dark smudges under his eyes as a man who'd found little sleep. I wasn't about to ask what activities had occupied his nighttime hours. The young lord popped a date into his mouth and straightened, leaning forward in his chair as Jachamin entered the chamber, ready to listen to his friend give his report.

"Alright, Jachamin, what news do you bring that Wimarc craves so much to hear?"

"Tugredd will not come. The messenger was whipped for his trouble before being sent away."

A growl of rage ripped from my throat, and I lashed out to smack the worn surface of the sideboard with a flat hand. "The man is a freeman and master of a non-existent guild!" I turned and stalked across the room. "The letters patent for his slave guild were repealed with the edict, and yet he dares defy the Crown in such a way?" I swung back on the two men.

Wimarc stood, his eyes dancing. "Casmir, the man knows your weak position. He knows you wouldn't dare come against him with force. It would start a war, and he knows you will not do it."

"Will I not?"

"Your Grace," Jachamin broke in, his mien unusually conciliatory. "If you would allow me to offer a suggestion?" I turned on him, my mood predatory. "Send me as a messenger. I will make a second attempt to order his attendance."

"And if he has you whipped?"

Icy coldness replaced the mercenary's previously conciliatory look. "He can try, but he will not succeed."

A silent message passed between us, and I gave a curt nod.

The door closed on Jachamin's retreating form, and I turned to Wimarc. "And you approve?"

"Does it matter?" he replied jauntily, picking up the dish of dates and crossing the room with it, stopping at a randomly selected seat and dropping into it.

I threw up my arms then swiveled my head back and forth as if searching for something. "There is no one else here, and it seems to me that you accompany your king in an advisory capacity. So yes, it does matter. I wouldn't have wasted my breath to ask otherwise." I jammed my fists into my hips, my eyes boring into the young lord.

Wimarc appeared unmoved by the caustic mood of his king. He tilted his head, sending his mop of dark blond curls bouncing. "Of course I approve. The Council in Prille, this journey of diplomacy..." he waved his arm around the room, "all have their place. But every king needs a man to do the jobs no one else wants to do. Jachamin is efficient. He will get you to your ends."

"Despite the means?" I studied Wimarc, searching for artifice. The young lord lived a very carefree life. Always quick with a joke, and an easy companion, nothing seemed to dampen his spirit. Perhaps this was the reason I found the man appealing. Did he see no darkness, only light in every possible situation? Maybe at such a time, this was good enough.

"I hope you are right."

Grimacing, I moved to make my way to the door. Wimarc jumped up and clapped a hand on my shoulder. "So serious. Come now, and you will see. Everything will work out fine, and you'll come out of this polished and gleaming like a shiny new cuirass! We'll be home to Prille in no time."

"Any word yet from Jachamin? It should not have taken a man with his skill this long to acquire the guildsman's cooperation. He is a professional, or am I mistaken?"

Another day had passed in the magistrate's hall, and while the time had been pleasant, little had happened other than the coming and going of city men bringing me their complaints and petitions. I grew ever impatient. Wimarc seemed little bothered, however, stood now in the light of a bright morning sun munching on imported fruits from the magistrate's board despite the older man's attempt to staunch the flow of the expensive delicacies when he thought no one could overhear his instructions to the servers.

Wimarc shrugged. "No, Your Grace, but I trust he will have news soon."

I narrowed my eyes. "You know something?"

"I wouldn't dare speculate, my king," Wimarc replied, his eyes glittering with poorly veiled eagerness.

I would have pressed the case more except that a man pushed into the hall, making haste for Ingólfer. Dropping to a knee, the newcomer caught his breath before speaking. "Ships, my lord. Cilgaron is here."

I turned my attention to the door, as if the baron would stride into our midst at that very moment.

"Thank you, Emeric," Ingólfer offered, then turning to his steward instructed, "Make ready the hall, and with haste!"

"No." I ran a hand along my unshaven chin. "I will receive Lord Cilgaron in the back garden rather than in the hall where the audience will be a casual one, of friends. We will save the more formal knee-bending for another time."

Ingólfer considered the plan, grasping his hands behind his back in thought. "As you say, Your Grace, but will the lack of ceremony feed any animus he may hold against you, to have his position dismissed so lightly?"

I lifted a brow. "Are you aware that he holds animus against me?"

"No, I know no such thing. I only thought..." He dropped his eyes.

"If the man claims loyalty, it should not matter. He will have his opportunity for show once we reach Croilton. I know his penchant for a display of wealth. He will be given the chance, I assure you. I simply want to talk with him. Until I know more from Tugredd, I will call him to task but will not accuse. It seems reasonable that as the lord of Cilgaron, he must have a finger on the pulse of the unrest in his honor, should he not?"

"Of course, Your Grace."

"My questions should not stir any suspicion. If he is as innocent as he claims, that is."

Situated under the overreaching bows of a centurion tree, I rested my head against a high-backed, cushioned chair. Tapping my signet ring on the polished mahogany armrest, I forced my breathing to slow, my legs to still their restlessness. Not normally one to balk at conflict, something about the coming encounter clothed as polite repartee twisted a small corner of my gut. Kings weren't supposed to be nervous, were they? Perhaps my decision to make the lord of Cilgaron wait to be received had not been a good one. Even so, it could not be undone.

After being notified of Cilgaron's arrival in the port, I'd retired to my chambers to have Andreu prepare me for the audience, and to design my approach to a conversation that would come off as entirely casual and spontaneous. Until more news came from Jachamin regarding Tugredd, it wouldn't do to rile the man. When the entourage pulled up at the gates of Parthley, I had asked Ingólfer to greet the man in the hall while I pretended to be busy. I'd wanted the older baron to grow anxious. The reality of the matter was that I'd paced my chambers, unsettled even as I'd hoped Cilgaron would be.

A group of men entered the back garden now, coming

around a neatly trimmed hedge, and I straightened.

Aksel, baron of the Honor of Cilgaron, led the way, his cloak flying behind him with each purposeful stride. As he drew nearer, he slowed, measuring his steps as would a miser begrudging the giving of a coin. When finally he came near enough, he lowered himself to a single knee, performing the obeisance with graceful flourish.

The game was on.

"My lord of Cilgaron, you surprise us with your unexpectedly sudden arrival."

"Your Grace, my deepest apologies for the lack of notice, for I had not intended to arrive as quickly as this. I was away when I received word of your coming. As luck would have it, events conspired to bring me here sooner than I anticipated. My daughter saved me two days' journey by agreeing to come directly to Lyseby from Croilton."

For the first time since his arrival, I noticed a young woman in the lord's entourage. Of medium height and with a rounded figure, his daughter resembled her father with her dark hair and eyes. She stood confidently at the back, watching the exchange between me and her father with fierce curiosity.

"How fortunate."

I switched my attention back to Aksel, Lord Cilgaron. The wealth of the man kneeling before me surpassed that of any other nobleman in Agrius. Dressed in the finest cut of cloth, and adorned with lavish ornaments, he'd spared no expense in making sure others knew all too well his power and status. Of an age with Ingólfer, his mostly salty gray hair still maintained evidence of its chestnut color from his youth.

"You know why I have come," I began finally, still not inviting the baron to stand. "I have heard disturbing reports out of Cilgaron, and Lyseby in particular. Cilgaron is your honor, my lord. Why have you not brought it to heel?"

Aksel flicked a dark look toward Ingólfer, but only momentarily before returning his attention back to me. "Tugredd," he began, but I cut him off.

"Tugredd is... *was*... a master of a trade guild, *not* a baron owed knight's service. He cannot summon an army, nor can he hold a manor for a king. You can. This is why you have your position, your lands and titles. Again, I repeat, why has he not been brought to heel?"

The baron kneeling before me shifted his weight, clearly uncomfortable with his extended obeisance. Still, I kept him there.

"Your Grace, if I may..." Cilgaron's daughter stepped lightly toward us, immediately dropping to both knees next to her father. Keeping her head lowered, she slanted her gaze up at me through thick lashes.

"My king, may I present my daughter, Helene?" Aksel introduced.

"Lady Helene, do you have something to say for your father?"

"Your Grace, my father would take more vigorous action, but I have cautioned him against a harsh chastening of the guildsman. It is in the best interests of the Crown, Your Grace, to tread cautiously lest a rebellion be stoked where diplomacy might succeed. He has done all within his power to try to garner an accord with the city and the guildsmen in particular."

I hid a look of astonishment at the eloquence of the young woman kneeling before me. Instead, I kept my face schooled into passivity. Something about her reminded me of Irisa. Her straightforward nature perhaps? And her keen mind? She certainly did not bear resemblance to Irisa, for she was dark to Irisa's light, her frame more rounded than slight.

Dark lashes framed dark eyes hovering over rounded cheeks pink with the exhilaration of the moment. Indeed, she presented a pleasing enough appearance to persuade any man to look twice.

"Your father is wise to consider the counsel of those around him." Motioning with my hand, I indicated that the pair rise to standing. "Is it common practice at Croilton to be advised by this lady of the manor?"

"When the lady is as wise as she, my king," Aksel said, a slow smile of satisfaction curling the corners of his mouth.

I returned his smile. "Please," I began, rising from my seat and inviting the lord and his daughter to walk the magistrate's gardens with me. "I would hear more of the mind of the Lady Helene on these matters."

Taking Helene's arm and falling into step beside Aksel, I peppered the pair about the events transpiring in Cilgaron since the edict.

❊ *35* ❊

Parthley Court
Lyseby
Honor of Cilgaron
Agrius

GOLDEN HAIR SPILLED DOWN *over a small shoulder. Her face turned back and beamed, an impish smile brightening her features. She flung her head, tossing the flowing locks in a manner like her mother. A carefree ripple of laughter spilled from her lips as she ran. "Lizzie! Lizzie!" she called. "Play like Lizzie!" I followed, my arms reaching as the girl danced and skipped, still laughing as she leapt out of reach.*

A chilly wind blew in, and the laughter deepened in pitch, Sybila's childish giggles turning somehow grim until finally, the laugh did not belong to her. The voice cut the air, like a shriek from a malevolent specter, and a fierce yearning ripped my chest. Shadow overtook the light, and the air bit my flesh like points of a dagger. Her outline faded inside a swirling fog, and as I pumped my legs to find her, grasping and straining to reach out with open arms, they came up empty.

"Casmir..."

The whispered words came right at my ear, the

softness of breath tickling the hairs against my skin. I sat up in an instant, alert to danger, and though the disturbing dream dissipated, my heart continued to beat wildly. Within a moment my head cleared enough to realize that danger would not have awakened me first to warn of its coming.

"Come with me, and put this on."

The room lay under a blanket of complete darkness save for the brightness of the light which Wimarc carried. After a moment for my eyes to adjust, I focused on the pile of drab-brown clothing in his hands.

"What is this about?" I rasped back at him.

"Just trust me."

The young lord of Dalery tossed the pile onto the bed. I looked at it, dumbfounded for only a moment then rose and dressed.

Without a word, Wimarc slipped out the door, and I followed close behind. The corridor outside my chamber stood empty, and the cool night air pricked at my skin through the thin fabric of the tunic. While my mind whirled with the confusing thoughts of the dream which had battered my sleep, curiosity drove me on. When finally we passed into the streets beyond Parthley Court, I stopped to demand an explanation.

He shook his head noiselessly, finger to his lips. "Do you imagine it would be good for you to be discovered alone, out here on the streets of Lyseby?" He turned back and continued on.

After nearly an hour of walking through deserted streets, we came upon what looked to be an abandoned inn. Going around to the back, Wimarc opened the door to the undercroft and led me into the darkness.

My step nearly faltered as the sole of my boot slipped in a puddle of something I was certain I did not want to identify. I swept my arm to the side to brace against the damp wall. Producing a key from somewhere inside his coat, Wimarc unlocked a thick door, pushed it open, then thrust his torch inside. A rush of fetid air greeted us as we entered the tiny chamber.

Jachamin waited for us, casually prying the point of a slender knife under his fingernails to clean them as he leaned his sinuous frame against a wall. The room was empty except for a table holding a burning oil lamp. A small door set into the back wall stood opposite to the one we had just entered.

"Why am I here, and why in the middle of the night?"

"Were you otherwise occupied, my king?" the mercenary asked, his tone waspish.

"I was asleep," I snapped back.

Jachamin straightened and flipped the knife back into the sheath at his belt. "Well, I have something to show you."

Turning, the mercenary took hold of the handle to the other door and pulled it open, swinging an arm to invite me to peer inside.

The second room was darker than the first, but enough light spilled through the open doorway to weakly illuminate the figure of a man, naked from the waist up. He sat shackled to a chair, head hanging on his chest. It didn't take a seer to prognosticate the identity of the individual in the dark gloom.

Tugredd.

I pushed a lungful of air through compressed teeth and turned, waving to indicate that Jachamin close the door. I wished I could hide my frustration and fear, but I knew my eyes hinted at my conflicted emotions.

Jachamin took my silence for what it was: an invitation to explain. "You wanted the man to attend you. He would not. I did what I needed to do."

"You beat him. He is still alive?" Jachamin's hard eyes

did not change, but his mouth thinned into a bloodless line. I took it as confirmation and sighed, turning away. I ran my hands through my hair as an aid to thought as I paced across the room. "Did anyone see you take him?"

"No, Your Grace." Jachamin's reply came through clenched teeth, as if affronted that I would even ask.

"Don't you think anyone will find it a coincidence that their king arrives at the same time this man goes missing? This man suspected of stirring rebellion?"

"Should it be an issue? You are king. You do what you want."

"I ordered discretion! We are here to put an end to trouble, not begin it!"

"Which is why we arrived with a show of force?"

I shook my head and expelled a sharp breath akin to a growl as I paced away from him. I could not argue his point. I had been persuaded before our departure to arrive in strength, showing the city a sign of my royal power. That I had sanctioned such a brutal action to one of the citizenry would complicate matters unnecessarily. Tugredd was a burr in my side, but the action reeked of something my father would have done. The people would not miss the connection.

I turned back. "And what have you found out?"

"Tugredd is a fool, just as Geres of Glenna was, but at least Glenna saw enough sense to back out when he sniffed danger. This one...." Jachamin flung a look over his shoulder. "He had a prime role in inciting the city."

"What was the end goal?"

"War."

I snorted. "Has ever a king sat a throne without someone trying to take it from him? What else?"

"He is not the man you are after. Not ultimately."

"Of course he's not. Did he name the author of this

sedition?"

"Lord Cilgaron," Jachamin confirmed. "Just as you suspected. Now you have proof."

"That *skingi*, that duplicitous, conniving son of *Rækallin!*" I bared my teeth as I spat the words in my fury. Even though I knew my suspicions would ultimately prove to be true, a small doubt had still remained that it might not be true. My fists curled into tight balls. "Take me back to Parthley. I travel with the beast back to his lair tomorrow, and we shall see whether or not he will choose to reveal the bones of his victims, or if he will continue this farce."

"And what would you have me do with this one?" Jachamin asked as I turned to leave.

I barely heard the man. Blood lust coursed through my body, pounding and surging like rushing waters as sung by the bards telling old warriors' tales. "I care not." I waved dismissively. "Do what you need to do, as you have already done. It's too late now in any event."

I pushed past Wimarc and made my way out to the fresh air of the still, dark streets, not stopping until I reached Parthley.

A familiar ache shot through my shoulder as Andreu fit my brigandine around me and adjusted the fastening straps. I grit my teeth and hissed, and Andreu eyed me. The man never missed anything, but rarely did he comment. I adjusted the lie of the linen shirt underneath by tugging to smooth it as Andreu fit a light, open tunic over top the brigandine.

A door opened behind me, and I turned, expecting to find Wimarc with news of our readiness to depart.

Another man stood in the door frame. I did my best to

hide my surprise.

"Bauladu is missing its lord," I observed casually.

Wolf returned my cool regard with his own banality. "And my king is missing one of his advisers."

Irritation wrestled with the comfort and familiarity of seeing my old friend. He was meant to be in Bauladu, should have taken my suggestion that he return home. Most men would take their king's suggestion as an injunction to obey. But not Wolf. He had defied the normal course of things as if by right of friendship.

As I remonstrated with myself, Wolf peered critically at Wimarc who had entered behind him and watched our exchange with passivity. Finally, Wolf drew a deep breath, standing tall, as if daring me to send him home because of his implied insubordination.

"You missed the first feast with Lord Cilgaron."

I said the words off-handedly before turning away, but not before seeing Wolf duck his chin, hiding a smile as he correctly interpreted my statement as an invitation for him to stay. I had not forgiven him, but we shared too much history together. I needed him even if I wouldn't admit it out loud.

"Yes, well, my apologies, Your Grace. It took me a couple of days to find a merchant ship heading north since you left without me."

I compressed my lips. "You are just in time to accompany us to Croilton. No need to unpack."

If he hoped to rest up, he would be sorely disappointed.

❀ ❀

The sun rose that morning into a fiery red sky. Rain would come later. Clouds moved in off the sea and would follow us, would even overtake our train of palanquins as we traversed the road to Croilton Castle, a day's journey from Lyseby.

I pondered the day from within the shadow of the manor's portico, lost in thoughts which echoed the augury of the rain. As was my lot of late, I had slept little the previous night, haunted first by the images of the guildsman in the makeshift prison then ruminating over how to extricate myself cleanly from the repercussions of Jachamin's reckless actions.

Whether Tugredd was directly complicit in treason or not didn't matter; at least not to the citizens of Lyseby. He was one of their own. Tribalism would always protect the guilty if he was one of their own. And soon enough they would find out that a leading member of their citizenry had gone missing. Once Cilgaron caught wind of what happened, the resulting tumult could only work in his favor, aiding his cause.

I knew that worrying over such matters now would serve no purpose, but trying to rationalize away the notion only worked in the daylight. I could not control my dreams.

Those of my men who had been lodged in the town rattled into the courtyard, and the peace of the morning shattered. I paced along the arcade to the far side to get away from the commotion, my fingers knotting and unknotting as I worked through the best way to approach the scheming baron on the journey to Croilton.

Helene approached from behind so quietly I did not hear her until I turned.

"Lady Cilgaron, did you sleep well?"

"Well enough, Your Grace. Thank you for asking. And you?"

"Not well enough," I admitted, though I couldn't suppress a smile. A person could not easily maintain a dark countenance around the Lady Helene. Lord Cilgaron may be a vile man, but his daughter was a ray of sunshine.

"I am sorry to hear that," she replied. And she did look sorry. With round eyes of concern, she studied my face, taking in the dark rings around my eyes. "But I do have good news for you, and I hope it will ease your weariness, even if only a little." She turned a brilliant smile on me. "My father has asked me to travel with you in the palanquin in his place while he travels in another. He suggested that my company might be more enjoyable than his own more august presence." Her smile turned conspiratorial, and she added, "That just means he is old."

I could not help but laugh at her surreptitious manner. While I had planned to ride with Cilgaron and Wimarc, beginning what would be a long discussion of our business along the way, I had to admit that the reprieve I'd just been handed was far more appealing.

"I would be delighted to accept your company," I replied, paying her back with an easy smile.

Grooms prepared the horses to bring along behind us, and I could hear their industrious preparations as they loaded wagons with supplies and our belongings to travel with the horses. Our route would take us through the foothills, higher into the heights to the fortress that was Croilton Castle. The journey would be much more leisurely and comfortable in the palanquins, and with the company of Helene, even more so.

As courtesy required, I took her hand and placed it on my forearm then escorted her toward the awaiting palanquin where burley palandiers stood at the ready.

I turned to the nearest man and patted him on the shoulder. "Deliver us safely, good sir."

The palandier turned startled eyes toward me. "It is my pleasure, Your Grace," he replied uncertainly, though the obvious pleasure of my gratitude showed on his face. That the king had addressed him directly would be a tale he would share with his friends and family and anyone who would listen for years to come. For my part, the kindness had cost me nothing.

Once Helene was comfortably situated, I boarded, followed by Wimarc and Wolf, and we set out, following the road west and into the fields green with early summer growth.

"My king, you are a most surprising man." Helene studied me openly. "Your wife should feel very fortunate, and I hope she knows the treasure she has in you."

I fought back a frown, wanting to keep the intent of her remark on the forefront of my mind. Somehow mention of Irisa seemed out of place here. And with that determination in place, I felt my spirits rise considerably, surprised that the approval of the daughter of Aksel of Cilgaron should matter so much to me.

❊ *36* ❊

Owl and Lute Tavern
Prille
Agrius

6 years ago

"CASMIR, THE COUNCIL HAS debated the subject of your marriage since you were knee-high to a grasshopper. Why this sudden recoil now that the discussion rages anew?" Wolf sopped up the last of his stew from the bowl and eyed me, waiting for my answer.

I brooded over his question. It was true that the Council had begun formal negotiations regarding my marriage to a young woman from foreign shores. There was no way to explain to Wolf that the event was not something I considered worth celebrating. If anything, it felt a trap, forcing me into an arrangement of misery and imprisonment, just like my own mother and father. Why would anyone welcome such a state?

Wolf reached forward to grab the flagon, but a passing serving maid noticed and grabbed it before he could. She offered me a beguiling smile as she leaned forward a little farther than necessary to fill my cup. I looked past her into the shadowed corners of the room.

Wolf studied me for a moment, confused. "Casmir, this has been coming all your life. It's a necessary part of being a prince. I cannot see why any man would balk at the choosing of a mate. Why has it set you off just now?"

Why indeed? It wasn't new. I had never anticipated the event.

The serving maid seemed undaunted by the conversation between us, and even less so by my disinterest in her. Rather than go about her business, seeing to the other patrons in the unusually packed alehouse, she leaned her weight onto the table, bending toward me to trail her fingers through my hair.

"Because," I began, pulling away from the serving maid's roaming fingers. I flicked her an irritated look, but she persisted. How to explain such a thing to a man who welcomed any and all female attention? It wasn't as if I didn't desire it, but I had seen my father overindulge his lusts too much. I wanted more than the casual affections of a tavern wench. By the gods, but swinging a blade in the training yard was easier than trying to explain myself.

"It's about your father, isn't it? You're afraid you are going to be just like him."

His suggestion sent my mind immediately to my father's latest distraction: a nicely-curved maid with piercing green eyes. I scowled at the image of her holding her hand possessively on my father's shoulder, and Wolf laughed, slapping me on the back. "Forget about all that for now. We came here to enjoy ourselves." He peered up at the serving maid and offered his own smile. "So enjoy yourself!" He waggled his brows at her, but the woman ignored him, offering the entirety of her attention to me.

Wolf flung up his hands. "How can I even begin to compete with a prince?" He sighed and slumped back in his seat.

"You don't have to," I returned, pulling the woman's hand from my collar and turning her toward Wolf.

"You are making my job as your friend much more difficult than it needs to be, but I'll go along with it for now."

Fighting back my rising irritation, I fired back, "I'm going back to the palace. Stay if you wish."

"You can't do this to me!"

"Do what?"

"As your friend and protector, I am honor-bound to come with you!" I rolled my eyes at the remark, but Wolf pressed on: "Why? Why can't you just stay and have some fun? Or, if you insist on not having fun, you can just sit here and not have fun while I have fun!"

"I am tired of being scrutinized."

"You say that as if it's a bad thing," he returned dryly, lingering a lascivious gaze up and down the woman.

I gave the woman a fleeting look. It was true her face was comely enough, her figure more than appealing, but I looked away and shook my head. Setting my goblet down heavily on the filthy table, I stood, turning to leave.

"Can I bring her home with me?" Wolf tossed after me.

I waved a hand over my shoulder. "I care not what you do."

❊ *37* ❊

Croilton Castle
Honor of Cilgaron
Agrius

A VELVETY WASH OF twilight purple cloaked the skies from one horizon to the other as our train of horses and palanquins traversed the sloping causeway into Croilton Castle, the ancestral home of the barons of Cilgaron. Royal pennants snapped in the rising winds carrying the tang of the oncoming rains, the musky yet fresh scent of moist air enveloping us as we reached the great gate. I thanked the gods that we arrived at the safety of this bastion just ahead of the downpour.

Despite the threat of the pursing storm, the journey had proved inordinately pleasurable. As the sound of trumpets blasted news of our arrival from the heights of the ramparts, a whisper of disappointment breezed across my awareness. Our journey had come to an end, and it would now be time to enter the pit of the viper.

"I hope you will find your accommodation suitable.

Your coming was sudden. With more notice I would have done more to prepare appropriately."

Helene dipped her chin, self-aware. While it was possible a more imperious king would take her comment as criticism as a lacking on my part, Helene had demonstrated her forthright manner, and I was convinced it wasn't possible for her to employ guile like most noblewomen. No, Helene was certainly an innocent, naive at best, and most certainly harmless.

"I am certain your preparations are more than adequate considering the suddenness of my coming. For that I am grateful. Now I look forward to washing away the dust of the road, changing into fresh clothing, and eating a hot meal."

She lowered her head again, a motion I had begun to realize she did habitually. A light rosiness colored her cheeks, another effect that my presence seemed to produce.

I mused on this only until we entered through the inner gate into the cobbled court, and the sounds of clattering hooves and the jostling of soldiers faded into the half-light.

Lord Cilgaron had only just disembarked his palanquin and now stood waiting to welcome his king into his hall. I resisted the urge to bare my teeth and instead pulled myself upright, placing a convivial mask over my ire.

"Your Grace, you are most welcome to my home," the lord said, dropping to a knee as he bowed his head formally once I'd descended from the palanquin. Behind me, Wimarc helped Helene down, and Wolf trailed just behind.

"It is good to have arrived."

I indicated that he stand. "Come into my hall and be welcome. When you have been refreshed, my steward will show you to your apartments. I hope you will find your time here well worth your long journey."

"You are very gracious," I added, the corner of my lip

curling into a snarl I was certain the man had not seen. "Indeed, it will be worth it."

Croilton's hall had been updated much over the years. Begun by one of the earliest kings of Agrius, Croilton Castle had long guarded the trade route from the port of Lyseby to the northern parts of the island kingdom for those coming by sea rather than over or around the mountains in the interior. The barons holding this castle had grown extremely wealthy, and most had not been shy about displaying that wealth by way of constant upgrades made to this thoroughly modern castle: its comforts, and not least of all its defenses. Having the lord of Cilgaron as an enemy was not an appealing prospect to any king of Agrius.

Despite Helene's warning that she had not had much time to prepare, the hall glowed with readiness. Aromatic and lavish beeswax candles adorned the length of the great tables up and down the hall while braziers burned herbed fragrance in the corners.

A simple but satisfactory meal had been laid for us, and we dined with little fanfare. A more extravagant meal would be laid the next night, as was tradition.

"Your daughter does not give herself enough credit," I said as we relaxed over the food.

"In what way, Your Grace?"

Aksel selected another morsel from a platter of partridge and hare between two delicate fingers, his eyes alight from both praise and drink.

"She claims that she had done little preparation, and yet I see a hall bustling with hospitality and a table spread with fine food. It would seem to me as though her supposed lack of preparation would humble many a great house."

I picked up my goblet and raised it in Helene's direction. She brought her fingers up to touch her neck, the flush of pink on her cheeks proving her pleasure. Roswen, the lord's mistress, sat farther down the table, boldly watching and listening. The angle of her head and the straightness of her spine showed she did not miss much, nor did she care to have her own contributions excluded.

"I am certain that she was guided by the expert hand of the Lady Roswen." I nodded in the woman's direction, and she repaid the acknowledgment with a genuine smile of her own.

Well beyond her prime, it still did not take much imagination to find hints of the beauty she had once been. Aksel's wife, Adenora, had many years since died, but in all the years she had been lady of the manor, she had endured the presence of Roswen as her husband's mistress. Adenora's beleaguered status had been public, for Roswen had been one of her own ladies-in-waiting.

"We are humbled by your kind words, Your Grace. And we would be hard-pressed to find more worthy company." Aksel smiled before taking another bite, but his look held less pleasure and more calculation. If a snake could smile, I imagined it would look like the lord of Cilgaron.

Time eventually came to retire. Bone weary and full to the brim, it was with great relief I greeted the castle steward who offered to guide me to my apartments.

"There is no need, sir, for I would be happy to show the king to his accommodation." Helene glanced over her shoulder at Roswen who stepped up behind her.

The older woman delivered a smile of encouragement rather than of censure. "And I would accompany you as well."

While highly unusual and questionably imprudent, I

nodded my agreement. "That would be most kind, thank you."

Wolf stepped in beside me, flashing me a look of warning, but I moved away from him and took Helene's hand on my arm as courtesy would have it.

The women led us outside the hall and across the Isle Court to the grand staircase leading us up into the private residence in the eastern-most range of buildings. A door opened into a luxurious outer sitting room with a plush carpet spread over gleaming wood floors. Intricately carved wood paneled walls hid behind thick tapestries. Two high-backed chairs embroidered with woodland and mountain scenes sat in front of a wide hearth. The west wall boasted two enormous bay windows with window seats and pillows for the comfort of its occupants.

"My father has given you his own rooms for your use while you are here."

Helene stood just inside the door, her hands folded primly before her. Roswen moved into the room to adjust a cushion.

"These windows face the gardens," Roswen added helpfully.

"I look forward to enjoying the view in the morning when the sun displays their splendor," I offered, smiling at Helene who returned my smile with a dimpled one of her own.

"I will send to check on you later, to see if you have any other needs."

She peered up at me with somber, innocent eyes as she spoke, and the room fell silent. It was only after she left that Wimarc and the rest of the men burst out laughing. "Needs indeed! I have needs! Would she see to them, do you think?"

Wimarc slapped me on the shoulder, and the rest of

the men ribbed me. Ignoring them, I poked my head into the bedchamber finding that, as with the rest of Croilton, not a speck of luxury had been overlooked. A solid wooden canopy surrounded the top edge of the bed with blue velvet hangings around it. Other chairs and chests, tables and furnishings had been finished with similar exquisite details as had the furnishings in the sitting room. Andreu had already laid out my things, and it looked as comfortable as my own apartments in Prille.

The men still told bawdy jokes while spinning overly hopeful tales of planned exploits when I returned. Wolf sat apart from the group, unusually sullen. I shared a cup with them despite my fatigue then excused myself to the privy. Another raucous joke flew in my direction and at my expense as I went, and I laughed good-naturedly, waving it off.

When I'd finished, Wolf waited for me.

"You walk a dangerous path, Your Grace."

I scrutinized his face, looking for the meaning in his words. He did not break his stare.

"It is the destiny of kings, I've found," I returned ambiguously, "to find danger in every shadow. Danger seems to me to be unavoidable."

"Always so enigmatic when you want to avoid talking about something, aren't you?" He crossed his arms and stood in the doorway, blocking my exit.

"And what subject do you believe I am trying to avoid?"

"Casmir, you mislead with your friendliness."

The accusation froze me. "You would have me be unpleasant toward my host?"

"Toward your host? Certainly not. Use diplomacy as you see fit. There is just no reason to be overly *enthusiastic* in your interactions with others of the household."

"You mean Helene."

I made to move past him to rejoin the other men, but Wolf put out a hand to stop me.

"Those men," he waved a hand in the direction of the sitting room, "may not expect much of you. In fact, everything they would sanction is probably common enough. But I do."

I barked a laugh. "You, of all people, dare to upbraid me on the subject of fidelity?" I turned and crossed the room, stopping in front of the window.

"I was not the man Addis deserved, it is true. But I have eyes to see, and so do others. You parted with Irisa in anger, and Helene is... here."

"This lady is not the first to conspire for my attention, I can assure you. And she will not be the last." I gripped the narrow ledge of the window frame, puffing out a blast of hot air to cloud the window. "You are like Lizzie who has chased her prey and lost it to the wrong thicket."

"And you are tempting fate."

I wheeled on him. "What do you mean? What have I done?"

"It's not what you have done, it's what you have encouraged. The entire journey here, you gave the young woman entirely too much of your attention, warmed too much under hers."

"What would you have me do, ignore her? There were only four of us!"

"Casmir, there is a fine line between praise and invitation."

I frowned. "I do not see how my congeniality could be misread in any way." A roar of laughter broke out in the other room and I glowered in that direction.

"When have I ever shown that I would act on such an

impulse?"

"When have you ever had something worth losing?" He moved toward me, his eyes serious. "I do not speak of intent but of breaking point. I only imply you are just a man, are not impervious to every enticement. I do not speak to accuse but as a friend."

"Then you should know when you push too far."

He made a face I could not decipher except for an element of wounding. He spun and left me standing alone.

❋ *38* ❋

Croilton Castle
Honor of Cilgaron
Agrius

THE NEXT MORNING REVEALED a grand view of the manicured gardens beyond my windows as the Lady Roswen had suggested there would be. By the time I dressed and prepared to ride out of Croilton with its lord for a tour of the surrounding countryside, a small entourage of my own men had finally gathered. There was no sign of Wolf.

Wimarc only shrugged, unconcerned, when I inquired of him. A groom overheard and offered, "He rode out at dawn this morning, Your Grace."

"For the journey home?"

"Not that it appeared, no. He did not say where he was going."

I felt provoked enough by Wolf's unusual and somewhat overbearing concern for me the night before to make me glad I would not have to face more of the same on the new day. I welcomed his companionship at Croilton, but not his censure.

"Your Grace, if it please you, I will take you first to see my new fisheries. I am most certain that the innovation of it will amaze you!"

Lord Cilgaron spoke in his smug way, and yet the self-satisfaction of his manner mixed with an innocent glee in his words, like a child in a bake shop viewing its delights. I almost forgot my anger with him.

That afternoon and the afternoons of the three days that followed found me closeted with the lord's advisers and officers, hearing accounts and reviewing summaries of the estate management, along with tales of the goings on throughout Cilgaron in the last months. Secretly I hoped that Cilgaron would implicate himself, cowering before me in a hasty, tumbling confession of guilt after the discovery of some unexpected proof; but in this, as with so much of late, I was disappointed.

At the end of the third day, another summer storm moved in just in time for the evening meal which, despite myself, I had found myself looking forward to more and more each night. Lord Cilgaron had so far proved himself to be a worthy host. I could not fault him for his generosity of provision or his choice of enjoyable entertainment. And though I would not admit it to anyone else, the real source for my eagerness had more to do with anticipating the presence of the delightful Helene who served a cure to the soreness of spirit her father provoked.

This night exhaustion threatened every sinew and muscle as Andreu fitted the last piece of my attire. Little had been accomplished, and my mood felt all the blacker because of it. The storm was just as well, for it mirrored how I felt inside. I all but stumbled to the hall for the evening meal, thinking my mood may be improved soon enough by the company.

Much to my great delight, I found Helene seated at my right hand rather than her father as had been the case the night of my arrival. When I asked her about it, she replied that her father thought I might be missing my queen and that while Helene was no substitute, I might enjoy the meal better in her presence rather than his own.

After her bewildering answer, I peered down the length of the table to the place Cilgaron sat next to Wolf, deep in conversation. They remained so throughout the meal, though now and then Helene's father cast surreptitious glances our way.

"Your Grace," Helene broke in, "if I may, I would offer you a cup of something you may not yet have had reason to taste in Prille."

A server stepped forward with a tray holding a delicate crystal goblet filled with a rich, golden liquid as minstrels played a jaunty tune. "This is normally served after the meal, but I admit that I am too impatient for you to try it."

I took it, curiously studying the color of the liquid. I took a sip.

"I have never tasted its like. What is it?"

"It is a distillation of the choicest wine of Elbra. My father has procured the vintage for many, many years, and only recently stumbled upon this concoction."

"What do you call it?"

"Raki, some call it, while others who have tasted it say it is named brandi."

"Lady Helene, I thank you for introducing me to raki!"

I toasted the young woman and took another sip, letting the rich flavor seep over my senses, very quickly leaving my limbs awash in a light, free feeling. Her father caught my eye and smiled, raising his glass of raki in salute.

The musicians moved off, and a storyteller took his place. Obviously, a man well-known to the lord's hall, the gathered assembly applauded wildly as he began his tales. As the evening wore on, he moved from the tales of heroism and high adventure to riddles with a broader appeal:

> *"I war oft against wave and fight against wind,*
> *do battle with both, when I reach to the ground,*
> *covered by the waters. The land is strange to me.*
> *I am strong in the strife if I stay at rest.*
> *If I fail at that, they are stronger than I*
> *and forthwith they wrench me and put me to rout.*
> *They would carry away what I ought to defend.*
> *I withstand them then if my tail endures*
> *and the stones hold me fast. Ask what my name is."*

"An anchor!" someone yelled.
"Indeed, good sir!" The bard applauded.
"Another!"

> *"My garment is darkish. Bright decorations,*
> *red and radiant, I have on my raiment.*
> *I mislead the stupid and stimulate the foolish*
> *toward unwise ways. Others I restrain*
> *from profitable paths. But I know not at all*
> *that they, maddened, robbed of their senses,*
> *astray in their actions --that they praise to all men*
> *my wicked ways. Woe to them then*
> *when the Most High holds out his dearest of gifts*
> *if they do not desist first from their folly."*

Many guesses came from various places in the hall, but

the answer was wine.

I sipped more raki, watching the festivities of the hall, the communal enjoyment of the lord's lavish hospitality. Wolf had disengaged from Cilgaron and sat watching me. I looked away.

> *"A thing came marvelously moving over the waves,*
> *comely from the keel up. It called out to the land,*
> *loudly resounding. Its laughter was horrible,*
> *awful in its place. Its edges were sharp;*
> *hateful it was, and sluggish to battle,*
> *bitter in its hostile deeds. It dug into shield-walls,*
> *hard, ravaging. It spread mischievous spells.*
> *It spoke with cunning craft about its creation:*
> *"Dearest of women is indeed my mother;*
> *she is my daughter grown big and strong.*
> *It is known to men of old, among all people,*
> *that she shall stand up beautifully everywhere in the world."*

"'Tis my wife!" shouted a drunk man at a lower table. The entire room burst into laughter, and several other suggestions flew, most of them with less than virtuous undertones.

Finally, someone called, "An iceberg!"

The singer proclaimed it to be true and moved on, but I had lost the thread of things.

A blessed numbness chased me with the flowing raki, bewildering the disunion of my spirit. One conversation after another blurred into the next, leaving me with the feeling that I watched my own actions from afar. At one point I realized that Lord Cilgaron had moved to my side, opposite Helene, though I had no memory of him having done so. The combination of drink and fatigue worked against me, and I tried hard to keep my focus on what the older man discussed.

Whatever the subject matter, I knew that it angered me, for an inexplicable fury heated my core even though I couldn't form a coherent thought as to why.

Cilgaron dismissed himself, and I turned to find Helene leaning in toward me.

"Your Grace, I'm sorry that my father upsets you so. I wish I could do something."

I shook my head, my thoughts cloudy. I knew a reply was necessary, but, for some reason, conscious words would not form on my tongue. I finally managed to utter something in return, but whatever it was could only have been meaningless, platitudes most likely. A thunderous crash sounded outside the hall, indicating the storm had increased its fury. Rattling rain blew at the window behind us, shaking the very frames.

"It must be so difficult for you," she added softly, her eyes round and full of sympathy. She leaned in closer to my ear, and I caught a whisper of scent on her hair. "Being away from your wife, your daughter missing. I cannot imagine the agony you must feel."

In the fog of my mind, I felt a delicate hand on my knee, found Helene peering at me. Something about the touch stirred a memory. That first night after I'd met Irisa, the night she came to my chambers in disarray. It had been far too late for propriety, and I'd been drinking. My muddled mind struggled that night just as it did now. Irisa had aroused a desire in me, and it was only my better senses that had beat down my impulses, and that only through enormous effort.

I pulled my thoughts away from the memory. I missed Irisa too much. Glancing around at the emptied hall, I realized it must be obscenely late. Wimarc and Jachamin, as well as Lord Cilgaron and a handful of my men, remained, sitting in opposite corners, each of them casting appraising glances from time to time. Wolf was nowhere to be found.

I turned back to Helene. Removing her hand from my knee, I mustered as much neutrality as I could and murmured, "My lady, I thank you for the wonderful evening. I must be away to my bed. The rigors of travel and your wonderful raki have taken their toll."

Without waiting for her reply, I stood, shakily making my way from the hall and into the Isle Court. I knew a guard followed, though the thought skirted only around the foggy edges of my awareness. A deluge had broken from the sky, and rain pelted the walkway, dousing my hair and clothes as I went. I'd made it only halfway across the court when my bladder screamed at me for relief, and I ducked into the darkness of a small alcove. When I'd finished, I re-oriented myself and steered in the direction of the grand staircase leading to my apartments. At the top of the steps, I turned and traversed the antechamber, turning onto the corridor leading to my door.

I had nearly reached it when I found my way barred, and I collided without thought into soft flesh. Rain dripped down my face and neck, running in a rivulet down my back between my shoulder blades as I uttered an apology as if through stranger's lips, my mind somehow oddly disembodied from my voice. I tried to move around the obstruction, but it moved with me.

Helene.

"Your Grace," she began, then added tentatively, "I... You left in such a hurry. And the rain... I was concerned for you, that you might not make it back safely." Her hair was as wet as mine, tendrils of it clinging to her cheek. A droplet of water ran off her chin and down her neck toward her wet gown which clung closely to her curves.

She leaned in closer, tilting her chin up. The paleness

of her face and neck showed milky white in the darkness of the corridor, and a thrill ran through me. I backed away from her, but she followed, and I found myself backed up against the coldness of the wall behind me.

She pressed closer.

I took a quick breath, perceiving for the first time her flesh, warm, soft and inviting. I breathed in more deeply and found her perfume intoxicating, stirring memories of Irisa.

Irisa.

Visions of my wife flooded my mind's eye... her lustrous hair falling about her shoulders as she stood in the light of the fire late at night...

My eyes drifted down to take in the rise and fall of her breasts with each breath. Heat flooded me.

She put a hand on my chest. "Your clothes are sodden."

Before I could make sense of my swirling memories, she trailed a finger up my neck, and her arms came around me, bringing our bodies tightly together. My mind felt muddled, the corridor swirling. Hands roamed my body, and I swallowed back a moan, my legs leaden, my body disobeying my better sense.

Why couldn't I think straight? I didn't want to think straight, but I couldn't escape the alarm ringing somewhere in my head.

This wasn't right.

Irisa's face swam before me. My resolve wavered.

Kisses, soft and light, trailed along my neck as hands fumbled to find the fasteners of my clothing. A precipice loomed, and I felt the earth give way, the edge crumbling under my feet.

The sound of a latch releasing...

"Your Grace? Is that you?" came a male voice.

A sliver of golden light poured into the corridor, revealing the upturned face of Helene before me. The cold dawn of reality washed over me like a bucket full of mountain spring water.

Thank the gods for Andreu, I thought as the logical part of my brain finally kicked in.

I caught Helene's hands, gently but firmly pulling them up and away as I eased her backward. Her breath came in uneven, ragged, gasps, her face flushed. She gave me a look of confusion turning suddenly to embarrassment and then anger.

"No, Helene. This won't happen. Not with me, at least."

She opened her mouth to protest, and I stopped her with a look that brooked no argument. "Go find your chamber and get some rest." I'd said it more calmly than I felt. My insides shook. "Find a bedmate if you wish, but I will be sleeping in my own chamber. Alone."

She snapped her jaw shut, then swirled in a tight circle and strode off.

Andreu held the door open, and as I passed by him to enter my chamber, the chamberlain would not meet my look.

"Shall I leave and give you a moment, Your Grace?"

"No, Andreu. Stay. Please stay," I said weakly, defeat seeping into my bones.

"Shall I help you prepare for bed?"

"No, not now. Find my lord Wigstan and bring him here."

No doubt he found my choice of Wolf's given name surprising, but as was his way, held himself in check. "As you wish."

I grasped for the nearest stool and slumped down onto it. Leaning forward, I thrust my dripping head into my hands to bury my face in my palms. My own breath was ragged, and

I worked to slow it.
How big a fool could I be?

❈ *39* ❈

Croilton Castle
Honor of Cilgaron
Agrius

HELENE HAD MOST CERTAINLY intended to waylay me, that much was obvious now. Had her father put her up to it?

The raki. It was a distillation, she'd said. Clearly, she understood its potency and had used it as a means to blunt my judgment, ease me into a compromising state of mind. And yet I had allowed it to happen, had not attempted to guard against it. That was my shame. Had Andreu not chosen to open the door at that moment...

Wolf arrived, and Andreu excused himself, silently pulling the door closed behind him as he went.

My friend had not yet been abed by the look of him. Still dressed in the same attire from the feast, he stood unmoving by the door, giving only a nearly imperceptible flick of his look toward the bed as if expecting evidence of some kind.

The moments passed.

As king, a liaison with the daughter of Lord Cilgaron would have been barely questionable behavior, raising few eyebrows. The keeping of a mistress was a common enough thing, as the lord of Cilgaron so readily displayed, and as the son of Bellek Vitus, it was almost expected of me. Or at least it would have been by those who did not know me well enough for it to matter.

The look Andreu had given me as I entered my chambers was bad enough. What would have been Irisa's reaction? How would I ever have borne the heartbreak I would have found there?

I took a shaky breath, running my hands through my hair.

"I have been a fool," I admitted at last.

"Yes, you have."

Wolf grabbed a flagon and pulled up a stool next to me as I explained what had happened in the corridor beyond my door. He listened in silence, his hand alternating between clenched fist and limp as an eel.

"I don't deserve Irisa," I admitted bleakly.

"I told her as much myself when last I saw her, as I have done many times in the past. And I would happily take her off your hands any time if you just say the word."

His lips twitched, the old Wolf back once more. He poured a cup and offered it to me, but I shook my head.

"What have you been about during your days rather than attend me with Cilgaron?"

"I thought my time would be better spent snooping about rather than add my nose to the backside of that puffed up mackerel."

"And did you find anything useful?"

"Rumors mostly, only scant suggestion of evidence."

When I looked hopefully at him, he added, "But I want to look into it more before I say anything. I can't have you do something rash before I'm sure."

I spread a slow smile, feeling somewhat better, even if only a little.

"I hope it turns into something, for I have made little progress here. The man is slippery as an eel." I stared at my hands for a moment to gather my thoughts. "If I could take back what happened tonight I would, but it has given me an idea. Since I know what Helene is about, I may have a use for her."

A look of both concern and amusement flitted over Wolf's face. "As you wish, but..."

"Just trust me in this. What I want you to do is to take Jachamin out with you tomorrow." He pulled a face, but I continued before he could argue. "I know you don't care for the man, but he is sworn to me. Say what you will of him, he is discreet, and as much as I hate to admit it, he gets results. I trust you to be the voice of reason. Keep him from being overly heavy-handed. I will see to things here."

"Ah, my king, you look as though you had a rough night! Sleep poorly, did you?"

Aksel, Lord Cilgaron strode toward me across the gleaming tiles of the hall, his smile broad, his arms outstretched as if in greeting. I did not rise from my seat.

Lord Cilgaron laughed and gave me a conspiratorial wink, as if he had every expectation that he knew what his king had been about in the wee hours following last night's carousel in the hall. It was likely he'd been the instigator behind Helene's intended night activities. Clearly, he hadn't seen his daughter this morning, or he would have known the truth of the matter.

I bestowed a thin, humorless smile on the man. *The miserable son of Rækallin.* "My chamberlain helped me prepare for bed before I spent the next couple of hours poring over missives from Prille." My look dared him to argue.

"Indeed?"

I heard doubt behind his words.

Good. Let the man wonder, and let his daughter explain to him later how she'd failed to trap the king.

I broke a piece of bread off the loaf and chewed slowly as he offered parting words and left me alone to speak with one of his men. I smiled to myself as I watched him. If the man wanted to play games, we would play more games. Today would bring the hunt, but my interest was not in hunting the hart but the traitor. We had the admission of Tugredd, but we needed more proof if Jachamin's overly harsh treatment of the guild master proved fatal. I only needed word back from Wolf and Jachamin who had ridden out well before the dawn.

It was very early still, and few had stirred from the comfort of their beds after a late night of festivities. A young servant bustled over with a plate of cheese and fruit, and to my great relief, the scant few who entered the hall after me seemed particularly inclined to conversation.

I had just brought a bit to my mouth when a crash sounded behind me. I whipped my head around to discover the source of the commotion and found a small child, not much different in age from Sybila. She had knocked over a stand with a basket of bread. A harried maid grabbed the child's hand and kindly but firmly redirected her before going about her wearied business.

I readjusted my seat so I could better watch the girl. She was small and very thin, wore a well-patched tunic and a light kerchief on her head. Stray wisps of hair escaped from under it, a darker shade of Sybila's. A pang of yearning pierced my heart as I followed the mite as she made her way around. Clearly not the child of a lord or any of his retainers because of her ragged appearance, no one seemed much concerned with her well-being. She was fed and clothed, yes, but that seemed the extent of her care and nurturing.

Just as I began to wonder who her father might be, the girl surprised me by making her way toward me, confident at first, but then more uncertain when she saw I had noticed her. I grinned at her in encouragement, and finally, she reached me, putting a hand on my thigh. I scooped her up, setting her lightly on my lap.

Once I'd settled her comfortably, a young maid shrieked her alarm, rushing over to me. Bobbing an apologetic obeisance, she uttered a shaky "Your Grace," clearly befuddled at her nearness to the person of the king, but also at a loss to know how to snatch the child away.

"Your Grace," she stammered. "Forgive me! Brigid should not have bothered you. She was causing such trouble in the kitchens, and we thought she could play up here in the hall for a time since the hour is so early. Just to give us a break, you understand. I will take her now if it pleases you," she stated, less a question than a fact.

"But why disturb her when she is so content?" I nodded down at the child who had settled back against me, snuggled into the crook of my arm. She fiddled with a buckle, entranced by its complexity. "She does not do my buckle any harm, and I am happy for her company. You do me no disservice."

The maid forgot herself for a moment and tilted her head to the side, opening her mouth to speak, only to close it again, self-aware at speaking so intimately with her king.

"Whose child is this?" I asked gently.

"Brigid is an orphan, born to a slave who died after..." the maid began, but then realizing to whom she spoke, stuttered to a stop.

"After?"

"Her mother died after the edict, after being freed. It was when everyone was upset and took it out on the slaves they were forced to let go. But the lord allowed Brigid to live here because Brigid's mother was his..."

She looked away embarrassed by what she was about to say, so did not finish the thought. I had a suspicion I knew what it was and did not press her. A stab of my own sort of guilt pierced me regarding the girl, for it was not the first of such stories I had heard regarding the treatment of slaves after the edict.

Once the maid regained her confidence, she continued: "We took pity on her, Your Grace, on Brigid, and have tried to raise her here, with help from all the maids. We do what we can for her, sire."

She dipped her head with a look of shame mingled with fear that she'd admitted too much.

I looked down at the child sitting comfortably on my lap. She had ceased playing with my buckle and rested her head on my chest, asleep. I wrapped an arm around her to keep her from falling then slipped a thin, gold ring off my little finger.

"Take this," I instructed. The maid's eyes widened into globes the size of a dinner plate. "Use this for her care, to feed and clothe her in the future. If anyone asks, tell them your king requires it, and that in addition, I will require a periodic accounting of her well-being."

She nodded mutely, and I moved my arms for the maid to take the child.

I watched them move off, a renewed pain surging in my heart. If I could not help my Sybila, perhaps I could help this little one.

Even as the pain washed over me, a new resolve formed itself in my spirit. I would settle the matters of Lyseby, and I would get home to Prille, back to Irisa and the business of finding Sybila. If my men were not back from Aksum, I would go myself. The foolishness of last night, while disturbing, had served a purpose, sharpened my resolve. I would tend to the traitor Cilgaron then shake the dust of Lyseby from my boots.

No matter how painful or wounding our dispute had been, I loved Irisa, and together we would work through it. We would tackle matters together as we'd always done.

❋ *40* ❋

Bellesea Palace
Prille
Agrius

Irisa

MOIST, HEAVY AIR WEIGHTED the night, and bolts of lightning streaked across the sky to the north. The rain would come soon, Irisa thought to herself as she brought a deep lungful of air into her body, smelling the tangy-sweet scent of the rain yet to fall. She closed her eyes and listened to the rumble, as if the gods themselves clashed in anger. Though thunderstorms were infrequent in Corium, she'd always loved them as a child, for the rage of the storm brought her an unexpected and inexplicable peace. She hoped the storm would persist through the night, for her nights of late could use some peace. Just then, a bulbous drop of rain splashed onto the balustrade of the balcony on which she stood. Turning around, she retreated indoors, back to the overflowing pile of correspondence awaiting her reply.

A timorous voice spoke from the other side of the room: "Yar Hátin..."

Irisa looked up to find a young scriptstóri standing uncertainly just inside the door, a stack of books in his hands.

"Thank you for bringing those to me. I admit that I have felt overly exhausted in recent days. Your delivery of these renews me, even if just a little."

She bestowed a smile on the young man, and in his uncertainty, his fingers fumbled around the edges of the books. Rather than try to engage him in more conversation, she directed him to set the books on a small table close to the bed so she could read them when the inevitable difficulties of finding sleep came as it did many nights. He stared at her wide-eyed, as if the thought of going anywhere near his sovereigns' bed terrified him.

A wave of pity overcame her. "Here, I will take them." Glancing quickly at the pile, she noticed several items she had not requested.

"Are you certain you intended all of these for me?"

"Yes, Yar Hátin. The Ballad of Trardreer is very much like the Ballad of Capaleon which you requested, except for a few subtle differences in style. I thought you might enjoy comparing the two."

He had spoken boldly at first, his interest and passion for the subject matter obvious. Quickly he turned self-aware, as if realizing it was not a close-acquaintance to whom he spoke. His previous confidence dissolved.

"I thank you, Master..." Irisa prompted.

"Annor, Yar Hátin."

"Master Annor." Irisa repeated the name to herself to help her remember it then offered a brilliant smile, intending to put him at ease. The gesture seemed only to make the young scriptstóri uncomfortable, for he fumbled with the folds of his robes, twisting the fabric between anxious fingers. "Thank you for your service. Your recommendation is most welcome. I look forward to reading it, though it might be quite late tonight." She gestured broadly to a nearby table piled high with parchments then added softly, "Ever since Sybila went missing, Casmir and I have been receiving messages from all over Agrius from people offering their comfort. I want to reply to them all, and as you can imagine, it takes a great deal of time."

She wasn't sure why she shared this with the young man, but he looked kind, and his quiet demeanor seemed to welcome confidences.

"So many condolences..." he sputtered. "Your daughter is much loved." He shuffled his feet awkwardly.

The comment surprised her coming from one appearing so ill at ease. Irisa nodded even so, and Annor took in the sight of the parchments once more, swallowing hard.

She walked toward the door. "I keep you from your rest, master. Likely you have had a long, hard day." A valet opened the door. "Thank you again, Master Annor, for your consideration and thoughtful recommendation."

When he had gone, Irisa looked to the pile of correspondence then back to the table at her bedside. A crack of thunder sounded overhead, rattling the windows. Rain struck the panes of glass outside with a fury, and she yawned. Turning to her bed, she sought the ballad Annor had brought her and decided to read instead. It would be a welcome distraction from the loneliness of another night with Casmir away.

The next morning she sought out the Bibliotheca.

"Grand Master Conrad," she greeted, offering the Grand Scriptstóri her hand as he bowed over it.

"My queen, I greet you." He released her hand and, searching her face, wrinkled his brow. "Your Grace, you needn't have come personally. You could simply have sent for me, and I would have been happy to attend you to provide updates on our work here."

"That's not necessary, Master Conrad," Irisa assured. "It has been far too long since I have visited, and I quite enjoy the break from my other duties."

"As you wish."

He swept his arm to the side as invitation for her to follow him across the cavernous main room, chatting about the various projects in process and the groups of scriptstórii who worked in earnest concentration. Finally, he stopped at a table near the bright light of an eastern-facing window where a small cohort of scriptstórii worked over piles of parchments in varying states of damage.

"The restoration work continues, though the progress is not swift, for the work must be carefully done." He directed her to a pile at the furthest end of the table. "These were the most heavily damaged in the fire, and we are not certain how much can be restored." Irisa nodded her understanding. "There were many fully burned, of course, but there is much that is only smoke damaged."

"Yes, of course, and my expectation is that you only do your best."

She knew the work would be slow, but it was also necessary. During the reign of Bellek Vitus, Casmir's father, the scriptstóri worked to purge the record of all traces of her family, the Sajen line. Nikolas Sajen, her grandfather, and the king who was overthrown by the coming of Bellek, had been a wicked man. Slavery, a long-standing trade in many kingdoms, had been expanded by Nikolas, the trade in human flesh broadened to involve enslaved humans as meat for bloodsport in public amphitheaters. Bellek put a stop to the practice, and the history of his predecessor had been all but cleansed from the Bibliotheca. This cleansing had enraged Irisa. While she did not approve of what her grandfather had done, she thought the practice of cleansing the history of its truth equally disturbing. It was this conviction which moved her to instruct the masters of the Bibliotheca to see how much, if any, of the histories had survived, and what, if anything, could be done to recreate what had not survived.

"What cannot be restored will be recreated to the best of our humble abilities," Grand Master Conrad continued, "from memory and our community knowledge."

In truth, the Grand Scriptstóri was being overly modest, for the scriptstórii of Agrius were known the world over for being elite intellectuals. While the Bibliotheca was not an overly large institution in terms of the number of scriptstórii working within its walls, it was highly selective, taking only the best minds. It was their knowledge which separated them from mere clerks.

"Our best scholars will work on the histories."

"Of course, Master Conrad," Irisa encouraged. "And please, remind those who work on it not to flower the truth with words designed to please me. I want as accurate an accounting as possible. We owe our children and their children nothing less. We cannot change what happened, but it would be folly to allow future generations to become ignorant of it."

"As you wish, Yar Hátin."

Irisa took time to peruse the work of the scriptstórii masters, and just as she was about to leave, she spied a familiar face working in the far corner.

"Master Annor, what a delight to see you this morning!" The young scriptstóri startled, nearly tipping over his small pot of ink. Grand Master Conrad watched curiously but said nothing. "I wanted to tell you that you were absolutely correct in your recommendation. The Ballad of Trardreer is indeed very much like the Ballad of Capaleon, as you suggested. In fact, I think the bard who composed it was even more clever! I am indebted to you for your wisdom in bringing it to me. I slept more soundly last night than I have in weeks."

Grand Master Conrad brightened at the praise of one of his younger scriptstóri. "Master Annor is a very promising young man, and we are very fortunate to have him here at the Bibliotheca, even if he was brought here by the former master, Orioc. Though Annor can hardly help that, can he?"

The grand master said the name Orioc coolly, with no more critique of the man's unworthiness. Irisa appreciated his restraint, for the reminder of the former master of the Bibliotheca, the man who had murdered his predecessor, Master Lito, brought a sour taste to her mouth. She smiled thinly.

"Grand Master, I have been thinking to acquire the services of a scriptstóri, to serve me personally. With the king away, much more rests on my shoulders, and it is all I can do to keep up even with clerks. I wonder if I might borrow Master Annor? I will not take him away from you at all hours. Perhaps just in the evenings. And only for a little while."

"Of course, Yar Hátin," the Grand Master replied. "I will send him to you this very evening, in fact."

"But Grand Master..." Annor protested.

"Annor," the Grand Master interrupted, patting the young man on the shoulder, "you have been granted an honor. To serve our queen directly... this is a duty that many in this room would welcome eagerly."

In fact, most of the scriptstórii sitting nearby appeared to fight feelings of jealousy for most could not hide the surreptitious glances they tossed one another and at Annor. Irisa felt slightly guilty for putting them in this position, but she liked the placid nature of the young man so stood by her choice.

"Thank you, Master Conrad." Turning to Annor, she said, "I will see you later this evening."

He offered her a weak smile, and she turned to offer parting words to Grand Master Conrad before returning to her chambers.

Much later after the evening meal, when Irisa had retired to her apartments to begin work on her nightly correspondence, a knock sounded on the great oaken door. An under-steward directed Master Annor to where Irisa sat working at a table near the cool night breeze blowing in from the outside.

Irisa looked up to find the young man standing uncertainly before her, a satchel strapped over his long white scriptstóri robes.

"Please take a seat, Master Annor. I would like you to sort then record these as I've already finished with them. You can take them to the Bibliotheca to record when you are finished."

The young man said nothing, simply nodded his head and got straight to work. After some time, Irisa realized the late hour.

"Once again, I must apologize to you, Master Annor. I have kept you far longer than I intended. Please forgive me." She rose and invited Annor to stand as well. He did, but he cast her furtive looks, not moving toward the door. "Was there something else?"

"Yar Hátin, my pardons, but..." Annor unclasped the satchel he carried across his body and reached inside, pulling a leather-bound book. "I came across this and thought you might like to see it."

"What is it?"

"It is a journal that belonged to the old Grand Master. I looked through it," he stammered suddenly cautious, "just enough to see what it was. It has a history of your family, and not one damaged by the fires. It was tucked away and not part of the current project, so likely you have not seen it."

"Where did you find this?"

"As I said, it was tucked away. Hidden." His eyes shifted when he spoke. Did she sense a spirit of guilt in the young man?

She ignored his seeming equivocation for now and took the bound journal with gratitude, examining the cover and remembering it as she had seen it the day Master Lito showed it to her.

"I thank you, Master Annor."

Perhaps in time, when she read through it, it might cast some light onto the mysteries of her parents, the stories Grand Master Lito had never been given a chance to tell her. She would set it aside for now.

The bigger question seemed to be why this young scriptstóri chose to bring it to her. Why were his emotions so conflicted over it? He knew more than he was saying, there was no doubt. It could well be, perchance, that Annor held a key to a mystery. She would discover it sooner or later.

❊ *41* ❊

Betem Jebili
Sékra
Aksum

Jack

FOG SWIRLED IN HIS brain, like carded wool, its fibers elongated, sinuous. As if swimming from the bottom of a murky pond back to the surface, it took every force of his will to push through it, to recognize real thoughts from the churning and roiling of confusion.

With a heave of effort, Jack tried to move what he thought was his arm. It felt somehow detached from his body, but the attempt met success, and he moved his other arm. How was it that he felt as feeble as a newborn kitten? Sitting up to take stock of his surroundings seemed like a good idea, so he focused on moving his legs, compelling his muscles to move the left one first. Immediate waves of fiery heat and agony coursed through his midsection, and the loud moan that issued forth out of the darkness must have come from his own throat.

A disembodied voice spoke from somewhere next to him.

"Jack, lie still, lad."

He knew that voice. If only he could piece together how he knew it.

Then he remembered he had eyes. He opened them painlessly. That was a good sign at least.

He scanned the room, but there was not much to discover. Darkness cloaked his surroundings, though whether it was the darkness of night or tight curtains to shut out the day, he could not determine.

"Rest easy."

The voice again. Except this time the fragments fell into place for him.

"Simon... what happened? Why do I feel as though I met the wrong end of a flanged mace?" he croaked through parched mouth and cracked lips.

A cup touched his lips, and he sipped, inviting the cool liquid to soothe and cool him.

"You are not too far off the mark, son. You were stabbed, though fortunately that young squire, Cai, found you almost immediately and sent for Melku. He ordered a court physician to treat you, the same churgion who attends the Negus himself. He examined and cleaned your wound then stitched it. You lost a lot of blood, and there was worry you would not make it. You have been given medicine to help you sleep. You will need it for all the blood you've lost. You're likely to be weak for some time."

"Isary. It was Isary." Jack croaked, nearly choking on the name as he said it. "He meant me dead."

Simon leaned in, and Jack could see the drawn lines of concern tighten. "You are certain it was Isary?"

"I am as certain of that as I am of my own wife's love." *He will try to do you harm just because he can.*

Simon smiled, his amusement at odds with the circumstances. "And it was your wife's love that saved you, most likely." When Jack appeared thoroughly confused, Simon laughed outright. From somewhere near his bed, Simon produced the wooden painted portrait of Kassia; the one Jack had been keeping just inside the folds of his tunic. "Fortunately for you, that *skingi's* motion deflected off this. His angle was awry, so the thrust did not go deep. There has been damage, yes, but you mostly bled like a stuck pig."

Jack adjusted his position and it felt like the dagger pierced him anew. He winced. "How long have I been here?" he rasped.

"Two days."

Jack shook his head, still attempting to remove the cobwebs from his brain. By the gods, but he felt weak! And the smell! He wrinkled his nose, noticing for the first time a ripe odor of moldy straw mixed with the sweet pungency of rotting humanity. He still could not see, but he knew he was not in his room in the *kifili*.

"Where am I?" he croaked, a terrible realization washing over him. "Simon, what is going on? Someone stabs me, and I am thrown into prison for the privilege?"

Before Simon could answer, a door opened and standing in the sliver of golden light spilling through the crack, a guard.

"Chancellor," the man stated, "soon."

Simon compressed his lips. "You are in the Negus' prison." Jack heard him grind his teeth as he spoke the words. "Aksum law requires this because you assaulted a prince," he finished, his words clipped. "Fortunately they gave you one of the more luxurious rooms in deference to your rank and your injury."

"But Isary is not from Aksum," Jack growled low in his throat. "How does their law apply to him?"

"It matters not. He is a prince, even if from Elbra, and that is enough."

"So a man could call himself a prince and be immune from all harm?" His bitterness felt palpable.

"There is some good to have come out of this. You know all too well how our attempts to be granted an audience with the Negus have been stymied since our arrival. I have learned it is all thanks to Kiros. Despite his great hospitality, something makes him reluctant to grant our wish. He controls access to the Negus like a porter, and no one gets to the Negus without his permission. It's hard to say if prior to your attack on Isary, that the Negus even knew we were here. But the law requires a ruling by Bazin personally. Whether or not Kiros would have ever granted us an audience with the Negus matters no longer."

"Kiros keeps a locked storeroom in the upper ketema. He keeps it guarded." Simon narrowed his eyes, and Jack continued. "Cai saw it too. Ask the lad about it. He meant to get inside, one way or the other."

"Cai? How would he..."

"It's best not to ask. The ways of Cai are often mysterious, and it's best not to know how he does what he does."

Simon nodded slowly. "There is much happening around the throne of Aksum, it seems. Men and women who fight for position, to make their claim on their father's favor. How any of it relates to Sybila, I don't know. It seems a lot to be a coincidence."

The door inched open once more. "Chancellor, it is time."

Simon pressed his hands against his thighs and stood. Jack made one more attempt to sit up, but Simon shook his head. "Just rest, Jack. I will return as soon as I can, once we hear word of your impending audience with the Negus."

If evil had a face, Jack was certain it would look like Isary's. Despite Simon's assurance, a nugget of doubt burrowed through his mind. Without knowing anything about the Negus, how could they speculate on the Negus' mood toward his situation? Consciousness slipped from him even as he formed the thought. His eyes closed in sleep.

He awakened much later to the sound of the door swinging in on its hinges. A figure moved into the room and Jack sensed that the person motioned to someone before sitting.

The feeble light filtering through the doorway hurt his eyes, and he squinted up at his visitor. He could not tell if he recognized the man or not. A moment later another figure entered, setting down a tray before them. Another brought a lantern, casting light into the shadows.

"I have brought you food, *Bitwoded* Jack, and wish to provide you with companionship."

This voice was not familiar. "*Bitwoded?*" He scrunched his face, willing his eyes to adjust to the new light.

"You are a baron of Agrius, are you not?" the man asked.

Jack said nothing in reply, simply eyed the food dishes. The man caught his glance and nodded to a servant who lifted the lids. A familiar aroma tempted his senses, and his stomach growled in response. Two other servants came alongside Jack, and with the gentleness of skilled healers, helped lift him to a sitting position. It felt good to sit up even if his insides felt like the furnaces of his father's forge. One of the servants prepared him a plate and set it carefully across Jack's lap, careful to give his bandaging a wide berth.

"I ordered our kitchens to prepare some dishes from your home. I hope they meet your expectations."

"You have me at somewhat of a disadvantage, le'ul, for you know me, but I don't know you," Jack prompted as he took a nibble of some bread.

The man inclined his head. "I am a son of the Negus."

"I gathered as much," Jack returned, hiding his irritation. "But which one, that is the question. I know Melku, have met Kiros. You are neither of them. Teklu, perhaps?"

"You are very astute, *getaye,* my lord."

"And what do you think I can do for you so that you come visit me in prison?"

Teklu sat back on his stool and made a shrewd study of Jack who returned his scrutiny in kind.

"I am sorry for your injury," the prince replied finally, avoiding the question. "This prince of Elbra, he is a man of a fiery temperament. Unpredictable and cunning..."

"He's a snake," Jack snarled.

The confirmation determined something for Teklu, for the Aksumite prince allowed a look of subtle joy to creep across his face. "Yes, very much like a snake." The prince took a sip of something from his cup then added, "And I presume he is not here simply to retrieve the Agrian princess he claims is here?"

"You know of his accusations?" Teklu spread his hands as if to ask *why would I not?* yet did not reply, so Jack continued. "He seeks a bride."

Teklu nodded. "Do not fear that you have revealed any secrets, my lord," Teklu reassured. "For the man's intentions are as clear as if he had sent a messenger ahead with the news. It does not take the skills of one adept at *salay* to figure this out."

Teklu took another sip, and Jack took the opportunity to do the same, uncertain as to exactly what information Teklu sought to acquire if he knew this much already.

"Teklu, you mention salay. I was a smith by birth. I am not used to, nor do I like, these games of court. I am no good at them, and they serve no purpose for me. Just tell me what you want. Plain-speaking."

At this, Teklu laughed outright, and a light of sincere regard flit across his eyes. "*Getaye*, I like you. And I am truly sorry for what has happened to you. That Elbran *wizili* deserved what you gave him."

"So you can get me out of here?"

"No, I am sorry. That is not possible."

"So what do you want then? If you are no good to me, why should I give you anything?"

Teklu's light-hearted manner dissipated, his posture hardened, his smile disappeared. "I want to succeed my father. I want to know who you support, who has the affirmation of your king."

He should have known it was something like this. Simon had said as much earlier. "Tell me how to get out from under this death sentence." By the gods, his midsection hurt. Even so, he leaned toward Teklu, his own face hard and unyielding. "Help me, and then we will consider helping you."

Teklu's face remained impassive, but only momentarily. When the muscles around his mouth twitched, Jack knew he had him.

✳ 42 ✳

Betem Jebili
Sékra
Aksum

Jack

"DID YOU ATTACK THIS man?"

The room fell silent at the question, all ears straining to hear what had been said and what would come.

Jack stood alone in the middle of the room with only a prison guard for companionship. For all his outward restraint, more than anything he wanted to turn his head, wanted to look around the room and scream at the assembly, to tell them how Isary deserved more than the broken nose he'd suffered, more than the black and blue bruise spreading across his cheekbones where Jack's ring had ripped across his flesh. The man had defiled his wife, by his words and intent even if not with his hands. As Kassia's husband, he was duty-bound to protect her honor, and if they knew anything about honor, they would understand this.

But he said none of these things. Instead, he steadied his breathing and pictured Kassia's face in his mind.

"Yes." And he would do it again too if given the chance.

Those who heard his blatant admission inhaled audibly.

Jack kept his gaze steady, his attention fixed on Kiros, who had asked the question, and Isary, who sat on a low stool at the foot of the Negus. Le'ul Teklu stood just behind Isary and watched Jack with impassive interest. Isary however, sat with his chest and chin thrust forward the way a vulture perched over a fresh kill. The Negus sat in shadow, allowing Kiros to proceed.

Kiros paced to his left, presumably considering his next question, as Jack willed his legs to remain firmly under him.

He had done little else but sleep in the day since Simon came to visit him in his cell, but the rest had done little to help him. Now that he stood fully upright for the first time, his injury throbbed. He felt as wobbly as a newborn lamb, and the floor threatened to open up underneath him, swallowing him whole.

"It is against the supreme law of His Imperial Majesty, the Negusa Nagast, Bazin Assefe Amare," Kiros continued, "to attack or otherwise assault or defile a prince in the Kingdom of Aksum. Were you aware of this law when you attacked this prince of Elbra?"

"No, my lord, I was not."

"Why did you do this thing?" Kiros asked, tilting his head as if confused. Did Jack detect a hint of disappointment?

"He was once betrothed to my wife, intending to wed her to gain the throne of Agrius for himself," he began, but his voice cracked with the strain of emotion, and he paused.

He glared at Isary and clenched his fists. When Simon had come to him that morning with the news of his audience before the Negus, he'd warned him to do everything he could to remain neutral. But now, in the moment, and without realizing he'd done it, he took a step toward the throne. The guard next to him put rough hands on his arm, stopping him. Jack gave the man a dark look but complied, turning his attention back to the Negus. "He did not honor or respect her, intending to use her before discarding her."

Anger flashed in Isary's eyes as his cheeks turned the color of mottled grapes. He pressed his hands down on the arms of his chair as if to stand, but Teklu placed a hand on his shoulder even as the Negus raised a hand to silence Jack.

"I know this story," the Negus said, breaking his silence at last.

Negus Bazin stood, ignoring the looks of surprise around the room. Kiros opened his mouth to say more, but the Negus simply swatted at him with an irritated twitch of his hand. He studied Jack as if he was a novelty, and Jack held his ground, keeping his eyes on the Negus instead of Isary. After a moment of scrutiny, Bazin moved so he was face to face with Jack.

"He did this to your wife, and yet you did not seek *bek'eli*, vengeance, at any other time?" He kept his voice low, a private moment in a public place.

Jack clenched his jaw and fists, furrowing his brows. "No."

The Negus' eyes went wide in surprise. "And you do not call this," Bazin turned behind him to indicate Isary's broken nose, "*bek'eli?* You did not do this to retaliate for what he did to her then?"

"Not for what he did then, no. This was the result of a

new insult. He called my wife a whore, Your Grace, to my face, and in front of Melku just before I hit him. It was not *bek'eli* but simply defending her honor, as a man of *wami ts'shekimi*. I did what I needed to do." He lowered his voice even more. "It was not my honor I intended to protect, but that of my wife. You are a people of honor. I know you understand this."

The Negus compressed his lips, but even with this apparent censure, a new light lit the points of his eyes. After a moment, he turned around, and holding his hands loosely behind him, paced back toward the throne.

He raised his voice once more, for the benefit of the entire room, and tossed over his shoulder as he walked: "You know that Aksum law rarely holds mercy for those who commit such a crime against a royal person? The offended person need not be Aksumite to be protected." He reached his seat, gracefully swiping his flowing robes behind him as he sat.

Jack swallowed back the bleakness of the truth. "So I am told."

The Imperial Majesty rubbed his chin. After a moment he waved Kiros over. The two men consulted together quietly, and the room stilled in expectation.

The Negus Bazin had not been the man Jack expected when he'd been escorted into the audience chamber. Awaiting his prisoner seated on a gilded throne, Bazin appeared old and frail. Thin-framed and small of stature, Jack would have taken the man to be a scholar rather than a Negus. Even so, his narrow face and wrinkled skin sheltered eyes burning bright with intelligence and wisdom. If he stood a chance now, it was because of this, not because there was any particular Aksumite law on his side.

A knot of anxiety twisted in his stomach. He had

promised Kassia that he would come back to her safely. The outcome, however, was not in his hands. The silence stretched on, and the room remained utterly silent. Now and then a foot shuffled against the polished floor of marble, yet if he was to close his eyes, Jack would have guessed that he stood before the Negus alone.

Jack flicked a look at Isary to find him smiling. A fire lit his soul. He could remain quiet no more.

"Did you know this prince of Elbra beds your daughter, Addis?" His words pierced the air like a flight of arrows across a sunlit sky. Jack saw Teklu suppress a small smile of approval, and it gave him the confidence to press harder. Kiros pulled away from the Negus and stared. "The same Addis who is already wed to the Agrian Lord Wigstan of House Argifu? The same daughter who plotted to kill my king and his queen, and who most recently conspired with Taibel Rebane of Haern to kidnap my niece, the daughter of my king and queen?"

A communal gasp sounded in the audience chamber, as if the very room sucked in its breath. Jack sucked his own in, right along with them.

The Negus stood in a whirlwind, his robes swirling. His eyes locked onto Jack's, and Jack was certain in that moment that the man could shoot bolts of lightning from them if he'd wished.

"Guards, take this man back to his cell," he ordered, his voice low but thundering. "And order my daughter brought before me at first light."

❀ *43* ❀

Betem Jebili
Sékra
Aksum

Jack

EARLY MORNING FOUND JACK awakened again by the arrival
of a guard opening the door to his cell. As his eyes adjusted to
the invasion of bright light from the outer corridor, another
man bearing a pan of tepid water entered. He presented Jack
with a towel, indicating he wash his hands and face. Once
finished with that task, the man offered him a comb to tidy
his hair.

When finished, the guard led him out of the prison and
past the feasting hall, into the Negus' private apartments by
way of an intimidating archway tiled with cobalt blue glazed
tiles. Guiding him into a much smaller room than they had
been in the previous day, Jack found himself surrounded by
men and women bearing tattoos of the royal house, to the last

of them. Simon and Luca had both been granted access, but no other member of either the Agrian delegation or the Aksumite court was present. Isary sat near the Negus as he had done the day before.

After a moment, the door opened, and Addis entered, gliding in with the confidence of one who has nothing to hide. Her glistening hair cascaded down her back, shimmering in the morning sunlight. Jack caught the scent of exotic spices when she moved. She held her head erect, her bearing straight and regal. The white material gathered at her shoulders left her arms bare to her wrists, revealing her own delicate and intricate tattoo, declaring her relationship to the throne of Aksum. She spared not a glance for Jack but continued to regard her father.

Negus Bazin got straight to the business at hand.

"Is it true, what this man claims about you?"

Jack did not turn his face toward Addis when her father spoke, but he was certain that she straightened even further, half closing her eyes, and offered a confident smile.

She refused to answer, and once Bazin seemed to note this, a side door opened. Cai entered. Isary transformed from placid observer to furious at the sight of his charge. Jack felt just as much surprise, and he willed the boy to look at him, but Cai kept his attention on the Negus.

"This boy is in the service to the prince of Elbra. He is prepared to offer witness. I ask you again: Is it true what this man claims about you? I would hear the truth from your own lips. Honor demands it."

"Isary Branimir of Corak, Lord of Brekkell and Prince of Elbra is my lover, yes. And we plan to wed."

If the Negus was shocked in any way by this, he restrained it with practiced ease. Only a raising of his brows signaled that he had feelings on the revelation, one way or the other. "You would dishonor your name and your house by doing this thing even though you are avowed to another? By your own word?"

Addis raised her own brows. "For your daughter to wed an Elbran prince, how would this bring you dishonor?" Addis tilted her head to the side, pursing her lips as if her father's answer could do nothing other than agree with her own conclusions.

"It would not be dishonor had you not already given your pledge to another. You are already wed to a nobleman of Agrius." Bazin narrowed his eyes at his daughter, and his lips pinched in the way of one who had just eaten a bitter fruit. "What of his claim regarding the king and queen of Agrius? Did you conspire to have them killed?"

"No, I had no part," she returned boldly, curling her upper lip.

"So, you say this man," the Negus pointed at Jack, "is a liar?"

Addis did not bother to reply. Instead, she snapped her mouth shut, held her chin high.

Bazin pulled in a slow but steady lungful of air, his chest broadening as he did so, and Jack could almost imagine what he might have looked like as a younger man. The Negus considered Addis for a long moment before he turned to Jack.

"You still do not deny that you struck this prince of Elbra," he stated matter-of-factly, pointing at Isary, "and that the damage to his face was the result of your own hand?"

"I do not deny it, no. I will take the responsibility upon my own shoulders, along with the consequences for such action."

Jack made his best effort to maintain a placid exterior as he watched the older man closely for any sign of what his ruling might be. Any outward show of impatience would do him little good. His decision to speak truth had probably ensured his own death sentence, but he would have it no other way.

After a time, Bazin spun around, a move so graceful and deft that Jack wondered if the man's fragile mien and elderly appearance served him well as a misleading facade. He was clearly more vigorous than Jack gave him credit for, and he wondered how many others had fallen into the trap of underestimating him because of it.

"Will any of my children speak for this man who was not born of the mesafint, despite his title? Will any of you share his fate as if it was your own, thereby offering him the weight of your own *wami ts'shekimi* as our ancient customs allow?"

This was a surprising development. It had been Teklu who had recommended to Jack that he raise the issue of Addis' indiscretions with the Elbran prince, and her meddling in the politics of Agrius to sway his father's opinion of Addis and against Isary in favor of Jack. But he had not expected the Negus to ask any of his own children to stand as surety for Jack's good character with their own reputation. But Teklu must have known this. Perhaps it had been his expectation and plan all along. Perhaps Teklu knew this would happen, had prepared to speak up for him. Jack carefully shifted his attention to Teklu, but the oldest Aksumite prince stood motionless and would not meet Jack's look.

Or perhaps he'd had no such plan.

No one spoke and no one moved, and a sense of panic twisted in the pit of Jack's stomach, waiting like a coiled snake to strike. Would his execution be immediate, or would they give him time to speak with his friends, to write one last letter to Kassia?

Isary smiled a serpentine smile. He had won.

"My Father, if you please...." Melku rose from his seat and stepped forward. "I offer my own good *simi* to stand for him, may it please Your Imperial Majesty." Melku knelt in submission at his father's feet, with both palms stretched out before him, flat against the gleaming marble floor.

The Negus looked down with surprise, and a light of approval shown in his eyes. "You would seal your fate with his?"

"Yes, Father."

Bazin turned to take in the room. As he scanned the shocked faces, he raised his arms as if to quell an uproar. He held them there, unmoving, as a man dressed in clerk's robes stepped out from the shadows. He handed the Negus a long, elegantly tapered spear, gilded and etched with elaborate designs up and down its shaft. "Unbind this man," he ordered, pointing at Jack with the lethal end of the spear. "He is found not guilty of all charges. He will not bear responsibility or punishment for the assault of which he is accused."

The room erupted into a clamor, though Jack couldn't tell if it was anger or a release of the tension that had caused it. Perhaps it was neither, and Jack felt more like a foreign visitor than ever before. He quickly scanned the room for Simon and found the older man watching him, smiling his approval.

Once more the Negus raised his hands above the crowd and raised his voice. "The law of Aksum is binding, and anyone who would argue this fact would not be wrong. But I am Negusa Nagast, Bazin Assefe Amare, and my word is supreme law."

Jack felt the floor shift under him, his knees grew weak, and he wanted to collapse. With every remaining strand of energy he could muster, he kept to his feet. Within the next intake of breath, Melku stood next to him.

"Come, friend, and let us get you a seat." He slipped his arm under Jack's for support, and Jack all but collapsed against him. Melku turned him to walk toward a chair.

They had made it no more than several steps when Isary lunged toward them, hot fury blazing across his face. He did not get far because Bazin noticed, pointed his spear at Isary, shouting, "Guards!"

Two t'ebaks moved in to take hold of Isary, one on each side.

"Place this man under arrest. And give him the cell most recently vacated." Bazin eyed Jack, a slight smile curving his lips.

"For what charge?" Isary cried, fury blazing hot across his cheeks. He pulled at the guards holding his arms. "I am a prince of Elbra and not under your laws!"

"And yet you would have this man held responsible to them?"

"You said yourself that your law as it applies to princes does not see the boundaries of a kingdom!" Isary bellowed.

"And thusly," the Negus reasoned, "we arrest you." Isary opened his mouth to argue then closed it again. There was little point. "You have dishonored a daughter of my house, an assault on a princess of Aksum." A smile of sheer pleasure spread the Negus' cheeks. The man clearly enjoyed the sentence.

"As for Addis..." the Negus continued, turning away from the convicted Elbran prince toward his daughter. The smile of amusement fled as a pinch of sadness settled over him. "Guards, take her." Addis had clearly not expected this outcome, and her rich complexion paled. "You broke your vow, your word of honor. If that was not enough, you are found guilty of conspiring against a prince of the blood."

Addis sputtered protests, maintaining her innocence, but the Negus held up his hands. "Even if you deny it, I know it to be true. I have heard the evidence, both from Aksumite scribes and foreign as well. The laws regarding the bodily assault on royalty holds true for you just as well for this man."

The Negus waved a hand, and both Isary and Addis were led from the room. When they had gone, the onlookers rose and began to filter out. Kiros remained at the side of the Negus, and Melku still stood with Jack.

Once the room was empty of his children, Bazin turned to them.

"My friends, I am sorry this happened to you."

"What will become of her?" Jack nodded in the direction Addis had gone.

"Tell your lord of Argifu that his connection to Addis is no longer valid. He is free to marry as he would. As for Addis, I will not execute my offspring, but she is no longer a daughter of mine. She will be sent to the *ma'idini*, our mines, to work out the remainder of her days."

He turned to leave, but Simon called out after him. "Your Imperial Majesty, a word?" Bazin turned back to them. "You have shown yourself a man of honor indeed, and we thank you. But we have come seeking news of a man called Taibel Rebane who has been accused of stealing away our young princess, Sybila."

Jack could not say for certain, but it seemed as if the Negus received the information as having heard it for the first time. His brows furrowed, and he turned to Kiros who whispered something in his ear. After a long moment, he came to stand alongside Jack, placing a firm hand on his shoulder. "Kiros assures me that your princess is not here." He smiled knowingly. "And Kiros would know."

"Then why was Aksum implicated?"

The Negus shook his head. "I am sorry. We cannot help you."

And with that, the Negus spun from the room, leaving Melku alone with Jack, Simon, and Luca.

"Do you believe him?" Jack asked Simon.

Simon looked to Melku.

"He speaks truth, my friends. Kiros would know. And I have done my own investigation as promised. She is not here. I am sorry."

Simon nodded.

"We must get word immediately to Casmir. And then we must depart. At first light, if possible."

Jack heaved himself to standing, pushing aside the exhaustion seeping into his bones. The thought of working to prepare to depart would take more of his already spent energy, but the thought of home felt a good trade-off.

"I will see you back to your *kifili*, my friends," Melku offered.

❁ ❁

They had been back at their *kifili* only moments when visitors arrived.

A nurse stepped into the room, along with a young boy hanging on her skirt. His lighter skin set him at odds with the richer hues of the Aksumites, though his curly, chestnut-colored hair reminded him of Addis. Kiros followed behind them.

"My friends, before you go, there is one more thing. A gift. The Negus requires it."

Kiros' words sounded polite, flowing from his lips with his usual polish. His face, however, announced the opposite. That the task was not of his choosing but was a command of the Negus was clear. He placed his hand atop the young boy's head then pressed him forward. "When you return home, I ask you to take Kalu."

Simon and Jack exchanged curious glances.

"A most unusual gift," Simon ventured. "I assume the Negus has his reasons? Surely this boy has a family? Agrius is a long way from Sékra."

"Indeed. But by returning to Agrius with you, he returns to his father." When neither Jack nor Simon could find a reply, Kiros continued. "His name is Kalu, son of Wigstan and heir to House Argifu after his father."

❊ *44* ❊

Croilton Castle
Honor of Cilgaron
Agrius

Helene

HELENE HAD SLEPT LATE. It had to be mid-morning at the earliest. When the first chambermaid arrived that morning to pull back the bed curtains, she'd swiped at the girl with a pillow, ordering her to leave. She felt ragged, having slept poorly after crying herself to sleep, and rasped at the maid ferociously.

What a miserable mess she'd made of everything! When the formidable Roswen arrived sometime later, she bore the brunt of the mistress's anger.

"Up with you, girl!" Roswen yanked back the piles of coverlets, exposing Helene's nakedness. Grasping for a sheet to cover herself, the girl swung her legs over the side and stood only to meet the disapproving scrutiny of the older woman.

"The fact that you are here, in your own bed, and not in the king's chamber, tells me all I need to know about your night's activities. Or the lack thereof." Roswen scowled, the corners of her mouth pinched in her usual way.

Roswen waved her hand and the maids rushed in to dress Helene. Now as she stood at the window, her long tresses being brushed and tended to in preparation for the day, her father's mistress stood alongside her, gazing out at the courtyard below and the assemblage of men gathered there.

"I would tell you to get down there to send off the men, but you would not make it in time. Your idleness has ruined this as well."

The king had not yet joined the men preparing for the hunt, but her father stood amongst the houndsmen, instructing them regarding the day. She admired her father more than any other man. He was bold, brave, decisive, and he knew his own mind. Despite being of Sajen blood, he had survived the overthrow of Nikolas those many years ago, long before she was born. He had supported Nikolas for certain, for Nikolas had made his family wealthy beyond reason. But then Bellek came, and her father had seen opportunity. Being as wily as a fox, he had been among the first of the barons to arrive in Prille to offer his sword and his allegiance to the new, Vitus king. It had been the only way to survive, to hold his name, his titles, and the wealth accumulated over generations.

"An allegiance is nothing," he'd said. "It is only words spoken to salve the open insecurity of the Crown." He had gone willingly to Prille and had come back with even more power than before.

The women behind Helene chattered, cleaning and

tidying the chamber. When the king emerged from his apartments on the far side of the Isle Court, the chatter quieted, and all the ladies flocked to the windows to catch a glimpse of him. A new kind of chatter rose up as they watched, their words not filtered by the presence of men or by the proprieties of polite society. The maids bantered back and forth, their openly admiring assessment of the king's attributes bringing a light flush to Helene's cheeks. A flutter rose in her chest, and she held her hand to her throat at the memories of the previous evening. She had been humiliated at his rebuff, but despite her failure, she still harbored hope. He'd wanted her. He couldn't have denied that fact even if he'd wanted to.

When the king moved, presumably, into the hall to make his way through to the cobbled court on the other side, the ladies all moved across the room to watch for him to emerge again. As they went, Helene cast a sidelong glance at Roswen who stood watching the king with the rest of the women.

Pools of brilliant sunlight poured in through the eastern-facing window, bathing the older woman in golden rays and highlighting the fine wrinkles around her lips and eyes, doubtless formed through hours of judging those around her. Roswen frightened Helene. Why else allow herself to be bullied into doing things as she had done?

Helene shifted her gaze back to the king, wondering what Roswen might be thinking just as he took the reins to his impressive courser. Doubtless, Roswen saw a handsome, powerful man. What woman would not notice these things? But for Roswen, it was first and foremost his display of wealth and the ultimate power of kingship which kept her attention. A carter could have a handsome face and she would not spare even a look. No, Roswen valued only status and power. And there was no denying that dressed in luxurious fabrics and sparkling jewels, the king cut an impressive figure.

Yes, Helene fancied these things as well. He was most definitely handsome. The rumors said that he had never paid much mind to his appearance, that he wore his cloak of appeal so casually. She found it difficult to understand since her father had always made certain that others could not miss noticing his fine clothes, wealth, and title.

But to Helene, it seemed different with Casmir. His wealth and position were certainly part of his appeal, but she had seen the man underneath. They had talked over a variety of matters covering many topics, so he had a keen mind. He could also be gentle with words and deeds. Her memories of the previous night sent a shiver through her, and she suppressed them with a quick breath.

Roswen's keen sense did not miss it. She smiled her approval.

"It is said he is not normally a man to make a show of pretense with his dress," Helene returned, desperately wanting Roswen to turn her intense focus away from her face and the intimate thoughts she knew displayed across her blushing cheeks.

"Perhaps in his own hall, but here he knows he has to showcase his immense power." Roswen turned bodily toward her, placing her hands on the girl's shoulders. "And don't forget for one moment that he has immense power, my girl, and that you must rein it in to your own designs. He is a king, but he is still a man after all." Roswen's lips curled artfully at the corners, as if it was a foregone conclusion in her mind that eventually, every man would cave to the lure of an attractive woman if given enough pressure.

Helene wasn't convinced. "It is also said that his wife, the queen, is a rare beauty, that she is like the very goddess herself."

Roswen flicked her wrist. "Oh, tut. You mustn't listen to every court gossip to pass through your father's hall. While she may be attractive, remember that she has also failed to give him another child. And with the young princess now missing..." Roswen countered, her lips puckering smugly. "The man in the king may yearn for the queen's comely face, but the king in the man is in need of another heir. That is the way of royalty and the continuation of a noble line." The older woman spun Helene around then adjusted the fit of her bodice. "He needs Sajen blood, yes. But if another Sajen was to give him one..." She shrugged.

"But his chamberlain..."

"Hush." Roswen pressed a single finger to Helene's lips. "So you have already explained. Poor timing, and it couldn't have been helped, though you must be cautious next time."

Roswen said the words as if trying to soothe a distraught child, her eyes solicitous, her lips pouting, but Helene knew the cold interior of the woman, the scheming ways in which her mind worked. No, she did not try to make Helene feel better for her failure. She meant only to humiliate her. The fact that it was only chambermaids to overhear did not matter.

"I do wonder though..." Helene pondered aloud. "If I was to bear him a child, it would be illegitimate, would it not? How does that help me?"

"He will realize he has no choice but to put aside the queen in favor of you, to make his offspring through you legitimate. He would have to take you to wife. There is no problem. You must only do your part, though I cannot think there is much hardship for you in that."

Roswen turned her attention back to the courtyard

below, and Helene followed the line of her attention to find Casmir mounting his magnificent horse. The beast tossed a spirited head in its eagerness to run, but the king managed him with practiced ease. With sure movements, he turned Sevaritza in tight circles then made him prance in place to ease out the courser's nerves.

No, there was no hardship for Helene, of that there was no doubt. She felt another flush of heat rise to her cheeks as she watched him, remembering her nearness to him in the dark of the corridor just outside his room, of what would have happened had they not been interrupted.

And then an unbidden image of the queen rose up in her mind's eye, filling her with dark loathing. Helene knew she was far superior to the queen, for the woman had been given a detestable upbringing among the dirty filth of poverty. Sajen blood flowed through Helene's body as well, and unlike the queen, she had been bred properly, knew how to behave. She also knew she could give the king what he most needed: an heir.

A signal sounded, giving the hunting party permission to move out. As the lead rider left through the gate, a man rushed in from the opposite direction, flagging the king. Casmir leaned down to take in the quiet words of the messenger, and as he spoke, the king grew visibly upset -- though whether it was with the messenger or the news he brought she could not tell. Helene shrank back from the window. She had seen her father furious many times, but there was a level of danger in the king's mien that chilled her to the bone.

Better to have him as a friend, not an enemy, she thought.

Casmir waved over his captain and issued him an order. As he listened, the man's top lip curled back into a snarl. Without another word, he spun his horse, whipped it into a frenzy, and rode away.

"What could that have been about?" Helene asked Roswen.

"It matters not. Come, my dear. You must see to our other guests. Make sure they have everything they need for the day."

Helene nodded, doing her best to return her focus and attention to the day ahead. Any wanton thoughts she might have of the king would have to retreat to the background of her mind for now.

She made her way through her apartments, to the upper-most floor of the great tower, and slipped a key from its hiding. Fixing it into the lock, she gave it a gentle turn and swung the thick door open.

Sitting in the comfort of the morning light, settled among bright cushions at a vast table spread with parchments, sat her father's guest, Taibel Rebane. He raised his face to her as she entered.

"Ah, my lady. It is good of you to come." The man leaned back in his high-backed chair and smiled warmly. He gestured at the tray before him and the empty dishes arrayed on it. "No one has been back to retrieve this, and I fear I need the space to work."

Helene bobbed her head. "My apologies for the oversight, my lord. I will send a boy soon. Is there anything else you require?"

Rebane glanced across the room, to the far side. "Yes, I think the child could do with some fresh air. Since the king is away, it seems this might be the best time."

Helene bobbed her head again, her gut-wrenching at the thought. Even so, she smiled. "It would be my delight." Stretching out her hand to the young one, she said, "Come, child, and we will play in the yard behind the kitchens for a time."

The coil in Helene's gut twisted even further as the girl grasped her hand with small fingers. The ever-present knot of anxiety and fear grew considerably each day the king dwelt in her father's hall. He played a risky game, did the Lord Cilgaron, and to put so much trust in the servants seemed foolhardy, even to Helene. Even though she took the girl to play in a sheltered area behind the kitchen and its gardens, trusting to the loyalty of those few servants who observed them, there was a risk Helene would not have undertaken had she been given the choice.

But she hadn't been.

She had never been given a choice.

About anything.

She glanced down to the child at her side. Lustrous golden hair spilled over her shoulders as she skipped along. At one point the child nearly tripped, and as she looked up at her minder, seeking affirmation, Helene took in the ethereal, radiant beauty of the mite's eyes.

If this child looked anything like her mother, the king was likely enchanted beyond reason. The queen would be a hard woman to supplant.

❈ *45* ❈

Croilton Castle
Honor of Cilgaron
Agrius

Helene

HELENE STOOD BACK AMIDST the stacked crates near the wall, with her back to the cold stone, hesitant to step out. She had made her way to the cobbled courtyard outside the great hall long before the sentries announced the return of the hunting party. She'd arrived early because she wanted enough time to still the panic rising in her chest before she had to act. It had been the same way last night too, prior to the feast and her role as hostess in her father's place.

Roswen had urged her to come, declaring her assurance that this was the best way to catch the attention of the king. Men in a jovial mood were much easier to manipulate, she'd said. And by the looks of the heavily laden carts lumbering past, the hunt had been very successful indeed. The returning hunters should be exuberant.

As she considered the evening ahead of her, a knife of anxiety cut through her anew, and she worked to still her hands which even now worried the braided cord encircling her waist. She glanced up at the sky and noticed that sullen gray clouds heavy with rain had moved in, replacing the brightness of the morning. Blinding flashes of lightning streaked across the sky in the distance just as the hunting party rattled through the gateway into the courtyard. She hoped they could make it indoors before the deluge opened over their heads.

Taking another deep breath, she fixed a smile on her face and stepped out. The task would not become any easier in the waiting. And if she failed, she would have the lady Roswen to answer to as usual.

Scanning the bevy of boisterous, clamoring men, she searched for any sign of the royal livery. Casmir had taken his own armed guard along with his friends, and his party should be easy to spot. She knew if she could find his men, the king would not be far away. Before long, she spied Sevaritza, the king's powerful courser, so pushed her way through the sea of men who parted for her as she came. She reached the large horse just as Casmir hopped down from the beast's back.

As he tossed the reins to a groom and cracked a joke over his own disheveled state, she took in his dirty and stained clothing, his tousled hair, and the bright red streak crossing his left cheek as if he had taken a fall. Finally he turned and noticed her. Flushed with high spirits, he flashed her a boyish grin.

"Your Grace," Helene demurred, dropping into a deep obeisance.

Casmir pulled off a glove and raised her up to stand.

"Lady Helene," he returned.

"You have injured yourself." She lifted her hand, wanting trace her finger along his cheek where droplets of blood had dried along the cut but checked herself.

He offered a kind smile then took her hand and tucked it into the crook of his arm. "It is nothing," he began as he turned them to walk toward the hall, "simply an overreaching branch where the game trail should have been. But never fear," he added conspiratorially and with a wink, "I have ordered the tree cut down and turned into firewood for its trouble." He cocked a crooked grin, and she giggled, relieved that he had received her well, despite her humiliation the night before.

In fact, his mood toward her was solicitous – dare she say flirtatious? – and certainly not what she had been expecting. It was a fortuitous sign, she knew, and she felt a brief flutter of anticipation. Perhaps her work would not be as difficult as it could have been.

"Now, I must wash and change, for your father has promised me I will dine heartily this night. I expect unrivaled amusement." He turned toward her, his eyes intent. "I believe he is right. I believe there will be plenty to keep me occupied this night."

She could not quite read his expression or meaning, but his words seemed to intimate another meaning. "Of course, Your Grace," she squeaked, her knees nearly buckling. The look in his eyes hinted at danger, and it was all she could do to resist reaching out to put her hand on his cheek. She forced her legs to continue to carry her forward, though the task was more difficult than it should have been.

❋ 46 ❋

Croilton Castle
Honor of Cilgaron
Agrius

AFTER PARTING WAYS WITH Helene, I turned my step toward the hall where Lord Cilgaron waited with the rest of the hunting party. I had no wish to join, for my fall from Sevaritza that afternoon had left me more sore than I'd let on, the tree branch which had knocked me off in the fury of the chase bigger than it had at first appeared. I swallowed back a bitter curse at the memory, though I was thankful no one had actually seen me do it.

I glanced overhead, eyeing the approaching storm, and smiled a grim smile, for it matched my mood perfectly while also heralding the coming of a different kind of storm. No, I would not join the other men for the celebratory drink in the hall. There was too much to be done, too many plans to set into motion.

Just as I determined to continue on through the hall, exiting into the Isle Court to make for my chambers, I noticed Ingólfer milling about just outside the door. I waved the magistrate over as I walked past, thinking his presence served as good an excuse to avoid the hall as any other. Ingólfer displayed hesitation, but just then the clouds burst overhead, sending down a torrent of rain, and the magistrate seemed only too pleased to escape the deluge.

Once we reached the safety of my chambers, Andreu opened the door immediately, and I thrust my gloves at him, stripping off my tabard as I went, tossing it absent-mindedly onto the nearest piece of furniture, and caring not that the soiled garment left its mark where it landed. Andreu helped me with the cumbersome brigandine jacket.

I was about to begin my interrogation of Ingólfer when I noticed a young kitchen maid heaving the contents of a bucket into a steaming hot bath on the far wall. So heavy was her burden, and so intent was she on fulfilling her duty, that the little maid only noticed my arrival when I approached her from behind to peer into the tub.

"Did you fill this all by yourself?" I asked her, genuinely surprised at the size of the girl compared to the weight of the bucket.

A look of awe commingled with abject horror flooded her face as she nodded mutely. Most likely she was meant to have this task finished before my arrival, for I was at this very moment meant to be in the hall, drinking with the lord of the castle. She had only managed to fill the tub halfway. Considering her small stature and young years, it was no surprise the job had been too much for her. I scowled.

"It is sufficient to my needs," I said gruffly, though before the words left my mouth, I realized my mistake.

The girl began to back away from me in terror, likely

thinking my mood and reaction a direct result of her failure to perform her duty.

"Lass," I began again, more gently this time, "you have done well enough. I only meant that you needn't bother to bring more water. I will make do. This is too big a job for you."

The girl still did not seem convinced. If anything, her frame shook with terror at my words, though she stopped backing away. "Your Grace, I was told to bring enough to fill the tub. This is only half, and they will punish me..."

I moved no closer to the girl but dropped to a crouch before her, trying to meet her at eye level. "I will send a boy with you to explain," I said softly, "to tell them that your king asked you to stop. It was my fault for interrupting your work, and you should not be punished for that. I will not have it."

At my explanation, the young girl raised tremulous eyes to meet my look, hardly daring to believe what she'd just heard. I watched her a moment longer then waved a page over, instructing him as to what he should say. "And if they give you any trouble, I want to know about it."

The boy nodded then led the girl to the door.

"Hold!" I called after them. "What is your name, child?"

The girl froze again, likely thinking I'd changed my mind regarding her reprieve. She turned fearful eyes to me once more. "Teryn, Your Grace."

"Do you know of the girl Brigid?" She nodded. "And is she well tended?"

"Oh, yes, Your Grace!" This question seemed to hit a happy note with her, for her mood turned from fear to delight in a heartbeat, and for a moment she seemed to forget to whom she spoke.

They turned to leave and I watched them go, thoughts

of my daughter filling me with grief once again. I knew that if I turned around, I would find Wimarc watching me, amused at the conflict he thought I felt for a serving waif. He had no children of his own, could not understand my devotion to my daughter nor the concern I felt for the kitchen foundling Brigid. Likely he found my interest in this young kitchen maid perplexing at best. I cared not. The man was not a father, nor had he had a loved one stolen out from under his care and protection.

After a long moment, I threw back my shoulders. "Right," I began, taking in the circle of men waiting for me to speak. "Ingólfer, thank you for joining me here rather than in the hall."

"My king, there is no hardship in it for me. I have partaken of Lord Cilgaron's generosity often enough."

I clapped the man on the back. "What news?"

"Riders returned only moments before you." The magistrate's look turned hard, cold and unyielding.

"And?"

"It is as you suspected, Your Grace. A small number of mercenary soldiers have been seen landing along the coast just south of Sarsala."

"And these men have been hired by Cilgaron, you are certain?" Ingólfer grew less confident at the question, and I already knew what the magistrate would say.

"Not exactly, no. There are rumors," he began, but I cut him off.

"We cannot arrest a man based on rumors. No, we will take a different route to nail the traitor to the wall." I spun and paced toward the far wall, aiming for the window overlooking the north side of the castle precincts. "Keep digging for now. I tire of this nonsense. Cilgaron and I reached an agreement this afternoon regarding Lyseby, though

I know his promises are merely smoke and sleight of hand. He wishes me gone from here so he can get about his business."

"What will you do?" Ingólfer asked.

"What he should have done long ago," Wimarc cut in.

I shot him a dark look, and the young lord subsided. "Just take care of your business, magistrate," I instructed Ingólfer.

"As you wish, my king," he replied before bowing his way out of the chamber.

When he'd gone, Wimarc snatched a flagon from the table and poured himself a hefty measure as I peeled off my boots and sweaty tunic, rounding my shoulders to stretch out my stiff shoulder in the process. Andreu produced a dish of soft soap as I removed the last of my clothing and lowered myself into the less-than-steaming bath. With a wry smile, I wished I'd allowed the girl to finish filling the tub, for the water barely rose to my abdomen. Even so, I sank back against the side, closing my eyes as the water worked its wonders on my muscles.

Wimarc handed me a cup, and I accepted it gratefully.

"Are you ready to follow Jachamin's advice to bring Cilgaron around to your way of thinking?"

I kept my eyes closed as I took a deep breath through my nose, clenching the cup more tightly in my hand as a vision of the battered guildsman, Tugredd, flashed before my eyes. "You have managed to presume many things, my lord of Dalery." I cracked an eye at Wimarc who leaned his slender frame casually against the stone fireplace. "I advise you to remember your place." His pleasant mien did not alter, but I knew my admonition struck home, for a waiver of doubt flickered across his eyes, though it was gone in an instant.

"So Jachamin is free to act upon his return? You saw how he got what you wanted from Tugredd," he pressed.

"First we will see what evidence he has discovered." Wimarc opened his mouth to speak, but I opened my eyes fully, growling, "And then we will do it my way. I have seen Jachamin's way of doing things. They were my father's ways too. I will not repeat the mistakes of my father. Is that clear?"

"Yes, Your Grace," Wimarc said then left his king to prepare for the feast.

A crack of thunder sounded just outside the window, shaking the very stones of the room. I considered what the evening would bring as another rumble rolled across the twilight sky.

"Andreu, close the shutters and alert the men to keep a sharp eye out for Guimer. I fear what this storm may bring."

❋ 47 ❋

Croilton Castle
Honor of Cilgaron
Agrius

Helene

HELENE SCANNED THE HALL with pride as she glided up the center aisle, taking in the bright torches lining the length of the ancient hall of Croilton Castle. Pillared candles resting on great candle trees placed at intervals along the tables provided a warmth of subtle light and offered a pleasing aroma of beeswax along with the scent of roasted meat and other delicacies. A troupe of musicians prepared their night's entertainment in a prominent place near the upper table. Her father had spared no expense for tonight's meal and entertainment, for he wanted a level of extravagance on display rivaled only by Prille itself.

"Tonight we will celebrate the accord reached between the king and the peoples of the honor of Cilgaron and the

---

people of Lyseby!" her father had declared earlier that day after the hunting party had returned.

Helene was disappointed that the king retreated so quickly to his chambers without coming to the hall for the usual refreshment after the hunt, but it had given her the benefit of more time to prepare herself for the evening's festivities. She smoothed her silk skirts with her palms, straightened her spine, and checked on the last details of the preparations before the guests arrived.

"More raki, Your Grace?" Helene asked, flagging down a passing servant without waiting for his response. He had enjoyed enough raki already for her to know that he would not object to more. She smiled a private approval to herself as she turned to offer him another cup.

"Of course!" He received the cup and raised it to his lips, smiling at her over the brim.

Did she detect a tremor in his hand?

While Helene had hoped the king would come to her this night as a result of his own decision, the raki could only aid her cause. She could not bear to face Roswen's or her father's fury if she failed again. She returned his smile openly and took a sip from her own cup while she watched him.

Luxurious soft fur lined the collar of his coat over which lay a wide necklace of gold and precious jewels. His silken tunic had been laboriously embroidered, and Helene could only imagine the immense time and expense that had gone into the making of his garment. Glittering rings encircled his fingers, and she watched entranced as the firelight hit the largest of the rubies on his right hand.

As he had done the previous evening, her father gave

up his rightful place of honor in favor of her, choosing a place several seats down instead. She sought out her father and found approval in his triumphantly gleaming eyes. Wind and rain howled outside as a ferocious storm raged with a frenzy, but none of that mattered. Not when her plans seemed to go so smoothly.

When finally the diners had eaten their fill, Helene stood and invited the musicians to begin playing. Servants barely had time to clear away the tables before men and women moved in to take up the dance. It was not often the king came to stay at a particular lord's hall, and the opportunity to be so near his person in a way the dance allowed would be the highlight for most present.

"My lady?" Casmir had risen to stand just behind Helene's shoulder, and now he offered his hand to her as the crowd waited for their hostess to begin.

They descended to the middle of the hall and began the first dance opposite one another. They spun and clasped hands, turned to new partners, and moved along the line, all the while maintaining the graceful rhythm of the chosen tune. She lost herself to the fervor, immersing herself fully in the thrill of the communal merrymaking as one dance flowed into the next, the tempo changing and varying as the hours passed. She did her best to keep an eye on the king who seemed to enjoy the revelry as much as everyone else. Now and then she would catch his eye, and he would offer her a nod, causing ripples of thrill to shoot through her.

It was at one of these moments, just as she sought his gaze, that Casmir did not notice her. One of his men, a captain in his palace guard and the same man who had raced away on his horse before the hunt, entered the hall. Casmir broke away from the dancers to hear the news his man brought.

It could have been nothing good, for the king looked fit to bring down the very stones of the hall with his bare hands as a result. With impressive strength of will, however, he quickly regained control of his emotions before uttering a sharp command to his man who turned instantly and left once more.

As he moved to rejoin the group of dancers, Helene placed herself in his path, smiling invitingly. To her great pleasure, the musicians began a slow dance, matching pairs of dancers for longer periods of time.

"My lady," he said and took her hand as the dance began.

She drew close. "You received disturbing news, Your Grace?"

"Yes." Casmir's gaze pierced her soul, and her legs turned to jelly. After a long moment he turned her in a slow circle, their arms upraised as the dance required. When she faced him once more, a peculiar glint lit his eyes. He didn't answer her question; instead, he pulled her closer, bringing his lips near her ear as if to divulge a confidence. "I have a problem, and I hope you can help me," he murmured. His breath felt warm, scented with strong drink. Her knees trembled, and a familiar flutter of anticipation floated to her throat. She closed her eyes, feeling heat flush her cheeks.

"Of course," she whispered. "It would be my pleasure to help solve your problem."

She knew the musicians played, that dancers danced around them, but she heard none of it, saw nothing except the rising hope of her dreams realized. She opened her eyes to gaze at him again and found the intensity on his face staggering.

"Your father plays a dangerous game, and I would know where you stand."

It was not what she'd expected, and her heart seized in her chest. She wanted desperately to pull back from him, but his arms gripped her like belts of steel. How did he know of her father's plans? She remembered the messenger that morning at the hunt, Casmir's look of anger. But just how much had he learned? Did he know everything? If he knew everything, truly everything, she and her father would have been arrested by now. No, he couldn't know it all. At best he'd found out about the ships anchored to the north in Sarsala, and her father had a plan to blame the guild master.

She could still win Casmir, but she needed to find a way to warn Rebane. If he was discovered now, when they were so close, it may mean death for them all. She would continue as planned, would reassure Casmir, tell him what he wanted to hear, then seduce him as her father wanted.

"I am yours, Casmir," she purred cautiously, "eager to please."

He looked deeply into her eyes, and she found in them that peculiar glint, the one that thrilled her so. "I am prepared to reward those who prove faithful to me," he whispered quietly, for her ears alone.

His eyes held a question, an invitation, she was certain. She nodded vigorously, settling in comfortably against him. "I have always been faithful to you, Casmir." And though he could not see her, she smiled a satisfied smile, knowing her future was assured. He wanted her, and tonight she would make him hers.

The song ended, and she felt intoxicated. He released her, and she nearly stumbled, accustomed as she had become to clinging so closely.

He raised her hand to his lips grazing her fingers. "I must bid you goodnight, for I have yet much to do before morning." He drew away, keeping his focus on her.

What did he mean? How much could she read into his words? Roswen would know, but the older woman had long ago retired. Neither was her father anywhere to be found. She felt so desperately alone, and she knew that she must make the right decision, for to choose poorly could ruin everything. She chewed her lower lip in thought. If she misread the king's words and meaning, it would mean disaster, for if he did not intend a liaison with her, his rebuff would be severe, final, and she would not get another chance. But if he had intended that she visit him... She brought her hands up to cover her thudding heart.

Wimarc, the lord of Dalery stood against the fall wall, watching her. He offered her a slow smile, lifting his cup in salute before bringing it to his lips. That was her answer. The king's man all but encouraged her, knowing his king's mind and desires.

❋ 48 ❋

Croilton Castle
Honor of Cilgaron
Agrius

Helene

THE STORM HAD MOVED on some time during the night's dancing, and a full moon hung high over the clear skies of Croilton. Silvery, luminous light spilled over the flags of the empty corridors as Helene slipped silently from her chamber. Eventually coming to the door she sought, she breathed a sigh of relief upon finding no guard on duty.

She set her hand to the ancient wood, caught at the latch with a gentle hand to lift it, and pushed inward. The door opened on well-oiled hinges, making no sound. She glanced behind her then entered. Giving herself a moment to adjust to the darkness, her eyes sought out the bed along the far wall near the window.

Lifting her skirts so as not to trip, she crept across the

room toward the bed, her heart beating with both uncertainty and excitement.

A form lay under the covers, turned away from her. She reached out her hand and placed it on his shoulder, shaking it gently.

"My lord, you must wake." The man stirred, and she persisted. "I believe the king knows you are here. You must flee; you should take the child and go before he sends to arrest you."

The man roused, and to her relief, did not lash out from being startled as she thought he might. Slowly he turned over, and as the pale light of the moon stole across his features, a knife of terror pierced her breast.

It was not Taibel Rebane, as she'd expected. It was the king himself.

She shook her head violently. No, this could not be! She made to turn and run, but before she could move, Casmir's arm snaked out, and he grabbed her hand so she could not flee. She tried desperately to pull away, but he flung his legs over the side of the bed to stand then snatched her other wrist, twisting it painfully in his powerful grip.

"No," she groaned. "No, you are not supposed to be here!"

"And where am I meant to be?" His teeth gleamed white in the luminescent light of the moon.

"I was going to come to you, you wanted..."

"I wanted... what?"

Helene dropped her chin, embarrassed and ashamed, angry and... terrified. Mostly she was terrified. It had all been a game. At least that is what she told herself, the only way she could bring herself to do the duty her father had forced upon her. No one would truly be harmed. She had taken care of the little princess as best she could. But now, facing Casmir in his wrath, she saw not the man, but the father and the king.

"Say it," he pressed, pushing her backward. "What did you think I wanted from you?" She clamped her mouth shut and would not meet his icy glare. "You thought I would bed you?"

He spun her and all but flung her down into a chair where she collapsed. She shrank away from him as he placed his hands on the armrests and leaned closer, hovering dangerously over her. The air around him sizzled with contempt, and she shivered.

She would not look at him, flicked her eyes to the right and to the left to see around him, anywhere but his face. "You said you hoped I could help you. I assumed..." she rasped.

"I simply offered you a chance this evening, Helene. Nothing more. When I asked for your help, I hoped you would tell me what you knew."

"Betray my father?"

"You knew my daughter was here, and yet you said nothing!" He shouted the words, fire flashing in his eyes, and she cowered as utter fear gripped her. His chest heaved with dark fury, and she was certain he would strike her as her father did when he was this angry. "You could have told me! You had every chance to, but you said *nothing!*"

"Casmir..." Wimarc of Dalery stepped behind him on silent feet and put his hand on the king's shoulder, breaking the spell. "I will see to the lady," he coaxed softly.

Casmir's breath came fast and hard, like a wild animal cornered by a hound. And though she watched through streaks of tears, she sensed a shift in the king. Where he had only moments ago been fueled with the fire of vengeance, now he appeared deflated, a husk of extreme fatigue and misery.

He turned away, saying nothing more.

Wimarc watched her, a look of combined pity and disgust on his face.

"Come, lady. Let us get you to your chambers. Tomorrow will be a very hard day for you, I warrant." The lord offered his hand, and Helene took it then stood.

Wimarc handed her off to another man waiting at the door to escort her away. He watched her go, but Casmir had already turned his back on her.

❀ ❀

Gone.

Rebane, Sybila, gone.

For the second time, I couldn't protect my daughter. She had been here the whole time! And in that time I had been made to look a fool by that duplicitous whoreson, Lord Cilgaron.

I shook with the exhaustion of my ire and collapsed down into the chair Helene had just occupied.

Something else made me shake besides the exhaustion.

That I had almost hit a woman...

I stared at my hands. It was what my father would have done.

I was not my father.

Would I have done it if Wimarc had not intervened? Perhaps I would never know.

I dropped my face into my hands, feeling the tremor of them as I did so.

News had reached me earlier in the morning of rumors regarding Sybila. Townspeople who had delivered supplies to the castle approached one of my men, telling him that they were certain they had seen the little princess playing in the meadows in the past week. Since few people this far from

Prille had ever seen her, I took the news as suspect. Yet it would have been foolish not to follow up on it.

I'd sent Jachamin to investigate and he'd returned just after the feasting to tell me the rumors were true, that she and Rebane had lodged here at Croilton. But by the time Jachamin had found proof, Rebane had already fled, taking Sybila with him.

This very chamber had been Rebane's hideaway. Sybila had been in this very room, and I was completely oblivious.

"Casmir..." I startled at my name and looked up to find Wimarc still standing there. "I have more news, and it's not likely to make your night any better."

"What else could possibly go wrong? Is it not enough that my daughter is missing yet again? Has Lord Cilgaron begun his rebellion already?"

"He's dead."

"What?!" I leapt to my feet.

"I took men to apprehend him as you'd asked. When we arrived we found him dead in his chamber. It was about the same time Rebane fled with Sybila."

"Was it Rebane?"

"Hard to say, but it seems likely."

I dropped back into the chair once more. "Thank you, Wimarc."

"Can I take you back to your rooms?"

I shook my head, and thankfully he did not argue but left, closing the door behind him.

Surrounded by darkness and utterly alone, I slid off the chair to the floor and onto my knees, clawing at the floor with desperate fingers as bitter tears streamed down my face and gasps of abject misery shook my body.

❋ *49* ❋

Croilton Castle
Honor of Cilgaron
Agrius

I WIPED RINGED FINGERS over my eyes, clearing away the grit of fatigue. The day ahead would prove to be long and arduous, for I meant to sit in judgment over the perpetrators of treason, and while I would be justified in my actions, I never found pleasure in taking the lives of others. And though the day would see an end to the trouble at Croilton, I had yet to deal with the shattered pieces Cilgaron had left in Lyseby itself, with the city leaders and merchants. Something must be done regarding Tugredd.

Once I was finally able to depart for home, I would face trouble of an entirely different stripe. There were pieces of my marriage scattered about, and next came the business of restoring what had broken. An image of Irisa rose up in my mind's eye, her long hair flowing free and set against the bright and burning hearth so that it glowed as if with fire. In such moments, she looked a very goddess. But the gods had seen fit to doubly bless her, for along with beauty and a sharp intellect, she also radiated a warmth and caring that was not native to nobility, could only have been bred from a history of hardship and scarcity, when survival depended upon neighbor helping neighbor. Indeed, the traitor Veris had found me a treasure, even if his motives had not been pure.

The heavy rains of the previous evening had cleared the air which had been heavy and humid during the day, leaving a light, fresh scent over the landscape. From over the wall at my hands, I looked north toward the Iron Heights where I had hunted just yesterday. Just then, the sun broke over the horizon behind me, slanting across the landscape with the brilliant rays of early summer, washing the hills with colors. A hawk flew high overhead, her sharp eyes scanning the ground for her breakfast. From my vantage point, I could see for miles to the north and the west, deep into the foothills.

Without Irisa knowing it, I had treated her abysmally, and if she had any sense she would not receive me back so kindly once she found out. But I knew Irisa, knew her kindness and compassion. The very things which gave me the freedom to take advantage of her were the same ones which would give her the wherewithal to forgive me, whether I deserved it or not.

It pricked my pride even more that she had been right all along about the very things I had bristled over, even though she had done all she could to gently caution me. While I could argue that never in my life had I been accountable to anyone in the way I was accountable to my wife, she held me to it, and the truth of my error stung like a wasp. Had I not dismissed Wolf so carelessly, had I brought him in the first place as I should have, Wolf would have helped me see reason before matters degraded. Perhaps that was why I had pushed my friend away in the first place.

My men would worry after me if I stayed away much longer, and so, with the sun a fair bit higher in the sky, I descended to the hectic castle grounds. As I crossed the cobbled courtyard, I passed the kitchens. From the corner of my eye, I spied a bright head, and the ambling, playful gait of the little girl, Brigid. She glanced up from whatever it was that had held her attention, and a large grin spread her cheeks. She wore a newer kirtle, I noticed. Before I had a chance to wave the girl over, a kitchen maid appeared from around the corner, calling the girl to her. A new stab of grief gutted me, but I continued on, arranging my face into a neutral mien. It was time to set aside Casmir the man in favor of Casmir the king.

An uneasy hush settled over the gathered crowd as the ladies of the castle, Roswen, and Helene, trailed an uneasy escort up the central aisle of the hall and to the place I sat in judgment over those who had plotted treason in my kingdom. Both women wore fine garments, likely the best their coffers had to offer. Possibly they thought that a display of extravagance and position would plead clemency on their part. When they stopped before me, Helene stood with hands folded before her, head dipped, and eyes downcast. Roswen made no such show of remorse. Lord Cilgaron's mistress stood with back erect, her eyes boring into mine as she stood defiant before me.

"Where is Aksel?" she demanded, speaking out boldly despite her circumstances.

Gasps of shock echoed up and down the hall at her

words even while I revealed nothing of my thoughts. I maintained a casual ease, leaning to the side of my chair, resting my chin against the balled fist of my right hand as Roswen waited for my answer. I did not mean to give her one. At least not yet.

Anyone who had the freedom to do so had come to the hall to observe this impromptu King's Court, and they pressed themselves into every available space in the hall so that it nearly overflowed. Eager necks craned to see, ears strained to hear the king's judgment over the lofty Lord Cilgaron and his women. Helene had yet to lift her face to look at me, and I felt a sense of pity wash over me. I rose and descended the steps to stand directly in front of them.

Coming to a decision over what I was to do, I turned on my heel, snapping my fingers to Jachamin as I strode from the hall. "Bring them and follow me."

I made for a sumptuous chamber behind the hall, not turning to make sure my command had been followed. I knew the women trailed behind me, for I heard the shuffling of feet even if they remained sullenly silent.

"Where is Aksel?" Roswen demanded once more after the door had been closed behind us.

Ignoring the woman's question, I paced to the far side of the gallery, running a finger along a table near the wall as I went. I picked up objects at random, replacing them before turning around to confront Helene.

"Was my daughter well cared for? Was she happy enough while she was here?"

Roswen opened her mouth as if to speak, and I silenced her with a look cold enough to freeze the deepest parts of the Tohm Sound. "I would hear it from Helene," I snarled. Fortunately, Roswen exhibited the sense to snap her mouth shut.

"I tended her myself, Your Grace," Helene replied, her words quiet but steady. "She was well cared for and content enough."

I struggled to catch hold of the elusive strands of my anger, for I knew that if I did not master the emotion, I would not last this interview. I could not let my grief overwhelm my better sense now. I could not risk losing my temper in the same way I had done last night.

I nodded in acknowledgment then swallowed hard before continuing. "Rebane fled at some point during last night's meal, taking my daughter with him. Do you know where he has gone?"

Helene shook her head. "No, Your Grace," she replied quietly, sincerely, and I believed she spoke true. "I was not aware of his going until last night when I discovered you..." She broke off, sucking in her lower lip. "You set a trap for me," she added uneasily.

"No more than you did for me, thinking you could turn the head of the king."

"But I thought..."

"You thought what you wanted to think," I snapped, and a tear formed on Helene's lower lashes, pooling then splashing down her cheek.

I had done nothing more than treat Helene with the respect due her rank, respect I would have shown any woman. And while I had become well aware of her designs on me after my failure to think clearly the night she blocked my path outside my chambers, my actions toward her afterward had been the essence of propriety. If she'd continued to envision more between us, that was on her head, not mine. Yes, I had baited her, but in the end, it was for her benefit, to see if she would run to warn Rebane, or if she would admit to her guilt. Even in that, I felt no shame.

Roswen could not stand quiet any longer. "The queen is base-born, even if she is a daughter of Bedic Sajen. She does not deserve you," she growled.

"My lady speaks true, Your Grace," Helene pleaded, finding a surprising well of courage from somewhere deep inside at the older woman's words. "I would make you a better match, you have to see. I can give you a son," she said in desperation, stepping forward as if to take my hand.

Roswen smiled approvingly, and Helene lifted her face, hopeful, encouraged by the support of her father's mistress.

Rising anger flushed my face, and I stepped toward her, stopping before I touched her. Once more Helene cowered. Roswen stood resolute. "You sully my wife's name when you speak of her so. I will not abide it. Not from you, who would steal her child, *MY* child, holding her captive for your own purposes!"

"What of my father?" Helene whispered, once more subdued, shrinking back.

"He is beyond help," I growled, my patience thinned to straining.

Helene tilted her head sideways, not understanding. Roswen grew pale-faced.

"Your father has fallen victim to his own scheming."

"What do you mean?"

"He is dead."

"You lie!" Helene screeched as Roswen sank to her knees on the floor.

I arched a brow. "Do I, indeed? Hardly. Rebane killed him before fleeing with my daughter."

"Why?" Helene whispered, wrapping her arms around her stomach as if she wanted to retch.

"Because traitors turn on one another, I suppose." I shrugged, my face a cool semblance of disregard. In fact, I felt anything but composed inside. My delivery of the news had been harsh. "And now he has escaped the king's justice."

She sank to the floor, and I made no move to help her.

"What will become of us?" Helene asked at last.

"I will leave a detachment of men to garrison Croilton as I have now taken it under the auspices of the Crown."

"You mean to take Croilton?" Helene cried.

"I have already taken it, my lady. You will remain here under guard for the time being. At least until I decide to whom I will grant the Honor of Cilgaron. Once that is settled, likely you will be sent away to live out your days in modest accommodation in one of your father's manors, at your cost, with an annual stipend from the revenues of Cilgaron. As for your father's woman," I said, turning to address Roswen, "I hope you have family who will show mercy to the doxy of a traitor."

I switched my focus back toward Helene who appeared nothing like the woman I'd first met in Lyseby. I should be angry with her, but the burning coal of my fury had burned itself out. In its place, I felt only pity for a woman who had been manipulated and used by an overreaching, power-hungry father and his mistress. It was likely she'd had no choice, a young woman beholden to do her father's bidding else suffer the consequences. No, I did not harbor ill-will toward Helene.

Even Irisa, had she known the circumstances, would have argued for mercy. I smiled inwardly at the irony. I ached at the thought of Irisa, so I swung away from them before any emotion could betray me.

"One more thing, before I go. How did news get to Haern and then to Elbra that Aksum was behind the disappearance of my daughter? Were those false reports intended to mislead?"

Helene looked as if she might speak, but Roswen silenced her with a hard, icy look. A light shifted in Helene's eyes, and she seemed to straighten a little. "Yes. My father wanted to assure that he would have enough time to gather his ships."

"Who was sent to carry the reports?"

"His name was Anton. Anton Mathiasen of Haern, he called himself."

"You know him?"

Helene tilted her head sideways. "I wouldn't say I knew him, my lord. He visited here many weeks ago, to see my father. I met him in town when he came to deliver news of the fleet in Sarsala. While my father would never tell me such things, I overheard their conversations, knew that he headed next to Haern and then to Elbra with the news."

❊ *50* ❊

Croilton Castle
Honor of Cilgaron
Agrius

"YOUR GRACE, THAT IS the last of the garrison and lower household."

I nodded. A yawn threatened to loose itself, but I fought back the urge. I was the center of attention in this horrific business, and I understood that men sought weakness, would find it in my fatigue and judge my own judgments as ill-considered. I waved away a servant offering me a cup, knowing drink would only dull my senses further.

Sorting through Cilgaron's household staff and garrison, filtering out those who were complicit and those who were innocent, had taken the majority of the day's working hours. A fortification the size of Croilton, presided over by a lord as wealthy as Cilgaron, required a vast number of people to run efficiently. Perhaps second only in Agrius to the palace in Prille. I had no desire to punish those servants who had no choice in doing their master's bidding, but I also did not want to excuse those who should have known better or who went along eagerly with their lord's plans. I had done my best to question each person carefully, immediately dismissing the lowest servants because they had no power over their fates. While I could have foisted the duty on my men, I preferred to act on this personally.

"Next is the lord's household staff, his steward, chamberlain," the clerk continued, but I put up a hand.

"We will take a break for now," I interrupted.

The day had turned to late afternoon, and beams of golden sunlight angled through the west windows, highlighting dust motes which swirled and swam high overhead. With the disruption of the normal activities of the castle, I had no idea what sort of meal had been planned; even so, hall servants needed to prepare the tables, even if the meal consisted of nothing more than cold meats and day-old bread.

"In fact, we are finished for today," I told the clerk. "Keep the upper staff under watch for now. Tomorrow is a new day, and everyone needs a rest."

"Yes, Your Grace," the clerk intoned as he bowed his way back then hurried off to do his king's bidding.

I pushed myself to stand, feeling stiff and wanting nothing more than a hot bath and nap. A group of clerks made to rush toward me, pushing parchments under my nose for my attention, but I breezed past them all, crooking a finger at the scriptstóri I had brought with me from Prille.

"See that the clerks record the names of each of the remaining household members so that none slip justice," I instructed.

"Yes, Your Grace," the man replied.

"And then I want you to personally oversee the review of Cilgaron's household accounts. Look for any evidence that he called for, or paid, mercenaries. When, to whom, and for how much."

"Yes, Your Grace."

I dismissed the man who bowed at the waist and swept away.

Quitting the hall, I made my way across the Isle Court toward my apartments. Flicking a glance at the sky, I noticed storm clouds rolling in once more and an involuntary shiver ran through me. It would be too soon if I ever visited Croilton again. Best to give the honor of it to a man who was loyal enough not to warrant a royal visit again in my lifetime.

By the time I reached my rooms, Andreu had a bath prepared, a skill the man swore was not an otherworldly talent despite the impression it gave. He simply had long-ago learned how to anticipate my wants and needs. I quirked a smile and patted the man's shoulder. There should be more Andreus in the world.

When I had washed and changed, I sat back in a padded chair, stretching out my legs before me. I couched a large goblet filled with a rich red wine on my stomach and closed my eyes. The rain had come again, and a cool breeze blew in from the north. I would stay here tonight. No need to visit the hall for whatever would pass for a meal. Food could be brought to me here early, and then bed.

No sooner had I begun to relax, allowing my mind to wander, than Wimarc arrived.

"Casmir, I have just received word from Jachamin."

My eyes snapped open at that, and I jerked upright, sloshing the contents of my cup over my fresh attire.

"Rebane heads north, toward Sarsala," Wimarc continued.

"And my daughter?" I stood, gripping my goblet as a lifeline.

"She is with him."

With a great roar, I swung my arm back and hurled my cup at the fireplace, an arc of blood-red wine in its wake as it sailed into the flames, dousing the fire with a great sparking hiss and billows of smoke.

"Andreu, send to have Sevaritza saddled!"

"Andreu, wait..." Wimarc rushed toward me. "Casmir, I know what you are thinking."

I swung on him. "Do you, now? You know me so well that you know what I am thinking?" I bellowed, shrugging off Andreu's attempts to offer me a towel with which to clean the wine from my sleeve.

"I know you want to chase after the man yourself. You would have your justice, and you would exact it with your own hand."

I turned eyes lit with burning coals to the young lord of Dalery, furious with his presumption even while knowing he was right. Indeed I did want to chase after Rebane, wanted to cut him down without mercy where he sat his horse. Would not any father?

"Let Jachamin get him, Casmir," Wimarc continued forcefully.

"And let him handle Rebane as he did Tugredd? I will have my vengeance, Wimarc." I smashed my fist onto the table, rattling cups.

"Jachamin has more sense than that. And Lord Wigstan is with him. His messenger said they were nearly on Rebane's heels, had the man in his sights. It wouldn't be long before they have him in chains and back in Prille. Finish your work here, Casmir. Then get home to your queen. Likely they are already making their way back to the palace."

I clenched my jaw and narrowed my eyes. "Send word to Captain Barta to have the ships ready to sail. I will finish up here in the morning then make for Lyseby and the port with all haste. We'll leave the palanquins here and ride. Time is too urgent. I want the ships ready to sail the moment I arrive. I don't care if it's the blackest of nights. I'm going home."

"Casmir, the storm has stirred the ocean and the waters are treacherous. Likely the fleet will have to hug the coast, and the going will be slow."

I swung back around, pacing across the room. "Then we'll make it as far as we can while progress is good. I'll ride the rest of the way if I have to."

"Even in a squall?"

"I'd ride to the *Realm of Rækallin* and back to get my daughter," I growled.

The next day dawned overcast, and a light rain fell even as lightning and thunder rolled in the distance toward the coast. I finished my duties swiftly before midday, leaving the more sundry details to be sorted by those I left behind.

A groom held the reins of Sevaritza for me as I gave my final instructions to the man I left in charge of the garrison. Then swinging atop the dark courser, I let my gaze linger on the windows of the chambers overhead. Faces watched through the panes of glass, and I imagined one of them must be Helene. Without another thought, I turned away and kicked Sevaritza's flanks.

"Hie!" I cried, setting off for Lyseby, the port, and the ship waiting to take me home.

❋ *51* ❋

Bellesea Palace
Prille
Agrius

Kassia

"HERE, SON, HOLD IT like so."

Kassia watched the blade smith come around the anvil and slip in next to the two-year-old Cailen. He gently rotated Cailen's hand a quarter turn so that the blade he held in his small fingers rested flat for hammering. The contrast between the two could not be more startling. The thickly sinewed and rawhide forearm of the elder man showed stark against the smooth, pale-pink skin of her son's arm.

In the days since Jack's departure, Kassia had been bringing Cailen here, to the smithy where his father was born, partly to let him fill his heart and mind with a connection to a way of life the young boy would never know now that his father held a title and a manor for a king. It brought her great pleasure to see the men of the smithy take to Cailen, knowing who his father was. Mostly though, Kassia did it to feel closer to her husband in his absence.

"You'll be a master before we know it. I will have to keep an eye on my job here, I will!" The smith grinned at Cailen, who beamed back a bright smile.

"Cai, it's been long enough that your aunt will worry for us," Kassia interrupted. "She has promised your favorite meal this evening, and you must be cleaned up before you will touch a morsel."

Cailen responded with a pout and seemed about to protest when the burly smith crouched down at Cailen's eye-level. "You could always stay here and let me take your place? I've always wondered what a great meal in the palace was like. It's possible your aunt may not notice the difference between us and think you've just grown over the course of the afternoon?"

Cailen's eyes grew wide and round, and the smith laughed, standing. He took the blade from Cailen's hand and returned it to the workbench.

With a laugh and a wave, Kassia took Cailen and led him out of the smithy and onto the street in the tradesman's quarter of the lower ward. They passed along the winding street leading to the upper ward and had nearly reached the hall when a familiar voice resounded from the antechamber just through the doorway.

Jack. He'd returned.

Slipping his hand from Kassia's, Cailen squirmed his way through the legs of the people in front of them and disappeared inside. Kassia rushed to catch up, slowed by the crowd gathered to greet the returning men. By the time she found them, Cailen was already seated comfortably astride his father's shoulders.

Jack appeared both happy to see her yet at the same time haggard and drawn. She moved in to hug him and he winced. It was only then that she noticed the flurry of activity in the hall. Irisa stood talking to Luca, her face as pale as Jack's, sending waves of alarm like a current through her.

"Jack, what is the matter? Has something happened?"

"Rebane and Sybila, they were not in Aksum after all. They were never in Aksum. The information was false, planted by someone intent on leading us astray."

Kassia furrowed her brows. "Do you know where they went?"

"No." The admission seemed to pain him. Even the simple word caused him to flinch, as if a knife stabbed his gut. "But Luca will head north immediately to Lyseby. Casmir must be told."

❋ ❋

"You were *stabbed?*" Kassia shrieked. "Jack! How could you let that happen?"

Jack crossed the chamber nonchalantly as he told his tale. The meal finished, their son put to bed, Kassia finally had a moment alone with her husband to hear his news.

"It wasn't my first choice, admittedly." He grinned, and she swatted him on the arm. "When I met you, I had no idea I would be taking up a life as a pincushion!"

Kassia picked up a cushion to throw at him, but he ducked. Then in one swift motion, he spun, swooping under her arm. He grabbed her around the waist and turned her to face him.

"Jack, I..." she began but got no farther. He kissed her hard on the lips.

"Enough, my feisty one. I am fine."

"But you were stabbed, Jack! You could have died!"

"I am aware of that. I was there."

She wanted to argue with him, to make him see that his behavior toward Isary had risked everything. And for what? Her so-called honor? What good was honor if she lost her husband because of it? She would never understand men. Not as long as she lived.

The fire of her fury left her, leaving only a fatigue which sucked the fight from her. In truth, she was more happy to see him than angry with him. She slumped her shoulders and leaned her head against his chest. Jack pulled her in more tightly. She snaked her hands up his shoulders, around his neck, and entwined her fingers behind his head. She hung there, clinging to him, as if her very life depended on it.

They stood unmoving for an interminable amount of time. Finally, Jack released his hold on her and she let go as well. She turned to seek out a chair. She needed to sit.

"Thank the gods for Melku," she whispered, shaking her head. "If he hadn't offered you his *wobbly shimmy*..."

"His *wami ts'shekimi*," Jack corrected.

"Whatever."

Jack sat in the chair next to hers, his jovial mood evaporated and replaced with the same look of fatigue and worry she'd seen on his face earlier in the hall.

"What of Isary?" she asked.

"You won't need to worry about him ever again," he returned flatly.

"Did he get stabbed too?" she asked while making a face, but Jack only blinked, his expression unchanged. "He did? Someone stabbed him? Is he dead?" The truth showed in his face. A squirming knot of unease formed in her stomach.

"After he was arrested, he was found by guards early

the next morning, dead in his cell."

"Who? Who did it?"

Before Jack could answer, the door opened and a valet ushered in the older Cai with a young boy in tow.

Kassia eyed Jack, raising a brow in question.

"This is the boy I was telling you about, Kalu, Wolf's son."

At the sound of his name, Kalu moved a half step behind Cai.

"He has taken to Cai, refuses to leave him. He is Wolf's responsibility now, though they are essentially strangers, the two of them, even if they share blood. I cannot imagine what Wolf will do with him."

Kassia took in the sight of the small boy, immediately noticing the obvious similarities between both his father and mother. With one hand he grasped the older Cai's hand, and with the other, he worried the front of his tunic. He kept his eyes downcast.

"Did he come with a nurse, with anyone he knows?"

Cai nodded. "Yes, but I want to keep him with me tonight if it's alright with you?" Cai dropped his other hand to place his palm on the top of Kalu's head. "He might sleep better near me as he did on the voyage here."

"Yes, Cai, I think that's a good idea," Kassia replied. "But why don't you both stay in our apartments? I'm sure beds can be made up for you. Go and find your things, and bring his nurse here too."

Cai nodded and made to turn around, but Kassia stopped him. "Oh, and Cai?" Cai turned back, a question on his face. "I was sorry to hear about Isary." She quirked up the corner of her mouth as she squinted at him.

He said nothing in return, but Kassia was certain she saw the mischievous light she knew so well sparkle in the deepest part of his eyes. The corner of his mouth twitched, and he turned, taking Kalu with him.

Kassia returned her attention to Jack only to find him watching her with a half-smile, half-grimace.

"Do you really want to know the answer to the question you have yet to ask?"

"But..." she stammered. How did he know what she'd wanted to ask?

"Kassia," Jack said, rising to take her hands and leading her to their bedchamber. "My father always taught me never to ask a question for which I don't truly want to know the answer." Kassia made to protest, but Jack continued before she could. "Cai was oath-sworn to Isary. If you were to ask Cai if he killed his lord, even out of his affection for you, and he confirmed your suspicions, would the information change the way you look at him from now on?"

"But if he didn't do it..."

"Kassia, let it lie."

She sighed and tossed her newly removed kirtle over a chest then made her way over to the bed, freeing her hair as she went. Propping herself up against the pillows, she combed through her hair with loose fingers, considering Jack's words. She began to re-braid her copper brown strands loosely over her shoulder as Jack slid into bed next to her. She scowled at the sight of his bandaged torso.

Jack caught her look and smirked then rolled to his side, propping up his head against his hand to watch her.

"Kassia, I'm fine. The wound is fine. The physicians in Aksum are more than qualified." He snatched one of her hands away and kissed her knuckles.

She pulled her hand away to keep braiding. "That's not what I'm worried about."

"Then what?" he asked. He moved in closer and

nuzzled his face into her neck.

"I had a thought."

"May the gods help us all," he muttered, not paying any attention to what she said.

She shook her head and fell silent for a time. She finished off her braid, tying the end with an efficient knot, then flung the braid back over her shoulder and turned to look at Jack who had managed to bury his face in her chemise, his fingers sneaking down her leg.

"Did *you* do it?"

Jack stopped his pursuit and froze. After a moment he raised his head. "Why would you even think that?"

"Jack, I know about the Morthingi."

"You *know* about that?"

She flashed a sly smile. "Of course. Why do you think I worried so much? It's not because you were incapable of protecting yourself but because I knew your skill might make you cocky."

"How long have you known?"

"Jack, I am the matron of the manor. There is little that passes under my nose that I miss. I found your dagger so carefully hidden away where you thought I would never see it."

"And you understood the significance of the symbol on the pommel? But they are a secret group..."

The confusion on his face made her chuckle gently. She leaned over and kissed the top of his head. "Mmm hmm... But you still didn't answer my question. Did you kill Isary?"

His confusion turned to a look of thoughtfulness. "You need to know why I joined them, the Morthingi." He looked down to study his hands. "I was young. We were exiled. I was angry for all I thought I'd lost. It didn't seem fair, and I needed an outlet for that anger. When the opportunity came up, I took it."

"What did Rem think?"

"My father didn't like it, but he didn't stop me. I wasn't involved with them for long before I grew sick of what they asked of me. I had an idea in my head of what it would be like, and when that idea didn't match the reality..." He shrugged. "I took the first opportunity to sneak away, an act punishable by death if they'd caught up with me -- which they never did, though I honestly don't think they really ever tried."

"That's probably why their existence is such a poorly kept secret." She smiled pensively. "When you killed those guards in Lynchport, the ones guarding Swine, I was horrified at your efficiency. You were too casual about it."

He nodded. "Yes, I knew it bothered you. I feared then you would press me too closely about it. I just didn't know what else to do. We had few options that day. I knew what would happen if they'd caught you."

"I guess I must have just known instinctively what Rem taught you, that you should never ask the question if you don't really want to know the answer." Kassia dipped her chin, her impish humor returned. But only momentarily. "It's a secret you should have told me," she whispered.

"Yes, I should have. I didn't want it to change your opinion of me. I didn't want you to be disappointed in me. I couldn't bear it."

She slithered down the pillows and more deeply into the bed then slid up next to him, pressing her face right up to his. "Jack, you have never disappointed me. Not ever."

She reached up to brush away the hair that had fallen over his eye then put her hand on his chest. Jack drew her in and kissed her slowly. After a moment he asked, "So... do you still want to know if I killed Isary?" A wolfish smile tugged at the corners of his mouth.

"Not really, no."

His look turned predatory, and he pressed her more deeply into the mattress, lifting himself over her and kissing her again.

When he paused for breath, she mumbled into him, "But did you?"

"Do what?" he replied before kissing her again.

"Kill Isary. Did you kill him?"

His lips spread a slow, sly smile, and her eyes grew wide with horror.

"I thought you didn't want to know."

"I don't."

"Good."

❊ *52* ❊

Bellesea Palace
Prille
Agrius

Irisa

SHADOWS DREW LONG FINGERS across the room as the last
petitioner left. Irisa stretched, easing the ache from the long
hours of sitting. Bringing her hands to her lower back, she
worked the tight muscles, thinking that a salt and herb-infused
bath would be just the thing after her duties had finished and
she'd eaten.

A light breeze brushed her skin, coming in through an
opening in the window just above her head. A section of glass
had broken in a recent storm, and for now, only iron bars
filled the space between the mullions and tracery as
glassmakers prepared the new window sections. The areas
around the missing piece had already been replaced, and the
fading light filtering through the many-hued panes caught the
light, showering the floor with a haze of soft colors.

The condition of the light and the rumblings in her

stomach told her it would soon be time for the evening meal, and as had become her habit during Casmir's absence, it would be taken in private. Her mood tended toward gloom these last many days, and overwhelming fatigue sought to dominate her waking moments. She tried her best to shove it aside, to keep busy, even if it grew more and more difficult.

Since Jack's return from Aksum and Luca's quick departure to find Casmir in Lyseby, she had every hope that Sybila had been found, but she would not rest easy until she knew for sure. Nothing was certain. She had learned that long since.

The last clerk cleared the room of his writing tools and records, and now servants entered to snuff candles and put out lamps. Irisa sighed, fighting back the mournful pang in her soul, and wiped a hand across her brow. She would speak with Kassia. Perhaps her sister could help her prepare an infusion of wormwood, mint, and balm to soothe her stomach.

Thinking of the final details to be tended before she could withdraw to the family apartments, she turned to make her way to the door.

And froze.

Casmir stood leaning against one side of the door frame with his left arm stretched out to brace against the other side as if it held him up. She was still too far from him, and the room too shadowed, to read the expression in his eyes or to draw conclusions from the set of his lips. But his sudden appearance, his silence, and the way he simply watched her, all worked to unnerve her.

He appeared travel weary, wearing a riding cloak and tall boots splattered with the mud of the road, as if he had ridden overland rather than by ship. Neither of them moved, and the moments dragged on.

When finally it seemed as if they must either break the trance or die here, Irisa took a step toward him. She continued on across the tiles, and as she did, she lowered her eyes, unable to meet his look. She knew she should not be so uncertain regarding him, for she was his wife, he her husband. They had shared a life and bed these past years. Was it simply that matters had been left in such a precarious state between them that seeing him again brought up many old insecurities? Or did she fear something else?

She felt rattled and knew that if she looked at him now she would blush, betraying how much she had missed him. She could not be certain he felt the same.

Instead, she fixed her attention on his coat hanging open at the front, revealing a finely tailored tunic of soft cotton dyed the color of night and embroidered with black silk filigree. His wide collar draped his shoulders askew, as if he hadn't thought to fasten it properly.

"Your messenger did you a disservice by not telling us of your exact arrival, my lord," Irisa said finally once she reached him, dropping into a formal obeisance, as if she was nothing more than a common petitioner of the court rather than a sovereign in her own right.

He straightened, removing his hand from the door frame, and she raised her chin to look at his face. Her heart lurched, for the despondency she found there transformed everything she remembered about him, from a face she knew into one she did not.

"That is because they did not know." He pitched his voice so low that through its hoarseness she could barely make out the words. "I abandoned ship at The Point after a storm damaged the rigging enough to require repairs. I ordered a horse saddled, riding at speed for home."

More servants entered the room with buckets and soap

to clean the floors. Casmir's eyes followed their movements, but still, he did not move either from the doorway or toward her.

Irisa inhaled slowly, wondering what else to say. "You look to be in need of a wash."

He broke his gaze from the servants and looked back to her. He opened his mouth as if to say more then hesitated. After a moment he said simply, "Yes."

She tilted her head, trying to interpret his thoughts, but as was often the case, she could not read him. "We should go back to our rooms."

A strange look passed over his face, and then overcome with an emotion she could not interpret, he turned away from her. Pulling his leather gloves from his hands, his shoulders heaved, and he walked from the room.

Irisa trailed after him, confusion mitigating the speed she might have otherwise had in following him. When finally they reached their apartments, a valet opened the door. After taking Casmir's coat and boots, he excused himself and left them, leaving Irisa even more confused than she had been.

When he'd gone, Irisa turned back to Casmir only to find him kneeling before her, his eyes red-rimmed and shimmering. She moved to stand in front of him, taking up one of his hands in her own.

"My love, can you ever forgive me?" he rasped. He dipped his head to rest his forehead on their conjoined hands.

A bell of alarm sounded in her heart, and she felt at a loss for words. Candlelight reflected off his hair, revealing hints of auburn in the dark brown, keeping her gaze transfixed. Instead of responding immediately, she lifted her other hand to run it through his hair. He closed his eyes and caught it, bringing it around to his face and tilting his head to rest his cheek in her palm.

"Casmir, you are beginning to frighten me. What have you done needing my forgiveness?" The possibilities terrified her, seemed as wide-ranging as her imagination, but she needed to know.

With his eyes still closed he shook his head as if trying to forget a memory. "I have been foolish. Stupid and foolish. Short-sighted, negligent, stupid and foolish."

Had something happened to Sybila that he feared to tell her? Had he been unfaithful? She resisted the urge to give in to her rattled nerves. When he stopped for a breath, she whispered, "Come, let's talk somewhere more comfortable."

Taking his hand, she drew him toward a wide seat on the far side of the room.

"Now, tell me, what is this about?" She reached out a hand to wipe the hair off his forehead, for the first time noticing the fine lines and drawn skin around his lips. He had only been gone weeks but looked to have aged years. "Did you ride through the night?"

He nodded. "And the day. I fear I am too exhausted to explain adequately with words."

"Then tell me with hand signals," she quipped weakly, soliciting a flicker of a smile from him.

"I thought she might be here, Irisa."

"You thought Sybila might be here? Casmir, what has happened?" Her heart sank, and a new lump formed in her throat even as her eyes pleaded with him to continue.

"Sybila," he cracked. Tears glistened in his eyes. "She was in Croilton, not Aksum. Simon went on a fool's errand, and all the while our daughter was held at Croilton. I was there. I could have saved her, but I was too slow. Rebane left with her before I knew of it."

"Simon and Jack returned with the news, but we did not know she was at Croilton. So what happened that made you think she might be here now?"

Casmir looked up at her with hollow, haunted eyes. After a steadying breath, he explained to her the events in Lyseby and then Croilton, the endless talking and negotiating, news of Tugredd and then of the posturing of Lord Cilgaron. He explained the fateful night they discovered Rebane missing, along with their daughter, and everything which led up to his mad ride back to Prille.

"So Lord Cilgaron used the guildsman Tugredd, hoping he would stir up a full-fledged rebellion leading to war? To what end? To wear the crown?"

"He is Sajen by blood even if he made an oath of allegiance to my father. So yes, it seems he wanted to make his own bid for the crown." An edge of bitterness made his words sharp.

Irisa shook her head. "I thought our marriage ended all of that. Will we always be fighting off the coming of war?" She'd not asked expecting an answer, and he didn't give her one. "Casmir, I don't care about the throne. I just want my little girl back, safe and in my arms."

He nodded tiredly. "And this is where I have failed you, Irisa. I should have been able to protect her. I was foolish to think I could."

Irisa put her hand on his knee. She didn't know what words would help him with his personal disparagement.

"I know how you feel about Jachamin Guimer, but I sent him and Wolf in pursuit of Rebane as he fled north to Sarsala with her, likely to the ships Cilgaron had gathered there. Wimarc helped me see reason, suggested I come home, that they may very well be here upon my return. But she's not, is she?"

"No, she's not. None have returned."

Casmir dropped his chin, studying his hands by the

feeble light of the lamp burning on the table to his left. "It's a lance to my soul, Irisa," he finished quietly. "I will always feel responsible."

She wanted to comfort him, but she knew that there was nothing she could say that would help him. A drowning man was not saved with words.

"What happened to Lord Cilgaron?" she asked instead.

"Rebane killed him before feeling."

Irisa shivered at the thought. Casmir clasped his hands into a tight fist, his knee bouncing. He took a deep shuddering breath and turned his face to meet her look directly. His eyes held a new emotion. A sadness, or a loss; fear, or pain of a like she could not comprehend.

"There's something else, isn't there?" she asked finally, and in the asking held her breath.

"Cilgaron has a daughter, Helene."

The pounding of her heart grew tenfold, and without realizing she did it, her hand fluttered to her throat, finding the delicate chain holding her sun medallion, the symbol of the house she had chosen by going into her marriage with him willingly. She waited for him to continue, her breathing shallow.

"Wolf was right about her, but I wouldn't listen."

Irisa's hands began to tremble. She needed air, though she couldn't force her lungs to draw it in.

"Cilgaron had a secondary plan -- that if his rebellion didn't succeed, he wanted his daughter to become queen." His voice steadied, his words sounding more angry than tired. His look bored into her soul, but still she could not breathe. "Wolf warned me that she would try to tempt me, to trap me into a dalliance."

Irisa opened her mouth to speak, but her throat tightened around the words, so she closed it again. Casmir picked up her hand and brought it to his lips. She resisted the urge to snatch it away. A tear broke free from the corner of her eye.

"My Adonia, she did not succeed. My failure was that I did not guard myself against her, instead put myself into a situation for her to try, heedless of the consequences."

Sadness filled his face again, and he dropped his chin.

"You have pushed so many away," Irisa whispered.

"Yes. And that is my shame."

They both stilled into silence, the sputtering of the lamp's flame providing a staccato commentary on their misery. A distant dog barked, perhaps Lizzie wondering why her master had not come to find her.

Casmir clenched at his knee. His fingernails were dirty, the one on his little finger cracked and broken. A tiny scar on the back of his hand, the one she'd bandaged the day Simon left for Aksum, glistened in the frail light.

"Casmir, I don't know how I feel about this right now. What you did was not infidelity or betrayal, I see that. But that does not make it any easier to hear, even so." She paused to swallow, wiping the tear rolling down her cheek. "You used poor judgment."

"Certainly."

"You have agonized over this, over telling me," she observed, and he nodded.

"And with Sybila not here..." He took in a long, shuddering breath. "I am broken, Irisa. All the while I rode to Prille, I pushed myself thinking she would be here. It drove me as nothing else could. And she's not here. She's not here," he repeated, as if still coming to terms with the loss. "It's as if the weight of a thousand lives has come to bear on my shoulders in a single moment of time. And I have been left alone to carry it."

He was weary beyond words. She could see it in the cavernous lines etched around his eyes and lips. Even his hair hung limp. Like her, he'd carried so much these last many weeks, and the strain of it showed. He had cracked in places, and his edges frayed bare. He'd been trampled and bruised, but the damage had stopped just short of breaking him, she was certain, despite what he'd said. And that, at least, was a testament to his character, the character she had always known him to have.

Her heart broke for him. She picked up his hand again and ran her thumb along his fingers, cracked and worn from the long, desperate ride home to a daughter he hoped would be there.

"You are not alone, Casmir. I am here," she whispered. "We will survive this, just as we have always done."

He took her comment with stoical consideration. "What will we do now? About everything?"

Irisa turned her head to look about the room, as if the furniture would give her answers. The evening had long since waned, and night's stillness replaced evening's gentle murmur. Nothing but shadows claimed the places she knew so well.

"Now we sleep. And we hope that tomorrow brings clarity."

❀ *53* ❀

Bellesea Palace
Prille
Agrius

A SLOW AWAKENING INFILTRATED my awareness. Just as the liquid light of morning dissolves the fog of night over the waters of a mountain lake, my dreams changed from hazy to corporeal. I opened my eyes, momentarily confused over where I was.

Irisa.

My wife slept next to me. I was home.

Fatigue marinated every fiber and sinew of my body, and sleep threatened to take me once more. In the same moment I was about to give in to it, Irisa stretched out her hand, likely seeking the place that for these last long weeks had been nothing but a cold, empty bed. But this time, rather than empty space, her fingers met with warm, yielding flesh.

She opened her eyes.

"You should feel ashamed, my Adonia. Taking

advantage of a man when he is vulnerable, sleeping soundly in his bed. It's quite unseemly."

"You were not soundly asleep, you fiend."

"Guilty as charged, Your Grace."

Irisa glanced over my head and beyond through the bed hangings to the windows. The sun was not yet up. She offered me a languid smile and said, "You should not be awake. Go back to sleep."

"I have had more sleep in these last many hours than in the last three nights put together," I replied in the deep, gravelly voice of one just awakened. "I feel as vigorous as a young lad." I maneuvered myself nearer and traced a finger across her cheek then down her neck and shoulder.

"As tired as you were last evening, I thought for certain you would not wake for another week," she quipped drowsily, closing her eyes again.

"So my wife has formed an addiction to rule?"

"Why don't you just go back to sleep?" she said smiling, nuzzling her head more deeply into her pillow.

"How can I sleep now that I have to worry about you plotting against me? You hoped I would sleep my life away while you continued to rule Agrius single-handedly. That is your dastardly scheme."

"Perhaps," she conceded, but her smile faded.

I knew her thoughts went to Sybila. My smile slid away as all the horrors of the last days came rushing back. My eyes softened toward her as a jeweled tear moistened her cheek.

"Casmir, we need to find her."

The light-hearted joy I'd just found dissipated as quickly as it had come. I pulled her close to my chest and we slept.

When dawn finally did come, its light bathed the room in the warmth of a freshly baked honey cake. I noted the rich hues reflecting off a stone column against the wall when I straightened to stretch my back.

I couldn't sleep, had risen well before daybreak to wash myself and dress, then to begin to work through the piles of correspondence and issue orders. Thoughts of all that had just come to pass in the last weeks and months continued to haunt me. Sounds of birdsong filtered in through the panes of the windows, and I stood to stretch my legs. The door cracked open, and the face of a valet poked through.

"A message for you, from the port master."

I took the folded note and read. When I reached the end, I heard Irisa stir in the other room so set it down. I entered our bedchamber and made my way over to the bed, sitting on the edge nearest her, leaning over to kiss her forehead.

"Good morning. Did I wake you?"

"I should say yes, but it would be a lie."

"I have just had word that the *Sjórinn Mær* has arrived. The rigging is fixed, and they made good time." I brushed a strand of hair away from her eyes.

"Have they brought more news?"

I compressed my lips. "No. They know nothing more than when I left them at The Point. I have already sent out scouts to watch for Wolf and Jachamin."

I paused to consider my next words. Irisa caught my hesitation, for her head tilted to the side.

"But there is something, isn't there?" She sat up, as if ready to pounce into action over whatever news she anticipated me telling her next. "What else do you need to tell me?" She furrowed her brows as she waited for me to continue.

"The *Sjórinn Mær* has cargo you should know about. I wanted to be the one to tell you about it before you heard it from other lips."

"Casmir, what..."

I put my hands on her shoulders and kissed her to stop her protest. "It's nothing so dire, my Adonia." I drew in a preparatory breath, uncertain over how she would react to my news. "While I was at Croilton, I encountered a small mite of a girl. She reminded me so much of Sybila. She was the daughter of a slave who was killed in the reprisals after the edict."

The complicated story of my emotions washed over my face: sadness, anger, and guilt. She remained quiet as I struggled to find a way to explain it all.

"Her name is Brigid. I thought simply to leave an allowance for her care, but..."

"But you didn't?"

I shook my head. "No, well, yes. I did leave a ring from my own hand with a kitchen maid for her care, and in return, I was to get regular updates on her well-being." Irisa tilted her head in confusion, and I continued. "When I was riding out of Croilton on my way to the port in Lyseby, I happened to glance to the side. It was mere luck that I spied her bright head peeking up at me over a barrel." I felt an unusual flush paint my cheeks, and I looked down to fumble my fingers in the bed cover. "My Adonia, it was pure weakness. I couldn't help myself. I walked my mount over to the barrel, opened my arms, and she climbed up into them as if she was meant to be there."

"You brought her here?" Irisa exclaimed, and I nodded, a look of both guilt and embarrassment mingling in my expression. "My love," she said, leaning forward to wrap her arms around me, "it was your best impulsive act to date."

"I was worried you might be jealous of her, with Sybila gone." I shook my head. "I didn't know if you would receive her so easily, thinking that if you didn't want her here, we could find somewhere to send her... I just couldn't leave her there. I believe she is Cilgaron's by-blow from his slave girl, and in so being, Brigid has Sajen blood. I feel a duty to her." I finally stopped talking and studied her to see if her true feelings matched her words. "So you do not mind?"

"Having another child in the house? No, of course not." She smiled shyly, a strange aspect lighting her countenance.

I eyed her curiously. "I feel like I've missed something. Have I?"

"I wanted to tell you later, and in different circumstances... I am happy to welcome this Brigid to be raised at court if you desire it, but we will soon enough have another child of our own."

I felt my eyes grow round and wide, like the moon hanging perilously over the farthest horizon.

"Are you certain?"

"It's still early, and much could yet go wrong, but yes, I am about as certain as I can be."

I leaned toward her, kissing her once more.

"Does anyone else know? Does Kassia?"

"No, you are the first I've told, though I cannot control the suspicions of others."

I brought her fingers to my lips and kissed them then rose from the bed. "Can it be our secret for a time longer?" Irisa nodded, and I smiled. "I want time to take in this news. Sybila..." I stuttered her name then shook my head, seeing an image of my beautiful daughter in my mind's eye. Irisa's face softened, as if she followed the direction of my thoughts.

"It will take time, Casmir. It will be alright." She smoothed her hands over her lap then smiled the secretive smile of a mother new with child.

"I must go now to meet with Jack and Simon, to hear the report of their trip." I wiped a hand over my face, clearing the fatigue dousing my limbs and eyes. "What will you do today?"

"I plan to visit the Bibliotheca this morning, to check on my Sajen histories. I received word yesterday that they are nearly finished, thanks to the work of a young scriptstóri named Annor. I hope to reward him for his efforts when they are finished. He has been a tremendous help to me."

I kissed her then left to find Jack and Simon.

Our long conference finally over, I stood and noticed the changing shadows of the room. Jack and Simon had done well explaining the events of their journey.

"I think I want to walk down to the quay, to inquire for myself of the port master, to see if anyone has returned."

Simon and Jack exchanged glances at my unusual decision. Without reason to protest, they each shrugged, agreeing to accompany me.

The truth of the matter was that I still felt helpless. Even a walk down to the water's edge felt like action. Remaining confined at court would accomplish nothing. Normally I would have felt free to ease my agitation with a long ride outside Prille, but I dared not. If word reached the palace while I was away, it would take that much longer for me to hear it. The last time I rode out, Sybila was taken.

I followed Simon out of the chamber as Jack answered more of my questions about the discovery of Isary's body.

"There is no question he did not take his own life?"

"None."

His face hardened with certainty, his hand reaching down to touch the pommel of his dagger. I glanced at the design upon it.

The *Morthingi.*

Jack had an association with the group.

He saw the realization dawn across my face and smiled knowingly. "He did *not* take his own life," he said finally, dispersing any shadow of a doubt as to Isary's end and who had caused it.

I held his look for a moment longer then nodded. His secret would be safe with me.

We stepped out from under the shade of the arcade beyond the administrative wing and entered into the large courtyard of the upper ward. As we passed the Bibliotheca, Irisa and a young scriptstóri descended the steps toward us.

"Casmir, has there been any word from Luca? Has anyone spotted Rebane?"

I shook my head, unable to hide my dismal feelings. "No, not yet." A strange emotion flickered across the face of the scriptstóri with Irisa. While I was uncertain whether this was the Annor she had told me about earlier, I made note of it as odd nevertheless. "Though now at least I understand why we were sent to chase after Aksum as the offender. It was a ploy to intentionally mislead so the vile miscreant had time to set his other plans into motion. I'm convinced that it was only my trip to Croilton which confounded him."

"Rebane, or someone else?"

"Rebane, yes, in league with Cilgaron of course. They must have sent a lackey to spread word to Torrine to cast suspicion on Ethew."

"Mathiasen."

It took a moment for me to realize it was the scriptstóri who had spoken. I swung around, taking a menacing step toward him. "What did you say?"

The young man backed up, nearly colliding with the wall at his back. "A-Anton Mathiasen... Your Grace."

"Irisa, who is this?" I asked, not breaking my visual hold on the scriptstóri.

"This is Annor, the one I told you about. He has been helping me in the evenings while you were away."

"How do you know that name?" I asked Annor.

Irisa must have sensed my rising fury and reached out a hand for my sleeve. A pallor of sickness washed over the young scriptstóri, and he cast terrified eyes on Irisa. Rather than step in to help him, Irisa stood resolute, waiting for his answer.

"I... I overheard it."

I pounced like a cat on a mouse. "Where? Where did you overhear the name?"

"In the Bibliotheca." Annor struggled to find air, grimacing as he sought the words while fighting off his terror. He fumbled with his hands, his fingernails digging into his palms in his anxiety. He could not bring himself to look me straight-on.

"Where in the Bibliotheca? Is it conspiring scriptstórii again?" Annor blanched once more as I grasped a handful of his robe in my fist and twisted, pressing my face so close to his that he had to turn to the side to avoid having his nose crushed. "Who has betrayed me?"

"My love," Irisa intervened gently.

She stepped up against my shoulder as waves of impassioned heat radiated off me. Beads of sweat gathered on my brow, and blood vessels bulged against my neck and throat. My hands shook where they hid tangled in the white robe of the scribe. Every muscle in my body thrummed with the tautness of a bow about to loose an arrow or a hound who strained at his lead to be released into the wood after game.

"Give him a chance to speak." Irisa placed her hand on my upper arm and gently tugged me. I would not be moved.

Before she could say more, we were interrupted by the sounds of an approaching group of people. I swung on the sound, and my eyes went wide upon seeing the members of the group.

I lunged toward them, pushing aside the men in the lead to get at the man in the middle. I brought back my hand bunched into a fist, swinging it forward and smashing it into the face of Taibel Rebane.

❊ *54* ❊

Bellesea Palace
Prille
Agrius

FROM THE EARLIEST DAYS of my childhood, I had been steeped in the tales of heroes of old as sung by the bards in the hall of my father, after feasts of celebration and mourning, after the hunt or the competition. It is a common enough theme in these epic tales to tell of that hot, red mist which overcomes a man when the blood lust is upon him in the heat of battle. The whole of his mortal world suspends, a veil is parted, and a multitude of lifetimes combine and consolidate into a single focus. The hero sees the world as if through a haze of blood.

It was in such a state that I found myself when faced with the author of my misery these last months. All the pain and fury of a thousand days found its voice at last.

Through the fog, I heard shouts coming as if from a long, distant place. Words, but no meaning. I swat the notion away like a fly. No force on earth could keep me from plunging my fist, over and over, into the face of the man who had devised my torment. With a nebulous awareness, I sensed someone scratch and grab at me. Then pain erupted on my face. I saw a flash before my eyes like a shower of sparks off a blade as it is forged in the fire. It stopped me no more than would a flea under the skin. My head burned with an intense throb, and a trickle of warm blood ran down my face in rivulets. Whether it was my own blood or that of the demon I battered, I could not tell.

And I didn't care.

My arm held the man Rebane around his throat, holding him as choking gurgles bubbled from his lips even as he heaved with his weight to try to dislodge then flip me.

Then, like a man waking from a dream, I heard Irisa cry out: "Casmir, you're killing him!"

My world focused, and I became aware of faces around me, of sounds and the activity in the corridor. The break in concentration allowed Rebane to land a driving elbow into my gut. I doubled over with a forceful exhale of breath, grappling to regain my hold on him. In so doing, my elbow flew out, striking Irisa who had just moved in to pull me away.

She staggered back dazed. I released Rebane, and in an instant he dropped to his knees, gasping for air. I sensed that armed men moved in to drag him to his feet, but my attention fled solely to my wife.

I opened my mouth to utter words of apology to her, but she paid me no mind. The entirety of her focus shifted to Rebane, and contempt billowed off of her like waves of heat rising from a desert. She pushed past me and lunged at Rebane. With a sound like the cracking of a whip, she slapped him hard across the face, snapping his head to the side and sending his body to sprawl to the ground once more.

"Where is my daughter?!" she shrieked, her voice tight and ripe with the same fury that had heated my own. The guards who had held Rebane watched her in shock, their faces mingling both horror and approval.

He stared her down, his eyes full of resentment, but made no answer. She turned to Jachamin who had watched silently in the background. "Where is she? Was she not with him as we were led to believe?"

"No, Your Grace," the mercenary replied, his voice soft and gentle with unusual deference.

She turned haunted eyes to me, but I had no answer for her. Just when I knew we needed to take Rebane somewhere for questioning, another familiar face arrived, panting and out of breath as if he had run all the way from the port.

"I think she might be here somewhere in Prille, Casmir," Wolf interjected, bending over his knees to catch his breath, "but I cannot prove it."

"What do you mean?" I pressed him, though I could barely hear my own words over the sound of the pounding of my heart.

"We trailed him all the way to Sarsala, but by the time we got there, we'd just missed him. He'd already set sail. Jachamin and I each commandeered a ship from the fleet Cilgaron had assembled and gave chase. At one point the pair of ships we followed diverted from each other. Jachamin followed one and I the other. If Sybila was not on the ship Jachamin followed, the one with Rebane, she had to have been on the ship I followed."

"Then where is she?"

Wolf shook his head. "I don't know. The ship broke away with speed as we neared the Tohm Sound. It landed before me, and tt was empty by the time I boarded it. I asked, but no one could tell me anything. The quayside was too busy for anyone to have noticed or cared."

I turned to find a triumphant Rebane smiling at me through bloodied lips. A bright purple bruise had bloomed over his right eye and along the length of his cheekbone. I imagined I didn't look any better.

"Who was on that ship?" I seethed, but I knew I would get no answer.

Finally, a tremulous voice spoke up: "Your Graces, I think I might know where she may be found."

I turned to find the scriptstóri whom Irisa had brought in tow, the young man who had known the name Anton Mathiasen. At his speaking, Rebane jerked against his bonds in an attempt to get at the young scribe. Using as much caution as I would speaking to a spooked mare, I breathed, "Show us."

He nodded quietly then moved past us and along the corridor toward the Bibliotheca.

❀ ❀

Inhale.
Exhale.
I forced air in and out through my teeth for fear my body would not do it without my help. Over the sound of my boots scraping the stone stairs below me, the only other noise to be heard was the blood pulsing through the conduits under my skin, pounding, flooding my ears with drumming beats.

My fingers brushed along the damp stone walls to help me keep my balance in the near-blackness. Annor descended just ahead with a single palm-sized oil lamp barely bright enough to show the next step just below. The way seemed overly familiar to him, for his feet did not falter.

Above us, in a disused room in the cellars of the Bibliotheca, I'd left my guard. Only Irisa followed behind me. I would have left her as well, but she would not have it. Her light hand rested on my shoulder to help her balance on the precarious stairs.

Finally, Annor stopped. A door stood before us, stout and solid, dark with age and grime. The idea that my daughter had been brought to this cellar below the heart of the Bibliotheca, in the very palace which had been her home, stirred a deeper, more primal anger.

My anxieties over her comfort and well-being had long built up even though Helene had promised that Sybila was healthy, happy, and well tended. Perhaps she had been in Croilton. This was not Croilton. This was a tomb deep in the heart of the earth.

Annor fixed a key into the lock and turned it. The mechanism operated smoothly and silently, as if the ages had not decayed the metals of its manufacture to the point of grinding and groaning. He pushed inward, and warm light flooded the stairwell from the room beyond.

My feet flew into motion and I pushed past Annor into the room.

A frantic scan of the room revealed a pallet on the far side and a small figure curled up upon it. A young woman sat tending her and raised startled eyes at our sudden entry. Whether she knew our identity or not, she reacted calmly, stood with a finger raised to her mouth in admonition that we not wake the girl she tended.

I slowed my steps and stopped just short of the mattress. Irisa came up next to me, grabbing at my hand. Her other hand she stuffed into her mouth to keep from crying out.

Sybila slept peacefully. She appeared clean, well-dressed, fed, and well-tended.

"How did you know she would be here?" Irisa whispered in a wavering voice to Annor who had come up alongside us.

"Because this is where I brought her when I took her from her play."

"It was you?" Irisa's voice cracked. "Why?"

"Because I told him to."

The voice spoke boldly from the shadows behind us. Irisa and I swung around together to find Orioc, the old Grand Master of the Bibliotheca and the man who had murdered Grand Master Lito. Once stripped of his position, I'd thought no more of him. Perhaps I should not have been so foolish.

"I don't even want to know why, you vile, malevolent little toad," Irisa snapped. Her face had turned bright red with rage. I wondered if I would have to hold her back to prevent her from slapping him the way she had Rebane. I wondered if I even wanted to if she should try.

"Spite, *Your Grace*," Orioc replied, his words oozing vitriol. "The purity of the crown was compromised with your coming. And that one," he added, nodding to the place Sybila slept on, "only further diminished the splendor the throne had only begun to regain with the coming of King Bellek. I cannot speak to the motivations or intentions of Rebane, nor did I care when presented with Cilgaron's plan. It was none of my business. The coin he gave me was reason enough. Life here in this hole can be rather difficult as I'm sure you can imagine." He smiled a twisting smile. "Oh, but of course you can imagine, can't you, being raised as you were in your own hole."

His shocking admission echoed about the chamber, loudly enough that it had alerted a vigilant Travian who appeared at the door. With immediate understanding, he took in the situation and seized Orioc, leading him away. The former scriptstóri shouted defilements at us as they went, but both Irisa and I had already turned away from him. For another person captured our attention.

"Papa?" Sybila sat up on her pallet. With balled fists, she rubbed at her eyes to wipe away the obscurity of sleep. "You won the game!"

Irisa dropped immediately next to her, scooping her up into her arms.

"What do you mean my sweet?"

"Hide 'n seek!"

"Yes," Irisa responded, looking up at me as tears ran down her cheeks, "Papa won the game. It's over. All over."

I staggered forward as a man drunk and dropped to my knees beside my wife and daughter then wept as I had never wept before.

❀ *55* ❀

Bellesea Palace
Prille
Agrius

I NEARED THE DOOR to our private chambers, and just as I reached for the latch, Elimar, the aged court physician, exited, pulling the door closed behind him.

"How is she? How is my wife?"

"The queen is in excellent health, Your Grace."

"And," I continued then paused, turning to glance over my shoulder to see that we were alone, "the baby?" I whispered.

"Also fine. There is no need to be concerned about anything." With an unusual familiarity, the man placed his hand on my shoulder and squeezed. "You will be a father again soon enough, my son."

With a lighter heart than I had known since the news came to us of Ethew's disappearance, I grasped the latch and pushed the door in. A flutter like the wings of a butterfly rose up in me, and I almost felt giddy as I crossed the room to the place Irisa sat in a light linen morning robe. One of her ladies attended her, and I knew our secret couldn't be kept for too much longer. She had yet to show the blossoming of her womb, but I knew it was only a matter of time. Chambermaids were not known to be secret keepers, not even those as devoted to Irisa as hers were.

I grasped her hands as she rose to kiss me lightly on the cheek.

"Thank you for agreeing to see Elimar, my Adonia. The reassurance does me good, even if you had no worries of your own."

"It does give me reassurance, for I have heard that extreme distress can cause a woman to be misled by the usual cues."

A warm breeze blew in from the balcony beyond, so I stepped out onto it. Coming alongside me, Irisa slipped her hand into mine as we took in the view together.

Sitting at the highest point of the palace complex and constructed on a portion of rock that directly overhung the Tohm Sound above a sheer cliff, our vantage went beyond the water gate to our far right and to the fertile lands dotted with industrious farmsteads beyond Prille's walls to the far left.

I closed my eyes and tried once more to convince myself that all the strife and strains of the last months were finally at an end. For too long had I lived with moment by moment anxiety that it was difficult to truly allow myself to relax into believing that we could finally rediscover an order of normality.

The late morning sun felt warm on my face, its rays caressing my cheek with fingers of security and hope. And at risk of being fooled, I believed it.

Irisa must have felt the same, for she stood beside me

quietly reveling in the peace of the moment. I hated to break it.

"I have just now come from signing the death warrant of Taibel Rebane."

She didn't stir, and for a moment I wondered if she had even heard me. I continued: "I have set the time for tomorrow, midday. I feel as though I must attend, my duty as the one who has sentenced him to death. I owe him that, even if it is just out of deference to the integrity of the laws of the kingdom and my responsibility to uphold them."

At this, she turned to me and whispered, "I will not go."

"I do not ask it of you." I brought her hand to my lips and kissed her knuckles.

She took in the sight of my cut and bruised knuckles, drew her eyes along the bruise on my cheek from where Rebane had hit me. "I have witnessed too much bloodshed, Casmir. Too many have died, and while it is justice, I will not watch more. But it is right for you to be there. You are *Loxias*, my love, and in this, you will have vanquished your *Ulfer*."

I eyed her curiously and she smiled. "You remember the story of the great wolf Ulfer who killed King Loxias' father? It was a story you told Sybila once when she was only newly born. Loxias sent his Furies after the wolf, but the great beast defeated each of them in turn. Finally, the king took it upon himself to defeat the beast by himself, as was his duty in the first place. He wielded his two-headed ax and separated the beast from its head."

"I do recall the story, yes." I gave her a lopsided grin. "It was my favorite as a child."

"Casmir, you defeated not only your adversary in Rebane. You also defeated what many men would not have been strong enough to defeat." I slanted my head to the side, not catching her meaning, so she continued: "Helene, my love. You were tempted by her, yes. And as hard as it was to hear of it, you realized what she was about before it was too late. Even if you were a fool by not listening to Wolf." She said this last part with a sad smile then added, "But if you dare to ever tell him I said that, I will deny it."

I looped a wisp of the hair trailing down her face around my finger. "Why I should have told a tiny babe a bloody story such as that I will never know. You chided me for telling it, as I recall."

She merely grinned, and my heart soared to see her levity once more.

"Why did he do it, Casmir?" she asked, her mood quickly turned serious. "Rebane. He was Veris' man. With Veris dead, I never imagined he would act on his own. Was he full of such hate as that?"

"Rebane held a grudge, it is true. And he is ambitious. Even if he hadn't been in prison, he didn't have the means to enact any form of retribution on his own. His estates on Haern went to Ethew. No, ultimately it was Cilgaron behind it all. He coveted the throne, felt entitled to it with his Sajen blood; and if he couldn't have it, he wanted his heir to sit upon it." I dropped my gaze. "Cilgaron simply used the coals of hatred already seeded in Rebane as a tool to accomplish his own purposes. He tempted your young scriptstóri with the promise of 'greater things' to appeal to his grand sense of the world. The boy was naive enough to believe him. But bigger than that, I think he also manipulated the boy, threatened his position in the Bibliotheca if he did not cooperate."

Irisa shook her head. "I feel so sorry for Annor, Casmir, even though he did what he did. He was truly a kind young man. I do believe he thought he was doing the right thing, even after it all. It is difficult for me to harbor bitterness toward him. He was manipulated, and it was promised to him that Sybila would only be missing for a short time before she could be returned. He did take care of her in his time. He was fooled as much as we were."

"My Adonia, you are compassionate to a fault, which is why I have only discharged him from his service to the Bibliotheca rather than charge him with treason as he deserves. He is gifted, and I would hate to see his skills go to waste, but he cannot continue in the palace. I have given him a letter of recommendation to Eron in Dremesk. I am certain your uncle can find him a position. Even while I think it's more than he deserves, I knew you would want it for him even so."

"Be careful, my king, or some might accuse you of benevolence." The twinkle in her eye belied her words.

"So noted. However, lest you accuse before you have a full hearing of all the evidence available, I should tell you there is more." She raised a brow in suspicion, and I mustered as much solemnity as I could. "I would charter the opening of a series of institutions across our island, safe havens for the children of slavery, the orphans who..."

"Yes!" Irisa shrieked, turning and throwing herself into my arms before I could finish. I staggered back.

"I would have the idea presented to the Fiortha Court later this year, for there are those who will be more greatly impacted by it than others, and I would have their support, but I wanted to ask your opinion before that happens. A general plan should be made first, so there is something to work with. And I would have you present it..." She kissed me, interrupting me once more "...lest anyone else see through my intimidating and gruff exterior to view me as benevolent." I gave her a half-smile and she shook her head even as she beamed her approval.

The outer door to our chamber opened.

"I saw Elimar leave only a while ago and have come to check on you. Irisa, are you here?" Kassia called.

Irisa sighed. "We may have to tell her, you know. She knew before I did last time."

"Surely she can't know this time? You have experience with such things now, are not as naive as you were then."

She cast me a doubtful look and spun to go welcome her sister. I followed shortly behind her.

Kassia had brought young Cailen and Sybila in tow and was now occupied by pulling her son away from a delicate statue in the corner. Irisa caught up Sybila in her arms, taking her away from fondling Lizzie's ears. The levrier came over to me and pushed her snout into my hand. I sat in the nearest seat, and the dog jumped up next to me to plant her head on my lap.

Without turning from Cailen, Kassia said, "So has Elimar confirmed your pregnancy, or is there some other ailment that mimics it so well to warrant his visit?"

I think, had my jaw been able to disconnect from my face, that it would have fallen into my lap then clattered to the floor.

I stared mutely as Irisa asked, "How did you guess?" Her tone bordered somewhere between baffled and incredulous.

Kassia straightened and turned, grinning smugly.

Irisa looked to me for an explanation, but I only shrugged and raised my hands in surrender. Standing, I went to her and kissed her. "I will leave the mysteries of such things to you and your sister, for I would have nothing helpful to add."

And with that, I left them to scheme and conspire together.

❋ *56* ❋

Bellesea Palace
Prille
Agrius

9 years later

I HAVE NO EXPECTATION that future generations will acclaim me as the greatest king known to Agrius. I am not wiser than most, and I am flawed like any man. My strength lies in the union I have with others: my queen, my council, and the people of Agrius. It took much for me to learn this, but I learned the lesson well.

It is true that the last harmonious reign, when the people of Agrius enjoyed prosperity and good rule, can be dated back many generations, even before our shared ancestor, King Ancin. It is said that prosperity also breeds a weak people, for prosperity breeds laxity, comfort, and self-indulgence. A people lulled into the belief that things will always be as they are and settle into lives of comfort, quickly turning into entitlement, when any adversity or hardship is viewed with disdain.

So it was with the people of Agrius, and the kings reflected this approach to pleasure and wealth. Nikolas Sajen, my wife's grandfather, was the last of these rulers. No, my father Bellek was not a good man. And whatever must be said about his hound Ildor Veris, he was astute in reading the moods of the people and the auguries regarding the throne. Nikolas needed to go. Change was in order. While Veris may have had the ultimate motive of wanting to seize more personal power, he rode the wave of reform which was spreading through the land, ultimately to the benefit of the kingdom.

The Sajens had nearly ruined Agrius, but now that the houses of Vitus and Sajen united with the advent of my marriage to a daughter of the house of Sajen, prosperity had finally returned to Agrius along with its fair share of responsibility to the community.

"Papa?"

I looked down to see my youngest child, my daughter of four years, peer up at me with clear, green eyes. Her copper brown hair glinted with a profusion of golden hues in the bright sun of late summer. She held up a small hand, offering me a tiny caterpillar.

"It was going to fall, Papa. I saved it."

I leaned over to see. "Briegan, you should find a safer place for him outside then quickly come back. We must leave soon."

She nodded solemnly and skittered away. Her brother, Sebastian, older than her by three years, watched with a glint in his eye. When it seemed as if he would make some mocking comment to Briegan regarding the nonsensical nature of rescuing a caterpillar, I shook my head in silent warning.

He turned sullenly back around to sit and wait with his older brother Finian. The pair shared a look.

Irisa caught the looks passed between her two middle children. "It's a good thing Kalu is not here, or else I would foresee trouble at tonight's banquet. It's a shame Wolf could not make it for this year's Fiortha Court. Kalu so loves the first day celebrations."

Kalu had been raised for much of his earliest years here in Prille, at court. Wolf did as much as he could to be a real figure in his son's life, but his home in Bauladu required much of his attention. For several months out of the year he would have Kalu come home to Bauladu, but the rest of the time he lived with us. While in Prille, Kalu had formed a bond with our second child, Finian. And as an eight-year-old boy, Finian had always looked up to Kalu who was two years his elder. Finian had always tried to keep up with everything Kalu did when he stayed, as he often did, in Prille. If Kalu caused trouble, Finian was likely there in his shadow.

"Finian and Sebastian will find enough of their own trouble without Kalu, I am certain of it."

I smiled a half smile at the two boys then turned my gaze next to the two blonde heads of Sybila and Brigid who sat together in the sitting room beyond our bedchamber. Of an age with one another at eleven years old, both showed signs of budding beauty. It would do to keep a close eye on them, though Sybila was not so much my worry as my ward. Already Brigid took notice of a handsome face, particularly those of the armored palace guardsmen, and would offer her own bright approval of them as a reward for any attention they paid her. Yes, she would require all our guile to watch over her as she aged into maturity.

Irisa's maid finished with the last bit of decoration in her hair, braided and coiled, then draped in such a way as if to make it look like it had simply fallen that way. When she stood and came over to me, her eyes took in sight of her sons again, and I found the usual sadness there.

"When must Finian go?" she asked quietly so the boys would not hear.

"When Wolf is next able to come to Prille. He must finish his present project at home in Bauladu first, but I've told him it must be before winter, while the traveling is good."

Irisa dropped her chin, nodding. While she had always understood the inevitability that our second son would someday leave to be fostered elsewhere as was the traditional practice with noble-born children, Irisa still tended to tear up over the thought. To her credit, this time she kept her composure. Perhaps it was the knowledge that he went to live with Wolf that made it easier for her.

"Your Graces," interrupted a page who had just been admitted by a door valet, "your steward has asked me to inform you that the procession is ready to depart at your leisure. The Seat of Kings is ready. The parade will begin with your arrival."

I held up my arms for Andreu to fit the newly fashionable lacings of my overcoat along the sides. "Thank you. Tell Rigard we will be there shortly."

The lad ducked out as Finian and Sebastian jumped up. "Father, may we go down now, ahead of you?"

I pretended to consider for a moment, looking to Irisa with feigned concern. She couldn't hide the amusement in her eyes. With a weight of gravity, I turned back to the boys. "Yes, but..." I said, holding up a single finger, "you must walk. The entire way. Remember that you are princes and will conduct yourselves accordingly. There are many visitors to our home this week, and you will present yourselves accordingly."

Their faces lit up with the excitement of the day ahead,

and with as much obedience as they could muster, nodded. They turned as one and proceeded out the door. Once it closed behind them, echoes of their running feet came back to us. I sighed and shook my head.

Irisa came up behind me and wrapped her arms around me. "Do you really think Wolf will be up to the task of bringing that pup to heel?" she laughed, pressing her cheek against me.

I turned in her arms, bringing my own around her. She peered up at me as I gazed down at her, momentarily taking in the way the sun shot through her hair. *Very much like Sybila*, I thought. *It is only lucky our Sybila was born first and will inherit the throne and not her brother.* I barely suppressed a laugh at the thought, imagining our precious Sybila, our competent, sensible, capable Sybila. Irisa caught a hint of my thoughts, though she imagined my thinking had to do with the idea of Wolf teaching impulse control to Finian.

"No, I fear not," I answered in response to her question. "But he will do his best, as is all that can be expected. Kalu will learn his duties, and as he does, so will Finian. Both lads will learn hard lessons in the running of Croilton, I'm afraid. Finian may see it as an adventure for now, but he will see it soon enough, once he is old enough to understand the ways of the north."

She shook her head, unconvinced.

"Jachamin commands the garrison as he has done since the days I took it from its traitorous lord, and his hand is firm enough for now." Her face soured. She had never grown fond of the man after I'd brought him to court, despite his mellowing these last years. He was not the same Jachamin he had been back when I'd hired him as a mercenary. "And as its new lord, Wolf has seen fit to keep him there. He will see that Kalu is a capable lord before leaving him to his own merits with full control over his inheritance. Trust Wolf."

"If ever there was a more laughable thing to say..." she quipped, her mood only marginally lighter.

"You know I plan to send Travian to watch over our son while he is at Croilton. All will be well, my Adonia."

She looked about to argue, so I kissed her instead. "We should not keep them waiting. The gods only know the trouble our boys have created in their eagerness to get to their spots for the ceremony. I am told there is a troupe of acrobats from Kavador who are able to perform feats never seen on these shores."

It wouldn't be until very late that night, when the spectacles and ceremonies, the feasting and the festivities had ended, that I found myself alone once more with Irisa. The hour was well past midnight, and we had both already prepared for bed. Our servants had long since gone off to find their own rest. Even while we both felt a weariness born of a day well celebrated, we still found ourselves standing together on our balcony overlooking the Tohm Sound as was our way most nights.

"Before I forget to tell you, Casmir," Irisa whispered as she rested her head against my shoulder. "A messenger arrived earlier today with a letter from Jack. He sends his greetings."

"He and Kassia have finally returned then?"

"Casmir, haven't you been paying attention? They were gone for only a month. Considering how the Aksumites love their ceremony, I'd say that was a very short visit."

I nodded in agreement. "I thought it was the wisest choice Negus Bazin could make to choose Melku as his heir. Kiros seemed a capable enough leader, but crafty. I'm sure the Negus realized this once he learned how Kiros had kept Kalu locked away and under guard to use him against Addis.

Compared to Melku who proved his integrity when he saved Jack's life – it had to have been an easy decision for him. I am glad of it for his sake."

"He has even requested that Kalu come to visit when he is free to do so. Will Wolf allow it, do you think?"

"Hard to say. Only time will tell." I thought it best for the boy to visit, to know that part of his heritage, but it was a difficult thing for Wolf after what Addis had done to him. I could understand why he might hesitate.

A half-moon had just begun to peek above the land to the northeast, over the farmers' fields and fruit groves as we stood watching. Irisa slipped her hand into mine as we watched in silence for a time.

After a while, Irisa spoke again. "Kassia also sends her thanks for the flock of sheep she found waiting for her upon her return home." I cracked a grin, and even the darkness couldn't prevent Irisa from sensing it. "She always had a fondness for sheep, though the reason for it has always escaped me."

"I am glad she found some pleasure in them." I rolled my shoulders, feeling the tightness of the muscles there and in my neck along with the chronic ache which inhabited the area of the wound Ildor Veris had inflicted on me.

Irisa squeezed my hand. "Come, my love. Dawn will be here soon enough, and we have a long day ahead with the opening of the Fiortha Court Assembly."

"I will come shortly. You go ahead."

She turned on a breath of lavender and left me to a moment of solitude.

I turned up my face toward the wash of stars spreading the deep night sky. Aside from a straggling few revelers still making their way home after the night's celebrations, all of Prille lay still and silent beyond the walls far below.

I wondered what my father would have thought of this Agrius. He had cared for it in his own way, but he was weak. And others had exploited his weakness.

I wondered what Irisa's father would have thought. But he had been weak too, in his own way. He had sacrificed his own daughters for the pursuit of a dream which had, in the end, killed him. Not with a sword or any visible thing, but with a broken heart that comes from a broken dream.

I had proved my weakness too, many times over. In my own way. But the difference was that I had others around me to help. Irisa leveled my hand, and I hers. It was best that way. If my children would learn this, if Sybila would rule the same way in our stead, I could rest knowing we had done our best for Agrius.

It was all I could hope to do. It was all any man could hope to do.

With one last, deep breath of the clean night air, I retreated inside to find my place next to Irisa.

Author's Notes

Inspiration for Croilton Castle came almost exclusively from Raglan Castle in Wales with some help from Gainsborough Old Hall in Gainsborough, Lincolnshire, England.

While my books are fantasy and not based on any real history, I try to echo certain realities of a late medieval Europe into the culture and characters. I do feel free to change those realities when it suits me (the beauty of writing fantasy). For instance, I intentionally alter the medieval and more historically accurate notion of primogeniture (firstborn legitimate son inherits) and substituted lineal primogeniture (gender is irrelevant) for my royal lines. But what about other gender struggles? In Casmir and Irisa's time, Agrius may have practiced lineal primogeniture (though that practice did not necessarily apply to Casmir's older sister... though I digress...), but midway through the story she is concerned that Casmir and the King's Council may blame her in taking too long to have a second baby. Should Irisa have been concerned that Casmir might hold her responsible for not bearing a second heir sooner?

One of the most important duties of a medieval queen was to produce an heir. And generally that meant a male heir. The pressure to produce a healthy male baby was enormous, and when this duty was not fulfilled, there came a risk for the queen to be set aside in favor of a new, more fertile queen. Think Henry VIII and his many wives if you still don't know what I mean. More than one child was preferred, the heir and the spare. While this particular historical practice is not overt in my story, the idea of it certainly drives the secondary plot – that of Lord Cilgaron and his daughter, Helene.

Casmir is portrayed as constantly balancing his role as king with his role as husband and father. Would he truly have blamed Irisa when it came down to it? I'd like to believe he wouldn't. Without a natural heir of his own, Casmir and Irisa would likely have named someone else the heir. Casmir's youngest sister Kathel perhaps, or even Kassia. Oh, what story that would have made! Kassia as a crowned queen? Poor Jack.

In the very last chapter of The King's Furies, we learn that Casmir and Irisa's son, Finian, will soon leave Prille to live with Kalu at Croilton Castle under the supervision of Wolf. He will be fostered. Readers not well read on the middle ages may not know what fostering was. Alliances and loyalties were secured by noblemen in many ways. A strategic marriage could unite families (like what happened with Casmir and Irisa) who otherwise might not have the motivation to remain civil. Another method was fostering, when a child, generally older than age seven, was sent to live with another noble family to be raised and educated. Not only did it help strengthen loyalties, but it also offered younger children a chance for a better future. Inheritances were generally handed down to the eldest male in the family, leaving the second and remaining children with nothing. Fostering gave children the chance to work into a position with another noble family. They learned proper behavior, how to run a household, and how to command those underneath them in rank. Who knows what sort of trouble Finian and Kalu might find for themselves in the wilder Honor of Cilgaron? Maybe someone should write a spin-off series about their adventures? Hmm...

And finally, the riddles at the feast in Croilton Castle came from the Exeter book, specifically riddles 6, 18, and 57, translated by Paull F. Bum, Duke University Press, Durham, North Carolina, 1963. This work is in the public domain.

Acknowledgments

I cannot begin to thank everyone who, in some way, provided me with help, encouragement, and support during the writing and publication of this book. When perusing the final version it seems odd to think that the process has taken me nearly two years. Not only am I a slow writer, but there are also so many moving pieces to creating a work of fiction. Thankfully I have quite a 'team' of helpers who have provided unending support.

Tricia Wentworth had a big part to play in the development of Casmir over the course of this book. Her admitted infatuation with the man provided a basis for Tricia to be my sounding board for most scenes involving Casmir. She was his moral compass more times than I can count. Samantha Wilcoxson has been a steadfast supporter during my writing, and her role as a beta reader provided necessary feedback. Kim Barton is another friend who often provided daily pep talks and who served as a sounding board for story and character ideas. She was also a beta reader, and helped me work through the sometimes overwhelming editing necessities. My mother, Linda Churchill, is a stickler for detail and proved herself invaluable as a proofreader. Nicky Galliers and Amy Maroney are two rock stars of the written word and provided expert editorial help, catching inconsistencies where I saw flawless prose. I will always be indebted to their graciousness. And finally, my mentor, Sharon Kay Penman. She provided feedback as a beta reader (pointing out several plot points with which she was uncomfortable, thus leading to a slew of changes – I mean why would I not listen to a *New York Times* best-selling author's editorial comments?), offering encouragement and an enormous amount of support even as she faced her own deadline dragon.

I LOVE my readers and am so grateful for their encouragement and support over the years. Thank you for following along on this journey with me. Without you, it would be very difficult to keep writing!

I would also like to thank the entire author community. I am friends with too many authors to name individually, both indie and traditionally published. Social media has become as vital to my career as an author as air, water, and food to the body. So to all my author friends and acquaintances, thank you for your continued support, encouragement, promotion, reviews, and taking the time to engage with answers to questions, research help, and general silliness.

And finally, as a requirement of using a castle graphic on my map of Agrius for Croilton Castle, I must credit Chanut from **www.flaticon.com**.

About the Author

I grew up in Lincoln, Nebraska, and after attending college in Iowa, moved to Washington, D.C. to work as an antitrust paralegal. When my husband and I were married, I moved to the Minneapolis metro area and found work as a corporate paralegal. While I enjoyed reading, writing was never anything that even crossed my mind. I enjoyed reading, but writing? That's what authors did, and I wasn't an author.

One day while on my lunch break, I visited the neighboring Barnes & Noble and happened upon a book by author Sharon Kay Penman. I'd never heard of her before, but the book looked interesting, so I bought it. Immediately I become a rabid fan of her work.

In 2007, when Facebook was very quickly becoming "a thing," I discovered that Ms. Penman had a fan club and that she happened to interact there frequently. As a result of a casual comment she made about how writers generally don't get detailed feedback from readers, I wrote her an embarrassingly long review of her latest book, *Lionheart*. As a result of that review, she asked me what would become the most life-changing question: "Have you ever thought about writing?" And *The Scribe's Daughter* was born.

When I'm not writing or taxiing my two children to school or other activities, I'm likely walking Cozmo, our dog, or reading. The rest of my time is spent trying to survive the murderous intentions of Minnesota's weather.

Follow Me

Website: www.stephaniechurchillauthor.com
Facebook:
https://www.facebook.com/stephaniechurchill
Twitter: https://twitter.com/WriterChurchill
Instagram: @schurchillauthor
Pinterest: https://www.pinterest.com/sllingky/

Other Books by Stephanie Churchill

The Scribe's Daughter
The King's Daughter

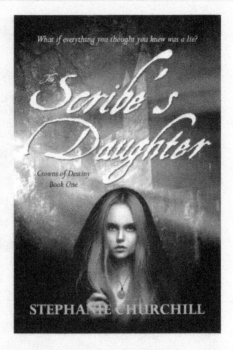

My necklace is my death warrant.

Show it to no one, my father told me. But then he disappeared. I assumed him dead.

The day a man showed up at my market stall to hire me for a job I couldn't do, my life changed forever. I came under the scrutiny of cruel men who would stop at nothing to gain the information I possessed.

Or what they thought I possessed. How was a scribe's daughter to know the secrets of kings and their thrones?

After escaping the abuse and privation of prison, my journey took me from high mountain vistas and into deep swamps, across the sea and into the sparkling palaces of princes. All of it would help me discover answers to the riddles about my family's mysterious past.

Everything I thought I knew was a lie. I am a scribe's daughter, but there is more to the story.

A destiny fraught with political intrigue, honor, family, love, and betrayal...

The King's Daughter

Crowns of Destiny
Book Two

STEPHANIE CHURCHILL

Irisa dreams of being overlooked.

And she manages to stay that way most of the time.

At least she does until the day her sister's strange customer reappears at her door. Kassia is away, working on his commissioned task, but now he is back and claiming Irisa's life is in danger. Can she trust him to keep her safe? How much does he know about the fate of her sister and father?

Only a voyage across the Eastmor Ocean to the land of her ancestors will reveal the truth about her family's disturbing past. Once there, Irisa steps into a future she has unknowingly been prepared for since childhood, but what she discovers is far more sinister than she could have ever imagined. Will she have the courage to claim her inheritance for her own?